This is a work of fiction. Names, characters, places, and incidents either are the product of the author's imagination or are used fictitiously. Any resemblance to actual persons, living or dead, events, or locales is entirely coincidental… mostly.

Canva Images

Cover Design by Primepgx on Fiverr

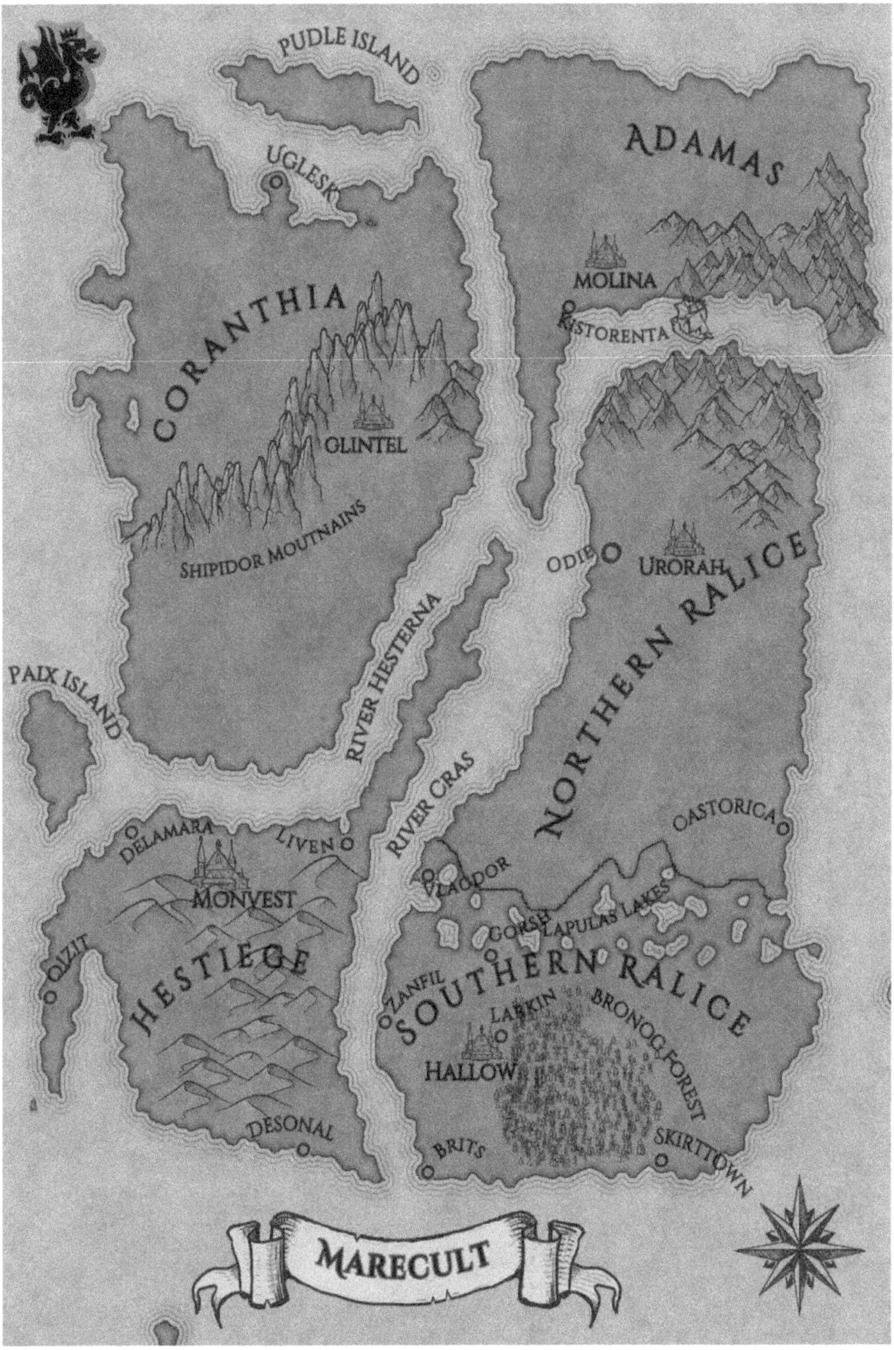

PUDLE ISLAND
ADAMAS
UGLESK
MOLINA
RISTORENTA
CORANTHIA
GLINTEL
SHIPIDOR MOUTNAINS
ODIE
URORAH
NORTHERN RALICE
RIVER HESTERNA
PAIX ISLAND
RIVER CRAS
OASTORICA
DELAMARA
LIVEN
MONVEST
VLAODOR
GORSH
LAPULAS LAKES
OIZIT
HESTIEGE
ZANFIL
SOUTHERN RALICE
LARKIN
BRONOG FOREST
HALLOW
DESONAL
BRITS
SKIRTTOWN
MARECULT

Fate of
Ruby
and
Throne

This book is dedicated to my best friend, Brits.

For listening to my crazy ideas.

For enjoying the soup.
You are far more precious to me than you can know.
BYYYEEE.

TRIGGER WARNINGS

Dear Reader,

This book contains the following things that some people may find triggering, or uncomfortable:

- Death
- Decapitation
- Brief mention of physical abuse
- Brief mention of physical abuse of children
- Mention of blood (minor)
- Poisoning
- Recreational drinking
- Violence
- Vomit

The intention of this note is to be as kind and courteous as I can, to any person looking to immerse themselves in a fictional world. If you have a specific trigger and would like to know beforehand if my book contains it, please reach out to me via my website monroewildrose.com, and I will happily answer your queries.

May all your adventures be pleasant.

Love shook my heart,

Like the wind on the mountain

Troubling the oak trees.

-Sappho

When we last left our heroines:

After being kidnapped by pirates, on her way to an arranged marriage to King Cyril Kosdel of Northern Ralice, Mercy found herself aboard The Siren, a pirate ship captained by two notorious pirate twins. It was made clear to her that they had been hired by her betrothed to return her to Northern Ralice, she reluctantly warmed to the idea of sailing on a pirate ship. She started to fall in love with the ocean, and with Elias the pirate captain as well. They were pursued by the evil King of Southern Ralice, and just when they thought they would escape him, Mercy fell ill. Right when it seemed her fate was about to change, and she wouldn't have to marry the King, the pirate ship was overtaken. Mercy was whisked back to her own country of Adamas. There, her brother informed her that the pirates she sailed with, and their friend Absalom, were murdered. Not only that, but King Cassius Dalion, of Southern Ralice was not the villain they feared and was helping Mercy's brother locate her after she was kidnapped. After grieving, her brother tried to tether her into being a token of war and Mercy made a public statement that she would no longer be a pawn in his political game.

In the aftermath of trying to sail Princess Mercy to safety, alongside her brother and childhood love, Absalom, Georgette found traitorous thoughts of life on land coming more frequently than she would have liked. After the devastating news that Absalom was betrothed to marry another, Georgette picked up the pieces of her heart to focus on evading King Dalion as he pursued them across the sea. Caught off guard at a port by King Dalion's men, Absalom attempted to explain the situation, but was killed by one of the men who had ambushed them. Georgette was dragged away grieving, having traded her life for her brother's and the rest of the crew aboard the ship. Once she arrived in Southern Ralice, she learned that the King planned to marry her. She defiantly approached the throne on her wedding day, but she saw someone unexpected seated there. The guard that took her from her pirate ship, who she had built a shaky friendship with, turned out to be King Cassius Dalion. Sworn to hate her husband for what his men did to her friend Absalom, she plots her revenge as the Queen of Southern Ralice.

Chapter One

Georgette

Three months.

I had been the Queen of Southern Ralice for three months. It had also been three months since I had spoken to my husband. In that time, not a word had passed between us. Not that I was complaining about that. If I never had to hear his dark, challenging voice again, it would be fine by me.

I *was* required to see him, however. We ate our evening meal together every night in a terribly long dining room. Places were set for us directly across from each other, and unless he was off on kingly business, he was in attendance, but hardly acknowledged me. The first month I didn't eat anything. I spent the entire time tipped back in my chair with my boot-clad feet resting on the table as I drank several glasses of wine. The food would go cold, and I would leave once he had excused himself.

I stopped when it became apparent to me that he was enjoying my rebellion. The more defiant I acted at the dinner table, the more he grinned as his gaze slipped over me, lounging across from him. So, after a month, I simply ignored him. I didn't let the incredible food go to waste. Some days I brought a book and would immerse myself in reading while in his company. Some days I thought over everything Devika, my principal lady, had taught me or what research I had done of my own.

Because I was still planning on taking Cassius' throne out from under him.

I soaked up information about his kingdom like a sea sponge. I greedily hoarded Devika's teachings and read all I could. I eavesdropped on guards' conversations and visited the market at High Hallow almost every day. Soon it would be time to move forward with my plan. A plan which was unformulated and unfounded as all the plotting I had done had been alone when I had brief moments of solitude. The plan would end with this arrogant king begging me to leave or me murdering him. I didn't have a preference on which it was. I imagined running a knife across his throat and watching him bleed out all over his fine gold plates. Or perhaps I would come from behind and run him through the way he had allowed Absalom to die.

I was sitting in the plush velvet chair, swirling my glass around after finishing my dinner. My mind wandered to when I asked Devika about the small town outside Hallow. The one I had seen people starving in when I had first arrived. The boy's face came to my mind and the way he thanked me for some small coins. I learned the town was called Larkin. Once, it had been prosperous, as it sat just to the side of acres and acres of land. Land that once held many orchards of fruit. It was where the palace and the city had, once, bought most of its produce. Then the orchards had dried up, and the crops failed, and now the people there were too proud to leave but were still starving.

When I had told Brees I planned on visiting Larkin, he had bristled and looked at me as if I were insane. He said he would ask for permission and I told him I would be going with or without Cassius' good tidings. He had let out a long breath and shot daggers at me. His hatred of me dripped from every salty look. Shortly after my wedding day, Brees had been assigned as my guard. He followed me around like a fly that would never die.

He hated allowing me to do things, but it seemed he wasn't in a position to question me. As a queen, I did almost anything I pleased. I had thought that I would feel imprisoned but aside from not being allowed to see where Cassius' chambers were (which was just good sense on their part), there was not much from which I was restricted.

I had only been required to attend three events at Cassius' side. Each time playing up my un-courtly pirate characteristics. He seemed perfectly content watching me put my feet on tables, drinking too much, and flirting with any man that happened across my path. I wore trousers and linen shirts and vests to everything and was never asked to wear any flouncy or feminine dresses. He was bothered by none of my behavior which was both interesting and irritating.

I had gleaned that Cassius was using me as some sort of display of madness. For, even his subjects referred to their king as *the mad king*. He wasn't mad. I could see in his eyes; he was haughty and infuriating, but he wasn't crazy. He was too intentional to be called mad. Everything he did was deliberate. Every one of his movements was calculated. I watched him out of the corner of my eye as he spoke, and his words were used as weighty things placed perfectly to sink whatever target was intended. No, Cassius, King of Southern Ralice, was no mad king, but he *was* dark and dangerous.

I started imagining how I would show up at Larkin looking for people who didn't know who I was. No one calling me *'my queen'*, no one bowing or curtseying. I could have a drink without someone curbing what they were saying to me because I was married to a king. I could get information about Cassius from some people who didn't serve him; this information was often much more useful. I just needed one weakness I could leverage. Everyone had one, and I would find his.

"You're in a good mood this evening." His inky voice startled me from my thoughts.

My eyes jerked up to meet his across the table. He had an eyebrow raised and a wicked smile starting to form at the corner of his mouth. After three months of silence, this was not what I imagined his first words would be. Normally my wit would have had something quicker for me, but I was startled that he spoke at all. He could tell, and his grin split his face.

"How have you come to that conclusion, oh illustrious one?" I asked.

Not king. Never king. I would never address him as king; I vowed it.

"Your emotions play across your features unchecked. Quite the failing, but at least it makes our silent meals together more interesting."

I couldn't argue his point. There would be no sense in denying it. Elias had said as much to me several times. Whatever I felt often flashed across my face unbridled, especially if I wasn't paying attention to controlling it. I wondered what he had seen flit across my features while I was thinking of finding a weak point in his armor and gouging it with a sharp stick.

"I am in a good mood," I said, leaning back in my chair and grabbing the golden cup filled with sweet wine.

"May I inquire as to why?"

"I was just thinking of when I escape you and this place," I gestured around with my glass.

"Have we been less than hospitable? You need only ask for what you want, my Queen."

My blood boiled at the name. He must have seen it because his smile widened.

"I want my freedom," I growled through clenched teeth.

"Ah, that is one thing I cannot grant you."

There was nothing left of the man I had shared a cart with those two days. Nothing left of the informal military man I had thought only a captain. There was only a king with his glittering black fingernails, holding the key to my gilded cage. I decided on a different tactic since it seemed he was gaining the upper hand.

"Whatever happened to Princess Mercy of Adamas?" I asked.

I hadn't heard of her imprisonment here in the castle, nor did any guard or maid chatter even suggest they knew of their king's pursuit and capture of her.

"That is the second time you've asked me about her fate. Tell me, wife, what concern is it of yours?" His eyes were suspicious, and they narrowed as he sat back in his own seat.

I hated the way he said wife more than I hated queen.

"I only wish to know how you have used her to incite war. I hear you itch for it the way a pet bird yearns for the sky."

I wanted news of Mercy's wellbeing. It seemed unlikely that she was even still alive. It grieved me to think of her face pale and lifeless.

"Princess Mercy Landlight of Adamas has been returned to her brother King Holt," Cassius said, and I was surprised at the anger that filled his features before he quickly hid it behind stone indifference.

"Alive?" I prodded further as he took a long-stemmed glass and drank a translucent green liquid from it.

"Last I heard, she was alive." His words had an edge, and I wasn't sure what it was I had said that bothered him, but I couldn't help but smile.

"And what pray tell did King Holt have to pay or promise for her return? His kingdom? Her life? Riches? Or perhaps men and alliance for a war. The bastardized lineage of Southern Ralice looking to retake its place as the head of both countries?"

"You should really stop sulking when we are at court gatherings and converse more, your viperous mouth would serve my purposes well." He looked angry and amused; perhaps he was mad after all.

"Don't make wishes in haste, Cassius the Liar. You might not like what's granted to you."

He didn't answer me. He just pushed away from the table, his smile never leaving his face. Now it held a challenge. *I was bred for war.* I remembered his words from our wedding day, and his look sparked a flame in me that I had cooled in the last three months. He braced himself against the table, leaning forward, and looked as if he was going to say something else.

Tomorrow I would double my efforts to find this man's foothold. I realized I had grown apathetic these past several months. The way he leaned toward me with that vicious grin on his face daring me to do my worst, reminded me of my goal. If it was a viperous pirate wife he wanted, it was a heel-biting snake he would get. With venom sweet as honey on my lips, I smiled at him, draining the rest of the wine in my glass.

Once I had dismissed myself from the dining hall, I walked back to my rooms accompanied by Brees. He was about as chatty as ever, and I rolled my eyes at his heavy silences. However, I was in no mood to talk either. Cassius had rekindled my anger, and the passion in my chest begged to be put to work.

When we reached my quarters, I walked inside without even saying goodnight to Brees. I doubted he noticed or cared.

"My Queen, I've drawn you a bath," Devika said.

She had stopped startling me by merely being in my room at unexpected times. She was like a ghost who moved about as she pleased. Tonight, she wore a white dress and gold earrings, and a matching heavy necklace against her deep brown skin. I couldn't help but marvel at her beauty every time I saw her. There wasn't a flaw in her that I had seen. Since my wedding, she had only worn white. It was some sort of Southern Ralice religious tradition I didn't understand no matter how often she explained it to me. According to her, she would have to wear white as long as she was in my service. The other grand ladies also wore white and would have to for the entirety of their service to me. I had dismissed the other ladies and did not see much of them. Only Devika attended to me.

She had become my friend. I wooed her into liking me almost immediately. It was a gift I had always possessed. I rarely met a person who wasn't malleable to the certain charm I had. My father called it siren magic. My mother called it shameless manipulation. Whatever it was, I had always found it easy to get a person to warm to me if they were not completely repelled by me being a pirate.

I got into the warm bath that was scented with almond and cinnamon oil at my request. It reminded me of The Siren, my home. It was a little comfort to still smell like the things I remembered. I grabbed the bar of soap Devika extended, and I began to scrub my arms with it vigorously. I hardly did anything all day and the bath at the end of every night was both pleasurable and unnecessary.

Devika began to rinse my hair and rub cinnamon oil through it. My hair had grown a little but still didn't reach my shoulders. Devika was the only one that could tame the cocoa-colored waves. I leaned my head back to look at her behind me.

"Remember when you wanted me to take a midday meal or tea with some courtiers?" I asked.

She hesitated before she responded. She was contemplative and slow to react, harsh, and honest, which I appreciated, and she didn't spin words to fill silences.

"Yes, I believe you said you'd rather be fed to a three-headed giant squid."

"A bit dramatic, doesn't sound like me at all." I smiled, and she narrowed her eyes, shaking her head. "Can we still do that?"

"Georgette, you are a queen; you must stop asking if you can do things." She huffed, getting tired of reminding me.

I smiled again at her use of my name. It had taken months, but she occasionally called me by my first name. Mostly when she was irritated with me, but I would take what I could get.

"I'm asking you if I've spurned people so badly now that they will be reluctant to meet with me."

"As I've said before, you needn't worry about that. If you send an invitation, they will come."

"Can you do that for me? Set up a small...teatime?" I grappled with the right term.

She laughed. "Yes, may I inquire as to why you have had a sudden change of heart?"

"Perhaps I have finally resigned to the fact I must fulfill my queenly duties for the betterment of the country, and my husband's good name." I looked back to see her raised eyebrows. "Was it my husband's good name? Did I take it too far?"

"I don't know what you're up to, but I'll send out invitations. We will start with courtiers that live on the castle grounds."

"There are courtiers that live on the castle grounds?" I asked as she leaned against a stone counter.

"I've told you this several times."

"I'm not an excellent listener if what the person is saying doesn't interest me at the time."

"That's a character flaw," she said, but a smile tugged at the corner of her mouth. "Yes, two women live here as guests of King Dalion. Bastil Scarele is a noblewoman from the southern part of our kingdom. Her father lost his life to a plague, and her mother asked our king to take her in to secure her a good marriage. Jessamine Vaxa is the daughter of the Duke of Puddle Island. He is King Jacob Vaxa's youngest brother."

"She's in line for the throne?" I asked curiously, and Devika snorted in response.

"She thinks she is, but Vaxa has seven brothers, and they all have gaggles of children. She is at least twentieth in line."

"But a Queen can rule in Coranthia?" I questioned, knowing it was the only kingdom that recognized Queens as heads when there was no king to take the throne.

"Yes."

"Why is Jessamine here?" I stood up to get out of the bath as Devika prepared a sheet to dry me off.

"Political alliances," she said simply, but a mischievous smile still danced at the corners of her mouth.

"There is something you aren't telling me..." I wrapped the sheet around myself.

"I think that makes us even, my Queen." She walked out of the bathing room ahead of me.

"Are you sure you've never been a pirate?" I called after her, "You savor of the salt of the sea."

I only heard her beautiful laughter from the room as a response. I turned to look at myself in the floor-length mirror in the corner, its gilded edges in sculpted gold. I dropped the sheet to view my full reflection. It wasn't as if I had changed terribly. My hands had gone soft as all my callouses had seeped away with no work to be done. My hair was shorter and always well kept. I slept so well that there was never a dark circle to be seen under my eyes. My skin was still olive-toned, but I didn't spend hours under the relentless sun, so it had lightened quite a bit. The curves I had were still there, the softness of them inviting, but I was beginning to lose the tone of muscle I was used to in my arms and calves from ship life. I scowled at my reflection. I looked like a queen. The harshness of the pirate captain had begun to fade, and I saw a high court female in the mirror. I stuck my tongue out at her.

"Vanity is one of the great sins," Devika said from the doorway, holding out a nightgown of deep green silk.

"Perhaps a great sin but not my greatest." I snatched it from her and pulled it over my head.

"I've set a few more books on Southern Ralice history on your bed, and there is a tray of tea set by your fireplace in your parlor, is there anything else you require of me, My Queen?"

"No, Devika, enjoy your evening. Thank you."

"Of course, goodnight," she said, walking out of the bathroom, leaving me in the large openness of my rooms by myself.

I hung the sheet I had dropped on the floor on a hook situated on a wall; though I knew a fresh one would be provided to me tomorrow. I walked into my bed chambers and heard the door from the main room click closed. My room was grand and large with a four-poster bed, a settee, and a small table. A vase of fresh white flowers was set on it, along with a fresh basket of fruits and nuts. The closet that housed too many clothes and jewels was attached to my bedroom and the bathing room. Just left of my bed was a dark wooden door. I had no idea where it led, and whenever I tried it, it was locked. No doubt more elegantly decorated rooms with more drapes and tables, something I had no interest in exploring.

I grabbed a book off the bed that Devika had provided for me and walked down the hallway to the main room. The small hallway was lined in oil paintings of oceans, landscapes, fruit, and even one of a couple of puppies playing. It opened into the main room, which was fully furnished with several velvet couches and side tables. The main door where a guard sat at all times led out into the hallway. I made my way into yet another room off the one that Devika called the parlor.

It was a smaller room with walls lined in books and a balcony that looked out over an opulent garden. A fireplace with an ornately carved mantle was situated into the wall. A single plush emerald wingback chair and side table were situated next to it. It was my favorite room. It felt like something I would have decorated. Simple but comfortable.

I set the book down next to the tea tray and made my way over to the double balcony doors. I opened them as the breeze blew back the curtains, and I stepped out into the night. The stars were marvelous, and the moon was half full and bright.

A noise to my right startled me a bit. I turned to realize the sound was of doors clicking shut on a balcony, yards away from my own. No other noises came, and the doors did not reopen, so I ignored it and went back to my view. Climbing up onto the stone ledge I hiked my nightgown up to my thighs. I stood up and walked the length of it and held still as a breeze blew, and I looked up into the sky.

On nights like this, I hoped Elias and I were looking up at the same stars.

Chapter Two

Mercy

"That is why I require the assistance of the throne to save my pig farm, your Majesties," the man spoke.

He was worn and haggard with a tunic full of holes wrapped around his shoulders. He was to be the last citizen allowed in the throne room today. Tomorrow, the grueling process would start all over again. My twin sisters and I sat on thrones as citizens were paraded in front of us with their problems, and it was up to the three of us to handle their requests.

Holt had set me to do this task as a punishment of sorts; for the rebellion I had held against him the last three months. Prudence and Temperance had been punished as well, as they had followed me in my defiance. However, it had backfired when it came to Temperance. She took to the task with vigor, and I was often thoroughly impressed with the solutions she came up with. She was fair but strict, and though I was the oldest, I found myself deferring to her counsel quite often.

I didn't mind the task either. It allowed me to learn a great deal about my country and the lives of our subjects. Prudence, however, was in anguish the entire time she was asked to sit and endure it. She squirmed like a schoolgirl waiting for a lecture to be over.

All three of us had taken to sitting for the citizen complaints all afternoon, and then rushing to our rooms to change into plain skirts and light leather armor to train in the castle's private training arena. This was one of the many things my brother did not approve of in my changed behavior since my time aboard The Siren.

For the past three months, I had been training in archery and was also instructing Prudence in the sword. Temperance had trained with me before, but we trained almost every day now, and we were all getting much more experienced. Temperance taught me close proximity combat, and Charity had even come to learn a little, though her governess wouldn't allow her to for very long. Holt had been so furious at first that he had tried to get my mother involved. She kept to herself mostly since my father's death and had barely acknowledged anything he had said. She certainly hadn't confronted me about it as he hoped she would.

So, it was my will against his, and he was displeased that I had grown a backbone.

I also spent a considerable amount of time outside. I tended a garden before, but if I wasn't training, filtering civilian complaints, sleeping, or eating, I was in the open air. I couldn't get enough of the sun on my face or the wind whipping through my hair. Even the few times it had rained, I stood outside in the downpour, reveling in the feel of the water. The phantom smell of ocean spray haunted me wherever I went.

Aside from Holt's initial report that Elias, Georgette, and Absalom had been killed, I had heard nothing else about them. I had a sneaking suspicion that the servants had been instructed not to talk to me about it either because whenever I tried to ask, I was met with uncomfortable silences.

"It seems as if your misfortune is due to your own negligence," I said to the man standing before me, having only half-listened to his woe.

"But Princess," he started to argue.

"My sister is right." Temperance's voice was rigid as iron. "Had you kept your animals better, the elements would not have taken them from you. Shall we reach into our coffers on account of your stupidity?"

The man sat mute before us; his mouth was a gate opening and closing in a storm. He stared at three princesses, two who had their gazes set on him waiting for a rebuttal and one looking out a window as if she couldn't be bothered with his issue at all.

"If we offer you livestock from our own barns, what then shall you offer us in return?" I asked him.

"I could offer a percentage of the meat sold at market when the pigs are slaughtered," the man grappled.

"No," Temperance insisted. "We will take a portion of the earnings from the market, but that is not all. We shall give you three pigs for the season, one gilt and two sows who have already born litters of piglets."

"Your generosity is humbling," he said, but there was an edge to his voice.

"All our livestock is exceptionally fed and healthy, so each female should be able to carry two litters before the year is up. We will take half of the piglets that are born as well as one-third of your earnings the coming year from your selling."

"Princess..." he balked.

"Sir, that you have come to petition us about your lost livestock sits oddly with me. Surely you have a neighbor who would allow you to borrow a sow or two. Perhaps you would borrow one for a price in town. That you are sitting before us means no one has any goodwill toward you," I allowed, and Temperance's nod was barely noticeable. "So, you either accept our terms and save your father's farm and your family from starvation, or you go try your luck in the next town over."

He stewed for a moment, and I wondered if he would give nasty looks to the King of Adamas, such as he was giving the three of us at that moment.

"Thank you, and I accept your generous terms." His teeth were grit as he forced the words out.

"Very well," I said, waving to Atticus, who was dutifully posted to the left of us. "Atticus, make sure this man is given his female pigs and that his debt is documented."

"Yes, Princess Mercy." He bowed low and the man in front of us followed suit.

Atticus escorted him out, and I breathed a sigh of relief.

"Please tell me we are done!" Prudence exclaimed, slumping in her chair so improperly I snorted.

"Prudence," Temperance said with thinly veiled irritation, "Must you so publicly show that you have no interest in this?"

"I stayed silent the whole time," Prudence argued.

I was reminded for a moment of Elias and Georgette and their bickering back and forth. I had no doubt my sisters had been like this for years, but I had never bothered to be around them long enough to see it.

"The garden fountain is done," I said, standing up and stretching my legs the best I could in the crimson dress I wore. "That means the garden is complete. Would you two like to see it with me before training?"

"I suppose, though that eats into our training time." Temperance got up, brushing off her black gown.

"I think Mercy is trying to get out of horse-riding archery lessons," Prudence sang as she skipped to the doors that would lead us out of the throne room.

I glowered at her, and she smiled. Prudence was the best archer of us by far and also the best rider among us. She was convinced that it wasn't enough for me to learn archery but to be so proficient that I could shoot on horseback as well. I had not developed any warmer feelings towards horses.

"We can change and meet in the garden and then train directly after that," I said, almost running to the door.

"Very well," Temperance said, "But only because my curiosity is so piqued by this mysterious garden you've commissioned that I'm letting it take over my better judgment."

I gave the twins one last smile before slipping out the door.

The castle I grew up in was rather cold for a place so familiar. The stone walls were lined with tapestries woven from the most luxurious of materials. There were tables draped in velvet and doors carved and painted in elaborate ways. It had always felt a bit wrong to me, and I had never known why. After spending time at sea, the feeling had only grown.

"Princess, where are we off to next?" Atticus' bright voice came to me.

I looked up as I had almost passed him, lost in thought. Atticus was the head of the castle guards. We were the same age and had grown up together, and I had often gotten into trouble running wild with him when I had been allowed to run wild. He was a tall man with wavy brown hair that bordered blond. He had been steadfast and longsuffering for as long as I had known him. When my brother had assigned him to follow my sisters and me around like a sheepdog, he had bowed and acted as if there weren't a greater task in all of Adamas. Though I'm sure, playing nursemaid to three princesses was not the height of excitement. He never let on if he was unhappy.

"To see the garden and then training," I said, smiling at him. "You could meet us in the training arena. Maybe you could help convince Prudence I don't need to learn to shoot a bow from atop a horse."

"I don't think I could convince any of you of anything that you didn't wish to be convinced of." He smiled back. "But perhaps I could convince her we needed a rematch in the sword."

"After you beat me so completely last time, my ego couldn't take it." I continued down the hall and was now walking backward, talking to him as I retreated.

"Beat you completely? Princess, I was sore for a week after our last match, and I barely won." He chuckled as we continued on our separate ways.

I took the stairs two at a time and even ran a little down the hallways to my room. I hadn't so much as glimpsed the garden after designing it and setting our best garden keepers to create my vision. It had been expensive. Though I think my brother had hoped it would help me get back to what he considered normal. I had taken advantage of his misconception.

In my room, Kiltore helped remove my proper corset and other things I couldn't get out of independently. Alita had formed a bond with Prudence while I had been away, and I hadn't been able to separate them upon my return. So Kiltore had taken Alita's place as my handmaid.

She left me to dress in my blue plain skirt and a linen shirt with a casual stay over the top. I strapped on my leather belt and struggled into my stockings and boots because of the hurry I was in. When I left my room once more, I fully ran through the palace's halls and down the stairs. The garden was located in the back of the castle, so I made my way to the kitchen and used a back door to exit the castle's side.

The garden was off to the left of the grounds, out a little way so that it wouldn't interfere with anything my mother had already done with the gardens. I only knew when I came upon it because where once there had sat a vacant stretch of grass, was now completely fenced off in evergreen shrubbery. I ran to it and found the front framed with a grand arched entrance just as I had instructed.

I stopped suddenly at the opening and took a deep breath. My sisters had beaten me to it and were looking around. I didn't notice their reactions at first because I was so taken aback by how close our groundskeepers had been able to recreate my vision. Temperance had helped me with some of the sketches and outlines as she was the only artistically inclined sibling I had. Still, I had expected less accuracy and beauty than what was before me.

The left wall of shrubs was completely covered with climbing roses in the most brilliant of colors. It was Georgette's wall after all, and the blooms exploded in assaulting colors of reds, pinks, and purples. The vines were both breathtaking and off-putting with their thorny branches. At the bottom, they gave way to a bed of soft bluebells, delphinium, and forget-me-nots. The floor of the blue buds wrapped around the garden representing the ocean. They were planted in stone beds of the deepest azure. And while this was all lovely, it wasn't what caused my heart to skip in my chest.

In the middle of the garden was a stone fountain carved from both the palest marble veined with black and midnight marble threaded with white. Half the fountain depicted a woman in white, hands outstretched, holding a sun in her palm. The other half was a man carved from the black stone with the moon held in both palms. Their backs were to each other, and a fountain of water sprayed around them. The water gathered around their feet in a large pool, and the stone sides of it met in the middle in a perfect contrast of dark and light.

I found myself moving to see the face of the Lord of the Night. Tightness gathered deep in me, and I had to bite my cheek to keep from making any noise. Immortalized in stone was Elias Baine with a moon in his hands and a mischievous smile on his face.

"Oh, Mercy, it's just lovely," Prudence breathed. "My new favorite garden in all the grounds. And the fountain you fashioned after that fairytale you told us. It's just magical. Isn't it magical Temperance?"

But Temperance was staring at me, and I caught her gaze out of the corner of my eye. Her eyes were clever and vigilant.

"It seems...intimate."

Her words allowed a few tears to slip onto my cheeks.

"Oh, now look what you've done," Prudence chastised her. "She doesn't mean it, Mercy. It's lovely, ignore her. All she wears is black and grey anyway. What would she know of designing a garden?"

"Her words didn't offend me," I said, wiping the tears away and both the twins looked relieved.

"Is this him then?" Temperance asked quieter, coming up to stand next to me.

We both looked up into Elias' stone face, and he didn't look daunted by the attention in the slightest.

"Yes," I sighed, breathing the truth to them, letting the slight summer breeze carry it away.

"He's very handsome," Prudence said.

"He's shorter than I imagined," Temperance commented and then let out a cry of pain as Prudence stomped on her foot.

"Really, Temper."

I chuckled at them both, silently promising the garden I would return when I was alone.

"Let's get to training," I said, turning on my heel and not looking back.

We were met halfway back to the castle by Atticus, who smiled at all of us brightly.

"Your brother wishes to see you, Princess Mercy."

"Which one?" I asked with a little sarcasm.

The only one of my brothers who would ever call upon me was Holt. The others had no need, and we hardly ever saw them.

"King Holt," he said, "He awaits you in the throne room. I will escort the princesses to the training room, and we shall wait for you there."

"Very well." I nodded and we all walked together back to the entrance of the castle.

From there, I left them to move to the formal part of the castle, and they went to the training arena. I was jealous as I would rather do anything in the world than talk to my brother. Whenever he called for my company alone, it was never pleasant.

When I reached the throne room, I took a deep breath and steadied myself. If I wasn't vigilant, my brother had a way of manipulating me into agreeing to what he wanted. I opened the doors and presented my best stoic face as he turned to greet me. As usual, he was impeccably dressed and cleaned up. Posture straight and noble.

"Brother," I said, bowing to him, and he nodded. "What do I owe the pleasure?"

"I have news that may upset you, and I thought it best to present it to you without anyone around."

"For your sake or mine?" I asked, smiling, and he scowled.

"As you know, when war is imminent, the kings' parlay to see if a peace agreement might be reached before definite declarations are made."

"Yes, though I thought it mostly a formality and not often an actual attempt at peace."

"It's often used as a meeting to intimidate other countries into submission," he agreed. "But I'm telling you because we are to host King Cyril at a formal ball in two weeks for one such visit."

"Oh," I said, startled though I shouldn't have been, for King Cyril was the one my brother was set on going to war with.

"And I didn't want to surprise you with the information. That he will be here, and you will no doubt have to interact with the bastard even after what he did to you."

I looked up at Holt, who had gone flush with anger. It was anger that he harbored on my behalf, and it softened me a bit. I couldn't see how this could be a ploy to manipulate me and instead only saw the concern on my older brother's features.

"Well, we shall be polite hosts and show him the best that Adamas has to offer. I will be kind and cordial. You needn't worry about my behavior?" I phrased it as a question, still unsure of his intent.

"I wasn't," he defended, "I just thought to extend the courtesy of telling you first."

"Well..." I said, taken aback. "Thank you."

Holt only nodded, leaving us to sit in silence for several moments. I curtseyed to signal my departure after it was clear he wouldn't speak again. He opened his mouth but closed it again and dismissed me with a wave of his hand. I wondered for a moment if I should push him to share whatever it was he was holding back. He had made it clear though, that he didn't want my input on anything he deemed a serious issue the past couple of months. Despite my efforts to improve my relationship with him, he remained distant.

So, I left him standing there with things unspoken between us.

Chapter Three

Georgette

A game I played was trying to see if I could lose Brees in Hollow Market.

He resented the fact that Cassius had assigned him to me as my personal guard. I found it rather funny and did my best to stoke that resentment until it was full rage. For my tall guard, with eyes as dark as the wood of The Siren, anger was never far. I had yet to lose him in the crowd of people, and his intuition was too good as he anticipated my moves. He couldn't yell at me, I supposed for rank reasons, but I could see the curses he wished to spew at me begging to be unleashed.

That morning was no different. I weaved in and out of stalls and tables. I bumped into people and wandered down alleyways. I glanced back to catch his withering stare as he hustled after me. People made way for him in a way they didn't for me.

I wore nothing to identify myself. My attire consisted of trousers and plain shirts with vests, much as it had been aboard my ship. The only difference was that I ordered them in obscene colors. My trousers that morning were violet with a matching vest and white shirt underneath. I looked like a colorfully dressed courtier. While it would be a little strange to the higher court that I was wearing trousers, I looked like a boldly dressed woman. It was strange to me how a few changes to my appearance and nobody could tell I was a pirate. I was wearing pants and a vest with a dagger at my waist, but Devika made me look polished as any courtier before leaving the palace. I wore my hoops in my ears and nose, but she always insisted on some other decadent piece of jewelry from my extensive collection.

Today my wrists were decorated with bangles of pearl, and small pins were affixed in my hair to match. Somehow these slight changes had turned me from a roguish pirate into an acceptable higher court lady. Even the dagger at my hip was ornate, the hilt decorated with deep purple stones and the blade a swirling metal as sharp as my tongue. I knew it had been a gift from my husband, and I tried not to think of that whenever I wore it, which was almost every day. My weapons had still not been returned to me, despite my asking.

Brees had almost caught up to me, so I quickened my pace down an alley. I shrank low and quickly scurried beneath a cart of fruit, hiding myself like a child. I squeezed my knees to my chest and dared not peer up until I was sure he had passed.

"Are you alright, lady?" a woman's voice came from behind me.

I turned to see a plump woman in plain merchant clothes; a dress of brown and an apron that was probably once white. She looked kind, and her face held no anger for me.

"Just hiding from my tyrant of a husband." I tried to appear distressed. "The tall, handsome man dressed in military blue, dark hair, and even darker eyes."

"We are all fools to fall for tall, handsome men. Such a rogue to treat you poorly; you are as lovely as a goddess," she huffed out. "You stay here, and I will let you know when he's passed."

"Thank you, madam. I am indebted to you."

"Of course, my lady." She stood back up, and I prayed that Brees hadn't seen me duck below the stall.

Though several minutes passed, and other than the sweet woman's voice calling to people how delectable her fruit was, there was no unusual interaction. I thought of how furious Brees would be if he lost me. I felt a little bad that he might get in trouble with Cassius for my misconduct, but not bad enough to betray my location. I wouldn't return to the castle without him, I told myself. I just wanted a moment of freedom.

"Madam, your husband is gone." The woman called to me, and I made an awkward show of getting up from under the cart.

"Thank you so very much," I said, curtseying to her, then realized I needed to dust off my pants.

When I finished with that, I looked up to smile and realized that she was holding out the ripest peach I had ever seen.

"Oh lady, I'm terribly sorry, but I have no coin on me," I said, cursing my stupidity.

"It is a gift, child."

"No, you've already been more than generous." I thought of something I could give her.

I looked to my wrist, slipped off one of the three pearl bangles, and handed it to her. She marveled at it for a minute, for even I had to admit that the bracelets were beautiful and worth much more than a peach.

"My lady, I couldn't. It isn't a fair trade," she insisted as she went to hand it back.

"I shall take one more peach then if you don't mind so that when I finished this one, I shall not be too sad."

She beamed and handed me another equally delicious-looking fruit. I curtseyed again and walked back the way I had come. I roamed the streets at my leisure, looking over stalls and treats. I had no money to buy anything but the minute of freedom I had was welcomed, and I enjoyed every breath of it. Higher Court Market in Hallow smelled of burnt sugar and oranges, and while Liven held a special place in my heart, this market was quickly becoming my favorite of the two.

I was walking down an alley darkened by laundry strung up between the buildings on either side. I was contemplating going back to the mouth of the gate that led to the palace estate when a stranger's rough hand pulled me into the alleyway. They were dragging me further down into the darkened place. The grip was strong, and I panicked, kicking against it, and tried to scream, but their hand moved to cover my mouth. I cursed myself for losing Brees.

I elbowed the figure in the ribs and heard the wind being knocked from them. I drew my dagger and, using their surprise to my advantage, shoved him against a wall. A deep hood hid their features, but I held my knife to the stranger's throat.

"You've picked the wrong woman to attack, sir," I ground out, pressing the blade deeper into his skin.

"Morning, Captain." A chuckle came from beneath the hood, and the weapon dropped from my hand.

I embraced him. Wrapping my arms around him and crushed him to me as his arms came around my shoulders. I cried. The tears were unintentional, but they poured forth from me as I sobbed uncontrollably. He held me tightly, not letting me go until my sobs subsided.

"Oceans, I missed you, George," he said, finally pulling away as he pushed his hood back.

The sight of his face almost caused me to start crying again. He had a full beard and mustache, and the grey eyes that mirrored my own sparkled back at me. I hadn't thought him dead, but I wondered if I would ever see him again. He held his arms out and grabbed me by the shoulders as I tried to wipe my face of tears.

"Let me look at you. A few months in the company of a king, and he's turned you into a courtier." Strangled voice and tears in his eyes, he looked me over.

Had he thought me dead?

"I'm so sorry, Elias," I said, tears threatening again. "I didn't know what to do to save the crew. I thought I could save you and them..." Tears spilled over as my heart twisted again.

"No, you did well." He gave me a small smile and pulled me in for another hug. "The crew is fine. Ported in Hestiege. I'm sorry, George. I'm so sorry about Absalom...I'm so sorry I wasn't there for you both. I'll never forgive myself for not being there for all of you."

"There isn't anything to forgive. We were ambushed. You made it out free. That is all I wished for. There wasn't anything you could have done."

"I'm sorry we fought. I'm sorry I didn't tell you how I felt about Mercy; I was such an ass, and you gave your life for mine." He squeezed me so tight I couldn't breathe.

"I haven't thought about that a single second, Elias," I promised, pulling away. "How did you find me? What are you doing in Hallow? What are you doing in the market?"

I couldn't get the words out fast enough. I couldn't say everything I wanted to say. I knew any moment Brees could happen upon us. He could have gotten more guards to look for me, and then our time would be cut short. The panic started to rise in my throat, and Elias could tell.

"I came to murder the King that took you. I came to avenge yours and Mercy's life. I came in a blind panic after you but then, you weren't dead. No one had been killed, not a princess and not a pirate. Then the news was that the pirate was to marry the king. So, I went back to the crew to formulate a plan and then came back here." His voice choked up.

"And Mercy was returned home," I assured him and watched as his shoulders sagged in relief. "Home to Adamas. I don't know more than that. Cassius told me and upon further investigation, he didn't lie. I don't know what game of kings is being played, but Mercy is alive. I've written to her, but I have gotten no response."

"Are you alright?" he asked, speaking quickly. "What happened? What kind of King marries a pirate?"

"An ass of a King." I rolled my eyes. "That man I fought on the pier at Liven?"

"Yes?" he asked with an eyebrow raised.

"That's the King. Cassius is his name, and he's as awful and crazy as everyone says he is."

"He hasn't hurt you, has he?" his tone went dark.

"No, he doesn't much speak to me, let alone touch me. He's using me as a pawn or a symbol of how deranged he is...I don't know. It doesn't make any more sense to me now than it did before."

"Kings," he cursed. "Once I found out you weren't dead, I have been trying to find a way into the castle, but the guard's presence is outrageous. What are they protecting up there? I have been in this city for almost two months. I just happened to spot you walking the streets with a guard three weeks ago. I've been here every morning since, but he's always on your heels. Until today."

"Brees, he's my personal guard."

"To protect you or to keep you in line?" He stepped back and leaned against the wall.

"Perhaps both."

"You look good, healthy, unharmed. I can't tell you how happy that makes me."

"I'm well fed and well-tended to, Elias; no need to fear for me. Unless Cassius tires of trying to bridle me, but I sense he has too much pride to give up easily."

"I almost pity the man," Elias smirked.

"He deserves everything he has coming." My eyes burned at the thought of Absalom and my forced marriage.

"How are we to get you out of here?" he asked, and my eyes snapped up to meet his.

They were the words I had longed to hear. The promise of true freedom and a way back to my ship. The life that was waiting for me as the captain of The Siren. Now my brother offered it to me on a silver platter. The freedom that had been stolen from me was close enough to taste.

"What is it?" he asked, reading the hesitation on my face.

"He'll hunt us," I exhaled, "His pride will demand it. He'll hunt us down if you take me; he's done it before. I don't want to spend my life running from him. I'd rather break him or kill him and leave a free woman."

"What are you saying?"

I stopped to think of what I was saying. There were so many things. We needed to go to Mercy. If she was the one my brother loved then, he needed to see her, to see if she was safe and offer her freedom aboard the ship if she wanted it. However, Elias would face the same struggles of getting into the palace in Adamas as he had here. We could never reach her with Cassius on our trail. Not to mention the fact that I had promised him a war in his own house I had not even begun to fight. I wanted him to beg me to leave on his knees, and if he did not beg, I would slit his throat when the time came.

"I am saying I can't come with you." I winced as the words left my mouth.

"Okay." Elias nodded, his faith in me unwavering.

"You have to go to Mercy," I said, "To make sure she is not in harm. I know she is home, but that doesn't mean she isn't in some sort of peril, and she's your love."

He colored a little but nodded.

"I have not yet finished with this soft-footed king. He will pay for what he's done to Absalom. There is no way we would make it to her with him after us, and I can assist you in getting into the castle much easier as a queen than I could as a fugitive pirate. I am in no immediate danger you needn't fear for me."

"I don't like the idea of leaving you here...with him. What if you're wrong and he kills you, and I've left you on your own?" he asked, "I won't allow you to be on your own again."

"Elias, with you alive and well, I am not alone." I stepped forward and set a hand on his shoulder. "Trust me to handle myself."

"How are you going to get me into the Castle at Molina?" he asked, finally nodding.

I was silent for several minutes, checking the mouth of the alley. He allowed me time to think. I pinched the bridge of my nose, formulating a plan. It wasn't a good one, but it was the best chance we had at getting Elias into the castle.

"Three days from now, buy copious amounts of whatever you like from the market and act as a vendor delivering them to me. I will let them know you are coming and insist on seeing you myself. Brees won't let me escape again in the market after today, so you'll have to come to the castle. Keep your beard until then in case the guards have seen your reward poster."

"What is your plan?" He raised an eyebrow at my growing grin.

So, I shared my plan.

When I finished, he was grinning along with me, and my heart ached when thinking of leaving him. We talked for several minutes until I was so nervous someone would happen upon us that I told him I had to leave. He hugged me tighter than he ever had, and we agreed to meet in the kitchens in three days.

I walked back to Hallow Manner's gates from the city. The sun was up midday, and I wondered what kind of commotion my disappearance had caused. I didn't need to wonder for long. When I walked up to the gates, the guard stationed at the top yelled something I couldn't understand as the gate opened without me having to ask. I walked inside and was greeted by at least twenty armed guards standing at attention. I nodded to them as I passed and looked up, realizing what the fuss was about.

Cassius and Brees were both a stone's throw from me on horseback along with dozens of other men. I walked to them at my leisure.

"Captain, I am sorry. It seems in my confusion, I lost you in the crowd. I am simply horrified that I worried you into accruing a rescue party." I batted my eyelashes up at him.

His rage was barely controlled as he just nodded once at me. Cassius' face was also tight with anger, but it seemed to soften a little at my words, and he looked sideways at his Captain of the Guard.

"Completely my fault, Your Eminence," I said, dropping a curtsey, and one of his eyebrows went up.

I had given him nothing but contempt since coming here, but I wanted to increase my chances of not being questioned about where I had been. He looked wary all the same. Even if he knew it was a mocking curtsey, it might serve me better than blatant disrespect.

"Quite all right, My Queen. I'm just grateful you have returned to me unharmed. I'll have to give Brees a few reminders on how to care for the queen of our kingdom properly." He challenged me with his stare.

I flinched away from the words. I knew Brees would be held responsible for my actions, and while we weren't fond of each other, I despised unjust punishment. Cassius also used every opportunity to remind me that I was his. His words *'my queen' 'returned to me unharmed'* irked me, and fire rose in my blood, but I was willing to bet he knew that.

"I'm sure my queen is tired from her journey, Brees. Would you accompany her back to her chambers? Are you able to manage that?" There was laughter from the men around them.

"Yes, my King," Brees said darkly as he dismounted.

I waited for him, and we fell into step beside each other.

"My Queen," Cassius called to my back, and I turned to face him. "Be careful not to lose your guard in the city again. If you do, I would be forced to revoke certain freedoms you have been allowed. For your safety, of course."

The words were cold, and I had no doubt he would make good on his promise. I only nodded my understanding before turning back to Brees, who waited dutifully for me. We walked in silence to the front entrance of the castle. Then, still in silence, we passed the serpent pool, and there was still more silence waiting for me as we ascended the stairs. My guilt ate at me.

"Brees," I called, but he didn't stop or even turn. "Brees, please,"

He stopped dead in the middle of a hallway and turned to face me. His nostrils flared, and I winced away from the anger that was pouring off him. There was no one around, so I dared to take a step closer.

"Yes, Queen Georgette."

"I'm sorry," I said, looking him in the eyes, as surprise washed over his features.

"You don't have to apologize to me." He narrowed his eyes. "I am your guard, and you are a queen; you shouldn't offer me an apology."

"I'm not a queen, and you know it," I quipped back sharper than I meant to; I was apologizing after all.

"I am sorry you will receive negative repercussions for my actions. I am sorry you were made to look like a fool in front of your men; I had men that answered to me once, so I know what it is to have your authority undermined."

He was silent. Taking in what I said and looking me over to gauge whether I was sincere or not.

"I won't attempt to run off in the market again."

Still, I was met with silence. The thing I loathed the most.

"In the market?" he asked finally.

"What?"

"You are only promising to not run off in the market but not promising to not run off at all."

"You are rather perceptive for a brute of a man," I said, smiling and walking past him.

He didn't speak until we reached my room. I was just relieved that his anger toward me had dissipated a little. I wasn't sure why I cared, but I did. Perhaps he reminded me a little of another military man I knew who had a keen sense of loyalty.

"Why do you despise me?" I asked when he started to open my doors for me. "Is it just that I'm a pirate?"

"I don't despise you, My Queen."

"Well, you dislike me at the very least. You are offended that you have to guard me. Is it my occupation that you detest?"

He hesitated on the edge of the truth.

"I am not a delicate court lady, Captain Brees," I said, crossing my arms. "Your criticism holds little weight, so there is no need to curb the truth."

"At first, perhaps it was your thieving nature and how coldly you admitted to murdering your own brother. However, it wasn't enough to elicit my dislike. It's your disrespect of my King and country that leaves a bad taste in my mouth," he breathed out, as if he had been holding it in for an exceptionally long time.

"I have no respect for your King or your country," I said, but kept any hardness from my tone. "I was kidnapped and brought here against my will, and my previous lifestyle didn't condemn me for my freeness of spirit."

"I understand, my Queen. Though while I understand your situation, it does not increase my sympathy for you. I told Cassius he should have killed you. You would not have been my first choice for Southern Ralice's queen."

"Nor the twentieth choice, I dare say." I smiled at him, and his eyebrows gathered together at my reaction.

"No, My Queen." A small smile played at the corner of his mouth.

"I appreciate your honesty, Captain. I am sorry for the humiliation I caused you today. I give you my word as a pirate. It will not happen again."

"How much is the word of a pirate worth?" He did smile completely then, and I felt I had won a small victory.

"Not much, but what else am I to offer you?" I walked into my room and closed the doors behind me.

Chapter Four

Mercy

I was staring up at the partly clouded sky through the glass of the training arena dome, as its imperfections cast rainbows on the ground around me. The hoofbeats of Belle, the mare I had just been riding had stopped, and I heard her snorting in the distance. No doubt telling Prudence what an idiot I was.

Atticus came into view and leaned over me. "Are you alright, princess?"

I grunted, sitting up, and looked around for the bow that I had let go of when I had fallen off the backside of the horse. I located it to my left and looked up to see Prudence leading the horse back to me. If she thought I was going to get back on the mare, she was wrong. I stood up groaning and hunched over as I felt every part of my body that had hit the ground. I glared at the horse being led toward me.

"Don't look at Belle that way. She hasn't done anything wrong. You are the one who lost your balance," Prudence said, stroking the horse's cheek.

"The horse sped up as I was losing my balance," I countered. "Maybe I'm just not made for riding horses, Prudence. I appreciate your patient instruction, but I don't seem to be improving."

"I disagree," Prudence said, pointing to the target I had attempted to hit in the distance.

I looked up and saw my arrow had landed in one of the outer rings of it, but I had indeed hit it. I smiled and stood up.

"Excellent, Princess!" Atticus beamed at me, and Temperance nodded at his side, which was as much pride as she expressed.

I stood there and started thinking that it had been almost a week since the conversation with my brother. Since then, he had asked me to coordinate the reception and ball for King Cyril Kosdel and his ceremonial army. Normally, it would be my mother's job, but she told my brother she couldn't bear the emotional burden, so the task had fallen to me as the oldest daughter.

It wasn't that I couldn't do it. I had been trained and raised to take on such things when I was married, to pick flowers and create a menu. It was just that I found myself apathetic about the idea. I didn't care about pomp and show. I didn't care what King Cyril Kosdel thought of our country. I thought my brother should run the treacherous bastard through when he sat down to eat. However, that is not how the game was played, and so now I was forced to choose between blush peonies or lavender roses. Would it be glazed apricot tartlets or decedent miniature chocolate cakes dusted with powdered sugar? The frivolity made me sick.

"Prudence, would you pick lavender roses or pink peonies for the ball? You have a better eye for it than I," I asked, feeling the tender spot at the base of my back that would no doubt bruise.

"The lavender rose is for enchantment, and a rose itself speaks of strength as a hearty flower. The peony means to honor and prosperity...I would go with the peony and perhaps some yellow sap buttons and green foliage to compliment."

The longer she spoke, the more out of depth I felt.

"Peonies," Temperance said with certainty. "They are harder to get this time of year, so not only will the flower speak its message but also speak of how we can afford such things when out of season."

"I'm convinced women have superior intellects to men," Atticus said, looking at the twins. "You all have to remember so much, and we are just taught to fight. All three of you might be better strategists than the board of advisors your brother has."

"Careful Atticus that savors of conspiracy," I laughed, and he smiled at me.

"Mercy, neither Prudence nor I wish to overstep, but we would be happy to help with preparations for the ball," Temperance said to me.

I felt a weight lift even though I had the same knowledge my sisters had, they seemed to wield it better in high court than I did. I could use their help, but I hadn't wanted to burden them by asking. It was my responsibility, after all.

"Oh, what fun," Prudence squealed. "Oh, please let us help Mercy, so we can show that Bastard King just what he is up against."

The rest of us looked after her in shock. Prudence didn't often have a harsh word for anyone other than Temperance.

"What?" she asked, coloring slightly. "He tried to use Mercy as a pawn to start a war with no thought to her safety. She could have been killed."

"I would appreciate the help," I said, smiling at my sister.

So, the rest of the day, they followed me about, or I would send them on different errands they handled with grace. Atticus stood by silently, smirking at something occasionally. We had table settings sorted; Temperance handled the Menu; Prudence ordered the flowers. I sorted the rooms that would need to be prepped and offered to house both the king and his gaggle of military men he would no doubt bring.

We prepped servants. The twins picked out clothes for me to wear during their stay that exuded health and strength. They looked no healthier to me than those I normally wore, but I didn't get in their way. By the end of the day, I was feeling much more prepared, so I asked Atticus to request Holt join us for dinner that evening so we could discuss anything he had reservations about.

We trained for a little over an hour right before dinner, so I returned to my room to bathe and change into something more appropriate. Kiltore was there when I got out, to help me into a corset and a violet purple gown with tiny violets embroidered into it. She set a delicate emerald tiara on my head and braided my hair around it. She colored my cheeks with powder and spritzed me with light crisp perfume of flowers.

The crown I had thrown on the ground in front of Holt and the courtiers all those months ago sat in my closet, but I never wore it. I sneered at it any time I opened the doors. I opted most days for light circlets or smaller tiaras. Though at the ball,

I supposed it would be appropriate for me to wear one of the gaudy crowns that sat within my collection.

Palace life had always felt a little strange. Like a stay that was a little too snug, I had never gotten used to it. I had assumed that in time I would grow to be more comfortable. Since my time on the ocean, it had only grown worse. Upon my return, it didn't feel uncomfortable anymore but had become stifling. I couldn't breathe most of the time as if the paintings, the drapes, and the fancy food would smother the part of my soul that had awoken on the deck of The Siren. The only time I felt free was in training.

I shook off the desolate feeling that had settled on me so frequently the past couple of months and headed out my door to go to the dining hall. My sisters were a few paces ahead of me in the hallway, and they stopped and waited. We walked the rest of the way together, with Prudence going on about some new courtier she fancied.

We mostly always ate dinner together in the formal dining room. My mother would join Prudence, Temperance, Herold, Charity, and myself. So, I was surprised when we reached the room, there was more chatter beyond the open doors than normal, and upon further investigation saw all three of my older brothers in attendance. They didn't often come to dinner. I had expected Holt as I had invited him, but Tobias and Langston were there as well.

Tobias was quiet and reserved and rarely talked. He was also the tallest of all my brothers, and his height and reserved nature made him seem formidable. Though as a child, he had also been the kindest and most sensitive of them. Langston was the most handsome, with a smile that could light up a woman's heart. He had slept with most of the maids in our employ and had the charm to win people over in a matter of minutes. He was reckless and brash, but one could not help but fall in love with him.

"There are our formidable planning warriors!" Holt boomed as we entered the dining area.

Temperance raised an eyebrow at me, and Prudence smothered a smile. Holt was either in an excellent mood, or he was drunk. My mother sat in a chair, looking up at us with an empty smile. Langston and Tobias turned to us, and Langston extended one of his war-winning looks and I couldn't help but smile back. Tobias only nodded.

"Quite the gathering," I commented, curtseying to Holt.

"I thought my brothers should be here to celebrate what an excellent job their sisters have done with our upcoming ball. I hear the three of you have been busy, and I couldn't be more pleased."

"It was Mercy, mostly," Temperance said, with Prudence nodding in agreement.

"Sit!" Holt commanded, ignoring her. "Let's eat and celebrate; I can't remember the last time we took a meal together."

"Mother, do you mind if I sit with you?" I heard Tobias ask her quietly.

My mother, Rosemary Eden Landlight, had once been a formidable queen and mother. After my father had died, day by day, we watched her spark of life fade, so now she was little more than a silent face at a table. It seemed a shame to me because she still possessed many great years. Her light brown hair was peppered with grey, but her posture was always impeccable, and to me, she looked lovely. I sometimes felt relieved her gaze wasn't trained on me constantly like before my father had died. I felt guilty for those thoughts whenever I saw her.

"Mercy, I can't believe how you've grown," Langston said, coming over to me beaming like a proud parent.

"You're only three years older than me, Langston, and it would be more believable to you if you bothered to spend any amount of time in my company," I said with an eyebrow raised, but I added another smile at the end to soften my harsh words.

"I'd heard your time away had sharpened your tongue." He leaned in to say, "I rather like it; it makes for better conversation. Sit next to me at dinner. I've caught bits and pieces of your pirate tale, but I want to hear the full epic adventure."

I rolled my eyes at him as we sat down. My brother said a prayer to Loripta, and the servants came out to start the first course. A deep burgundy bubbly wine was poured into a crystal glass in front of me, and a server poured water into my other glass. A silver dome was removed off a plate that had been set in front of me to reveal a gold soup with sliced and fanned pears on top. I hoped the soup didn't taste like pears. I was a firm believer that soup should be enjoyed warm and should never taste of fruit. We all waited for my mother to take the first spoonful and then followed suit. To my dismay, it was cold and did taste of green apple and pear.

I took a long drink of the sparkling wine and looked over to Holt, who was staring at me. I raised an eyebrow at him, looking down at the front of my dress, wondering if I had spilled some wine on myself.

"Have you seen Mercy's garden, mother?" Prudence asked from where she sat across from our mom.

"I have not yet ventured," Mother said demurely, "Not that I'm not interested, Mercy dear. I am glad you are using your time to do more than training like a man."

There it was. Just like that, I wished I were anywhere but at that table.

"It's quite lovely," Prudence interrupted before Mother could say any more, "I'll have to show you."

I shot her silent thanks, and she nodded back to me as I ingested another spoonful of fruit soup.

"While I am very proud of you three for doing such a marvelous job on the preparations for King Kosdel to come, there is another order of business to discuss," Holt said, keeping his voice casual.

It was his courtier voice again. Like he was peddling furs in the middle of summertime. My eyebrow raised, and I sat back in my chair. I wondered if he always had ulterior motives for everything he did and if he ever grew tired of living that way.

"So, you didn't call us to dinner here to talk about flower arrangements and what fruit should be offered in our guests' rooms?" Langston asked, and Temperance coughed over a chuckle.

"Decidedly not," Holt said, taking his glass and sitting back in his chair. "As you all know, I intend to go to war with Cyril Kosdel and his country for the grievous offense he has committed against us. He lied to me and used Mercy as a pawn to entice me to start a war with King Cassius Dalion of Southern Ralice. While Cassius helped me locate Mercy personally, King Cyril Kosdel continued to lie and manipulate me into war while unaware I knew of his treachery."

"We know all this," I started clenching and unclenching my fists under the table, my mouth going dry.

"Yes, my point here is that if Cassius is anything like his father before him, and I've heard they are cut from the same cloth, he will want something in return for his assistance in this war."

"Shouldn't he want to defend his honor in the war anyway?" Langston asked, "After all, King Cyril tried to frame him for Mercy's kidnapping?"

"Cassius is hesitant to go to war with him, being so new to the throne, and Southern Ralice has a long history of staying out of other country's wars. Their military is the strongest in Marecult, but they only use it when necessary."

"What would you offer him in exchange for his alliance?" Tobias asked.

"That is why I wanted us all here, as this will require us to unite as a family. Upon our victory, I shall offer him a jewel of Adamas. Our own sweet Mercy will make a fine bride for him and live in a palace of splendor. Hallow Manor has no equal in beauty."

I was glad I didn't have anything in my mouth at that moment because I would have spit it out. Temperance's mouth was slightly open, and she was staring at Holt in disbelief. Prudence's eyebrows were furrowed, and she sat back in her chair hard. My younger siblings looked from our mother to my brother and then down into their soup. My mother smiled distantly, nodding her approval. Tobias was biting his bottom lip and looking over at me worriedly.

"Don't you think it's a little too soon for her after...her previously botched engagement for you to ask this?" Langston was the only one who spoke up, but I didn't even have it in me to look at him in appreciation.

Holt's eyes were locked onto mine in silent command. My nostrils flared, and I pursed my lips together.

"I wouldn't underestimate our little sister, Langston. Since she's returned, she trains every day like a warrior. She is resilient," he replied, but his brown eyes staring into mine, were cold as the winter ocean and focused on me.

"Holt..." Temperance didn't get a chance to finish her thought as I stood, pushed my chair back loud against the stone, and gripped the edge of the table.

"No," I said to him, a word I was starting to feel comfortable saying.

"I wasn't asking your permission," Holt said, standing as well.

"I will not. You can't," I said, fighting my anger to form coherent thoughts.

"I can and I will; you'll make a marvelous queen."

"But he already has a queen..." Tobias said, and Holt broke eye contact with me for a brief second to shoot Tobias a murderous look.

"Mercy Sophia Landlight, you sit down and know your place!" my mother shrieked, and I was almost impressed that she'd summoned the energy.

I thought of so many insults to hurl at her to make her quiet, but I held my tongue. My fight was not with her.

"I am the King of Adamas, and your hand in marriage is within my right to use as I please, and you will accept with a curtsey and a smile." Holt's voice was deep and angry now, and I wondered if he had thought I would be too timid to disagree with him in front of everyone.

He was wrong.

"You're not a king. You're a boy playing at king, and you're doing it poorly." Lies mixed with truths as my mouth worked faster than my brain. "Father would be ashamed of you."

"Mercy!" my mother repeated my name like a curse word.

"I trusted you once with my hand in marriage, and I smiled and curtsied like a good little princess. You sent me to be married to a man who would have killed me without a thought, for his gain. Now you plan to send me off to be a wife to a king with a reputation for cruelty. No, Holt, I will not go with a smile and a curtsey, because you have proven you aren't worthy of the power bestowed on you. If you force me to do this, and you are right, it is within your power; I will kick and scream and fight you every minute until I am gone. Then, when I get to Southern Ralice, I will be nothing but a thorn in your side until King Dalion gets so sick of me, he either has me killed, or he sends me back to you."

I turned to go, regret already filling my stomach. It pooled there with my anger, hot and white. No one said a word to me. No one called after me, and I left the dining room without so much as a backward glance.

Chapter Five

Georgette

It had taken me the full three days to procure documents renaming Elias as Lord Tristan Kaloqey. I had found it surprisingly easy to assign land to him and to get papers and documents to that effect written up for me. I was still shocked at how easily people gave me what I asked for because I held a title. There was a plot of land near the Lapulous lake right on the ocean, thirty square miles and unoccupied. The record keeper had assured me it was a good place to choose for its proximity to freshwater for cattle, and one could create their own port there if they chose. He deemed it a perfect gift to bestow for someone I wished to thank for their deep generosity (as this was the excuse, I gave him). He was more hesitant to answer my questions about titling a person, but he said if I wished to bestow the title of Lord on someone there was no one standing in my way, save the king himself.

Perhaps Cassius would find out what I was up to, but it was the only plan I could concoct. I hoped reviewing title changes was low on his list of things to do. I would deal with him when the time came.

I also had the foresight to send a post out to King Holt Landlight letting him know that I was sending Lord Tristen Kaloqey as a friend of the crown. With the excuse for him to stay in Molina for a few weeks on a trading scout.

I was disappointed with my second meeting with Elias. Brees seemed to hate me a bit less, but he never let me out of his sight after the market incident. So, when a merchant came to the cellar doors with a large order in tow, I had Brees breathing down my neck the entire time.

"Thank you so much for delivering these yourself," I said, and he bowed to me.

"I wanted to make sure nothing was damaged, my Queen. It isn't every day that I get such a large order from such authority." Only I could know he was mocking me.

"I have brought some of my art renderings to you as promised. I am afraid they are not my best work, but I didn't want to disappoint." I handed him what was actually his titles and papers wrapped in twine.

"You honor me with this gift your Majesty." He bowed again and it took all my willpower not to kick him in the shins.

He had kept the beard but had trimmed his hair and was wearing high court clothing. He cut a fine figure even if I was tempted to laugh at him.

"I'm sure once the kitchen makes its way through this store, I will be contacting you for more."

"I will be waiting."

That was it. No embrace. No proper goodbye and I bit the inside of my cheek to keep from crying. He winked at me and went out the way he had come.

"You were busy the day you lost me at the market," Brees said, an unspoken accusation lay beneath his words.

"Yes, I just love..." I turned to see what Elias had brought me.

I looked on shocked, scowling and then a fit of laughter bubbled through me that filled the cellars. The staff who were taking the food Elias brought to be stored, stopped dead to stare as I continued to laugh doubling over.

"Mushrooms, asparagus and goose," I managed to get out as Brees cleared his throat.

Elias had brought every food I loathed. There was more beyond those I listed, and I hated every single item I laid my eyes on. I could almost hear his voice *Think of me when you are eating your meals for the next weeks George.*

"You mean to tell me that you've killed men and plundered vessels on the high sea, and you are nervous to take tea with women of your court who hold titles lesser than yours?" Devika made fun of me as I fiddled with the brown leather belt I wore.

"I'm not nervous," I said, shooting her an irritated look.

"You are. You're pacing." She raised an eyebrow at me.

I stopped pacing.

"And you're wearing skirts, a stay, and a blouse," she said, and I looked down at my clothing.

I had ordered the tailor to make me three sets of simple clothing worn in lower courts. I had plans to use them later but wore them today just to see how they would feel. Though I had asked for plain clothing, the black stay was embroidered with small white flowers. It was secured over the softest silk shirt I had ever worn with billowy sleeves. Of course, I had worn skirts before, but they always seemed itchy and uncomfortable. The castle tailor must have been a magic worker and the rust-colored skirts breezed across my legs with no more effort than a pair of trousers. It wasn't high fashion, but I supposed I looked more feminine than most days. Especially with tiny clear crystals adorning my hair and gold bangles at my wrists.

"High court women make me more nervous than thieves and murderers," I said, sitting down on one of my chairs with a sigh.

"Definitely understandable."

Her hair had grown out a bit from when I first arrived, but she still kept it rather short. She wore white again, a dress accented with gold jewelry, and her lips stained a dark berry color.

"Lady Bastil is very pleasant. I think you'll like her and Jessamine... well, she's the loveliest woman I have ever laid eyes on, but I should warn you..."

"Surely not more lovely than you," I interrupted, and her rich laughter and a shake of her head were the only response I got before there was a knock on the door.

Devika motioned for me to stand up, and so I did, as she went to the main door of my chambers. She had been right. I was nervous about entertaining these women, and it was a feeling I hadn't been privy to before. I couldn't say I liked it.

"Ladies, please come in," I heard Devika say as several women entered the parlor part of my room.

Both women had three ladies' maids with them and eight women coming at me at once was overwhelming. The amount of satin, lace, and beading alone almost caused me to panic.

Devika had told me that in Coranthia, the assistants to ladies were ladies' maids. The women that came in with Lady Bastil would be called principal ladies, as was the tradition in Southern Ralice. These women held their own titles and were not dependent on their position for their fortune.

The ladies' maids and principal ladies fell back so that Lady Bastil and Lady Jessamine could come forward. Lady Bastil was a thin woman with brown hair and freckles that cascaded over her face, down her neck, and spilled onto her collarbones. She looked delicate and innocent with eyes a soft blue. She wore a dusty purple gown that looked to be entirely made of tulle.

If Bastil was innocence, then Jessamine was pure sin. Devika had said she was lovely, but lovely wasn't the right word. Perfectly sculpted with attractive curves, which she was happily displaying in her metallic crimson gown. Her golden hair was shiny and perfectly set. Doe brown eyes sat in a face over a small perfect nose and pouty pink lips. Her skin was flawless and golden honey-colored that spoke of her heritage.

I found myself feeling insecure, which also was not something I was used to. I cursed this palace and these high women and finally Cassius for putting me in this position.

"Queen Dalion," Bastil said, dropping a perfect curtsey.

"Or do you Prefer Queen Georgette?" Jessamine asked, and I saw a sharp look across her pretty face. "Perhaps your given name makes you less uncomfortable, here in a place you feel like you don't belong."

I tilted my head a little at her and raised an eyebrow. A rare beauty this woman might be, but I saw cruelty waiting to strike just behind her powdered features.

"Queen Dalion suits me fine, Lady Bastil, thank you. And Lady Jessamine, I am touched by your concern for my comfort, and I thank you. I feel as if we are the best of friends already."

Devika had told me not to correct them when they called me a queen or insist that they call me by my first name. I had fully intended to ignore her advice until Jessamine had looked like she had been slapped by my title of *Queen Dalion.* They both also looked astonished that I spoke like a well-educated woman. No doubt they were expecting a wild pirate with sea slang on her tongue.

"Please call me Bastil, my Queen," She came forward and took my hand in hers. "It is such a pleasure to meet you finally. I must admit I have been rather curious as the last time we saw you was on your wedding day."

"Well, here I am," I said as I gestured to the couches behind me. "Would you all care to sit?"

"Ladies, you are dismissed," Jessamine said coldly, and the three women that had accompanied her nodded and stepped outside.

I gave a wide-eyed look to Devika, who shook her head at me to say nothing.

Lady Bastil's Principal ladies sat with us, and they talked to Devika. Jessamine and Bastil sat on a small couch across from a chair I sat in as straight and proper as I could manage. Bastil looked slightly uncomfortable which was a relief but Jessamine looked quite in her element.

"Thank you for the invitation, Queen Georgette," Jessamine said, eliciting a smile from me as she completely ignored my previous request. "You've caused quite a stir in court, and we awaited the day when you would grace us with your company."

My gaze kept shifting to Devika, whose lips were pursed. She had known something she hadn't told me, and now I was stuck in a room with this woman who was more predator than lady.

"Tea?" I inquired, trying to smother my smile, thinking this might be a more interesting meeting than I originally thought.

"Please," Bastil said, Jessamine simply nodded.

I waved Devika away when she tried to pour the tea for us and did it myself.

"Your rooms are lovely," Bastil said, and I could tell she was straining to keep the conversation light.

"Cassius' mother had excellent taste," Jessamine said, addressing Cassius by his first name, surprising me.

It also seemed to surprise Bastil, who looked at Jessamine in horror. I tucked away questions I had for Devika. *Cassius' mother had slept in these rooms? Was Cassius' mother alive? I knew his father had died, but I hadn't heard about his mother.*

"I am unaware of the original designer of the room, but thank you. They are quite opulent for my taste but still lovely."

I handed a cup to each woman and sat back in my chair with my cup as Devika spoke quietly with Bastil's ladies as if they were previous friends.

"You aren't quite what I expected," Lady Bastil went on, her fair skin, coloring pink at her words. "Not that that is a terrible thing Queen Dalion."

"I am surprised by how many people hold strong opinions of pirates who have never met one." I smiled at her, and her face went from pink to red. "I don't mean to chastise you, Lady Bastil. How could you guess that your king would choose a pirate as a wife?"

"Truly," Jessamine said darkly.

"I meant no offense my Queen," Bastil said, looking sheepish.

"It takes a great deal more than an honest curiosity to offend me, Bastil."

"Cassius would have had his reasons, of course," Jessamine started in, "Taken with your exotic nature or perhaps a certain appeal of danger that you hold though..."

She stopped mid-sentence to appear as if she had tact enough to think about not saying it. I had known plenty of women in my life exactly like her, and she was merely giving her next words the dramatic pause they deserved before she attempted to flay me open with them.

"...rumors around the castle are that Cassius doesn't share your bed and that you don't warm his either."

"Jessamine," Bastil said, her eyes going wide as she looked at the woman.

I set my cup of tea down on a table near me and sat forward in my seat, entwining my fingers together and resting my elbows on the chair.

"Oh, you know how servants talk," Jessamine said, her tone still holding the vicious edge of a knife blade.

"No, I don't." I smiled at her. "Tell me, what do the servants say?"

She looked panicked for a moment which I counted as a victory, but she wasn't a woman to be trifled with and regained her composure quickly.

"Oh, Queen Georgette, I wouldn't do you the disservice of telling you such gossip. I only meant to warn you as a friend that there are laws in this country about marriage that you may want to be aware of."

"What laws are those, you treacherous snake?" My tone was clipped, my patience grew thin, and the talk from Devika and Bastil's ladies went silent.

Jessamine seemed unfazed by the insult.

"For a marriage to be fully realized by the priests of Southern Ralice, your marriage has to be consummated. If Cassius refuses to share a bed with you, one could question the validity of your marriage. Heaven forbid another woman caught his eye, and he decided to bed her and turn you out cold."

I was speechless. Not because I didn't have many things that came to my mind to say, but because I was questioning the authority of what she was saying. One look at Davika, and the cringe on her face, and I knew it was true. Bastil's eyes were wide, and her ladies all stared at me, waiting for my response. I could laugh at her. She meant to get under my skin by implying that she might steal my husband from me. If I ever needed to assert my authority as a Queen, I couldn't behave solely like a pirate in front of women like her. I needed to be a pirate queen.

"If you are so eager to warm my husband's bed, I wish you all the luck in the world. Some women have been gifted with no more than what is between their legs to improve their station in life. We must all use what weapons we possess. Hear me well, Lady Jessamine, I care nothing for Cassius Dalion other than what his title and power provide me. Your childish threats of marital sabotage are inconsequential. So, whore yourself to him if you see fit. Perhaps he'll tell me about it at one of our daily meals together. But until you indeed win his heart, and usurp me as queen, you will do well to remember that I currently hold the title."

Her response was silence, and a hatred that burned, lingering in her eyes the rest of the uncomfortable gathering.

When they left and all women had shuffled out of my room, I got a glimpse of Brees outside the door who had a mischievous half-grin on his stupid face and a sparkle in his eye that caused me to slam the door on him. Though mostly to cover my smile that he felt comfortable enough to make fun of me.

Still facing the closed door and my back to Devika I asked, "What was it that you were going to tell me about Jessamine?"

"She came here nearly a year ago and has been a guest of court," she said.

"Okay, but why does she hate me with such fervor?" I turned around and accused her as if she were the cause of all this.

"She came intending to become the next queen of Southern Ralice. Her father requires power and, on his behalf, she has been trying to seduce King Cassius into marriage."

"For a year, and it hasn't worked?" I looked to the door as if I still might see her beautiful features.

"No, he does little more than spend sparing minutes with her when she arranges it," Devika said, walking down the hall to my room as I followed her.

"Sparing moments in public perhaps..." I said under my breath.

Devika stopped and whirled on me. It was an indication that I had said something offensive.

"Jessamine would lose all credibility as a lady if she were to make good on her thinly veiled threats, and our king isn't the sort of man to take a woman to his bed without thought of the consequences," she huffed.

"Devika, have you known very many men in your lifetime?" I met her steel tone with my own as I breezed past her. "Or been in the heat of the moment when someone you fancy wraps their hands around your waist?"

She might have blushed, but I only heard an outraged objection get lodged in her throat as I went to remove some of the jewelry I was wearing and set it on my bed.

"My insult to her intentions was not a judgment of who she beds. A woman ought to choose who she lies with and when. It was an insult to her intent. To lay with a man for power or petty jealousy alone is below what we as women are capable of."

"I'm sorry, my Queen, I spoke out of turn." I looked over at her.

That fire still burned in her eyes. She was a strong woman to apologize when she still felt I was wrong.

"I'm sorry to have offended Cassius. Not for his sake but for yours. I suppose if I had tried to get a man to marry me for the better part of a year and he ended up marrying a pirate woman, who I thought myself superior to, I would hate me too."

Her shoulders relaxed. "She's awful. I would never try to encourage sympathy for her. She's rude to her ladies and treats the staff here like little more than whipping servants."

"So I saw. Perhaps next time we could just invite Lady Bastil. She seemed pleasant enough and I admire curiosity in a person."

"I'm surprised you would agree to another tea with them at all," she said, reaching out and taking the jewelry I had discarded.

"I think it's time I stop feeling sorry for myself, Devika. I can spend my days here walled up in my room, and walking the market alone with Brees playing watchdog, or I can make the most of the situation."

"I would say I was proud of you if I wasn't scared some devious plan against the crown was behind this sudden change." She rolled her eyes at me. "We need to tell the tailor what you plan on wearing to the ball to celebrate your ascension to the throne."

"Tell me why that has to happen again and why do they wait five months to hold this celebration?"

"By Southern Ralician Law the Queen is not announced into court in front of all Lords and common folk alike until the fifth month in case anything is to happen to her."

"In case anything is to happen to her?" I asked.

"In case our ruler decides he no longer wishes to be married to her," she amended.

"In case he decides to murder her?"

"Sometimes." She nodded. "You should wear something grand..."

She went on as if she hadn't just told me Kings in this country could murder their wives with no repercussions for five months after they married. I took a deep breath and assured myself that if Cassius wanted me dead, he would have surely killed me by now.

Right?

Chapter Six

Mercy

He'd come with more than just a ceremonial military. It was a show of power. It was a threat. He had at least fifty men with him, which wasn't enough to overthrow us from the inside but enough to make a statement. For now, my brother had forgotten his anger with me and was seething at the implied force and threat from King Cyril Kosdel of Northern Ralice.

A man I had been intended to marry but had never met.

My sisters had picked my dress. Something about opulence and femininity. The fitted bodice was crafted from sensuous green velvet with a single flounce around the bustline and thin velvet straps that tied at my shoulders. The skirt was embroidered with delicate golden flowers and a single thin green tulle layer laid over them, making it look like you were viewing a garden through a haze. My hair had been rag curled and pinned up and I wore a full crown of black diamonds and emeralds. The points of the crown jetted up like spires of a prison tower. A dash of color across my cheeks and a stain on my lips made me look older and somehow more formidable. I looked more confident than I was.

Kiltore dabbed some white flower oil on my wrists and left me alone to stare at my reflection. My sisters knew I was nervous so they said that we could walk together to the ballroom. Temperance said I should walk down the stairs by myself with my head high as if I was next in line for the throne, and Prudence said as soon as I reached the bottom, they wouldn't leave my side again. I took a deep breath and for the hundredth time that day, I told myself I could do this without crying. The loss I had felt months ago threatened to bubble over at this most inopportune time.

Originally my brother was going to have my sisters and I greet King Kosdel alongside him. When the messenger had come to say King Kosdel had fifty military men in tow, that plan had been thrown out. My brothers met him and his men by themselves. So, the first time I would see him would be when I descended the ballroom stairs. I tried to imagine what I would feel looking into his eyes. They would be the eyes of the king who I once was betrothed to and now was nothing more than my brother's enemy. My grief reared its head and reminded me that it was his fault that Absalom and Georgette died. It was his fault that...I pressed my fingers to my lips.

My door opened gently, and I turned to see Prudence smile at me from where her head peeked in. I smiled and waved, and she retreated, shutting the door behind her. There would be no delaying this another moment, it was time to be the fearless survivor my brother hoped to present me as.

I stood and walked out of the comfort of my room and was faced with my flawless sisters, both as beautiful as I had ever seen them. Prudence was dressed in a pure white satin dress with billowy sleeves and cloth capped buttons down to the floor where the fabric pooled and shimmered like snow white water. Temperance wore an identical dress, but the satin was nightmare black that seemed to swallow all light. While Temperance wore a tiara decorated with clear shining white diamonds, Prudence wore the same tiara with black diamonds set into it. Two halves of a coin and not a duo I would attempt to disturb.

"You both look so lovely."

While they both smiled, that is where their similarities ended. Prudence beamed at me with thanks and twirled her satin skirts about her whimsically. Temperance's smile was almost vicious; one that could take over a kingdom.

"You do too," Temperance said, "You look like a queen."

"I'm not a queen." We started toward the ballroom.

"Rumors have spread to the other kingdoms of Mother's...condition." Temperance went on though her back was to me now.

"What condition?" I asked, "How do you know this?"

"Trust me," Prudence interrupted, "You don't want to know."

"Mother is fading, her soul has stopped living since father died and rumors of our vulnerability circulate the waters." She said it cold and distant as if she didn't speak of anyone she knew.

This wasn't my brother trying to cram something down my throat. This wasn't a scare tactic being used to make me behave. It was Temperance trying to impart something important if I was smart enough to listen.

"And?" I asked quietly.

"You are the eldest. While you may not like it, and I don't agree with Holt's methods, you are one of the beacons of strength in our family."

She was chastising me. Not for standing up for myself or rebelling, but for shirking my responsibilities and acting as if I could run from them. I took a deep breath as I followed behind them.

"I hear you Temperance," I said, and Prudence looked over her shoulder to give me an apologetic smile.

We were silent the rest of the way, winding through hallways to avoid the main entrance. There was a foyer and a staircase behind a set of open doors that led to a grand marble ballroom floor. We could hear music, raucous laughter, and conversation. My brothers would already have been announced as well as King Kosdel and most of the guests. It was traditional for the women of the castle's family to be introduced last. I hadn't asked if my mother was attending because I had been afraid of the answer. If Temperance were right and rumors were already milling about, her absence here would be noticed.

We stopped off to the left as a herald came to take my sisters, leaving me to the left of the door. I took another breath as they walked away. I hadn't realized how much I had been relying on their company to make it this far. Prudence tapped her chin up at me once; a reminder of how I was to hold myself. Then they both disappeared as the herald announced them to the party below.

After a few short moments, the herald gestured to me to take my place in front of the doors. *How would Temperance walk into a room?* I asked myself. Strong and silent as if she knew every one of your secrets and wasn't afraid to lay you bare. *And how would Georgette walk into a room?* Like she owned every pair of eyes on her and she wouldn't hesitate to fight them all off with her bare hands. I attempted to embody that energy though I felt it warred with my instincts to sit in the corner and observe.

I was barely aware of the herald saying my name as I descended the stairs and roleplayed a fearsome princess capable of ruling a country and a pirate experienced in running a ship. I allowed my gaze to linger on some people giving them curt nods and small tight-lipped smiles. I didn't falter, though I could feel my fingers trembling with so many eyes watching my every move.

Then Langston was there at the bottom to meet me with his hand out to receive mine. I gratefully accepted as the room went back to its music and laughter. I let out a pent-up breath and scanned the room for the infamous King Kosdel.

"That was immaculately done," Prudence said, bounding up to us and Temperance gave me a nod.

"Would you like me to take you to him?" Langston asked.

I opened my mouth to say yes, intending to rely on him the entire time but then I stopped myself. I would face him on my own. He would look into my eyes and know that his deviant plans to use me as his spark of war had failed and I would not be shackled to him. I wanted my brother to walk me there, but it was something I needed to do on my own, for myself.

"No," I said, shaking my head. "Point the way and I shall introduce myself."

"Unorthodox but you deserve nothing less," Langston said, pointing to the corner of the room where a large table was set for the royal family.

To one side, my brother spoke with a tall handsome older man with chestnut brown hair that was peppered with grey. The man was wearing gold and crimson, the colors of Northern Ralice and he had a dark metal crown sitting atop his head.

"Do you want us to follow behind you?" Temperance asked, as her eyes too wandered to King Kosdel.

"I can do this," I told her, but I was mostly reassuring myself.

"He doesn't deserve your respect," Temperance said.

"That he does not," Langston seconded.

"The respect I show people of the high court is not for them but myself," I said, quoting one of my mother's prose.

So, I soldiered over. Willing myself to channel the same regality I had come down the stairs with. My brother caught my eye first and I swore I saw a smile tug at the corners of his mouth as I came to meet them on my own. Women were usually required to have a male companion to introduce them. The queen was the only exception to that rule, but Holt didn't look as if he intended to stop me or even scold me for it.

"My King," I said, curtseying to my brother when I arrived in front of both of them.

I did not curtsey or even nod to King Cyril Kosdel. He licked his lips and looked at me like a cat might eye a mouse he was thinking of playing with. It gave me the chills, but I did not lower my gaze from his.

"Cyril, may I present to you my eldest sister Princess Mercy," Holt said my name with authority as if it meant something.

"Ah, my beautiful ex-betrothed." He reached out and went to reach for my hand, but I pulled away from him.

He didn't seem to be too offended as he smiled like a predator, his lips splitting into a grin I could have never learned to love.

"A shame you did not make it back to me, what a fine addition to my crown you would have made."

"Fortunately for us, your backhanded plot did not succeed," Holt bit out and I shot him a thankful look.

"If we could but come to a peaceful arrangement Holt, the Princess here would certainly still make a lovely bride to secure an agreement."

"My sister can speak for herself on how she would feel about that, but I would never do her the dishonor of ever entertaining such an idea."

"I would do many things for my people and many things for my brother, King Kosdel, thankfully a future with you is no longer my fate." I hoped the words sounded cold and sharp.

Holt looked shocked and King Cyril Kosdel looked mildly irritated.

"I forget other countries don't know how to keep their women in check." King Cyril coughed. "King Cassius has that advantage over you. His father had a way of keeping his women in their place and I do not doubt that he will treat that wild new queen the same."

"My brother is a respectable man and King," I said, hoping my words would act as an apologetic balm for some of the angry words I spoke to Holt at the dinner table. "You are a coward. If you mean to silence me into submission, perhaps it is you that is fortunate not to have married me."

Holt smiled at me.

"Would you take the next dance with me?" King Cyril asked holding out his hand.

It was more than a little surprising, seeing as how I had just insulted his character.

"You needn't," Holt said, addressing me.

"It would be my pleasure," I said, curtseying to King Kosdel.

I nodded at Holt that I was okay as King Kosdel lead me to the dancefloor as one song ended, and another began. I breathed a silent sigh of relief that it was a short song. So, while I would be in the bastard's hands it wouldn't be for long and I would have done my duty.

"I appreciate a woman with such candor," he said as his hand felt a little too low on my back and I narrowed my eyes at him.

I didn't give him the satisfaction of responding, instead I focused on the dance as the music came. I tried to block out memories of dancing with a striking pirate under a bright sky of stars. I ached for the ocean and the ship I had only known for a fortnight.

"Perhaps when I overtake Adamas I will still make you my bride after all," he threatened and again I met him with silence willing the song to end.

"Did you meet Commander Absalom Church when you were aboard my pirate ship?" he asked casually, and my eyes shifted to him slowly with more than a little venom building on my tongue.

It wasn't your pirate ship you vile man. Still, I stayed silent.

"Such a *young* man to have lost his life but that is the cost of war," he said, looking directly at me as I tried to keep my composure.

I knew he was only trying to get a rise out of me. Though how he guessed I would have formed a bond with any of the crew of The Siren I didn't know. Perhaps he was just blindly attacking in the hopes of ruffling my feathers. I was wishing my brother could kill him on the spot.

"I can't say I remember him," I said with a voice as steady as possible.

"He wasn't the sort of man to make an impression," King Kosdel went on, "A little too meek. My Army master tells me he took after his mother, unfortunately. The woman was as crazy as a sewer rat at a banquet. I didn't intend for him to die but perhaps it was for the best."

"I do not envy the men under your rule," I said, breathing deeply not letting my anger surface.

He smiled down at me. He leaned in uncomfortably close to me so that his sickeningly warm breath was too close to my ear. My stomach churned. He had pulled me tighter against him so I could feel the press of his body against mine. My instincts were screaming at me to push him away and yell at him. To tell him Absalom wasn't mad and that he didn't deserve to die for his loyalty to Elias and Georgette.

"If your brother can't convince King Dalion to aid him in this foolish war against my kingdom, you might get to see how I would rule over your country quite soon. I knew Aamon Dalion quite well and he trained his son to be the same kind of ruler he was. King Cassius Dalion will never agree to a war he gains nothing from. I'll take over your kingdom and turn you into my prize whore."

"May I cut in?" It was Holt who had a rage built behind his eyes, and though he was only a few inches taller than King Kosdel, he seemed towering at that moment.

"Of course!" King Kosdel said jovially, releasing me and I welcomed the space between us. "What a fine dancer you are my lady."

He bowed and walked away leaving Holt to take his place who took my hands gently as a new song began.

"You were right," he said and my eyes snapped up to his. "I am not worthy of your trust after I almost betrothed you to that man. I hope one day I might earn your forgiveness."

"You did what you thought best. I've never resented you for it. I'm sorry...for what I said." I patted his shoulder where my hand rested.

"Let's not speak of it now," he smiled. "The music is too lovely and the wine too sweet."

"I want him dead, Holt," I said darkly, letting out part of what I felt when King Kosdel had held me in a dance. "I want him run through, and I want him to pay for what he's done. I don't care what we have to do."

He may have assumed I meant revenge for my own sake. Not that I wished cruel and final justice for Absalom, Georgette, and Elias. I would let my brother make assumptions about my intentions.

He nodded as a promise passed between us.

Chapter Seven

Georgette

"I swear you know when he's away and plan your stunts accordingly," Brees said, looking at the front of the ragged tavern I had instructed us to.

It was only him and I; he was wearing middle-class clothing as I was. No jewelry adorned my sleeves, and no intricate pearls were woven into my hair. So, dismounting our horses and tying them to the post in the front of the tavern, we looked as if we belonged. Though I doubted even people from the middle class visited this desolate place. It seemed as if it were just an unfortunate stop on your way to something better. It had also rained the morning before, so the ground was muddy slop.

"I cannot get away with anything too dastardly with you beside me, Brees." I stepped forward, no longer hesitating at the doorway and he followed.

While the inside of the place was just as dilapidated as the outside, I immediately sensed comfort. A comfort that was broken once two strangers walked into the crowd gathered for their last meal of the day. All heads swiveled to us, and I decided that the people of Larkin did not like strangers. Every single face trained on us with a critical eye almost willing me to step back out of the establishment.

Except, the reputation of these embittered people is exactly why I had come. The rumor was that the people of Larkin hated their royal family. Once they had been in good favor but when their orchards had burned down, they had nothing but hatred for the Dalion line. You could trust very few people to tell the truth in the world, but angry and bitter people were some of the few.

I kept my chin raised, making eye contact with anyone that met my gaze. Brees kept close behind me, and I didn't doubt his hulking presence was keeping me safe. We sidled up to the bar and placed ourselves on two empty benches. A woman eyed us from the far end of the bar where she was talking to a man who looked to have been more than a little intoxicated. She did not hurry over and in fact, seemed to be making a show of taking her time.

When she came close enough, I recognized her as the woman I had offered my money to when Cassius and I came through this place months ago. When I had been taken from my home and thought I would perish, I offered the last of what I had to her. She had rebuffed me and instead I had given the coins to her son.

I panicked. Would she recognize me now? If she did, she didn't show any sign of it. She eyed Brees and I with the same cold glare that the others had given. She stopped in front of us, not offering any greeting or warm tavern owner welcome. She simply stared and looked irritated that we hadn't said anything.

"Well," she demanded, "What do you want?"

"Some ale?" I asked, "Perhaps a meal."

"You have money?"

Brees huffed and set a small bag of coins on the counter. He gave her a look to let her know he wasn't impressed with her tone, and she returned his gaze with one of the same.

"Spiced ale and rabbit stew." She turned to fill two metal mugs with ale from a barrel.

The room was still silent as the people inside the tavern listened to our every word and stared at the back of our heads.

"We don't get much company." The woman all but slammed the cups in front of us so that some spilled on the counter. "My name is Dola; I own the place."

"With such a warm welcome I can't imagine why people don't frequent," I challenged, taking a loud sip from my mug and found it to be very watered-down spiced ale.

"Like I said we don't get people often." She leaned forward on the bar throwing an accusation at me.

"We're newlyweds." I grabbed Bree's arm. "We've traveled from Vlagdor to see Hallow."

I smiled wide and placed a swift kiss on Bree's cheek. He turned a sunburnt shade of red but didn't pull away from me. When the woman nodded and walked down the bar to get us our stew, he turned to give me a look that said he wouldn't marry me for all the spice in Hestiege. I slurped my ale at him intentionally loud.

"When did you get married?" Dola asked when she set two bowls of muddy-looking stew in front of us.

"Not a week ago yet," I looked up at Brees batting my lashes lovingly.

"Congratulations." She smiled slightly and she seemed to have softened a bit after deeming us non-threatening.

The room had also gone back to quiet conversations at tables over lantern light. I surveyed the crowd behind me. No doubt they all lived in Larkin. They looked as rundown as the rest of the town did. It wasn't just their appearance either but the way they held themselves. Their heads hung low; marks of people who had been trampled and now resided in that dark place.

"My husband said when he was a boy there was a great orchard outside these castle walls," I said, turning back around and stirring my steaming stew. "Can it still be found somewhere around here? I'm from Puddle Island and we don't grow much of anything there."

"No." Her tone had gone back cold, and Brees' eyes slid to mine waiting for the rest of the words to my scheme.

"Shame, he talked of its beauty, and I wished to see it. What happened to it?" I asked taking a tentative spoonful of the soup into my mouth finding it full of wild sage and fresh pepper.

"It was burned down." She leaned back watching me eat.

"Lightning? Rogue bonfire?" I asked casually as Brees dipped his spoon into his bowl.

"King Aamon Dalion had it burned to the ground." She spat his name out like poison.

"Quite the accusation." Brees' tone held an edge of anger I was sure did not escape Dola's notice.

"Ah, a loyalist." She looked at him with distaste.

"Why did he do it?" My curiosity piqued.

Brees shook his head once at me which made Dola laugh.

"Not too fond of our Royal family yet then miss, good on you."

"I've not met them. Though I do know the greater power a man holds, the greater opportunity for evil."

"Darling," Brees warned under his breath. "This savors of royal slander."

"Kian tells the story best," Dola said, jerking her head toward a man who was sitting a few seats over from us at a bar.

"I'm tired of recanting the tale," the man's voice came across to us with no humor.

"Oh, come now Ki, don't let our guest go without hearing the tragic fall of Larkin." There was a sharpness to her voice, and he lifted his head to glare at her.

"Will you leave me alone then?" he asked her, raising his head to look at us.

Brees and I looked over at him as he straightened and turned. He took a deep breath as if preparing himself for the tale he was about to weave and Brees looked just as curious as I to hear what he had to say. The man drained his mug of spiced ale and slammed the empty mug on the counter.

The tavern had gone silent again but now the patron's attention were not on us, but the man sitting before me. He looked to be old enough to be my father with light brown hair peppered with grey at his temples. His face was handsome with soft brown eyes and a mouth that looked as if it once smiled. The edges of his eyes held wrinkles of arduous work and age.

"The tale goes like this," he started, looking at us both. "Once there was a man who whispered to trees. He tended an orchard outside the city, and it flourished. News of his gift reached the king and so he called the man to come to tend the trees in the palace gardens. The man worked in the palace during the day and brought home honor at night to his town. He did well, the king's gardens flourished, and the king was well pleased. Until the man that spoke to the trees fell in love with the king's prized flower he kept locked away in the palace. The man took her for himself, and they fell desperately in love. But one cannot take even a flower from a king without a price. So, the king burned his town's orchard to the ground and banished the man from entering the city and from ever reseeding the land that once held the beautiful trees. Then he forbade the trade of goods with that man's city and the traders inside the wall."

"A hefty price for a flower," I said when it was apparent his story was over. Elias would have liked his tale.

"I have never found her equal." He turned back to face the counter and the looks around the room had grown more dismal, if that was possible.

I was surprised that the man telling the story was the main character, but the woman behind the counter stared at him with anger. Perhaps she was still punishing him for the fall of the town.

"Perhaps men should stop comparing us to flowers and some of their heartaches could be avoided." Her words were directed at Kian who had just told the story, and even *I* flinched away from them.

There was bitterness between them. A deep-seated resentment that had not healed, though I knew the orchard had burned nearly twenty-three years prior. Brees was still looking at the man with his brows furrowed as if the story was new information to him.

"On the contrary," I said, suddenly feeling sympathy for Kian. "A flower is a diverse comparison because while they are pleasing to the eye one might carry thorns, or another contain poison. Flowers are integral to nature and the roots of flowering trees can topple stone buildings. A flower is a mighty thing."

The woman behind the counter scoffed but the man who had told the story looked over at me with the barest hint of a grin on his lips.

"What type of flower was your love?" Brees asked, surprising me with the question.

"A dahlia," he answered without hesitation. "What kind of flower is your lovely bride?"

"Probably one of the poisonous strains." Brees smiled and I attempted to shove him off his stool good naturally; he did not move an inch.

A few men laughed at his joke, and I went back to eating my stew. The room had lightened and the woman at the bar seemed to relax. She even offered Brees a bit more stew when he finished his, which he accepted gratefully. I refused a refill on food and instead sipped the weak ale and eavesdropped on conversations around the room.

I wouldn't push these people for more information tonight. I could tell they were a wary bunch. I planned to take Brees back every night for the next two weeks to keep up our newlywed facade and slowly use the time to start conversations and overhear anything that might be useful to me. Tonight, I had already learned a great deal. Mostly that Cassius's father was the villain that all of Marecult made him out to be. So that left me to wonder who the King's precious flower had been. My mother had told me stories of how King Aamon Dalion had kept a woman on a metal chain with him wherever he went. That he hadn't ever married her. Was that woman Cassius' mother? I had inquired about her a couple of times, but Devika refused to divulge any information about her, and I could tell she and the other staff had been ordered not to speak of her to me.

"Mom," a voice came from around the side of the counter, and I turned to see a round-faced girl with stringy brown hair up on her tiptoes, looking at her mom.

"Clarice Glister." Dola scolded the young child, who looked less than chastised.

"Sorry mom, she got away from me," a boy's voice came from a little further off and I assumed there were stairs somewhere that led to rooms on the second level of the place.

"Thomas, I told you and the boys to keep her upstairs," Dola said, as three new heads popped into view.

The oldest one who I assumed was Thomas was the boy who had taken my coins that day.

"I'm sorry mom but she kept going on about how she heard new voices down here and I told her that she shouldn't bother you, but she kept nagging at us." The boy complained and I smiled as Dola walked out from behind the counter. Presumably to return them to where they were supposed to be. That was until I noticed one of the younger boys held a wooden sword and wore a makeshift eyepatch over his face.

"I'm surprised you let such ruffians into your establishment," I said, tone mock horrified. "Pirates sleeping upstairs, I'm shocked."

The children were drawn to the accusation, and they avoided their mom's grasp to come around the bar to look at me. They were all three siblings, of that I was sure. They all had the same round face and upturned nose. The oldest, Thomas, made eye contact with me and his eyes went wide. I winked at him and put a quick finger to my lips hoping it was enough to keep from exposing me at that moment. The sharp lad nodded at me.

"They aren't real pirates." Clarice came forward.

"Could have fooled me," I said, eyeing the boys warily.

"Don't be scared," she reached out to touch my hand reassuringly. "They just play pretend pirates."

"And which pirates are your favorites?" I directed the question to them all.

"Baron Valloe!"

"Nathaniel Baine!"

"Captain Dirty Rooster!"

The boys all shouted at the same time and my chest squeezed at the mention of my father.

"Did you know that our queen is a pirate?" Clarice asked me, as her brothers made their way closer to Brees and me with their mother's disapproving gaze behind them.

"I'd heard that, but I didn't know if it were a lie or not," I leaned back.

"I wish it were," Brees said, and I turned to give him a salty look.

"No! it's true! Our King captured one of the famous Captain's Baine and married her!" One of the younger boys exclaimed, like he couldn't keep it in anymore.

"You don't say?"

"I hear she's terribly ugly with a wart on her nose like a witch," Brees said.

"I hear she walks around the castle in pants," James said.

"You're kidding me," I gasped, and Thomas smiled at me.

I wondered if he had put together that the woman who had given him coins that day had become his king's bride. Did this young boy know who I was? Kids were often more aware of things than adults gave them credit for. I never underestimated children.

"I hear she's perfectly terrible," Dola said sourly. "I also heard that if you four don't get up to bed that you'll all be hung by your toenails."

"I heard she's lovely; a gardener from the palace I know says she gives them all trouble," Kian said from the other side of Brees.

"Uncle Kian!" Clarice shrieked, leaving my side and running to throw herself at the man.

Siblings. The bitterness of sibling resentment was what I had sensed earlier, I realized. I turned back to look into my empty stew bowl. The tavern had gone quiet again and I wondered what the patrons were listening for now.

"I hear she once dueled with your king on a pier in Hestiege, bested him, and escaped," I said, turning to look at the boys, but they were looking beyond me now at the door to my back.

Their expressions were curious except for Thomas who looked stricken. I looked up to Dola who had bowed her head. I realized the eerie quiet that had come over the tavern was on account of someone entering.

"What a creative version of that story." The dark voice came from behind me, and I took a deep breath before I turned.

Cassius stood before me. A dozen guards stood behind him, intimidating and radiating authority. Cassius also held that same authority and it shimmered off him in waves. He looked around the tavern before his gaze came back to rest on my face.

"I remember that duel quite differently, my Queen."

A murmur went through the tavern as Cassius exposed me for who I was. Brees stood up and bowed to Cassius going to stand next to him like the good soldier he was. I narrowed my eyes at him.

Traitor.

Though he wasn't a traitor. He just wasn't loyal to me.

I surveyed the people around me who had, just moments before, been comfortable with my presence. Now they looked at me like I was an invader, like I was their enemy. I looked back at Dola and she glanced up for the briefest moment to share a hideous scowl that was just for me before she went back to bowing her head. The three boys behind me stared at me in wonder which was slightly medicinal on my wounded pride. I turned back to Clarice and Kian. Kian wasn't quite smiling, but he wasn't offering me a scowl as his sister was.

"You're the queen?" Clarice asked, looking up at me.

My response to her got stuck in my throat because what I wanted to say was no. No, I wasn't a queen. No, I wasn't *his* queen. He had turned me into this thing that I wasn't. Made me into this courtier that was so appalling to me. Their faces of docility because of my title repulsed me, but the truth was, I was a queen.

"Aye," I said, smiling at her. "That I am."

"Are you a pirate too? Are the stories true?" James asked from behind me.

"She was once." Cassius answered for me, and my eyes whipped to him and the smile that spread across his face.

"Thank you for your hospitality," I turned and dropping a curtsey to Dola who didn't so much as acknowledge that I said something.

I walked past Cassius in silence and the guards parted for me as I made my way outside. I stopped dead as I surveyed a gilded carriage that was parked in front of the tavern. It was out of place amongst the run-down buildings and dismal muddy streets. My anger grew. He had come here like this on purpose. It had been a strategic move.

"I don't think you've ever seen the royal carriage," he said, having come out of the tavern to stand behind me. "Quite grand to bring out all the time but for special occasions, I do prefer it." He breezed past me and got into the carriage holding the door open with his foot.

The other guard mounted horses that had been tied to the front post and two guards climbed onto the front of the carriage to drive the horses. I took a deep breath, convincing myself that throwing handfuls of mud into the ornate interior was childish. Part of me didn't care and I looked down into the muck at my feet.

"Just get in," Brees said, coming up beside me. "He's in a mood and he won't let you win this one."

My face was hot, and I worked my teeth against each other.

"Coming, wife?" he called out loud, and a few of the guards laughed.

I looked down the road back to the route leading back to the castle.

"Please do not walk off in defiance," Brees begged.

I didn't know if he was requesting it for my sake or his, but I had made him a promise not to humiliate him in front of the guard again. Even if that meant humiliating myself, I would not break my word.

"Just because you asked nicely," I said, smiling wide at him making a show of touching his arm lightly.

"Thank you, Georgette," he said under his breath, giving me a slight reprieve from my anger.

However, the moment fled as soon as I stepped into the ostentatious carriage and found Cassius eyeing me smugly from one side of it. I sat down on the opposite side deliberately not making eye contact with him as he shut the door. We rode in silence as my anger bubbled. He had asked me to behave like a pirate and yet he showed up in all his finery when I crossed over an invisible boundary. I wondered if it was just to show me that I belonged to him now.

My pride railed against the idea. I belonged to no one.

I looked up at him finally when we were close to Hallow Manor after letting my emotions swell into an insurmountable mountain. His brown eyes met mine and his mouth began to form the grin that seemed to destroy all my control. I wanted to scratch his eyes out of his head.

We finally reached the back of the manor and I got up to exit the carriage as fast as I could, unable to be in such a confined space with him a moment longer. I meant to walk straight into the cellar and into my room. To not give him the satisfaction of my outburst but his conceited grin flashed in my mind, and I whirled on him as he climbed out of the carriage with the guard there to witness.

"Why? If you had such a problem with me going to Larkin, why come and get me in such a fashion?"

"Because you meant to go somewhere in my kingdom where you could still be Georgette the pirate captain. I don't think I have to remind you that I've stripped you of that..."

He didn't get to finish his thought as I flew at him in a rage. To my pleasure, he looked startled at first but caught me easily enough by my arms. He grabbed me firmly and gave me a hard shove that unbalanced me as I fell to the muddy ground on my backside. I glared up at him, willing the flush of humiliation not to creep over my cheeks.

"You're untrained and sloppy. That crude fighting might work in the back alleys of common streets, but you needn't waste your time on me," he disparaged. "But while you're down there let me make a few things clear to you that you seem confused about. This is my kingdom and my castle, and the people here are my people. You, my darling wife, belong to the crown of Southern Ralice. I am using you as a display of power, but you are nothing more than a pawn played for my end goal. You do nothing without my blessing. Your horrendous clothing isn't ordered without my consent. You don't hand out titles and land without my approval. You do not continue to breathe outside of my good grace. So please, give the people a good show and stalk your cage like the feral cat you are. But remember, my queen, who put you in that cage, and who holds the leash you are on. I will parade you all across Southern Ralice, to every single soul that lives within its borders to show them what I have turned you into. A once infamous pirate reduced to a king's pet."

"I loathe you," I spat.

"That's a good girl." He stalked off leaving me with shame still flushed on my cheeks.

I decided then that I wouldn't leave peacefully. If I didn't get to slice Cassius Dalion's throat open before I made my escape from this place I would not be satisfied.

None of the guards laughed at me now and they all moved about as if they didn't see me wallowing in the mud. I sat there until Brees appeared in front of me looking off to the direction that Cassius went. He reached his hand down to help me up and I took it.

"He shouldn't have knocked you down like that."

"I would have done the same to him had I gotten the opportunity, no need to fault him for that bit." I tried unsuccessfully to brush the mud off my skirts. "Would you teach me to fight? Properly?"

He looked at me startled for a moment and then seemed to contemplate it.

"I suppose I could. It was painful to watch you just then. I could at least give you a little more of a fighting chance. Though his father made him train from five years old. You fluster him, which you can use to your advantage."

"What he just displayed didn't seem flustered. He seemed mildly annoyed like I was a fly in his glass of wine." I stomped after him as he made his way toward the cellar doors.

"I've known Cassius for a long time." He chuckled, and I was startled he referred to him by his first name. "He never asserts his dominance verbally. He's never had to. Trust me when I say, you have thoroughly agitated him."

"Why are you telling me this." I stopped to stare at him trying to gauge if it was a trick or some form of mocking.

"I..." He stopped to smile back at me, "find it amusing to see him in such a state."

Chapter Eight

Mercy

I had survived King Cyril Kosdel. He had taken his men and fled, or at least it made me feel better to act like that is what happened. My brother told us that he would wait for King Cassius Dalion's invitation into his court to discuss terms with him. Meanwhile, Holt was in contact with King Dalion to discuss his assistance in a war against Northern Ralice. From what I could understand, he was hesitant to enter a war with my brother, despite his grievances with the King that ruled the land just above him.

My brother had brought up the idea of my marriage to King Dalion only a few times in passing and his face was always guarded against my rage. Though my original anger had dwindled. If we did not have King Dalion's support in this war, we would never win with the river between us and Northern Ralice. His assistance was necessary for our triumph, and with my want of vengeance still fresh in my mind, I had started to contemplate the idea of agreeing to Holt's idea.

After a couple of weeks, Holt informed us he had received a letter from the new queen of Southern Ralice. She was sending a Lord to stay with us and we were to welcome him as warmly as one could be welcomed. He said she gave some vague trading reason, but he suspected that King Dalion was sending him as a spy to be sure of our intentions. We were all instructed to be on our best behavior while the Lord was around. Holt planned to sway this ambassador to our side and send him back with a good word about us to his King.

So, we all sat in the throne room one afternoon waiting for Lord Kaloqey to arrive. I was dressed in a crushed velvet dress that made me look as if my body actually held some shape. A long silver chain with a daisy on the end was between my fingers as I rolled it back and forth in boredom. My twin sisters sat on either side of me and were both sensible enough to bring something to pass the time. Prudence was embroidering a tea towel with a shocking purple lilac, and Temperance was reading a short history of the civil war in Ralice that had caused it to split centuries years ago. We had all been sitting to the left of the thrones in a short section of pews that were intended to hold us when we were forced to go to religious ceremonies.

My brother Holt sat on the throne with Tobias next to him. My mother was evidently too weak to show up again. Langston who was growing more irritable by the second was pacing behind the both of them with increasing fervor. My two younger siblings had blessedly gotten out of this, and their governess was teaching them their daily lessons. I envied them and wished I was twelve years old again.

"You may read over my shoulder but if you cannot keep up with my pace, I will not slow for you," Temperance said quietly to me.

"Generous," I said, but obliged her and started to read about the great war over her shoulder.

She did read faster than I, and I often missed whole paragraphs of material because she turned the page early. Though this was better than sitting on the uncomfortable pew with nothing to do. I was just reading about how both the king and his bastard brother started starving their people as a means to control the other when I heard the doors to the throne room open.

Temperance and Prudence looked up and turned their heads back, but I took the opportunity to keep reading. I hoped that I might finish the page before Temperance meant to turn it. I found the information rather interesting, and I thought I might have to ask her if she would let me have it awhile after she was finished.

"He's handsome," Prudence said in a whisper.

"You think everyone's handsome," Temperance chastised, and I smiled because it was true.

"Your disposition is going to leave you a spinster, Temper, I swear it," Prudence hissed. "Look Mercy, don't you think he's handsome."

I straightened up and rolled my neck around. I had now gotten a kink in it from having it craned over Temperance's shoulder. Lord Kaloqey passed before I could get a good look at his face. I saw the flash of a beard and then his backside as he followed the herald up to the thrones.

"He's got a rather nice backside," I whispered in Prudence's ear, and she shook with silent laughter while Temperance shook her head in disapproval.

"May I present Lord Tristan Kaloqey, your highness. Here from Southern Ralice on behest of his Queen," the herald said before stepping aside and heading back toward the doors.

The man bowed to my brothers perfectly.

"Lord Kaloqey," Holt Stood, "We are beyond pleased to extend hospitality to you as long as you are here on your queen's need."

"The pleasure is mine, your highness." The man spoke and the hairs on the back of my neck prickled up.

"My brothers Prince Tobias, and Prince Langston," Holt said, gesturing to my brothers but I was staring at the back of the stranger's head. "And my sister's Princess Mercy, the oldest and Princesses Prudence and Temperance."

He turned too slowly as I held my breath. My chest restricted and I told myself that I had been mistaken. I did not know the voice. In my boredom, my mind was playing tricks on me. Though when he turned, I almost began to weep. Both my sisters had stood to curtsey back as he bowed to us, but I was glued to the pew staring at his face. That rakishly handsome face was now hidden behind facial hair.

Temperance turned slightly and nodded her head to remind me to stand. I blinked and hastily got to my feet as her eyes narrowed at me with their quick knowing. I dropped a curtsey and when I came up his grey eyes caught mine and the hint of a smile whispered across his face. He turned back to face my brother and I almost stepped forward but caught myself.

Prudence was sitting back down reaching for her embroidery, but Temperance's eyes were trained on my face as her gaze slid from me to Lord Kaloqey and back again. I took a breath and sat back down, plastering a princess smile across my face.

"Please let us know if there is anything you need while you are here. We have had a spectacular room made up for you with an excellent view of the lake," Holt said. "Langston can escort you and I do hope you will join us for dinners in the evenings."

"I'll escort him." I jumped up and all but shouted causing every single one of my siblings to stare at me in shock.

Lord Kaloqey turned to me his smile barely contained and my heart sang in response.

"I mean," I took a breath and curtseyed to my brother, "If it pleases you, brother, I have been reading of Southern Ralician history and the majesty of Hallow Manor. I would love to hear more from Lord Kaloqey."

"Indeed," Holt said with a raise of an eyebrow but as I had hoped he offered me an encouraging smile.

He took it as an attempt to woo this man to see our devotion to his country. That I was finally agreeing to behave better by entertaining his wishes. I knew that if you gave men even the slightest hint that you were doing what they wanted, they turned a blind eye to a lot of things.

"I would be honored, Princess. Hallow Manor is splendid indeed and it's king and queen as well." Lord Kaloqey offered his arm to me.

I looked to Holt who was now looking at the man with arm extended with concern and then he looked at me with the same face. Could he have already judged some conspiring between us by my actions alone? But he wiped the concern off his face easily enough and nodded for me to take my place at the Lord's arm, which I swiftly did.

"Lord Kaloqey, I heard my brother invite you to dinner, but I would be remiss if I did not extend another invitation personally," I said as we walked away from the thrones to the door at the end of the corridor.

"Personal invitations from a king and a princess how could a man refuse?"

The herald who was at the door opened it for us as we stepped through and continued through the halls. I dared not say anything to him until we were in his room with the door closed. We passed portraits and tapestries and large stone walls that had seemed built to keep me in. At that moment I did not care. I was arm in arm with a man that had made me feel free. A man that had told me I could choose what I wanted to be. I did not notice the stone walls or heavy woven rugs. I noticed only his face as I snuck glances at him during our walk to his room. Every time he caught me, he smiled or winked at me but also stayed silent.

We reached the room that had been prepared what seemed like a lifetime later and I opened the door and ushered him into it. I looked around suspicious of any guard who was walking their rounds but saw none as I followed him through the door. I shut it behind me and leaned back against it. I stared at him for a long time and his face shifted into a half-grin as he stared at me with what I could only describe as adoration.

"You look exceptionally lovely, though I think I prefer you in pants," he said, breaking the silence.

"Is that all you have to say, Elias?" I asked breathless still using the door to support my weight.

He walked toward me. I found myself holding my breath yet again at his presence. I stood up straighter, backing my spine up against the door. I smiled as he stopped before me and reached his hand out, so the palm of his hand was against my face.

"No, my love, there are many more things I intend to say to you. Though I shall not waste them all at once."

My hopeful eyes met his and the tears that had started to build in my eyes spilled over. *My love* played over and over in my mind as he gently wiped tears off my face. I closed my eyes against the feeling and let the fact that I had grieved this man for months wash over me. I had thought him dead, but he wasn't, and not only that, but he had come for me.

"I thought..." I said, trying to get the words out.

"Yes." He put both his hands on my cheeks and pulled my face forward so he could place a kiss on my forehead.

After he did, he stepped back and away quickly and I frowned at the distance between us.

"I do not mean to overwhelm you." His tone was apologetic. "To take advantage of your surprise and force my feelings upon you."

A smile formed as he took another step back and I wondered at how my opinion on pirates had changed so drastically. I stepped forward to close the distance between us and grabbed the lapels of his moss green jacket and pulled his face down to meet mine.

It was just like I remembered, kissing him. Him grinning against my lips before his hands wrapped tightly around my waist. It felt like being out on the ocean. His mouth on mine was like a breeze through my hair and the sun on my back.

I stepped back quickly covering my mouth and blushing red.

"I'm sorry." I was surprised with myself as it had been the first time *I* had kissed *him*. My body seemed to think I had been made to kiss him and my mouth and hands took over before my brain and manners could catch up.

"You need only be sorry if it was a poor kiss," he said, stepping forward to meet me again and I wondered if it felt as natural to him as it did to me.

I looked away from his face, but he tilted his head and body to meet my eyes.

"Was it poorly executed?" he asked, and I shook my head dropping my hand, sure that the color on my cheeks was still there.

"I'm not thoroughly convinced, so let me attempt it again." He threaded his fingers through mine and tugged me to him with no resistance on my part and kissed me again. His mouth was slower and more deliberate. His teeth caught my bottom lip and tugged on it gently before he pulled back once more. "How was that?"

"Perfect." I pulled away and rested my head on his shoulder as he held me for a moment.

"Do you have to go?" he asked when I had just begun to think if I didn't meet my sisters in the training arena they would start to wonder.

"Yes," I sighed. "Atticus will come looking."

"When can we speak freely?" he asked still holding me and it didn't feel as if he would let me go.

"Tomorrow," I said, pulling away and his arms fell to his sides. "Tomorrow after breakfast I'll show you something and we can talk."

"I look forward to it, Princess." He bowed.

"Lord Kaloqey," I said, winking at him as I retreated to the door, but turned back to stare at my ghost pirate captain dressed in high court clothing.

"Don't stare at me like that or I won't let you leave," he warned, and I smiled, slipping out of the room with the warmth of happiness on my face.

I all but ran to my room and changed as quickly as I could, with Kiltore's help, into my training clothes. I grabbed a bow that I had taken to my room to try to improve my form and headed down the stairs like a woman weightlessly swimming. There were so many questions to be answered but at that moment I didn't care about a single one of them.

I skipped into the training arena and as soon as I saw my sisters and Atticus were not there yet I went to the wall to pick up a few arrows. All three came in as I knocked the first arrow into the bow and aimed it at a far target. I let it fly and it missed by seven hands, but I smiled over at them unable to care about my obvious failure.

"What are we doing today?" I asked.

"Hand-to-hand combat," Temperance said, and I nodded as I returned the bow and arrows to where they belonged.

I ignored her gaze on me, fearful that my exuberance would give too much away but unable to keep a smile from my face.

"So?" Prudence asked stepping in front of me expectantly.

"So?" I asked back.

"The Lord Kaloqey?" she insisted, nearly bouncing with the idea of gossip. "What's he like?"

Oh, if I could only tell her.

"Well," I searched for words that wouldn't give me away. "He seemed adequately pleasant."

"Yezreth's blade!" she cursed. "It's like I'm the only female among my sisters. Well, don't worry Mercy for I have determined to win our fair Lord's heart for the crown of Adamas."

The words brought my euphoric headspace to a crashing halt. I shifted to her and opened my mouth to object but remembered that I shouldn't have much of a reason to. This brought me to the realization that I was going to have to decide if I was going to trust my sisters with Elias's identity. If Holt found out, Elias would be hanged for sure. I might have warmed to the idea of pirates, but if my brother found out he was hosting a pirate parading as a Lord, then he would fly into a rage that would end up with Elias' head on a golden platter served at his next feast.

"We don't know anything about him," I objected lightly.

"I know he's dashing," Prudence said. "I would know more if you even so much as bothered to gather more information than 'he's adequately pleasant'. Perhaps if I get him to fall in love with me it will make his king look more favorably upon our cause."

"Prudence I don't think that a promising idea," I said, racking my head for a suitable reason.

"Because you don't think he would love me?" she asked, looking wounded, and I felt guilty for my words.

"No that's not it," I amended. "Of course, any man worth anything would see how lovely you are. I just mean maybe you should ask Holt about this first, and we should see what kind of man this Lord Kaloqey is first before you sign up to be his bride."

"Good idea Mercy," Temperance said, coming to stand next to Prudence. "I shall go with you in the morning to talk to Holt and we shall see if he thinks any good coming of you wooing the handsome Lord."

It was a tone she never took and when I met her eyes, she stared at me with fire. She knew something but she didn't know what she knew. She was trying to force a fox out of its hole with fire, but I would not be forced just yet. Not until I was sure Elias would be safe if I revealed his identity.

"That sounds perfect," I said, hesitating only slightly.

Atticus was off to the side and looking between all three of us as if he just happened upon a dog with a fifth leg.

"Good," Temperance spat.

"Good," Prudence sang, not noticing our silent battle.

"Good." I turned and shrugged going to browse the rack of weapons wondering how I would focus on training for the entire afternoon.

Though she had previously agreed to talk to Holt, when I came to the dining hall, Prudence had placed herself right next to Elias and was speaking to him with her clear blue eyes batting up at him, enraptured. A fit of jealousy flared up in me that I tried to tamp out as I sat across from them keeping a tight smile on my face the entire meal. Prudence talked to Elias the entire time, asking him question after question about his land in Southern Ralice which he answered flawlessly and without hesitation.

He conversed with my brothers easily about trade routes and the influx of certain commodities. If I didn't know him, I wouldn't believe him to be a pirate but a polished court Lord, well versed in his craft.

"Are you fond of gardens Lord Tristan?" Temperance asked after Elias had insisted we stop using his surname.

I swallowed the bit of wild boar I had been chewing and my eyes slid to her as she ignored my stare.

"As a matter of fact, I do," Elias said smiling. "I find flowers, and plants understand me better than most people."

"We will have to show you around the ground tomorrow," she went on, "there is one garden I think you would enjoy particularly."

Her eyes fell to me finally, and deliberately. I shook my head once slowly at her and she raised an eyebrow at me in a challenge.

"I would be glad of it. I do not have business in town until the afternoon so I would be glad to oblige."

"Do you like sculptures as well?" she went on.

"Temperance!" I barked abruptly causing Elias and Prudence to stare at me.

Thankfully, Holt was occupied in a conversation with Tobias.

"I believe you and I are taking tea tomorrow morning so we can show Lord Tristan the gardens after that," I begged her with my eyes and Elias looked between us knowingly.

"Yes of course," she smiled which was rare and quite unsettling. "After our tea, of course, sister."

Chapter Nine

Georgette

It had been weeks since the incident at the tavern, and weeks still since Cassius and I had spoken. He was gone more often than he had been before, but whenever I asked anybody why, they became silent and awkward. It was something I was beginning to tire of. I wasn't allowed to know anything of importance. It wasn't as if I blamed Cassius for being so suspicious of me, he had every right to be. With the right information, I would become a more dangerous caged animal.

Like the feral cat that you are.

The words bounced around in my head. Some days they made me smile and some days I scowled at the invisible king who was hardly ever present.

I had gone back to my routine of going to the market in the morning, since my plan to use the tavern in Larkin had been thwarted. I searched for another route to glean information about Cassius and his family. If I had known that the answers I sought would wander into my bedroom, I wouldn't have suffered about it for so long.

I woke up one morning to the sound of a door being shut. I left my eyes closed for a moment enjoying the down comforter and the way the sheets were warm where I had slept. Though when I rolled over to greet who I thought would be Devika, I was struck with a small person right next to my bed. I made a startled sound but didn't move from my side-laying position.

The girl said nothing either, and her wide eyes scanned me without fear of being caught. She squinted a bit and I suddenly felt as if I were being judged. She couldn't have been more than eight or nine with pale skin and freckles across the bridge of her nose. Brown eyes that looked familiar stared back into mine, and dark curls that were untamed framed her face. Her small hand reached up and she took a bite of some jam toast she had brought with her.

"Hello," she said first.

"Hello," I said, raising an eyebrow.

"I'm Camber."

"I'm Georgette."

"I know."

I chuckled a bit and sat up in my bed as she stepped back. The necklace at her throat caught my attention with four eight-point stars surrounding three inter-lapping circles with only one filled in, as opposed to Cassius' two.

"What are you doing here?" I asked her after another long bout of silence.

"Cassius and mother told me that I couldn't meet you," she explained as if I would understand. "So, I waited until Cass was gone and my governess was using the private."

"Smart plan, but why come to see me?"

"You're the queen," she said, taking another bite of toast, getting some on the front of her dress which was already muddy and grass-stained.

"Me?" I gasped. "Oh no, I think you have the wrong room, I'm just a pirate."

The girl chuckled and then helped herself onto my bed. "You're funny, Cass said you were funny."

"I'm glad to know he enjoys my humor."

"He also said you were lovely, he said you were prettier than Jessamine. Momma said that you couldn't be because no one is prettier than Jessamine."

"She is lovely." I tucked away all the information she was giving me freely.

"Are you Cassius' sister?" I asked, wondering first if she was his child, but she seemed a little old.

"Of course I am," she said, furrowing her brow and looking at me like I was an idiot.

"Of course, and your mom is Cassius' mom as well and you both...live here? In the castles?" I stood up out of the bed and tried to sound casual. The girl exhaled hard.

"No, we live in our own arboretum that is hidden on the grounds. For safety, we can't live in the castle."

Smart.

"So, you're a princess?" I asked.

"No, my father and mother weren't married, so he made Cassius an heir but not me," she explained and then after a pause said, "Because I'm a girl and mom says kings don't like to have girl children."

There was a knock on the door of my room and the girl's eyes filled with wide panic. I knew it wasn't Devika because she would have just walked in.

"Who will that be?" I nodded toward the hallway.

"Lady Gistel, my governess, and probably my mother's guard."

"What do you want me to tell them, Lady Camber?" I got out of bed and started walking toward the hallway, with her quick on my heels.

"Will you tell them I'm not here?" she asked hopefully.

"I'm not a terribly good liar," I sighed reaching the door. "But, with Cassius gone and Brees gone with him, I'm almost certain no one can tell me no. That is if I request something within reason."

"That's true," she said thoughtfully, "I'm glad you aren't as stupid as people say pirates are."

"I'm flattered, at least I know the arrogance is hereditary." I yanked open the door in my nightdress.

Standing before me were two guards; one that had been charged with guarding me when Brees left with Cassius and the other I didn't recognize. This also raised the question in my mind of how a child had managed to get past him in front of my door. There was also a woman with a thin pointed nose and thin lips. She had hard wrinkles around her eyes and reminded me of an old bird that refused to die.

"Yes?" I asked as the two male guards colored at my state of undress and turned their backs to me.

"I'm so sorry to disturb you, my Queen," the old woman said, and emphasized the queen in a way that was meant to make me feel inferior. "But we are looking for a young girl who may be hiding in your chambers."

"Cassius' sister is in here with me," I said, and the woman's eyes flashed surprised and then went back to glaring.

"Would you please send her out?" she asked.

"No, I won't. Lady Camber is going to be spending the day with me." I went to shut the door, but the woman put her foot in it and gave me a sneer.

"I will have to speak to the King about that."

"Well, go speak to him then, and when you travel to wherever he has run off to tell him if he has a problem, he can come speak with me." I shut the door hard but she moved her foot just in time, her mouth opened in protest.

"Camber?" I asked still facing the door. "Do you know where your brother is?"

"He's gone to check on soldier camps," she said as I turned. "Mom said that our father never checked on his soldiers, so that makes Cassius a better king."

"Why is he checking on soldier camps?"

"Cassius says a war is coming. The king that lives above us wants Cassius on his side and another King across the river wants Cassius on his side too. Cassius hasn't been king for a very long time, so he doesn't want to go to war but the King above us keeps pushing into our borders with his men. At least that's what he told mom and I don't think I was even supposed to be listening."

I had learned more in the last five minutes in the company of this child than I had in the last four months of living in the palace. I smiled at her and made my way down to the hall to get changed. I remembered that it was the third day which meant Devika was doing some religious ritual. On those mornings she came late which had worked out well for me.

"Is it true that you wear men's pants?" the girl asked, following me into my wardrobe of clothes.

"Yes." I smiled as I pulled out a pair of deep blue pants and a matching brocade vest. "I wore them on a pirate ship and so I find them more comfortable than skirts or dresses."

"I hate skirts," Camber said, looking down at her own.

"Well, we will have the tailor make you a pair of trousers," I said, grabbing underclothes and a silky white blouse. "Though, I think your brother might be upset."

"Cassius doesn't get mad at me," she said, tilting her chin up, proud of the fact.

"Very well then, that's what we shall do first," I went to my bathroom to change as she sat on my unmade bed.

"What else shall we do?"

"Whatever you like. I suppose me being married to your brother makes us sisters. I don't think it's right to have a sister you don't know, do you?" I asked, feeling the slight pang of guilt as I manipulated a child.

"You should meet my mom too," she said after a pause, which had been my intention, but why did I feel so bad about it. "Since you are related to her now too."

"If you don't think she'd mind the visit."

I pulled on my clothes and attempted to put pins in my hair the way Devika did, but my hair did not obey me as it did her. It had grown a bit and become slightly more manageable, but I did not know how to bind it other than two tight braids on the side of my head. So, I braided them like I once had when I captained a ship, only when I tied each of the braids off, they now ended at my shoulders. I splashed some chilly water on my face to clean it and rubbed some almond oil on my wrists.

"Well to the tailor first and then to see Lady Dalion."

"Lady Lolista," she corrected. "But she prefers to be called by her first name so Lady Amara. You can just call me Camber; Cassius calls me Cam but only he's allowed. What do you like to be called?"

"You can call me George since we are family."

"George is a boy's name."

"So, it is."

"I like it," she decided.

I heard my door open and close and a set of quick but sure steps come down the hall. I smiled and came out of the bathroom to find Camber staring at Devika at the entrance of my room.

"Hello, Lady Devika!" Camber called like they were old friends.

"Lady Camber," Devika curtseyed then turned her gaze on me. "What pray tell, is this?"

"We are off to the tailor," I explained.

"To make me some trousers," Camber said excitedly and Devika gave me a hard stare which caused me to chuckle.

"Why is it that whenever Brees or I are not here to watch you, you find trouble my Queen."

"I didn't find this trouble," I said, looking at Camber. "This trouble found me."

Devika had opted not to come with us to see Lady Amara. She came with us to the tailor and gave heavy sighs the entire time as Camber picked out fabric for three sets of new trousers and shirts to go with them. We took tea in my parlor, and I drank up everything Camber said. She talked about her days and her mother and Cassius. Devika looked on with a concerned expression as I prodded the girl about everything I could think of. She was delighted to oblige me; the child was a natural-born entertainer as some children are. I asked for the kitchen to prepare a special lunch to be served to us in the arboretum and the kitchen staff exchanged worried glances but of course, no one told me they wouldn't.

So, I walked beside Camber past all the gardens I had been shown. It was an awfully long walk indeed to the hidden place and I was almost startled as we came upon it as it was so well concealed by a half wall of brick and trees. A house made of glass and brick covered with all manner of vines and plants.

"Can I ask you a question?" Camber asked as I stood in front of the small home marveling in its romanticism.

"Seems only fair." I looked down at her as she slipped her small hand into mine.

"Why doesn't my brother want you to meet me or my mom?" Her eyes stared up at me with honest curiosity.

"I suppose," I said, trying to find something true to say without devastating the sister that had spent the day idolizing my worst enemy. "I suppose he doesn't trust me."

"Why?"

Because I'm looking for a way to cripple him.

"Because we don't like each other," I decided on.

"Aren't married people supposed to like each other?" she asked as I took a step forward to evade more questions.

"I don't know, this is my first time being married."

"Well, I like you, George, I think we will be good friends." The shrill scream of guilt racked me again and I silenced it.

I hadn't asked for this. This was Cassius' fault. If he didn't want me using his sister and mother as leverage, he shouldn't have brought me here. He shouldn't have locked me up.

We walked up to the door of the glasshouse and it opened before Camber could reach the knob. I looked up and met the hazel eyes of a woman a few inches taller than me. She had long, almost black hair, and one grey strip ran through it on her left temple. She was beautiful and besides the crow's feet at her eyes and a few lines around her mouth, I would not have been able to guess her age.

"My Queen," she said, bowing to me.

"Lady Amara," I curtseyed back.

"She likes to be called George," Camber said, not feeling the weight of the moment as I was. She let go of my hand and waltzed past her mother into the house.

"I am informed a meal will be served here." Amara was staring at me with an intensity her son must have inherited from her.

I felt like my soul was on display and she was judging what it was made of. Mothers, true mothers, always had a way about them of making you feel five years old. I wasn't put off by it as it was rather comforting like you were in the presence of someone much wiser than you. Though they also always had a way of knowing exactly what you were up to with a simple look.

"I should have asked," I said, feeling sheepish for the first time since I had been at Hallow Manor.

"Nonsense, the queen asks no one what she may do, save the King."

"I do most of what I want when the king is gone." Honesty being pulled from me by the sheer weight of her presence.

"So, I hear." She smiled wide.

For reasons unbeknownst to me I almost began to cry. Because there was not a single drop of judgment or malice in her gaze, only curiosity, humor, and a bit of admiration if I was gauging correctly. She reminded me of my own mother, with eyes as deep as the depths of the ocean.

"My mother," I stumbled out, "My mother told me a story once, of seeing you in Coranthia."

"Lady Hazel," she nodded.

"Did you know her?"

"No, but I loved the tale of her running off with a pirate. I envied her in my youth. I imagine she was a brave woman indeed."

I slowly nodded wondering how I was going to go through with my plan. On Amara's neck were scars that ran in rings all the way around. The metal collar my mother told me she wore was no tall tale and it had left behind its marks. The collar the King of Southern Ralice had made her wear the duration of his life. I thought the story was too cruel to be true and the evidence of it made me cringe.

"Welcome in, you are my daughter after all. I hope you don't mind me saying that. I am well pleased to be able to take a meal with you."

She reached her hand out to touch my shoulder and I saw a tattoo on her wrist. Four stars surrounded the same three circles, all three of which were filled in.

"My son is a good man, Georgette," she said, picking apart my thoughts before I had pieced them together.

"I hate him," and to my horror tears welled up in my eyes and spilled over my cheeks.

"I understand the hatred a bird has for its captor." She smiled and the soft brush of her fingers on my shoulder felt like a touch I hadn't felt in many years. "And you must do what you feel you have to, to be free."

I invited the two of them to dinner after our lunch. It had been very pleasant to sit with them, and I found myself laughing as I hadn't in weeks. Though in the end I still resolved to do what I had set out to. There would be no harm that befell them by making my point to Cassius. I had told Lady Amara that I didn't know if Cassius would be dining with us but that was a lie. I had heard the guards talking about when he would return, and I knew he would be back for dinner.

I wore the red vest and pants from our wedding and a ruby tiara woven into my hair. I kept my white undershirt so the clothing didn't hold the same sentiment that it had the first time, but it would be reminiscent enough. Devika brushed pink powder over my cheeks and a tin of stain across my lips before I dismissed her to whatever better things she had to do than dress me.

I made my way to the dining room slowly building my confidence and anger by recalling all Cassius' offenses against me. I needed only to remember Absalom's lifeless hand falling from mine, and the spark was rekindled. Then the wicked smile Cassius had flashed me when my eyes met his on our wedding day. It didn't matter how much I liked Camber or Lady Amara.

I would not be kept prisoner by that bastard any longer than I had to be.

I opened the doors to find the two seated next to each other properly. They rose when I walked in to give me a curtsey.

"Please don't," I said, waving the gesture off.

"Look, George," Camber said, bounding off her chair to show off a pair of golden tailored pants with frilly buttons on either side that mimicked men's fashion in a feminine way.

"Lovely." I smiled at her. "Did you give them a good test?"

"Oh yes, she ran nearly the whole way here panting on about how she was never going to wear a skirt again." Amara gave me a shake of her finger but there was a lightness in her eyes.

The doors at the other end of the dining room slammed open. I took a deep breath to face who I knew I would see. No doubt someone had informed him the second he came home who was in the dining room.

Sure enough, Cassius' eyes were alight with panic as he took in the scene before him. His arms were wide having opened both doors at the same time and he took one step forward very quickly. He scanned his mother and finding no harm had come to her, focused on Camber who he also found in good health. That left his gaze to travel to my own. I shifted my thoughts from lunch in an arboretum to a prowling cat staring at her captor behind immovable bars. I let a cold smile slip over my face and his mouth pursed into a frown. A predator finding another predator in his den.

"Cass!" Camber cried rushing to him, and he broke eye contact with me to offer a warm smile to his sister. She crushed herself to him and remorse filled me as he squeezed her back.

"Hello sweet Cam, how are you today? I see you've been busy."

"Oh, please don't be mad, look at my lovely pants."

"Very lovely," he said, stepping closer to me, his eyes slipping to mine every few seconds. "Mother," he said, having made his way over to kiss her cheek.

"I wasn't sure you were going to be able to join us, but I had them set your regular seat for you, your highness," I said, walking over to the other side of the table and pulled out his seat gesturing for him to sit.

His mother's watchful eyes shifted between the both of us as he slowly walked over to the seat I stood behind.

As he reached me, servers came out and began to fill glasses and lay down golden trays of food. Mushroom soup if I was correct, and I cursed my brother for the hundredth time in so many weeks. As Cassius sat, I slid his chair in behind him, his fingers gripping the arms making his skin tight, and paler than normal. I leaned in over him as two servants were setting trays in front of Lady Amara and Camber. I pressed a kiss to his neck just under his ear and watched as his clenched hands flexed out, putting his stars and circles on display.

"Might be best to pull up on that leash you have me on, darling husband," I whispered.

I pulled away and walked to my side of the table with my head high and a cautionary smile on my lips.

Chapter Ten

Mercy

"I don't know where to begin," I sighed looking at my two expecting sisters across the parlor.

"Who is Lord Tristen Kaloqey," Temperance suggested.

"Elias. Elias Baine."

"The pirate?" Prudence asked, eyes going wide. "Of the captains Baine who you sailed with?" She jumped up but she didn't look upset, her face was exuberant.

"What is he doing here?" Temperance asked.

"I don't know. I haven't had a chance to ask."

They were both taking it much better than anticipated, and I probably misjudged them which made me feel a little guilty. It reminded me how long it had taken to open up to my sisters and how before I had left to be married to King Kosdel, I had not attempted to deepen our relationship at all. I cringed thinking of the conversation with Elias aboard his ship where I had told him I didn't like my sisters. It was one of many things I needed to thank him for. Because of how much I admired He and Georgette's bond for the brief time I was with them, I had come home and seen my siblings in a new light.

"I cannot believe *that man* is Captain Baine," Prudence said wistfully.

"I'm meeting him in the garden after the first meal," I explained. "He might already be there. I was going to take him to my garden for some privacy and ask him about his last four months."

"Can we meet him?" Prudence asked suddenly shy. "I mean, meet him again?"

"Of course, you can come with me. I'm sorry I was hesitant to tell you I... if..." I couldn't finish the thought.

"If Holt found out he'd kill him." Temperance nodded. "We may believe that the captains meant you no harm on your journey, but I think Holt still thinks you went a little mad."

"You've already lost him once," Prudence said, nodding in the same understanding.

"Perhaps we will give you a moment together," Temperance said, "And come find you in a bit."

"So, you can show him the garden," Prudence said, nodding at her sister.

Logic and love. Standing before me my fanciful sister dressed in cerulean blue with her hair free and her color high on her cheeks. Then the other sister was punctilious in her soft grey dress with hair pulled back and away from her face to display her hawklike eyes. One coin two sides, or perhaps they were their own coins altogether.

"Thank you." I nodded to them and all but ran out the parlor doors to meet Elias in the gardens.

I wasn't sure if my heart was pounding with nerves or excitement, and I tried to sort the tangled feelings on my walk to the gardens. I hadn't stopped being thrilled that Elias was so near to me; near to me and alive. I hadn't slept much the night before with all the possibilities running through my mind of what Elias being alive meant. Were Georgette and Absalom alive too? My brother had been so sure that they were dead that I hadn't allowed myself to hope. He said that his guard ran Absalom through himself and delivered his head to King Kosdel. No, I decided, King Kosdel had confirmed that Absalom had died.

I came to the first garden out the back stairs of the palace. It was surrounded by an evergreen hedge with a giant fish fountain in the center of it. Though when I looked around, I couldn't find Elias anywhere. So, I moved on to the garden just beyond that and smiled as I spotted him lying flat out on the brim of a fountain. As I got closer, I realized his eyes were closed against the sun beating down on him and some of the water was splashing on his face which wasn't bothering him in the slightest. I saw the pirate; despite the matching trousers, vest, and silver cravat he wore. Despite the foreign beard and the lack of silver rings he had once worn on his fingers.

"Would you prefer me to stay still so you can continue to stare?" He popped his head up and his mouth twisted into a teasing smile.

"I'm looking for my pirate friend." I smiled back. "I can't see him behind all the finery."

"Can't you?" He sat up but didn't move toward me.

"I can," I conceded, "I just didn't want to admit that I was staring."

"Oh, Princess." His grin split his face now causing me to shake my head at him. "I do love to be stared at, especially by beautiful ladies."

It lightened something in me. I had felt as if I was suffocating for the last four months but his smile set something free. I could breathe again. I wasn't worried about my royal responsibilities or my brother trying to wed me off for alliance. It was just Elias who had told me that I could be whatever I chose to be.

"I want to show you something," I said, walking past him and nodding for him to follow.

I wanted to grab him by the hand and pull him along with me, but we were too close to the castle. There was bound to be a lady's maid or a guard who would see us, and gossip in a castle spread faster than any fire.

"Very well Princess." He stood up and followed me across the palace grounds.

I often had to stop for him as he admired flowers, vines, and ponds. He marveled at a white stone garden with green ivy wrapping around large trunks of trees. Then he stopped at the corner where the beekeepers kept our hive. I enjoyed watching him take everything in and enjoy the part of the castle I liked the most. When we finally reached my garden, I stopped just outside and gestured for him to go in.

"What's this?" he asked.

I didn't say anything as I felt a slow blush creep over my face. He raised an eyebrow at my response but sauntered into the garden anyway with his hands clasped behind his back. I paused for a moment outside, not following him right away. I'd had a recurring dream the first two months that I had been back in Molina. Elias was walking the grounds with me, and he started running and I began to chase him. He teased me as I laughed. In this dream he came upon the garden I had made for him and wandered inside alone. When I finally caught up to him, he would meet my eyes and say, *there's my pirate princess* and then I always woke up. I wondered if the actual moment would live up to the dream.

I walked into the garden and caught him turning slowly in wonder. His eyes were wide in amazement and his face lit up by a genuine smile. It caused my heart to burst with happiness as I realized what a wonder it was that he was standing here admiring the garden I made for him and Georgette. He walked over to the fountain and stared into the woman's face before walking over and looking into his own. The statue was not an exact likeness and obviously had no beard, but it was enough for him to recognize himself. He turned to me and walked over with an unreadable expression on his face. He pulled me to him and spun me around.

"It's magnificent Mercy, I've never seen something like it." He had stopped spinning but I was still in his arms against his chest.

"Do you like it?"

"I've never been another place on land that I've loved more. I can see all the water and, Georgette over there with the brilliant colors, and the fountain. Ocean's deep! It's incredible. I feel as if you've taken my mind and turned it into a tangible place."

The sound of someone clearing their throat came from the entrance of the garden. Elias dropped me faster than he had picked me up and stepped away. He ran his hands through his hair and looked at me worriedly and I saw his mind reeling for an excuse for the scene that had just unfolded.

"It's alright," I said, nodding to Prudence and Temperance who watched us from the opening in the hedges.

"Prudence and Temperance may I introduce Captain Elias Baine of The Siren."

He looked shocked at first, his hesitation etched in his features, but his posture softened almost instantly. Instead of Lord Tristan with rigid posture and withdrawn words, He was my pirate captain, all mischievous grins and relaxed attitude. He bowed to my sisters, sweeping and dramatic as Prudence giggled.

"The pleasure is mine." He stood back up and ran his hand absently through his hair.

"We've heard all about you," Prudence bubbled.

"Don't believe anything your sister says about me and if she mentions that she happened to best me in a duel, that is completely inaccurate."

I scoffed, turning to him with my mouth open and he winked at me.

"She spoke of you fondly," Temperance said, and I saw hesitation behind her eyes as she judged him in her way.

He did not shrink from her gaze nor the way she threw the words out like an accusation. Instead, he offered her a closed smile letting her make what she would of him.

"You saved her from drowning," she said finally, once she seemed satisfied.

"If I am being transparent, I must say at that juncture, I saved her merely because I felt pity for her and the reward returning her would get me. Though I am awfully glad now that I did, for a myriad of reasons."

"You came for her. You're in love with her," Prudence said, bringing her interlaced fingers to her chin.

"Yes, I am," he said, and my cheeks warmed again as my eyes slid to his.

There was no hesitation. He said it like it was a fact that had always been. He met my eyes and his mouth quirked up as we shared a look. I had both melted into nothing and wanted to hold him forever, but I was suddenly very scared. I had never known love before, and it seemed a weighty thing to discuss after I had just learned he was alive. Though he wasn't looking at me like he expected a response. So, I smiled at him which was all I could offer him, and it seemed enough.

"Is your sister alive?" It was Temperance who broke the silence to ask the question I should have asked the day before.

"She is. I thought you would know that." He looked at all of us confused.

"Why would we?" I asked, tilting my head in response.

"She's married to a King. King Dalion of Southern Ralice. He's the one that fought with her on the pier. The one that took her off the ship. He was the king, and he took her back to his court and married her."

I watched as both my sisters took in the information and felt a little relieved that they hadn't known. Their surprise was genuine. I was relieved she was alive and then felt a heavy weight of anxiety as I realized who she was bonded in marriage to. The cruel king of Southern Ralice. There was no way that my brother had not known this, which means he purposefully kept it from me and my sisters. A plan that would have involved getting others to stay silent with the information as well.

"You didn't know?" he asked gauging our faces.

"No," I said, the cold edge of anger in my voice. "We did not."

"She seems well enough. She wants to exact her revenge on King Dalion for taking her as his bride and for taking Absalom from us." He walked to a stone bench in the garden and sat as his tone went sad at the mention of the military commander.

"Elias." I couldn't reign in the emotions that were flowing through me, but I needed to tell him the truth that I knew. "King Dalion didn't kill Absalom."

"Yes, Jones recounted the tale, one of his men did." His shoulders had slumped, and I almost couldn't bring myself to say what I needed to.

"No," I said, going to sit next to him. "Elias, one of my brother's personal guards killed Absalom."

His head snapped up and for the first time since he had been angry with his sister on the deck of the siren that one early morning, I saw anger flash in his eyes. Though he did not jump up or demand that I explain. While the fire raged in his eyes, he allowed me to continue uninterrupted.

"King Kosdel lied to you both, he was the one that had me kidnapped. He staged the kidnapping to frame King Cassius Dalion for my abduction. When my brother confronted him, King Dalion denied it and even agreed to help rescue me alongside my brother's men."

"Why? Why send us to retrieve you then?" he asked.

"You were actual pirates, that he knew no one could connect back to him. He told my brother he had no intention of harm befalling me, but Holt suspects he intended to kill Absalom and me by ambush and then blame my death on King Dalion."

"Why?" he asked again seeming no more understanding than before.

"To start a war. He wanted my brother to assist him in a war against Southern Ralice. Now my brother has issued intent of war against him and is seeking King Cassius Dalion's assistance in his side against Kosdel."

"He used us," Elias said, his fists clenching at his sides.

"Yes," I exhaled, and Prudence and Temperance stared in discomfort. "And the man, the man that stabbed Absalom, was Adamasian. They thought Absalom a traitor working for a King who intended to harm me."

"He would have never!" Elias did stand up then as he defended his friend. "Absalom was a good man. Loyal to that bastard of a King but he would have never wittingly put you in danger."

"I know that," I breathed and cast my head down and away from his anger.

After a moment he sat down. His eyes were filled with tears and his breathing was uneven and slow.

"King Kosdel, Cyril, is responsible for this?" he asked and I nodded, unable to say any more; to bring him any more pain.

"He is responsible for taking Absalom from us and for my sister being taken away. It's our fault too, for making a deal with him. He used our friendship with Absalom to manipulate us all." He slammed his fist into the stone bench.

"I'm sorry, Elias."

"Did Absalom's father, Gerald, know?" he barely whispered.

"I don't know. He came with King Dalion when they were here for negotiations and King Kosdel insinuated he knew. Though I wouldn't trust a word he said."

There was a long bit of silence before he stood again.

"And this King Dalion helped your brother retrieve you without asking for any sort of reparation? He did not ask for payment or require marriage?"

"Not that I'm aware of. I think he did it to clear his name of the charges King Kosdel was trying to accuse him of. As far as I know, he did not require payment of any kind for his assistance."

"If only my parents could see us now, my how disappointed they would be." He ran his fingers through his hair.

I wanted to contradict his words. To tell him that I didn't think his parents would be disappointed at all. Then I realized that I didn't know his parents, and saying that would be overstepping. I hated myself for not having the right words to comfort him and I hated that I had to tell him a truth that caused him pain. So, I said the only things that I knew to be true.

"I am not disappointed in you. There is no way you could have known his plans and his willingness to use Absalom's love of you makes him a villainous wretch."

"Thank you," but he didn't smile at me then. "I have to write Georgette. She deserves to know the truth."

"Yes, of course." I nodded.

"Can we be sure the letter will reach her?" he asked. "She said she tried to send you a letter, but it must have never gotten to you."

Anger spiked my blood again as I imagined the torrent of fury I would unleash on my older brother as soon as I could have a private moment with him.

"I will make sure it gets there," Temperance offered and my eyes lifted to hers. "I have a way to get the mail out that I don't want anyone knowing I'm sending. Though there are no guarantees King Dalion will allow it to reach her."

"I have to try." He nodded and walked to Temperance taking her hand bowing to her and kissing the top of it. "I would greatly appreciate your assistance, Princess."

I don't think I had ever seen Temperance blush, but she just nodded and pulled her hand away quickly.

"I will look forward to dining with you all tonight," Elias said, bowing once more and saving a smile especially for me before he turned and walked out of the garden. He was too lost in his thoughts to offer any more and none of us would fault him for it.

"Why do you have a way to send mail outside of the palace?" I asked.

"I don't want everything I receive and send being scrutinized by Holt." She shrugged and I could tell by Prudence's lack of response that she had already known about it.

"I'll make sure the letter is sent without interference," she assured me again.

"I'm just," I said, pausing. "How could I not have learned to be as quick as you. How did I do everything they asked of me without trying to think of a way around all the stringent rules they had set in place?"

"Your obedience offered the cover we required to learn another way," Temperance said.

"And you learned your other way aboard a pirate ship," Prudence offered with a smile.

"I only wish it hadn't taken me so long."

Temperance nodded as she stepped to the fountain and looked at it a while before speaking.

"We all have to be true to our own road, for no one else will walk them for us."

Chapter Eleven

Georgette

I hunched over and started to dry heave into the grass below.

For three weeks I had trained with Brees, and I didn't seem to be learning anything other than he was a much better fighter than me. Also, I had lost a bit of my stamina in the last five months I had been here. I had gone soft with no ship work to keep me active. At the end of every day, Brees would work me so hard that I would either vomit or dry heave for several minutes. I learned to stop eating before I came.

"Your stance is better today. Not so erratic."

I nodded as I let myself roll to the ground and look up at the cloudless sky above.

The weather was beginning to feel a little crisper as autumn came to Hallow manner. The trees and their leaves hinted at the promise of change. I had always liked the autumn and harvest time. People seemed happy to be seeing the fruits of their labor and in many places, it meant a reprieve from the heat of summer.

"You won't get so winded every time," he assured me, reaching out to offer me a cup.

"Easy for you to say, you're like an oak tree lodged into the side of a mountain."

It was true. Brees was broad-shouldered and tall, not quite as tall as Absalom had been, but tall. He was even taller than Cassius who seemed an inch or two above six feet. Brees also seemed to be made of stone. No matter how many times I came at him, he held his ground without moving. He assured me it was just Southern Ralician military training, but I doubted I could ever learn to be a mountain.

"Cassius lifted the ban of trading with Larkin when his father died," Brees said as I sat up and took the cup of water.

I eyed him taking a long sip as my throat ached at the contact.

"Why are you telling me that?"

"Just making conversation." He shrugged taking a drink of water himself.

"Well stop." I stood up. "I don't care how you are trying to humanize him. I don't like the man, so you can save your energy."

Brees only nodded, not seeming fazed by my verbal outburst.

"Do you want to go again?" he asked.

"While I would love to endure more physical abuse that we are pretending is training, if I don't get back to my rooms Devika will kill me. I have a ball in my honor to attend."

"Ah yes and a particularly scandalous outfit as I hear it."

"How did you come by that information?" I asked raising an eyebrow at him.

He barely hesitated before speaking. "The tailor comes to Cassius with all your clothing choices. I think she's afraid she will be punished for your outrageous choices."

"Poor woman," I said, picturing the round-faced tailor who paled whenever I told her what I wished for her to create.

"I'll save you a dance," I said, walking away, throwing the metal cup at him which he caught without flinching.

"If you dance with me without dancing with Cassius first, your outfit won't be the only scandal!" he yelled back.

I looked unconventional. Beautiful but unconventional, which suited me fine.

I turned to my reflection in the full mirror with Devika looking on, shaking her head in disapproval. My ball attire was a bodice that mimicked a captain's coat like the one I had worn to my wedding, only this one was black and sand-colored. The buttons on it gleamed gold in the light. I was wearing tan trousers tighter than any I had ever worn as if they were a second skin. Over the top of the pants were two layers of see-through, shimmery black tulle. The whole ensemble suggested I wore nothing underneath, and though it would be obvious I wasn't naked under the thin mock skirt, I knew it was inappropriate for court.

"Somehow it's so much worse now than when you described it to Sissa," Devika said.

As always, she wore a white gown. Her billowing sleeves had slits in them which showed off her flawless skin and a skirt that moved like a slight breeze carried her everywhere. She had gold shimmer paint at the height of her cheekbones making her look more like a goddess of Hestiege than ever.

"I rather like it."

"Of course, you do." She came up behind me and I held still as she secured the ruby-encrusted gold crown that had been placed on my head on my wedding day.

She told me that it was traditional for me to wear it and I rather liked the ornateness of it against my suggestive dress.

"Would you like to wear the necklace Cassius gifted you at your wedding?" she suggested.

"No," I snapped at her.

The ruby-eyed siren reminded me too much of home and the malicious intent behind the gift caused bitterness to surge through me.

"Very well, just your hoops then."

"Thank you, Devika," I answered and stepped away from the mirror as soon as she had finished. "Who will you dance with tonight?"

"I'll know when they ask me." She smiled. "When you wish to retire, I shall accompany you back."

"No, you shall not," I defied. "You shall dance and drink and be merry as long as you so wish. I won't require your assistance to remove this outfit so as soon as we leave this room your many talents are no longer required."

"Yes, my Queen." She stood next to the hallway that led to the main door.

"Well, let's be off then," I said, though nerves fluttered through me.

The ball was being held in front of Hallow Manor. I was told it was a splendid sight, and I could not have been prepared for the spectacle before me. We exited the front of the castle and were stopped by a herald who announced Devika first, and she went down the stairs as the partygoers stared at her gracefully descending the stairs. I had also been instructed to wear no shoes and now I saw why.

There was no proper dance floor, but a massive expanse of grass that bore all kinds of couples dancing barefoot in the cool evening. Flower petals littered all surfaces, and fresh flowers were strewn delicately about. Strung between trees were tiny candles encapsulated in glass suspended on twine. Tables covered in silk were bulging with food and people held goblets brimming with wine. The night air was warm but not cloying as summer bid us ado and autumn swept in with its milder evenings

Across the lawn and past all the twirling couples, were two large thrones set apart against the whimsical nature of the festival. In one, sat my husband but he was not looking at Devika, he was looking at me. I wondered if he had been watching me as I admired the splendor of the scene before me and I scowled.

"Lords and Ladies of Southern Ralician High Court!" the herald yelled, breaking my glare. "I introduce to you your crowned queen and wife of our benevolent ruler, Queen Georgette Baine Dalion."

He stepped aside which I took as my cue to walk down the stone steps to the grass below. I kept my head high trying to focus on the lights and the food, and not the man across the dance floor whose gaze I knew was still on me. The crowd had stopped dancing, and everyone was silent. When my feet reached the small dirt path to the side of the grass a great cheer went up through the guests. It was a sort of small thrill to feel dirt on my feet after so many months of polished floors and luxurious baths.

Long live Queen Georgette. The cry went up like a praise to the goddesses

"Anasia take me," I heard a deep voice curse and turned to see Brees standing by Devika staring at me.

He looked as handsome as I had ever seen him with a blue vest and grey silk cravat with sharp trousers. I was surprised the soldier could look so polished. Even his hair which he normally wore tied back was down and pushed away from his face. The only thing that caused me to pause was that he too was barefoot, I looked from his bare toes back to his face and grinned.

"Don't comment on the dress you'll only encourage her," Devika scolded. "Shall we go pay our respects to the king?"

"Must we?" I asked staring up at the trees where lanterns and candles dotted the sky making it look like a close blanket of stars.

"I thought you had decided to be over your petulance."

"Perhaps I've undecided."

"Let's go," Brees said, taking my arm in his. "Don't make me tackle you in front of all these people and show them just how defenseless you are."

"That seems like it would be much more scandalous than a dance," I said, raising an eyebrow at him and he flushed for a moment before turning his face away.

So, with my arm in his and Devika at his other arm, we made our way to the thrones. The closer we got, the more I wished I had defied this plan a little harder. Cassius was poised on his throne like a hawk looking for a mouse in a field. He wore mostly black as usual, save a white shirt underneath, and the cravat he wore that night had a busy and colorful floral pattern.

His black painted nails tapped against one arm and his smile never wavered as we approached.

"My King, I present your wife and my queen, and her Principal lady." Brees let go of us and stepped back.

"Your highness," Devika said, bowing low.

"Lady Devika, what a marvelous sight you are tonight under the lights." He smiled at her, and I was surprised to find it a genuine smile. I found myself wondering if he harbored feelings for her. Quickly dashing the thoughts aside, I chastised myself. What did I care who he fancied?

"And my darling wife," Cassius addressed me, and I scowled at the endearment as it was the one he used most frequently, knowing how I loathed it. "I got quite an unobstructed view of you, as did everyone else in attendance."

"I hoped you enjoyed the show," I said, crossing my arms in childlike defiance.

"I would be hard-pressed to think of something I enjoy as much as I enjoy your performances." He winked and though the skirt and trousers had been my idea I hated the smirk on his face. My face heated under his scrutiny.

"Brees?" I asked and could almost feel him begging me not to do what I was about to do. "Might you dance with me? It seems I am swept away by the glory of this celebration."

I looked back at him, and he was looking at Cassius warily. I looked back at my husband who nodded at him once. I threw a rude hand gesture used by pirates his way before Brees pulled me away to dance.

"I thought," he said, pulling me close. "I told you not to do this."

"I'm sorry," I answered not feeling sorry at all. "I don't know what comes over me but when I see his face I am filled with uncontrollable irritation."

"I thought Devika was going to burst a vein at your vulgarity before I pulled you away."

"I have a feeling I've shaved literal years off my principal lady's life. She deserved a good queen, not the vagabond she got."

"So, be the queen she deserves," he offered, and I looked up at him.

"I'm not a queen."

"So, you've said, but the herald announced you as one, and the lord and ladies of high court cheered to your rule."

I went silent then, unable to answer his call for me to rise to my title.

"However, Devika can handle herself," he said, gracefully changing the subject. "Did you know she's in line for the throne of Hestiege?"

"What?" I asked, eyes flickering to where a young handsome Lord was extending his hand in an offer of a dance. "Devika is royalty?"

"Indeed." Brees was looking at her now too as she began to dance with more grace than I would ever possess.

"Why is she here, serving as a principal lady?" I asked, eyes shifting back to him.

"That is her story to tell," he responded. "I only told you so you can begin to see other stories surround you that are not your own."

The words stung but they hit their mark and I knew they were well deserved. Since I had been here, I had heard many stories of loss and love that lyric writers would pen with glee. I had always tended to be inwardly focused and miss other people's quandaries.

"I'm sorry my Queen, I spoke out of turn." He began to apologize, and I shook my head.

"No, it's alright."

"I don't mean to alarm you," he said in a quieter tone than he had used before as the music swelled and he spun me around to face what he wanted me to see. "Cassius has come for you."

There was more than a little humor in his tone as Cassius approached us and Brees stopped dancing leaving me defenseless.

"Might I steal your partner, Captain?" he asked as Brees bowed and gave me a look that I couldn't decipher as being an apology or mocking smirk.

Cassius stepped into his place, one hand on my waist and one behind my shoulder blade to support my arm. I supposed it would have been out of the question to pretend like I didn't know how to dance. So as the song shifted to a slower tempo melody, I sighed, realizing I was going to be in his arms for an agonizingly long time.

"You don't look pleased that I've come to dance with you, wife."

"Why would I be pleased?" I asked, trying to keep my tone bored instead of irritated.

"You once called me handsome, is it not a pleasure to dance with a handsome gentleman even if you loathe him?" He was goading me, and my irritation was turning to anger.

"No, the fact that I loathe you completely nullifies the fact that I find you attractive," I said as he spun me out and then pulled me back into a sway in the song.

"With your lack of self-control and male company, I'm surprised you haven't taken me up on my offer to be bedmates. You would need only woo me slightly."

I stopped dancing and turned to leave but he pulled me against him so that my back was to him, and we watched as the other couples danced. Luckily, we had ended up on the outside of the floor, so we weren't creating a giant spectacle, though I saw a few heads turn our way. His hands were wrapped around my waist like a vise.

"Please," I said through clenched teeth as the flush of rage crept over my face. "My palette may not be as refined as yours, but a soft-footed king is not the sort of bed company I keep. You wouldn't have any idea what to do with me, darling husband."

"I'll tell you what I think," he said, head dipped low by my ear. "I think you carry yourself like a woman who knows the way around the male sex. I wager you have more than your share of experience and I am also willing to bet that you take men to your bed who are henpecked and compliant."

The spike of heat his words shot through me made me slightly dizzy, and I tried to jerk away again but he held me tighter still.

"I think you're afraid I would know exactly what to do with you." His voice was heavy with desire now. I shivered as goosebumps covered my skin.

I exhaled hard as he worked his hands from where he held me, and slowly moved them up my arms. He kissed my neck, just once under my ear, where I had kissed him at the dinner table weeks before. My eyes fluttered closed, and my pulse quickened. I realized he wasn't holding me to him anymore, but I was leaning back into him on my own. This realization snapped me out of whatever haze I was in, and I pulled away from him and this time he let me go.

His smile was fiendish as he bowed deeply and turned to leave me where I stood; face flushed, heart thudding in my chest. I also realized that more people had been watching than I had originally thought, which sparked both shame and hostility in my chest. I avoided eye contact with everyone on the dance floor as I stalked to a corner where Brees was standing.

"Well, that was..." he said, and I glared at him coldly enough to freeze the River Cras. "...something," he finished, offering me half a glass of spiced wine.

I took it, drained it, and handed it back to him. I fumed silently, staring at all the celebrations and to my dismay, my gaze slipped to Cassius more than once. He sat on his throne and each time my eyes wandered to his, he was smiling, self-satisfied and not bothering to hide he was looking at me. I hated him.

"Such an interesting choice of attire your highness," a voice said from behind me, and I couldn't help the soft groan that escaped my lips as Jessamine saddled up beside me.

She was all white lace and gold jewels.

"I wish I had the energy for you right now, Jessamine."

On any other night, I would have brushed her thinly veiled jabs aside with little effort and maybe a little humor. Tonight though, I had been humiliated by my actions, and by the man I hated most. My face was flushed and there was an angry throbbing behind my eyes.

"Though I suppose we can't blame you for not knowing court etiquette. There would not have been the opportunity for you aboard a pirate ship to be properly educated so we must make allowances," she went on as if I hadn't spoken. "And dancing with your guard Brees before your king and husband, well people will start to talk."

My fists clenched as I tried to remain calm.

"Lady Vaxa, you would do well to leave my name out of your mouth and be careful how you talk about my Queen," Brees ground out.

I caught Devika's eye from where she was dancing, and something must have tipped her off to my current situation. She stopped dancing with her partner and gave him some excuse to leave.

"Though, we must also make allowances for that as well. For while your mother was once a high lady of title and money, she chose to run off with an unscrupulous pirate making her no better than a common street dove."

I turned to her and with a clenched fist, hit her square in the face. She tripped backward on her dress and did not catch her fall as both her hands went to her now bleeding and broken nose.

The people in our general area stopped dancing as I stalked over to where she had fallen.

"My Queen," I heard Devika say out of breath from running over to me, but I ignored her.

"Listen well Lady Vaxa," I said, putting a grass-stained foot on her pure gown to keep her grounded. "I would be incredibly careful how you disparage those around you when you have more than your share of shortcomings. You are from the poorest part of your kingdom and your father is nothing more than a power-grabbing snake, who sent you here to trick a king into marriage with your beauty alone; for certainly that is all you possess. A task you couldn't even complete and lost to a pirate woman. My mother was indeed from Coranthia, and I was born on Puddle Island myself to a whore who had so little to her name that she was forced to give me up. You are nothing, you'll always be nothing, and perhaps given your father's reputation we might have been born of the same whore on that island you call home." I did not know if that bit about her father was true, but she flinched away which made me suspect it was. "If you ever speak of my family like that again I'll break more than just your nose."

I lifted my foot and left the lovely grass dance floor, fleeing to my room where I could cry in peace.

I was feeling rather bad for myself while also despising the way I had handled everything. It was truly a paradoxical feeling of pitying myself while realizing I had also behaved like an ass.

Cassius had tried to unnerve me, and he had done just that. I had let my temper get the better of me and lashed out at Jessamine which meant I would get an earful for the words I had spoken from Devika. I hadn't meant to come off fully deranged, but I was afraid that was what happened. What kind of queen punched a lady in the face? Not a queen at all, but a pirate.

Both Devika and Brees had come separately to check on me and I offered them both an uncomfortable apology for leaving early but insisted they return to the party.

I had changed my clothes into a comfortable skirt and blouse and sat on my balcony letting the breeze shift my hair across my face as I rested my chin on my knees. I listened to the music for hours until the songs had died out and the sound of revelry faded. I didn't know what time it was, but I wasn't tired and doubted I would be able to sleep.

I looked up to the beautiful full moon that lit the back gardens of Hallow Manor.

Full moon? How many full moons had passed since I had been here?

I panicked trying to think. This was the fifth month but had five full moons passed? *Yes*, I realized in horror and the hatred for myself grew. How could I have forgotten this? So wrapped up in myself I couldn't see anything else just like Brees had suggested.

I rushed back into my room, to a small glass vase that I kept dried flower petals in. Every time I thought of a memory with Absalom, I would pull a flower from the garden, let the petals dry and then crush them up to be placed in this vase. I tried to convince myself the ritual would be just as meaningful with dried petals instead of ashes to spread but I really didn't have any choice. I knew Absalom's spirit if it rested peacefully, would not disparage the substitute.

I held the vase tightly to me as I opened the door to my room. My night guard was asleep slumped in his chair. I did not envy the man if Brees found him that way. I shut the door silently, expecting him to stir, and prepared an excuse, but he didn't so much as breathe differently. I slipped past him and down the dark hall of the corridor.

I went out the back steps of the manor and onto the brick walkway that took me past several gardens. When the bricks ended, I continued to a small lily pond I had seen on a walk to the training ground where I went with Brees. When I came upon it, I realized that a small stream led in and out of it so the water wasn't stagnant, which would also make it colder. I walked to the edge and set my petals on the shore of it as I reached to take my shirt off over my head.

"What are you doing?" a familiar voice called behind me and I nearly jumped out of my skin.

"Oceans deep!" I shrieked turning around clutching my shirt to the front of me.

"You know you can ask for a bath to be drawn for you no matter the hour," Cassius said, and I located him sitting under a willow tree that bordered the pond.

"I'm not bathing."

He looked different than he had at the party. It was almost as if he had removed a mask of himself and was now just a regular person. His posture was softened, and his hair was messy. He no longer wore his crown and had donned a light black coat.

"Then what are you doing?"

"Won't you ever leave me alone? You haunt me like the unrequited song of a siren." I glared thinking of how much I did not want to do this with him sitting right there.

"I was here before you," he said, and his tone lilted up as if he found it all rather funny.

I made an aggravated sound in the back of my throat. "I don't have time for this."

"Don't let me stop you." He waved a hand at me. "Proceed."

"Would you consider leaving?"

"No, I feel as if I have an excellent, if not unexpected, view of whatever will unfold right here."

I stared at him for a moment longer and he did not back down from my challenging glare. If I had to do this with him spectating I would. It wasn't about him, it was about Absalom. I could put aside my disdain and pride for my friend who deserved so much more than some petals and a song, but this is all I had to offer.

I shook my head, tossed my shirt to the ground and stepped out of the skirt leaving me only in thin undergarments with a slip over them. I had planned to undress further but I wouldn't with an audience. I felt his eyes on my back and I refused to turn around. I took the vase of crushed flower petals and walked as far as I could reach into the water. There was a drop-off six feet out where the water went over my head. I scattered the petals on the surface of the water and then waded back to put the vase on the dirt. The water was frigid and my fingers shook with its cold.

I took a deep breath willing my voice not to waiver and sang the song for lost loves.

I waited too long to sing of your praises.
Sun-kissed hair, your eyes in their phases.
I speak of the dazzling wonder of love
All of the magic that comes from above

I pray that you won't let go of these things
I pray this because the emptiness stings.
I pray that you'll hold onto them tight
I pray this because it's over tonight.

The sea has taken that which I cherished
My stormy eyed lover tragically perished
The waves are merciless, their reaping of life
They took a man and gifted me strife.

I pray that you won't let go of these things

I pray this because the emptiness stings.
I pray that you'll hold onto them tight
I pray this because it's over tonight

What would I give for a moment of time?
To speak of your qualities all so divine
Or perhaps I might just hold you and weep
For now, I can only touch you in sleep.

I pray that you won't let go of these things
I pray this because the emptiness stings.
I pray that you will hold onto them tight
I pray this because it's over tonight.

When the song was done, I held my breath and plunged beneath the water's surface crossing my legs as I sank deeper and deeper into the murky water below, just now wondering if there were any manner of life in this small pond beyond fish.

The sailor's legend had it that you sang a song of parting to the deceased on the fifth moon after their passing. Once done, you plunged below the surface to connect with their spirit. Some said that their soul could speak to you, but I wasn't naive enough to think I would see Absalom.

I drifted further until I reached the silty bottom and allowed my lungs to burn as I held my breath. The pressure of the water pulsing around me. I lost track of time until my lungs screamed with lack of air and my brain threatened to ingest water if I did not resurface.

I love you Absalom Church. Until I can make you smile once more, rest peacefully.

My prayers were left at the bottom of the pond, and I broke the surface of the water with a loud gasp. The water masked my tears so that no one would be able to distinguish between them. I breathed deeply a couple of times as my lungs remembered how to work. I was facing the shore and a few feet from me Cassius stood thigh deep in the water looking so horrified that I almost laughed.

"What is it?" I asked pushing my hair out of my face, I turned to look but saw nothing in the dark.

"You were under there for a good length of time."

"Were you worried?" I walked past him and up onto the shore.

He didn't respond.

"I was raised on the ocean, Cassius. I can handle myself in the water."

He walked up beside me as I picked up my dry clothing and stuffed myself back into my things dripping wet. He picked up his jacket and boots which he must have removed before he went after me.

He still said nothing, only stared at me as I shoved my wet feet back into my boots. I turned to face him waiting for some quip or insult but saw only hesitation. He opened his mouth to speak before closing it again, making him look even more human than he had before. He stepped forward and my posture went stiff waiting for whatever would come next. He took the jacket he had just picked up and draped it over my shoulders. He held the collar of it around my neck and I still sensed him hesitating, but I was too thrown by the act of kindness that I had forgotten to breathe. He placed a kiss on the top of my head into my wet hair and I stepped away from him, fresh tears springing to my eyes.

"I'm sorry," he said, doing me the favor and turning away. "That you lost him."

Tears spilled over and I hated him more than I had ever hated him before. Hated him for not acting how he was supposed to. Hated him for showing me kindness on a night I desperately needed it but hadn't thought I would receive any. I hated him for humiliating me earlier and then covering me with his jacket just now.

"I hate you," I said through my tears and my voice broke partway through.

"You should." He walked away toward the castle leaving me alone.

Chapter Twelve

Mercy

He had been delaying my request for an audience for two weeks.

I had tried to catch him at dinner, but he evaded me. It seemed he did not want to discuss the truth about the Queen of Southern Ralice he had kept from me. When I wasn't seeking an audience with my brother, I spent every waking moment with Elias, showing him bits of Adamas that I loved. Otherwise, he was regaling my twin sisters with daring pirate adventure stories. Herold and Charity had also grown rather fond of him in the short amount of time and while they didn't know his true identity, they begged him almost every day to play KostoBall with them on the large expanse of lawn in front of Molina Castle. He almost always obliged them, and often had them in such a fit of laughter by the end of the game that they were both heavily reprimanded by their governess. He hadn't known the game when they first played but he picked it up quickly. Once he,

Langston, Tobias, and Holt had played a gentlemen's game and Elias had bested them all.

His confession of love still hung between us, but I was not suffocated by it. It caused me no anxiety, nor did he pressure me or insist on talking about it. He seemed completely at ease passing the time in my company, passing me sly grins, and winks which made my cheeks color with intimacy. I had thought that perhaps the feelings that I developed for him on the ocean had been a young girl's fancy born from new experiences and open air. Though the more time I was in his presence, the more I wondered what I would do when he was no longer around.

Had he come here to take me back to the sea with him? Back to The Siren with him and Georgette? How could I leave my home? Holt may have seemed a little more amicable to my independence but there is no way I could convince him to let me go to be a pirate. Simply thinking of that conversation seemed mad to me. I imagined his face alight with rage thinking of his oldest sister wearing trousers behind a ship wheel as a wave hit the broadside of the vessel. Still, even if I couldn't imagine a way that it would ever come to be, my heart ached for it.

We had gotten his letter sent off to Georgette, and Temperance assured us it would make it to Hallow Manor unseen by curious eyes. Not long after that, Elias had invited me to sit with him by the fountain in the garden I had created, under a full moon. When I had asked why, he had told me that it was traditionally on the fifth moon after the passing of a sailor that you honored their memory by spreading their ashes out to sea. Since he had no ashes, we sat around the fountain drinking some tea from Northern Ralice. He told us stories of He, Georgette, and Absalom as children. He dumped out a bit of dried tea into the fountain.

Until the stars dip below the ocean, mate.

He had said it into the water; Prudence, and I brushed tears off our cheeks. Temperance had no tears, but I spied her blinking much more frequently than necessary in the lantern's romantic light.

So many questions still hung about us. How would he rescue Georgette from King Dalion? How long would Elias stay? and when he left, would I feel the gaping hole I had before? Even knowing he was alive sailing without me seemed an impossible future. Especially as I watched him across the dinner table. A dinner table that my brother was mysteriously missing from. It was as if he could feel my anger for him and it kept him at bay.

Elias looked up at me and caught me staring at him for what seemed like the hundredth time. Though the smile he gave me when his eyes met mine had not lessened. I smiled back, blushing down into my plate of roasted boar and honey glazed carrots.

"When shall we lose the pleasure of your excellent company?" Langston asked.

Since Elias had come, both my brothers had taken to eating most dinners with us. My mother had been to a handful, but I saw her condition worsen every day. Once I had come outside to meet Elias and found them walking the gardens together. When I had asked what they talked about, Elias had just said 'love'. I knew if my mother knew Elias was a pirate, she would be mortified, but I was glad she had been able to speak with him.

"Where is Holt?" I asked the table, and my brothers passed a look between them.

"He's meeting with the archbishop," Temperance answered for them and they both looked over at her with wide eyes.

"What about?" I asked her, seeing as how my brothers wouldn't release any information.

"King Dalion's answer to our request for allyship came." Temperance speared a carrot with a three-pronged fork.

"How do you know that?" Tobias asked concerned from across the table.

"Women know a great deal more than we do my good man. We would do well to treat them as allies instead of delicate things to protect," Elias said, taking a long drink of wine. "Your sisters seem especially capable."

Tobias said nothing to that, and Langston burst out into a good-humored laugh. Prudence beamed at Elias, and Temperance nodded her head to him in thanks. I stood up and pushed my chair back from the table.

"I bid you all goodnight." I curtseyed, lifting my peach embroidered skirt the slightest bit before turning from the table.

"I feel a little sorry for Holt once she finds him," I heard Langston say.

"The ocean has no tempest like that of a woman wronged. The sea itself lends them its rage," Elias said, eliciting a laugh from Prudence as I shook my head smiling to myself thinking of seeing Georgette mad at Absalom.

I stalked the corridors thinking that my brother and Archbishop Deelis were most likely in the throne room discussing whatever King Dalion's letter held. When I reached the large double doors, I hefted one open and was rewarded with voices that echoed across the nearly empty stone walls.

"Sire, I must respectfully disagree," said Deelis before stopping when he heard my footsteps.

Both men looked up and watched me approach. The archbishop with irritation and Holt with a strained smile. He knew I had come for him.

"Princess." The archbishop of our castle bowed to me as well as he could in his emerald-colored robes.

Deelis was an older man. He was prone to drink, though the sacred texts of goddesses prohibited it. He had also always been very unkind to us as children. My father had called him a slippery bastard on more than one occasion while my mother chided him for speaking of a goddess blessed man in such a way. He had calculating eyes the color of the cold blue mountains that lined our southern shores. His pale skin was wrinkled around his eyes and in the frown lines on his face. He was also my brother's most trusted and closest advisor.

"Archbishop Deelis." I bowed my head to him with my hands in front of me as was traditional.

"Sister, I must finish this conversation with Deelis, but I promise I will be with you shortly," Holt said preemptively.

"Fine." I walked to the pews to the left of the thrones and sat down. "I'll wait here."

"Very well." He sighed turning back to Deelis.

"Your majesty," The archbishop said outraged. "Is it wise to allow the princess to listen to our conversation? Surely this topic is outside of her skill set and will do nothing but confuse her."

My hands tightened on my dress and my eyes narrowed at the man. He was speaking about me as people had my whole life. Like I was a weak child in need of coddling. I decided I had not grown out of my dislike for our holy Archbishop.

"Mercy has proven herself loyal to the crown of Adamas more than any of us have," Holt stated. "She has proven herself as capable as any, and you have stepped out of your place to suggest otherwise."

My eyes shot up at his words. I also felt a slight pang of guilt ricochet through me as I had just been thinking of leaving my duty as a princess to become a pirate.

"Very well," Deelis ground out frowning his displeasure. "As I was saying my king, I think you are wrong to turn away the generous offer from King Cyril Kosdel."

"I will not entertain any offer that man has for me. Firstly, it would be dishonorable to collude with him in a war against King Dalion, after he was the one who rescued Mercy. Secondly, King Kosdel tried to force my hand in helping with his war by way of deception, so there is no amount of gold, exports, or promise of land that will coerce me to take sides with him. It's a war he wants and a war he shall have, but it shall not be with me at his right hand."

"Your highness, if your father was alive, he would consider such an offer to better Adamas despite his wounded ego, you are being childish," Deelis said, and my eyes drifted to Holt who stared the man down without hesitation on his face.

"I will not accept an offer from a man who intended to murder my sister as a plot. The full weight of our army will come down on him. I received word from King Dalion today and he has agreed to help us while setting some of his own terms. I have every intention of agreeing to all of them and as soon as he accepts, we shall move against King Kosdel in full force."

"I beg you to reconsider, this isn't what your father would have wanted." Deelis was sounding hysterical at this point.

"That's enough Archbishop. My father isn't here and you are no longer his advisor but mine. You are dismissed." Holt waved his hand and Deelis balked at him, opening, and closing his mouth like a mute dog trying to bark.

Eventually, he huffed and stormed out of the throne room with Holt and me watching his departure. Once he had gone, Holt sat down on his throne and pinched the bridge of his nose breathing deeply for several seconds. Most of my anger had already depleted but if I had any left, the sight of him overwhelmed on the seat my father left him, took everything from me. I relaxed in the pew allowing him a few moments of silence.

Holt had been seven when I was born and I could faintly remember the child he had been, all freckles and copper hair. He had loved doling out hidden sweets and he would build elaborate tents in my room for me with sheets that I would crawl under, my giggles uncontrollable. He doted on our mother always, and as he got older, I had watched as his shoulders had become heavy with the task of living up to the crown. Right then, I could see the brother I had known many years ago.

"Would you allow me to walk you to your room?" Holt asked and I nodded standing up.

He linked my arm in his as we walked down the entrance to the throne room. We left the room behind and walked silently for a little while wandering down corridors and hallways.

"You have every right to be angry with me. I knew you would learn that Cassius had taken your captor as his wife and I should have told you before Lord Tristan arrived. I hoped neither of you would spend much time together but that seems a foolish thought now."

"Why did you lie?" I asked, trying to keep my voice kind.

"At first it was to protect you. Then when you started telling stories about how the two pirates that kidnapped you hadn't been all that terrible, I was angry and assumed you would try to contact her. I thought you were delusional," he admitted.

"The first men that took me were as cruel as any pirates that father told us of. They were the very embodiment of the warnings told. But these pirates were a different sort, not proper but not mindless criminals either."

"I've treated you so terribly. Treated you like I thought a king should treat someone. I hope to be like Father to hold the same respect he did but..." He stopped walking and looked into my eyes. "I don't wish to treat you like father treated you. These past months I have seen how you have been training and handling things, Prudence and Temperance as well. You are more than pieces of royal jewelry to be handed out at the country's whim. You are warriors, women, and my sisters. I'm sorry Mercy...I... I have no defense for myself, only that I know I have surely become Adamas' most disappointing king."

"We've had some much more disappointing ones." I smiled at him and began to walk again at his side.

"I was angry with Cassius Dalion for taking your pirate captor as a bride and making her his queen. Our bargain was that he would kill the pirates, without trial for their crimes as pirates and your kidnapping."

"I am glad he did not kill her," I said honestly. "I know you cannot understand it, Holt, but the Captains Baine became my friends during that voyage."

"I cannot understand it. Nor can I promise to make any amendments to my judgments about pirates, but for your sake, I suppose it ended well."

One step at a time, I told myself. I did not need Holt to understand every part of me, I was only glad that it seemed he was trying. He was trying in the face of centuries of tradition as a king who was only twenty-six years old. I could not expect change so complete. The change I was witnessing now was nothing short of miraculous.

"What were King Dalion's demands to assist us?" I asked.

"A fifty-mile border increase if we take Northern Ralice. He has no desire for more land than that. He only wishes to give his people in the Lapulous lakes reprieve of border wars."

"Is that all?" I asked thinking for a king who had a reputation for malicious intent it seemed rather minimal.

"That is all." He nodded. "He thinks we should seek a peace agreement again with King Kosdel's son Hamish who would assume the throne if King Kosdel were to pass. He thinks neither of us can accommodate acquiring such land, with each of us being so new to the throne."

"Is he right?"

"Yes, I think he is."

We walked the rest of the way in comfortable silence as I pondered the threshold of change that was before us. Not only my journey but for our kingdom as well. We hadn't been to war in nearly a hundred years and now it seemed it was just a few days away. We would be allies with a king I had thought cruel but he had returned me home with no signs of using it to his advantage, and his only request for the spoils of war was more room for his people. Unless there was something else we didn't know about, he seemed reasonable.

We came to my door and my brother bowed to me.

"She wrote you a letter, the pirate woman, months ago." He pulled the letter out and handed it to me. "I'm sorry to have kept it from you. I will call on you and all our siblings tomorrow. I will not send a response to King Dalion's letter without consulting all of you."

"Very well," I said, curtseying. "Goodnight, Holt."

"Goodnight." He smiled like the older brother I once had.

Once I was inside, I went to the bath that Kiltore had drawn for me. She helped me undress and get into the rose-scented water where I didn't linger long. I dismissed her as soon as my hair was tied back and I had donned a night gown.

When she was gone, I went to sit at the desk by my bed. and opened the letter which had been opened prior as the seal had been broken. The handwriting was scratchy, quick, and represented Georgette so well I almost laughed.

Dear Mercy,

I've never been good at letter writing; Elias is much better with words than I. I feel you would find the sight of me in my ruby crown of queens rather comical, I must admit when I catch sight of my own reflection I chuckle.

I wanted to extend my condolences on the loss of our friend Absalom. Sorry, you could not have gotten better acquainted with him for he was a good man.

I also wish to know about your well-being. I hear you have been returned home and I hope the illness you had, passed.

Please return a letter to let me know how you are doing.

Georgette

She had written to ask how I was, and also to let me know Elias hadn't died as I might have incorrectly thought. Referring to him in the present tense and wishing condolences for Absalom's death alone. My heart swelled for I wasn't sure if I had ever had a friend write me a letter before. I pulled out a blank piece of parchment and dipped my pen into the inkwell to begin my letter.

Dear Georgette,

I hope you'll forgive me for when I first found out you had been crowned the queen of a country my first instinct was to laugh. Not because I thought you would look ridiculous with a crown upon your brow, for even though we spent little time in each other's company, I never met a woman I thought could bear a crown as well as you. I only laughed thinking of the man who thought he could tame you.

I am well, Lord Tristan is in good spirits and acclimating well, and I find myself missing you as one misses a friend of many years. I wish I could offer you some wisdom of crown, but alas I have nothing to offer that I think you lack. Be true to who you are. The benevolence you showed in

Liven will serve you well as queen as well as the firm hand you used to run your ship. I think, unintentionally, your husband chose his queen quite well.

I should not laugh at you in a crown for you always walked as if you should be wearing one.

Write me of your wellbeing and of Hallow Manor for I have never been.

Your friend,

Mercy

Chapter Thirteen

Georgette

"I have a plan," I said to Devika.

She leveled a perfectly balanced knife in her hands and threw it at a target under Bree's watchful eye. I could say with confidence I would never want to be on her bad side within knife-throwing distance.

She had started joining me for training with Brees and had been teaching me to throw knives which seemed to be her specialty. I had picked it up easier than I thought I would and welcomed the reprieve from the physical contact training Brees had been putting me through.

"This should be interesting," Brees said, smiling down at me.

"Isn't it always?" Devika teased, picked up another knife and handed it to me.

I took a deep breath, aimed at the target, and flicked my wrist the way she taught me. It landed about three inches from her perfectly thrown one and I beamed at her.

"You can do better," she insisted as she handed me another and I frowned.

"You're a harsher critic than my mother," I said, throwing the knife and it ended up being a worse throw than the first.

"Again," Devika said extending a knife and I shot her a deadly look.

"Are you going to ask about my plan?" I asked, turning and breathing through the throw and it landed closer to hers.

"Honestly, my Queen, I don't really want to know," Devika said and Brees snorted.

"I think my ideas are brilliant," I said, crossing my arms.

"The last time you had a brilliant idea, we ended up with Lady Vaxa in the healers with a broken nose. Also, you accused Prince Vaxa of siring her illegitimately," she reprimanded, and I winced.

"That wasn't so much an idea, as it was an emotion that got away from me."

"I see," she said, not seeming to approve at all.

"I thought it was about time that someone punched her," Brees said and Devika whipped around to fix him with a disapproving stare which he countered with a charming smile.

"She's now telling everyone you are as savage as everyone would assume."

"Maybe she should, let her tell them." I turned to Brees. "We are going to Larkin today."

"Cassius won't like that," he said, but turned away to prepare for us to go, leaving Devika and me alone.

"Devika?" I asked, too much of a coward to look into her eyes when I asked the question.

"Yes, my Queen," she said, having taken a step to retrieve the knives from the target.

"Why are you here, as principal lady, if you are noble-born in Hestiege?" I turned to face her, and she looked at me, working her mouth from side to side.

"My country is very devout to its religious views. A woman can never be anything more than what her husband has amounted to. So, while my uncle might be the King of Hestiege I would never be looked at as more than a pretty token for my father to pass on to a man of power. Although my uncle has no heirs and I am the closest in line for the throne if he does not sire an heir. Not that I believe he would allow that to happen but as it stands now, after my father, I am the closest heir."

I nodded, hoping she would go on. She didn't often tell me about herself, and I wished to understand her better.

"My choices for suitors were extremely limited as my father thought my worth too great for a common Lord of Hestiege, but in our culture, it is frowned upon to marry outside of our people. Eventually, my uncle asked my father if he could have my hand."

"Your uncle?" I asked horrified.

"Yes, my father was entertaining the idea when I wrote Cassius. I had met him a couple of times when my father had taken me along on his ambassador travels here. He wrote back to my father and offered me the position of Principal lady in Hallow."

"Why did your father agree to that?"

"My uncle is a cruel man, mostly to his wives. My father did not want to send me to be married to my uncle but there was no reason for him to tell him no. When Cassius offered me this position in his castle, my father used it as leverage for our treaty with Southern Ralice. I came here to serve Cassius' future wife and he renewed his peace treaty with King Ning, my uncle."

"Your uncle agreed?" I asked.

"Yes, he ultimately saw me as little more than a pawn and if Cassius' only stipulation for a peace treaty was his niece serve in his court, then it meant little to nothing to him. Our country is struggling and we could not sustain any sort of war."

"Are you happy here?"

"My life was very boring before I had a queen to attend, but I was happy."

"And now?" I chuckled a little.

"Well, you are the most unconventional queen I could have imagined but I am grateful to watch and assist you as you become a great queen."

It was said with too much genuine thought. She turned away and finished her path to retrieve the knives we had thrown. I wished I could laugh at her for the faith she seemed to have in me. I couldn't help the overwhelming feeling that I would no doubt disappoint her.

Brees and I went to Larkin and I walked into the tavern with my head high in skirts with pearl and crystal bangles on my arms. I wore a tiara, not trying to hide who I was. Dola had been behind the counter and I saw her bristle and give me a look one might give rotten food after having tasted it. I sat across from her and explained my proposition. She had flat out rejected it at first with *my queen* at the end of her refusal. I told her I would be back in a week; she could present my offer to the town but if she decided not to because of her pride she would be responsible for her town's suffering as much as her brother was.

We came back to Hallow Manor, and Brees was called to speak to Cassius, so I went and pulled all books in my small library on fruit trees. There was very little and I found myself frustrated with the information and stacked the books up on a chair on my way to dinner. I planned on going to the larger library the next day. Perhaps I would ask Lady Amara, she seemed deft with plants and would have been alive when the orchard flourished outside the castle walls.

"Busy day?" Cassius asked as soon as I walked into the dining room.

He was sipping his pine flavored liqueur looking at me with an expression I couldn't quite understand. He hadn't mentioned the night by the lily pond, and I was thankful for it. His hair was tied up on the top of his head and he looked tired.

"Quite," I said, walking past him and around to my seat where my food was already waiting.

"What has my esteemed queen been doing today?" he asked, an edge of something dark beneath his words.

"How do you feel about orchards?" I asked, not bothering to hide my intentions.

"I think we have enough of them." He all but growled following me with his eyes.

"If I may respectfully disagree, your worship..." The slight didn't get a chance to leave my mouth.

I had reached my plate and saw a letter in familiar script resting against my dish. I reached down to pick up the letter. It was still perfectly sealed in the back with no evidence of tampering.

"You didn't open it?" I looked at him in surprise.

"Had you taken a single moment longer to arrive to dinner, I'm afraid my manners for your privacy would have given way to my insatiable curiosity."

He didn't sound curious. The dark undertones I had detected in his words earlier savored almost of jealousy or possessiveness. I figured it was the latter. It would be just like him to think I was his property. I turned the letter back over to read the front.

"From our newly titled Lord Tristan," Cassius said from across the table and I sat down slowly trying to gauge how much he knew. "Who is now in possession of a valuable piece of property off Southern Ralice's shores. He must be rather important."

He just stared at me, and I looked away hoping he couldn't read anything on my face. I opened the letter with him watching. Unfolding the parchment, I sighed at Elias' easy and calm handwriting.

Queen Georgette,

I hope this letter finds you healthy and well-fed.

I rolled my eyes and continued.

My travels to Adamas on your behest have been quite fruitful, having gained many great pieces of information on trading and commodities. So, it disheartens me to bring some news to you that I have come upon during my stay with the very welcoming royal family here at Molina. Of course, I mean not to upset you but it had been brought to my attention that when you were being pursued by King Dalion, he was pursuing your vessel at the behest of Princess Mercy's brother, King Landlight. Respectfully, I wish to make you aware also that King Cyril Kosdel, who you and your brother had been working for, was the hidden villain in this game of kings. Rest assured that I have assessed this information and found that King Cyril Kosdel had Mercy kidnapped by his own hired men and then send you and your brother to retrieve her as an unmarked vessel so that he could be duplicitous and blame the kidnapping on King Dalion. You must be told now that King Dalion and King Landlight have been friends since childhood and when King Dalion heard that King Landlight thought he had kidnapped his sister, Princess Mercy, he offered his assistance freely.

Getting this news must be very difficult for you, yet I have another burden to add to this unfortunate letter. Even while you believe that your friend Absalom was killed by men that worked for King Dalion, this is not true either. Other trustworthy sources have confirmed that the man responsible for Absalom's death was a soldier of King Landlight's, who thought Absalom complicit in King Cyril Kosdel's plan to kidnap Princess Mercy. Regretfully, I have confirmed this as I have spoken to the soldier myself. Goddesses only know what kind of twisted game is at play here, but you needed to know the truth.

Effortlessly I offer my respect and adoration.

Your Servant,

Lord Tristan

Princess Mercy sends you her warm regards.

I read it again, and then again and again trying to catch my breath. My heartbeat pounded in my chest and tears welled up in my eyes. If anyone's hand but my brothers had written these truths, I would deny them, but the childish message system we invented as children was displayed in the letter. It was why it was so oddly written. The first letter of every sentence between the greeting and the farewell spelled a message.

IM SORRY GEORGE

Only my brother would know to put this there for me. It was him validating the information and apologizing for its truth.

Our friend. My friend had not died at the hands of the man sitting across from me but at the hand of a King Landlight's soldier who was sent to save his Princess. The villain of

Absalom's story was not Cassius the Liar, but King Cyril Kosdel who had used us to start a war by deceiving people into thinking Cassius had kidnapped Mercy. Cassius had been helping Mercy's brother. He had been pursuing pirates looking to send Mercy back to her home the entire time.

King Cyril Kosdel used our bargain with him to attempt to start a war. In an attempt to kidnap Mercy, or worse, and it had cost Absalom his life. The commander who had been so loyal to him. I looked down and realized the letter was crumpled in my hands where I gripped it so hard my knuckles were white.

What hurt the most was that I realized I was more responsible for his death than my husband I loathed for it. My connection to Absalom was exploited. He was dead because he was friends with pirates. Bile rose in my throat.

I looked up at Cassius who was frowning with concern.

"Perhaps I should have read it after all," he mused but there was no humor in his voice.

I stood up. "Has Brees retired for the night?"

"I believe so."

"Where might I find him?" I asked my voice sounding small and broken.

"His quarters are in the bottom part of the west side of the castle. Next to the library. His door is red with a gold lion knob."

I didn't stop to ask why he was giving me the information freely. Perhaps he saw the distress on my face. Perhaps he knew what was in the letter and he wished me to finally know the truth. The truth he had kept from me. He had lied to me. He was Cassius the liar after all.

I left the dining room, the letter still clenched in one hand as I made my way to the part of the castle Cassius had specified. The library was tucked away and hidden almost in the serving part of the castle. Beyond its doors were rooms where Devika slept as well as Lady Bastil and Jessamine. I had never been in any of them, as I had never had a need. Now I searched for a red door with a lion keeping its privacy with wild panic. I passed the library and as sure as Cassius had said, a red door came into view with an ornate lion knob.

I knocked hard on the door three times in a row before impatiently opening it, surprised to find it unlocked.

"Brees!" I shouted into the room before surveying the scene inside.

A very startled Brees was half-covered by a sheet and leaning against the headboard of his bed. What had startled me was a very naked and surprised Devika who was draped, breasts bared, across his lap as casually as I had ever seen her.

"I should knock, then wait. My brother was right," I said by way of apology before I stepped back out into the hall and closed the door.

Had I been any less determined to get the answers I sought; I simply would have left them alone. I owed them that after barging in unannounced, but I knocked again instead of waiting at the door for someone to answer it. Thinking to myself how much sense it made for Devika and Brees to be in each other's company. I wondered if they were in love. It was the sort of story Elias and my father would have devoured.

Brees opened the door and leveled me with the most unhappy stare I had ever seen him give, which was saying a lot.

"I am terribly sorry, Brees," I winced.

"You needn't be sorry, you are a queen," I heard Devika say from somewhere behind the door.

"You still need to be sorry." Brees leaned in and whispered to me still glaring.

"I am, very," I said, and he nodded opening the door to let me in.

"My queen," Devika said from where she sat on Bree's bed now covered in a robe.

I decided not to comment on their situation as it was none of my business and not why I had come.

"Was Cassius helping King Landlight find Mercy when he was pursuing my brother and me?" I turned to Brees who wore only trousers and went to sit on a wooden chair next to an ornate dresser.

He stared at me while sitting down, taking a deep breath and leaning back.

"Don't you think you should be asking him this?"

"I am asking you and I expect an answer."

He sighed. "Yes." He leaned forward on his knees. "Yes, King Landlight sent men to the castle to accuse Cassius of kidnapping Princess Mercy, which he did not. So instead, he took the men King Landlight had sent, and some of our own, and went to find her and offer his assistance."

"King Cyril Kosdel had her kidnapped?" I asked as soon as the first answer left his mouth.

"Yes. He made it seem like a Southern Ralician attack, had some riffraff wear our colors, and left just enough men alive to sail the ship back to Adamas to report it to King Landlight."

"Then he asked us to retrieve her..." I said, willing my eyes to remain tearless.

"Hoping you would deliver her to him before anyone caught you, given your ship's reputation. Then when he got word you were being pursued, he hoped for you to drop her off in Brits. He had men waiting just outside the town to ambush her and your friend, to kill them and make it look like Cassius' doing."

"How do you know this?" I asked, stepping back to lean against the door while Devika looked on with pity.

"Some of it came from messages we intercepted from you to him and some messages from him to his men stationed in our country. Some are from a woman we have working for us in King Kosdel's castle."

"Who?" I asked though it made no difference.

"King Kosdel's youngest wife is from Southern Ralice. She is a lady of the high court and loyal to us. We supply her family with money and she has a private house that awaits her when King Kosdel dies."

"And the man that killed Absalom?" My voice broke.

"Not our soldier, He was one of King Landlight's, blinded by anger when your friend said he worked for King Kosdel. Had he been Cassius' soldier he would have killed him for disobeying an order, but he wasn't under our authority."

I sank to the floor and closed my eyes breathing deeply.

"Also," Brees went on. "While I am shifting your perspective, just know that Cassius made a promise to bring you and your brother back to Hallow Manor and execute you for kidnapping the Princess. King Landlight requested it to be done here because we have no system of trial. If King Landlight found out you lived, it would have been within his right to extradite you and have you killed for kidnapping and piracy."

"He married me to protect me?" I scoffed and Brees just shrugged.

"I don't know. I just know he was supposed to kill you but made you queen instead, which is the only way King Landlight would have no authority to kill you."

"Why not just tell me himself," I said, rubbing my eyes with my finger. "Why let me hate him for the past half a year. Why let me think he was the villain?"

"I can't answer that," he said, shaking his head. "Though Cassius has been raised to think he needs to be the mad king. His father was before him and ran a country successfully. Cassius writes himself as the villain so perhaps he is most comfortable with people believing that he is. Though perhaps he did it for the exact reason he says he has, and marrying a pirate woman that defies him at every turn makes him look just as mad as his father."

"But he's not mad," I said, my eyes close to prevent any tears from slipping out. "Is he?"

"Depends on who is weaving the tale."

They both let me sit in silence for a few moments before I stood up to leave.

"I'm so sorry I interrupted your..." I faltered looking for words, which usually wasn't a struggle for me but at that moment I was drowning.

"It's alright George." It was Devika that spoke to me using the name my friends called me.

I smiled over at her and nodded. I hoped the nod communicated that her secret was safe with me. Though I knew I would have the opportunity to tell her, I hoped she wouldn't worry about it this evening.

I walked out nodding at Brees. I took my time walking back to my room and when I finally reached my door, I nodded at my night guard and closed the door behind me. I padded down the hall and threw myself on my bed and let out a loud unladylike scream into the down duvet.

The next morning my head was still swimming with too many emotions for me to sort through. I decided I needed to visit Absalom's pond to clear my head and possibly work through wounds I was still nursing. I walked out before the sun was up, making my way through the gardens as the promise of light was barely beginning to whisper along the leaves. I trudged across grasses and through hedges. The guard that stood at my door at night was standing at the bottom of the stairs of the castle upon my insistence, though he looked uncomfortable to let me go.

I came upon the pond and stopped a few feet away cocking my head to one side. Something seemed quite different about the spot than how I remembered it. I had only been there in the dark so perhaps my memory wasn't serving me well, but as I took a few steps forward I realized what it was.

The pond and the surrounding area had been tidied up. A line of rose bushes had been planted to act as a sort of fence to make the pond look more like a destination spot and less of a forgotten bit of water on the back of the manor. The pond had been cleared and I could now see the water lilies that floated along the top and could admire the beauty like I hadn't been able to the night I came for Absalom.

There was also a stone bench that had been placed under the willow tree that Cassius had been sitting under when I found him. I walked over to it and knit my brow as an inscription had been carved into to seat.

To the man who caused the pirate queen to sing a love song. This place belongs to you.

I ran my hands over it, knowing that no one but Cassius could know about my song to Absalom and perhaps knew that I was the only one who would see this. I wasn't sure if it was for me or Absalom like the inscription suggested. I sat down hard on the bench pulling my knees up under my chin.

"Why must men be so difficult," I sighed out to the serene pond beyond.

Chapter Fourteen

Mercy

There was a knock on my door the day after my talk with Holt, just as I was lacing up my boots for training. I opened it to find Elias standing on the other side. I couldn't help the way my heart swelled at the sight of him. He had something laid flat in his hands wrapped in a large cloth.

"Might I come in princess?" He smiled as I stepped inside to let him cross the threshold.

"I've brought a gift." He extended his hands as if I hadn't noticed.

I stepped to him and pulled the fabric aside to reveal the two swords Jones had given to me when I had won the duel on The Siren. I heard myself take a sharp breath in and reached out to touch them. They were still the most beautiful thing I had ever seen. The swirled steel of the blades melded beautifully into the twin handles. Light and beautiful, the swords had been a cherished gift. They laid atop a leather harness of sorts I hadn't seen before.

"Oh, Elias," I said, tearing up.

"Jones insisted I bring them to you, and I was looking for the right moment to give them back to their rightful owner."

"Why is this the right moment?" I questioned, picking them up and extending them both in each hand.

"I thought you might be gracious enough to duel with me again." He tapped the sword he wore at his side.

"Is that right? You must enjoy being beaten."

"At your hand Mercy, I might enjoy more punishment."

I colored and shook my head at him as he set the cloth on the bed and held the harness up that I realized was a double sheath to be worn on one's back. I set the blades on the bed as he helped me into it. He adjusted it using a series of metal rings and pulled leather straps until it fit snugly against my back, before putting the blades into the crossed sheaths.

"How does it look?" I rolled my shoulders getting used to the weight and feel of it.

"Magnificent." He stepped to me and pulled me to him with his hands on my hips.

"Hello," I said, feeling another blush creep over my face.

"Hello." He leaned in and my eyes closed as his lips brushed against mine. "What shall we wager on our duel?"

"You want to place a wager?" I laughed.

"What's the fun in a duel if there is nothing at stake?"

"Okay," I conceded. "If I win...You tell me what happened to your parents and what was so important for you and Georgette to find that you made a deal with King Kosdel to get it."

He looked at me openmouthed as I looked into his eyes. Secrets were The Captains' currency. I was crossing over a line, testing the water of our relationship. He did not disappoint as he pressed another kiss to my mouth which I accepted and returned one of my own.

"You're more ruthless than you look, Princess. Very well, but if I win you will agree to marry me."

"Elias!" I exclaimed pulling away from him, but his ever-present grin was still on his face. "Don't jest about that sort of thing."

"I assure you, Mercy, I'm very serious."

"I cannot wager that."

"Why not? I shall seek your brother's permission if that is what it takes. I am titled and papered with property after all. I'm a lord. I have more money than the goddesses themselves."

"It's not about money or title," I said, feeling both overjoyed and stunned.

"What is it about?" He stepped forward again and brought me to him once more.

"What am I supposed to tell my brother? I will live on a ship most of my life?"

"If you would prefer to live on land Mercy," he started, and my eyes went wide at what he was saying, "I will adjust to that."

"Elias, no. I would never take you from your ship. If anything, I would want to sail with you, not tie you to the land." I was going off spilling secrets I kept in my head and realized it as his eyebrows went up.

"So do we have a wager then?"

"You are impossible, there is so much to be sorted before..."

Before what? I asked myself, tumbling over my words. Before I agreed to marry Elias Baine the pirate captain? My heart thudded in my chest. Even then I knew my answer, though I couldn't get my mouth to form the words to tell him.

"So, we will sort them," he said simply.

Tell him yes. I chastised myself, but I felt so overwhelmed I couldn't.

Another knock came at the door, and I lingered in his arms a moment before stepping away to answer it.

"Princess, your brother is requesting you and Lord Kaloqey's presence in the dining room." The guard that had come to deliver the message said.

"Thank you, Brinton." I nodded as he walked off.

I leaned against the open door taking a moment to myself with Elias at my back.

"You needn't answer now," he said, and I jumped a little, not realizing he had come up behind me. "I'll ask again, and again until you say yes, or that you wish for me to leave you alone forever."

I couldn't tell him yes. My anxieties wouldn't let me, but I slipped my hand into his and squeezed it.

"Please don't leave me alone forever," I said, looking back at him.

"Yes, Princess." He leaned in and placed a soft kiss on the tip of my nose.

"Mercy, Lord Tristan." Holt greeted us as we walked into the dining room.

All my siblings were there along with three of my brother's advisors including Deelis. There were six guards with

Atticus standing on the outside of the room. He nodded at me. Prudence and Temperance were sitting next to each other dressed in training gear. Langston and Tobias sat on either side of Holt. Even Herold was there in a chair that looked much too large for him. Though Charity and my mother were not present.

Temperance nodded to me, and Prudence smiled. I acknowledged them both before turning my attention to Holt.

"My King," I said politely, curtseying to my brother. "I apologize for my appearance; I was not planning on you to call us so soon."

"No mind, sister," he said, gesturing to a chair where I took a seat.

Elias went to stand next to Atticus and turned to him saying something I couldn't hear. Atticus nodded and answered as they both turned to listen to what Holt was going to say. They had formed a bond of comradery the past couple of weeks, and I had watched it grow into a friendship.

"I have asked you all here, my advisors as well as my siblings, to discuss our countries next course of action."

There were mixed responses to his statement. His three advisors looked at me and my sisters with some contempt for having been included. Even Tobias looked a little hesitant at our presence. Langston only nodded in understanding.

"King Cassius Dalion has answered our request for his assistance in the war against Northern Ralice. He has requested a borderland increase as payment which I intend to accept if there are no great objections by anyone seated at this table."

No one spoke.

"To be transparent," he said, directing the words at me. "I also will inform you that King Cyril Kosdel still wishes us to join him in a war against King Dalion and has given me very strong monetary and trade incentive to say yes."

"Snake," Langston spat. "After what he did to Mercy, how can he expect us to help him with anything?"

"I agree with Langston," Tobias said stoically and I breathed a sigh of relief.

I hadn't been sure if either of my brothers would agree with Deelis about aligning with King Kosdel. They both sounded sure that they wouldn't consider such a thing. Holt nodded at them both.

"I was hoping that you both would feel that way. So, I will respond to King Dalion's letter today and within the next couple of weeks we will close in on King Kosdel's sides. We will send our army by ship, and they will come up on the northern border. Northern Ralice has a sizable army, but their numbers cannot defend against us and Southern Ralice coming from both borders. King Dalion's army is more formidable than ours and King Kosdel's. Once we infiltrate Urorah and kill King Kosdel we shall negotiate with his son for another peace treaty. This treaty will include monetary reparation and trading that will strengthen and enrich Adamas."

"I think that prudent my King, as it would be hard to rule over a country across the river Cras. Best to take something else from them to enrich our people and lands," one of my brother's advisors said, I thought I remembered his name being Hilton or Hamlin.

My other brothers nodded at the words, and I was so focused on their reactions I hadn't realized that five of the guard had moved to be positioned around the table. The only reason I noticed was that Temperance sat forward, her posture going more rigid than normal. I looked over to her as her eyes shifted to each guard that seemed to be moving casually but stopped behind each of my brothers, while the other two stepped behind my brother's advisors, save Deelis.

"Holt!" Temperance slid her chair back and shouted as the guards drew daggers.

Holt hardly had time to turn to look behind him. With surprise on their side, the guards pulled heads back against chairs and dragged the blades against their necks, my heart shuddered as bright blooms of blood opened on my three brothers' necks, spilling down their chests.

Time slowed and my breathing became shallow as I watched my brothers grip their throats with their blood pouring over their fingers as they seemed to be gasping for air. Prudence had tears that slipped down her face and Temperance looked on in horror. I turned to see Elias draw his sword and then turned back to Temperance who looked to me and nodded.

"Now Lord Kaloqey, I would be careful." Deelis' slippery voice slid across the bloody scene as we watched our brothers still dying in their seats.

"I cannot allow this country to go to war with Northern Ralice," Deelis said, standing and looking at my brothers with no more concern than he would give a trapped animal.

It wouldn't matter if we called the healer. Tobias' eyes already fluttered as the life left his body. It was too late to save them. I willed my tidal wave of grief to wait until this was finished.

"As your brother's soon to be only living advisor, I shall take my rightful place as the steward of this country. Then I shall tutor young Herold and we shall raise him to be a pious man of the goddesses and our vision of uniting all the kingdoms under one religion shall be realized. Kill the lord." He finished by gesturing to Elias who had his sword at the ready with a face set for battle.

As the guards turned to deal with Elias, Atticus drew his weapon against them as well.

"Atticus you shall lay down your weapon, as your steward, your oath to the house of Landlight commands you to serve this country."

"Choke on blood," Atticus spat, standing at Elias's side.

"Very well." Deelis sighed. "Kill him as well."

Three guards turned to attack them before two daggers found themselves lodged in their backs and they dropped to their knees. I turned to Temperance who had gotten up on the table and was now taking another dagger that Prudence handed up to her. She ran across the table and jumped down to attack another guard that looked as shocked as if she had turned into a viper.

I stood, unsheathing the swords from my back and slid one hard across the table to Prudence who picked it up and stood with as much fierceness as I had ever seen her wield. My blood boiled as I focused on the men crying in pain and reaching back for the knives that had been embedded in their skin. I stepped from behind my chair and with as much force as I had ever used, I took off the first one's head with my sword. I freed the dagger from the back of the second and dragged it across his throat as he fell to the floor. Elias nodded to me once as he and Atticus attacked the third guard. It was a quick fight and the man fell with Elias' blade through his chest.

Temperance was just standing up leaving the guard she had attacked dead on the floor. That left one guard, who had his sword raised in front of him. He looked panicked, eyes shifting from Deelis to each of us as we closed in on him. He dropped his weapon and raised his hands in surrender. Before he could say anything, Prudence took the few steps it took to be in front of him and thrust one of my twin-blades into his gut. She withdrew it and thrust again as the man cried out falling and curled up on the floor still screaming in pain.

All five of us turned to face Deelis who had gone white as a sheet.

"You should have brought more than five guards, or did you assume the women of the Landlight name would not defend themselves?" Temperance said wiping some blood off her dagger onto her skirts.

I walked over to Deelis who was unarmed and shaking, looking at us in bewilderment. He went ahead with his plan even seeing that I had come in armed. He hadn't seen us as a threat. It would be the last mistake he made.

"Kneel," I commanded.

He did and dropping to his knees slowly he used his hand to brace himself against the floor.

"Why?" Temperance demanded.

"The high priests will not stop until Marecult is united under one religion. The goddesses' servants will be rewarded for their faithfulness," he recited like a hollow worshiper.

By this time, my brothers had all passed with their hands on their throats. The other two advisors were also slumped in their chairs in puddles of their own blood. I looked to Herold who I had forgotten in the nightmare and saw him with his knees pulled up to his chest, tears streaming down his face as violent sobs racked his body. I was overwhelmed with anger so hot and pure it consumed me.

"This nation will crumble under the rule of women!" The archbishop went on. "The people will revolt, and you will fail.

When you are weak, the faithful will strike and you will fall just like your corrupt brothers."

I couldn't listen to him anymore. I turned and swung my blade making contact with his neck. I didn't swing to decapitate only to slash the front of his throat. So, he could slowly suffer the way my brothers had.

He gripped his neck and attempted to yell but couldn't. We all watched as blood-soaked the front of his shirt. Eventually, he fell to the floor. No one moved until he had stopped twitching. Until his blood pooled on the granite floor of the room where we took our meals. I doubted I would ever be able to eat again.

It was Elias who moved first, to my brother's bodies, where he closed their eyes out of respect. Atticus went to the two other men shutting their eyes as well. I supposed this wasn't Elias' first encounter with murder or blood. I knew Atticus was a soldier and had no doubt seen deaths this brutal, but Temperance, Prudence, and I stared at them as they moved about not knowing what to do. The adrenaline had left my body and my sword fell from my hands clattering to the floor.

Elias walked over to Herold, who was still curled up in terror where he sat on the chair. Elias kneeled before him and pulled his knees and hands away from his face.

"What a brave man you are," Elias said as the tears I had held back gave way to the sound of the tenderness in his voice.

Prudence walked to a chair and sat down hard, as her tears came as well. Temperance merely looked to Atticus, who walked to her without hesitation and embraced her tightly as she too began to sob. I was too washed over with grief to be surprised.

I walked over to Elias and sat on the floor next to Herold, reaching my hand out and slipping mine over his smaller one. Elias put his hand around my shoulders but said nothing.

For what was there to say?

Adamas' three eligible rulers had been murdered as well as their advisors. Three royal sisters stood in grief with blood on their hands and a little boy had witnessed too much murder, for a lifetime, in so many minutes.

"What will we do?" My voice came out shaky and quiet.

"What you must," Elias answered.

Chapter Fifteen

Georgette

Dola and all of Larkin had responded to my proposition.

I had spent the day training with Brees and then with Amara, talking about the intricacies of transplanting orchard saplings. Both she and Camber had joined me for dinner as Cassius wasn't to be back until later that evening. The letter had been waiting for me when I arrived at the table.

Most Esteemed Queen,
The people of Larkin will accept your generosity. However, it comes with one condition, that one-fourth of our crop for the next ten years will be given to the palace in exchange for your kindness.
Your Subject,
Dola Noon

Other than the fact that it was dripping with sarcasm, and I could almost see the tavern woman writing it with a sneer on her face, I was pleased. The pride of the town would insist on a portion of the crop being returned and I could live with the bargain.

At dinner, Amara told me a few stories about Cassius when he was a child. I found myself laughing at some of the tales of his iron will that had manifested at only five years old. It was evident by her tone that she doted on him, as mothers did with sons. Even my mother had forged a special bond with Elias growing up. I spent longer at the dinner table with them than I ever had before. Amara and I talked so long that Camber fell asleep in her chair with her head lolling to one side and a bit of drool coming out of her mouth.

Brees picked her up and offered to escort her and Amara back to their plant-covered home.

"Goodnight, George." Camber's eyes peeped open, though they were weighed down with dreams.

"Goodnight my love." The words flowed from me without thought. I shut my lips tight after they left, but not fast enough for the quick Amara who gave me a slight smile.

I almost skipped to my room clutching the letter in my hand. I was as giddy as a temple girl on too much wine. I felt like I had won something. Not only would I be able to help the people who I had pitied when I first arrived in Hallow, but the outcome would enrage Cassius, and that alone was worth the effort.

I turned a corner and was confronted with a scene of two people passionately kissing against the wall. One I knew was Jessamine's lady's maid, and one was the guard that stood guard at my door at night. I cleared my throat. The two sprang apart like two halves of wood that had been split.

"My queen," the guard spoke, and a heated blush raced over the lady's face.

"Good evening," I chimed as I passed them.

"Indeed." It seemed as if my guard could think of nothing else to say.

I smiled at them both, not looking back as I passed.

When I reached the hallways that led to my room, I looked up to find someone who might be able to ruin my good humor. Jessamine was stalking toward me with as much determination as she ever had. I scanned her face and aside from her nose which was now slightly more crooked than it had been, there were no other signs left that I had punched her. Devika had told me she refused to come out of her room for two weeks because she had gotten two black eyes.

"Queen Dalion," she spoke in a tone so polite it made me stop walking.

"Lady Jessamine," I responded as she curtseyed to me.

"Have you seen my handmaid Cleoette? I am trying to locate her."

"No," I said, taking pity on the girl I had just seen with my guard. "I have not, I came from that way and have seen no one."

I pointed behind me and Jessamine nodded.

"I shall have to look somewhere else then, thank you, your highness." She curtseyed again and didn't so much as turn her lip up at me as she spun on her heel and returned the way she came.

I stared after her as she passed the doors that went to my room and beyond until she reached a staircase and made her way down. I shook my head at the wonder I had beheld and continued to my room. Once inside I took off my boots and threw them haphazardly to one side as I undressed from the trousers and light stay I wore. Devika was attending some sort of religious ritual that evening but told me she would have a bath drawn for me.

True to her word my principal lady had a bath drawn and small whispers of steam rolled off the top of the water. Lavender petals were swirling on top, and the smell of almond oil filled the bathroom as I finished undressing. I tossed my clothes on the floor, a habit Devika loathed, and sank into the warm tub. I looked to a small wooden table to the left of me and smiled with delight. A small golden box was wrapped with ribbon and displayed on the table. I reached out and opened it casting the ribbon on the floor and the lid as well.

Inside were delicate truffles rolled in cocoa powder that looked as divine as anything I had seen. They were all stacked up in a beautiful mound and I immediately popped two into my mouth and set the box back on the table. The cocoa on the outside was bitter but it gave way to creamy smooth chocolate that I enjoyed as I slipped beneath the surface of the tub.

I stayed in the warm water for a while before stepping out and drying off with a sheet. I was getting a little dizzy as I slipped on an ankle-length satin robe and tied it around my waist. I leaned against the opening of the bathroom door as I became very disoriented, and my knees buckled together.

I fell on the tile floor shaking my head to get rid of the faintness that had come over me. I felt my stomach turn and start to riot. I turned back to the chocolates sitting on the open table and frowned. My legs were not cooperating, and I had to drag myself by my arms across the floor. I knew I couldn't make it to the door down the hallway to the main entrance to my room. My only hope was to get to the door that was set into my bedroom wall. I had tried to open it several times before only to find it locked. Devika said she didn't know where it went and so I left it alone.

My arms began to weaken as I pulled myself one more time to lay at the bottom of it. The contents of my stomach threatened to come up as I took a very weak fist and started hitting the door as hard as I could. If anything, perhaps the guard stationed outside my main door would hear something and come looking.

I thought of Jessamine, face so polite and blank. No, there had been no snide remark, because she had thought she had bested me. It seemed at that moment that she had. I may have broken her nose, but she was going to take my life from me. I could no longer lift my fist to knock on the door and I rolled over on my back. I knew if I opened my mouth and used my stomach muscles to scream, I would vomit. I was contemplating covering myself in puke to be saved when the door I had been knocking on opened inward.

I lifted my head as much as I could, and my stomach rolled again.

"Oceans deep, not you," I moaned as Cassius' face came into view over me.

For the briefest moment, he looked amused and then taking in the situation his slight smile turned into a frown.

"What's happened?"

"I don't want your help," I said. "Leave me to die."

"Not very courteous after you knocked on my door." His humor was back.

Of course, he slept in the adjoining room to mine. It would be the only reason Devika hadn't told me where the door led. She had been told to keep it from me. I couldn't even blame Devika for not telling me. The vile way I had been when I had first arrived here, I might have tried to kill him. Up until a few weeks ago, I might have killed him. Now, he was still a villain but not my villain. He was simply a wretched man with a crown placed on his head.

"Did you, do it?" I said as it became hard for me to talk. "Did you ask her to poison me?"

"You were poisoned?" he asked and stood up straight looking around my room. "With what?"

"This is how you kill me?" I asked as I started becoming delirious.

"No, if I wanted to kill you, I would just have you beheaded in the throne room, no need to be secretive about it. Where is the thing you ingested?"

"Bathroom," I managed to get out before a heave of vomit come up my throat and I rolled over to deposit the contents of my stomach on the floor. Cassius disappeared from my line of sight.

I closed my eyes and waited for darkness to come. It wasn't coming quick as I felt my insides revolt at the toxin from within.

I heard Cassius yell and more footsteps followed. I couldn't tell how many.

"Go get the healer," he barked out. "If she dies while you are on your way, I'll have you tortured and then killed. Tell him it is death thistle, and that I'm putting her in my bed."

"Not a very original name," I said, having rolled on my backside once more.

I kept my eyes closed, breathing the best I could though my throat had started to close.

"Georgette." It was Cassius at my side, in my ear. "You better not be dying."

"Seems like it would solve a lot of your problems," I said, and my thoughts grew very heavy, enticing me to the deepest sleep.

"Don't you fall asleep you dreadful woman. You've made my life miserable for the past half of a year. Fight this damn poison as you fight me every day of your life in this castle."

"You can get a new wife," I mumbled out and felt myself being lifted off the floor.

"One wife is plenty, if you don't survive, I'm never getting married again. With all the trouble you've given me."

"I've saved the female sex then." My eyes fluttered open and closed against my will as I tried to see what was happening.

"Captain Georgette Baine," he demanded, and my eyes flew open to meet his. "You stay awake until the healer gets here." He set me down on what I assumed was his bed.

"You aren't in command of me," I defied.

"That's it," he said, "Tell me how much you hate me."

"A lot." I managed to blink my eyes hard as my limbs started to tingle. "I hate every drop of blood that runs through your arrogant, selfish veins."

"Good." His sigh sounded relieved.

I soon realized it was because someone was in the room.

They spoke to each other, and I caught pieces of the conversation, but I couldn't understand everything they said. My eyes were so heavy with sleep that I closed them despite Cassius' insistence that I shouldn't.

"My Queen," a steady and calm voice came to me, and my eyes fluttered back open. "I am going to shove something into your mouth, and I need you to swallow it despite how difficult it might be."

I nodded because it seemed I had lost the ability to talk. I laid there for a few more moments. My eyes had gone dark despite me having them open. A twisting ache gnawed at my stomach. I felt a warm paste of sorts being forced into my mouth. It tasted dreadful like ground-up toad eggs and dirt. I gagged several times but managed to swallow the mouthful I was given. Once I had swallowed one mouthful more was shoved between my teeth. I groaned but swallowed that too. A hand force-fed me the goop until my stomach could hold no more, and I rolled away from whoever it was.

"What now?" I heard Cassius ask.

"Let her sleep. The snake intestine will work while she sleeps. If the thistle didn't reach critical points, it will save her. If it did, she will die."

"Thank you Saltoe," Cassius said and I heard shuffling.

The rumbling in my stomach kept me awake despite the exhaustion. I kept my eyes closed and breathed deeply. I felt a warm cloth wipe across my face. It was wet and comforting and made several passes over my mouth and cheek. There was a brief break and then I felt fingers running through my hair as someone pulled it away from my face. When it stopped, I opened my eyes, but I still couldn't see so I closed them again.

My stomach had started to settle and wasn't sloshing about with the contents. I tried not to remember the woman's words, *snake intestine*. Thinking about it made me sick all over again. I felt a blanket settle over me, and the bed shifted beside me. I felt a tingle of touch on one of my hands, a light caress across my knuckles, over and over.

"Don't die, Georgette, if you are only going to listen to me once in your life, let it be now."

I awoke with the worst taste in my mouth. *Snake intestine,* my brain supplied and my stomach rolled.

I tested my body and found I was able to move my toes. I could feel my legs and arms and when I opened my eyes I could see. Other than my body aching, and intense nausea, I felt alive. I pulled myself up on my forearms to look around. I was in a large bed, in a room with heavy curtains and dark wallpaper. The sun streamed in through the cracks of the drapes, and I saw gold and crimson accents decorating the walls. The wallpaper depicted large ornate birds with golden feathers.

I turned and was startled by a man sleeping next to me. He was propped up in a sitting position, his dark hair had fallen in his face. I also noticed he was wearing only trousers. His bare chest was exposed giving me a view I hadn't wanted. My cheeks heated and I shook my head. I had seen plenty of men without their shirts. I had seen plenty of men with no clothes at all. There was no reason for me to get flustered like a virgin in a shipyard suddenly.

Though I kept staring, because against Cassius' sculpted chest was a deep black snake tattoo that took up a large amount of space. It started with the snake's gaping mouth as if the creature was about to attack in the middle of his sternum. Then the snake's black body wrapped around his chest, down his ribs, back along over his pelvic bone and the tip of the viper's tale disappeared below his trouser line.

I looked back to his face and froze as his eyes were now open and he was staring at me with one eyebrow raised and one side of his mouth quirked up in a grin. I swallowed hard, unable to keep a blush from settling on my cheeks again.

"Feeling better?" he asked, and his voice still held the light gravelly tone of morning.

"I've been worse." I let myself fall back into the bed letting my arms rest at my sides.

"Death thistle tastes like cocoa powder only more bitter," he said after a brief pause.

"Excellent, I shall hold onto that piece of information for the next time I'm handed a golden box of chocolates."

"Why would you eat food that hadn't been tested first?" he asked, and I turned my head on the bed to look over at him.

I was sure I looked an absolute wreck, but I wasn't sure why it mattered.

"This is my first time being poisoned. I've never had cause to check my food before."

"Poison is the easiest way to kill someone if you are a coward. All your food is tested before you eat it."

"What an unpleasant job that would be."

"Though if you're stupid enough to eat chocolate laying around in your room perhaps you deserve to die." He looked up at the ceiling as if contemplating.

"If it would have gotten me out of this marriage, perhaps I should have eaten more than two." I groaned as I shifted to sit up.

My stomach revolted and it felt as if every muscle in my body had been bruised by Brees himself. I moved my legs so that I was on the edge of the bed with my feet dangling off. I closed my eyes and pressed my fingers into my eyeballs as a pounding headache began to form.

"Do you know who poisoned you?" he asked and the teasing that had been in his tone earlier was gone.

I stayed silent because I didn't know what to say. Of course, I knew who poisoned me. The reality of it was too obvious now. Jessamine being in the wrong part of the castle. Her lady in waiting pulling my guard away from my door. I was an idiot for not having been more suspicious. He took my silence as an omission of knowledge.

"Who?" he asked firmly.

"What will happen to...them?"

"They will die." It was a blunt and final nod; I winced a little.

It wasn't as if I hadn't taken a life before, but there was something different about a duel or a fight where one person bested another, and another thing entirely for me to send a woman to her execution for being jealous. If she could wield a blade, I would have challenge her to a match to the death. Though it would hardly be fun if she had never held a sword before.

"Would you consider handing their punishment over to me?" I turned to look into his eyes.

His eyebrow went up again as he considered my question.

"Please," I added, and his eyes went wide for a second before he replaced his expression with passive curiosity.

"Very well, their life is yours to do with as you please."

I nodded and fell back on the bed, not being able to sit up anymore. I closed my eyes again taking deep breaths and willing myself not to vomit again.

Cassius got up and I watched as he gathered new clothes and changed with no regard to my presence. I stared up at the ceiling when his trousers came off. Though I should have enjoyed the view as it seemed the back of him was as well-formed as the rest of him was. When he had fully dressed, he pulled his hair back away from his dark eyes with a leather cord.

"Georgette," he said as he went to leave his room into a hallway, that I supposed dumped into a receiving room as like mine did.

I lifted my head to meet his eyes.

"You are not to go back to Larkin again. You will not offer those people any more assistance than they've had, and you certainly will not continue this insane mission of replanting their orchard." His tone was cold as steel and as final as a blade in the chest.

It was the kind of tone that shot the wall back up between us. The invisible barrier that had seemed like it had crumbled a little bit. Both of us were now defensive and my pride swelled in me at his order. I stared coolly at him.

"And if I do continue my insane mission?"

"This time there will be consequences for your actions."

"What sort of consequences, darling husband?" I sat up again defying him with my glare.

"The sort you shouldn't be foolish enough to try and test." His tone had gone as dark as mine and any softness he had for me the night before had vanished.

So, I reached for the thing I knew would hurt him. For it seemed, though I wasn't sure how he had wounded me, and I would not be the only one made to feel this way.

"What will the consequences be Cassius? Will you lock me in my room? Or perhaps..." I paused knowing the words I was going to say would destroy whatever lingered between us. "Perhaps you'll put a metal collar on me, the way your father did to your mother."

"Georgette," he warned, and I heard the black anger lying beneath the way he said my name.

"Will you beat me? Like he beat her, Cassius? Will I wear your scar of abuse around my neck for the rest of time?"

"Enough!" he shouted, and his eyes were wild with something like fear and rage.

He took one step toward me and never broke eye contact as I challenged him. He sneered and looked me over as if I were a disease that inflicted him. He turned without another word and stormed out of his room.

While the words had hit their mark, I did not feel satisfied. I felt sick to my stomach.

Chapter Sixteen

Mercy

We all agreed we had to keep it quiet. If the word got out that all three men of the Landlight line, old enough to take the throne had died, it would cause a panic that would sweep our kingdom. So, the guards were sworn to secrecy, and no one was allowed to leave the castle as we laid my brothers to rest.

There was a family crypt in the back of the castle where they were put in marble and sealed forever. We had no archbishop to say words over them or perform the religious aspects of the ceremony. A boy who was training under Deelis did the best he could but he stumbled over his words as the crypts were sealed. He prayed to Ysmir to give my brothers a prosperous afterlife.

I hadn't been able to stomach looking at their lifeless faces again after we had moved them from the throne room. Something was haunting about seeing them dead so young, their life ripped from them too early. When my father had died there had been a sense of peace about it as he had struggled with his health for years, but Langston had been only twenty-two and his bright smile and effervescent personality plagued me. Tobias with his quiet listening and his contemplative glances. Then there was Holt who had just reached out to try and heal our family for the first time. Our loss was devastating.

We wept for weeks as tradition had it there would be no discussion of who would become the steward of the country for that time while we were in mourning. Not that there was anyone eligible by the standards of our law. Our archbishop had been killed along with both my brother's other advisors. It left no one to take the throne.

On the morning of the ninth day of grief, we woke to yet another tragedy. It seemed the burden of losing her sons was too much for my mother to bear, and her ladies maid found her with lacerations up her arms in a drying pool of blood on the carpet of her chambers. So, we mourned my mother too, her death ripping open the wounds of my father, my brothers, and for me, Absalom.

Three weeks passed in dreary and dismal silence. We mechanically moved about the palace as Elias made sure we ate but beyond that, it felt like the presence of darkness itself hung over the castle. Until the morning that marked the third week came, and Elias had us all gathered in the throne room together. We all sat in silence sitting in the pews waiting for him to tell us why he had called us there. Atticus stood off to the side. The captain of the guard had been one of the guards that had betrayed us and had paid for that with his life. We had appointed Atticus to the position, and he had done an excellent job thus far.

"It is time to decide what is to be done, Princesses," Elias said finally.

We all looked up at him and Prudence's ever-present tears began to slip down her face. Temperance's hand slid into my sister's lap, but she nodded at Elias in acknowledgment of his words. I knew he was right. We could not keep this silence for long.

"You have a wolf gnashing his teeth at your door and he will take this kingdom from you with blood and claws if he must. While we have done all we can to keep the death of your brothers a secret there are always cracks in the wall. Soon your enemies will be upon you. If you do not meet them on your terms, they will rip you to shreds."

"Yes," Temperance said standing, pacing now. "He is right, if Cyril hears of this, if he hasn't already, it will look like we are ripe for the picking, and he will no doubt come for our weakness."

We had sent a reply to King Cassius Dalion the night my brothers had died. We signed it for our brother and used his seal. We agreed to his terms and told him another letter would be coming with more information. While he would have surely received the letter by now, he had no other word from us, and we had no more information to give him.

"Mercy will take her place as the steward of the kingdom," Temperance said and my head snapped up to meet her eyes.

"Me?" I asked, panic and anxiety knotting itself in my stomach until I thought I would wretch. "There are laws that prevent me from taking the throne even as a steward until Herold becomes of age."

"It is time for new laws Mercy. If one of us does not do it, then we look weak to others." Temperance's tone was cold as steel, and I shrunk back from it.

I wasn't sure what I had been expecting to happen, but it wasn't this. I felt so ill-equipped to run a country. I hadn't been trained to be a ruler or a swordswoman princess. I was not graced to rule a country. Herold wouldn't be old enough to take the throne for six years. Was I to be the steward of this country for six years until that time came?

I didn't want it. My heart rejected the idea. Not only did I not want it, but the people deserved more than a princess who was only half committed to them. A princess whose heart belonged now mostly to the ocean and a pirate who sailed it. I couldn't, could I?

"We will continue with the war that Holt has started, I have a feeling if we pulled back now, Cyril would only come for us," Temperance said, still pacing as Prudence and I looked on.

"Atticus," she said, looking up to the captain who had anticipated her call and come to her.

"Yes, Princess," he said, as dutiful as ever.

Since the day in the throne room, I had not seen a single moment of intimacy between them, but it had opened my eyes to tension and passion that I had not seen before. The way he looked at her and the way she tried not to look at him.

"Are the camps ready to be dispatched by boat to the shores of Northern Ralice?"

"Yes Princess, Master Hestor Fortunnic is ready, and as always, dedicated to the house of Landlight."

"Will the men stand?" I asked him across the expanse. "If I take the throne until Herold is old enough will the guard and the soldiers stand behind us?"

If our armies fell, we would fall.

"Princess Mercy. Every man in your army has pledged their service to this house. Whether it is you on the throne or one of your brothers your army will stand behind you, and we will not let that bastard king take anything else from us." He had come to kneel before me and again my stomach rioted with anxious nerves.

It didn't feel right.

"Very well then," I sighed. "Shall we formulate a plan?"

We talked, we took a meal and talked some more. We strategized bringing Master Fortunnic and Atticus in on the deliberation, as we came up with a plan. I would go with Elias back to Southern Ralice. We would explain what happened to King Dalion and see if he has any qualms with allying with us now that a woman would be on the throne. Our kingdom hung in the balance of his answer. Temperance and Prudence would stay and carry out military action when the orders were received via letter.

Master Hestor Fortunnic agreed to prepare ships and companies to be dispatched on the first word and left to start the preparations. Ships would be readied, armies would be prepared, and our country would go to war with me on the throne. The guard was doubled in the castle, and we deliberated on how we would spread the news of our brother's deaths.

We decided that the day I was to leave for Southern Ralice, a decree would be sent out to all major towns in Adamas. The kingdom would grieve as they went to war. Anger was a large part of the grieving process, and its cold grip would arm our soldiers to the teeth with vengeance.

Elias had sent word to Jones a week after the bloodbath in the dining room for him to sail the ship to Adamas. He informed me that it would be docked and ready for our journey in Kistorenta, a port town south of Molina. It would take us half a day to travel there by horse and then with the river's down current, we would arrive in Southern Ralice in about a week. We had sent a letter To King Dalion to expect us, but it would probably only arrive a few days before we did.

I packed for our voyage late into the evening. My hands trembled with what I knew I had to do. Hoping I had the strength to explain myself well. I left in the morning, and I had only this evening to talk to my sisters and convince them of my plan. So, I mustered my courage and made my way to the room my twins shared. It was likely that they were already in bed or at least getting ready to go to sleep, but I had wanted to make sure that we wouldn't be interrupted.

I nodded to their guard and knocked on the door. It took a few minutes, but Prudence opened the door, curiously looking out. I held the copy of the decree to be spread through the country in one hand and I gave her a small wave with my other. She opened the door so I could come in and I stepped inside.

I realized immediately that they hadn't been sleeping. They had been in the middle of a game of kings and horses. A strategy game played with small wooden pieces to look like war. I had never quite taken to the game as Temperance had taught me to play and I never seemed able to best her.

"Mercy," Temperance said from where she sat. "Is everything okay?"

"Yes," I said smiling. "I just thought I would bring this for you to read over before it is dispersed."

I handed the parchment to her with the looping and neat handwriting that would be plastered all around our kingdom.

"I'm sure it's fine," Prudence said, and she read the letter over Temperance's shoulder.

It was much the same as we had discussed before, only the name of the Princess assuming the throne as a steward had been changed. I waited patiently for them to get there. Prudence audibly gasped and Temperance threw the parchment on the table, disturbing some of their playing pieces in the process. Her eyes slid to me, and I saw the anger there that I had thought might surface.

"You did this without asking," Temperance asked in an accusatory tone.

"Exactly as you volunteered me for the same position without asking," I said calmly, but it did nothing to soothe the outrage.

"You are the oldest, the choice was obvious, you cannot do away with tradition..."

"Tradition dictates I cannot take the throne at all, Temperance," I defied. "Father had no brothers and no sisters, therefore, we have no cousins to defer the throne to. We are making our own rules. We've broken so many laws why should this one be any different?"

"The people deserve..." She stood up, shouting at me now.

"The people deserve you Temperance," I said, not raising my voice to match hers but keeping it steady.

She just stared at me as if she didn't understand.

"I might be the oldest, but my place is not on that throne. The people deserve the one who will do the job the best. The one who will know their needs. A strong hand and an iron will. A clever mind and a steady temper." I stopped, holding my hands out. "Except for right now."

Prudence smiled at me with all the understanding in the world and looked to Temperance whose mouth hung open.

"You are the right choice Temperance. You know the most about our people, you are strength in human form. These past six months I can't count the number of times I have deferred to you for royal matters. You are the right choice," I reiterated.

"I would never think to usurp you of your place," she said, quiet tears forming in her eyes.

"I'm making the choice. For our family. For our people. You are not taking anything from me. I am simply placing the crown where it belongs, and it isn't on my head."

"What..." she stumbled out as her tears fell from her face. "What if I fail them?"

"You might fail every day, just as everyone before you has. Though, I know you have it within you to be a good ruler Temperance, and when Herold takes the throne, he will have you as an ally and advisor to guide him as he ages."

"What will you do?" Temperance asked, sitting back down in the chair with hunched posture and a wide-eyed expression.

"She'll be on the ocean," Prudence answered for me hugging her sister from behind.

The next morning, we were preparing the horses for our journey. I packed a bundle of clothes and little food. We would be to the harbor in six hours and Jones had been instructed to stock the ship for a weeklong journey.

I wore my training skirt and a simple blouse with the harness on my back that held my two blades. My hair was pulled back and plaited from my face as I looked back to find Temperance, Prudence, Charity, and Herold walking toward me. I had told myself I would not cry during my departure. After all, I would see my family again soon, but I still found a sorrow spring up in me that I couldn't lay to rest. The tears came when Herold and Charity latched onto my skirts and began to sob.

"Oh, come now, come now," I said through quick tears. "When I return I shall have so many new pirate adventures to share with you."

"Don't stay away too long Mercy," Charity insisted, her tears leaving tracks down her cheeks.

"I shall not, I'll be back before you know it. Perhaps I shall bring a treat for each of you then. Something wondrous and exciting."

"A dagger!" Herold exclaimed and I smiled after him.

"Certainly not," Prudence chided him as she embraced me in a hug. "Thank you," she said in my ear.

"For what?"

"For bringing us together, I hadn't thought we had it in us." She stepped away and Temperance rushed in for a hug in the most un-Temperance-like fashion.

"Be on your guard and do our kingdom proud. Our very own ambassador," she said.

"Shh," I said, shaking my head at her. "I haven't yet asked Elias if he will have me aboard. Pirates don't like working for kings."

"It's a good thing I am not a king then." She smiled and stepped back.

I climbed onto the horse and pet her, like Prudence taught me to.

"Listen Cherub, just take me six hours without bucking me off and you and I shall be fast friends," I said, patting her.

Elias joined us looking much less like a high court man and much more like a pirate than when he first arrived. He had his gold hoops back in his ears and his silver rings all slipped back onto his fingers. He had also shaved and looked every bit as dashing as the first time I saw him.

Atticus had nearly lost his eyeballs when he found out who Elias was and then had a particularly good laugh after that. Herold had been thrilled and asked Elias so many questions about the dirty misconduct of pirates, and I thought Temperance was going to keel over.

"I rather like you as a pirate," I said as he mounted his horse.

"Good because I was starting to get stuffy in those noble clothes," he said, smiling as his mare hooved the dirt in anticipation of our trip.

"Write as soon as you can," Prudence said, waving.

"I love you all." I smiled down at them as we kicked our horses into a trot. "Don't get into too much trouble while I'm away."

"I think it's you we have to worry about," Temperance called as they all waved us off and our horses left the gates of Molina Castle.

We were silent for the first few hours of the journey which I appreciated because my mind wound itself around ten thousand things. Had I decided on this path because it suited me best? Was the choice to have Temperance take the throne a selfish one and I had only been manipulating her to make it seem like it was unselfish reasoning? No. I reminded myself for the thousandth time. Temperance was right for it. She had proved herself and would serve our kingdom well.

Then my mind wandered to the conversation I would have to have with Elias. About being the ambassador for Adamas. While I knew it would involve traveling and sailing most of the year, I would have to be ported some of the time and I did not mean to bind him to the choice that I made.

"Your thoughts run deep, my Love." He spoke casually and my heart leapt at his endearment.

"Yes." I looked over at him as we rose side by side.

"Where do they wander?"

I was not ready to tell him or ask him what I needed to. So, I found something true to say instead.

"The ocean, can you hear it calling?"

"Almost always Mercy, almost always."

Chapter Seventeen

Georgette

"My father used to say something to my brother and me," I started as I paced in front of Jessamine who was kneeling before me having the good sense to look slightly afraid. "He used to say that a sailor doesn't seek to fight a shark."

Her defiance blazed in her eyes but there was a worry there too, as there well should be.

"Devika," I called, and my principal lady brought over a silver tray with an opened golden box on it.

Nestled in the box were chocolates coated in cocoa powder. I took the tray as Devika glared daggers at the Lady kneeling before me. Devika had asked if she might be able to strangle Jessamine to death and my two-day recovery was the only time I had ever seen her truly angry.

"Eat one." My demand echoed across the hallway walls.

Jessamine shook her head, a look of terror crossing her brow.

"Now." My voice thundered again, and Jessamine reached out a hand, picked one of the chocolates up putting it in her mouth and chewing so slowly it was painful to watch.

Brees stood behind her. He was the one who had brought her here after she and her ladies' maids had been held in the castle keep for three weeks. It had taken me as long to think of a suitable punishment after I recovered from being poisoned.

"The lesson my father was trying to teach us by warning us against starting a tussle with a shark is this; while the sailor might be smarter and more evolved, the shark has bigger teeth."

Jessamine swallowed and I watched as two tears spilled down her cheeks, tears I could not muster any compassion to feel for. Her hands were trembling, and she clutched them together. Large dark half-moons had formed under her eyes, and she was as unpolished as I imagined she had ever looked.

"Now Jessamine." I squatted in front of her. "You might be of higher birth than me, you might be more beautiful, and conniving than I am, but I have bigger teeth."

Her shoulders started to shake. The chocolate she had eaten was not poisoned but one's mind was as strong as any toxin one could concoct.

"My husband has delivered your life into my hands," I explained, and her eyes hardened as betrayal shot across her features. "He wanted to have you publicly executed but it's a little garish for my tastes."

Devika brought forward my jeweled dagger and held it out to me by its ornate sheath. Jessamine had started with straight posture and pride, but she had sat back now and looked at me in terror while I slid my dagger from its sheath. No one was ever ready to die. I reached out and grabbed a large chunk of her honey-colored hair and yanked her to me. She strained forward, tears coming faster and faster now. I saw a girl there. A girl who had been sent to wed a king and instead found herself at the end of a pirate's dagger.

I lifted my hand with the dagger back and she took a sharp intake of breath before closing her eyes tight. When my blade swung through the air it made contact with the strands of hair I had pulled tight, shearing them close to the scalp. I took up another section and cut that one as well. Jessamine kept her eyes closed the entire time as I lopped off her golden glory, watching it fall to the floor below. When I was done, I stepped back and she opened her eyes looking down at the hair she had lost.

It was no great loss as far as life went, but to a woman whose vanity meant everything to her, it was. She still trembled and she fell to her hands in front of me and a bit of pity started to bloom in my chest as her shoulders shook with sobs.

"You'll crawl back to where you came from," I said, turning away from her. "Instead of gaining a king, your father will have a daughter returned to him with her hands empty. You will never return to Southern Ralice for as long as you live. And as your hair grows out, and it will, you will be married off to a lesser man and live out your days knowing that you were bested by an uneducated filthy pirate woman."

I didn't look back at her as I left even as her cries got louder. I walked out the door of the throne room and closed the door, leaning back against them and letting out a long breath. I hadn't seen Cassius in three weeks. Since I had asked if he would collar me as his father did to his mother. Words that when I remembered them, tasted much more bitter than the poison had on my tongue. He was still in the castle walls, just keeping away from me. He didn't take any meals with me or check on my healing progress once since then. I didn't blame him, it had been the intention of the insult, so why did I feel so empty?

I vacillated between anger and melancholy. One second, I would be filled with rage at everything he had done to me. He had lied to me, letting me think he had a hand in killing Absalom, letting me think he stole me away as some sort of twisted punishment, he ordered me about as if he were to rule over me. Then suddenly the part of my brain that loved a good argument would fire back with: *would you have believed him if he told you?*

No.

Then my words, harsh and painful, would bounce around my head, *shall I wear the scar of your abuse around my neck?*

I thought of the tattoos on his knuckles. The matching one on Amara's arm and the necklace that Camber wore around her neck. They were his weakness and I had used them. In a moment where I had felt vulnerable, I had wanted him to feel vulnerable too. Though he had never raised a hand to me, nor did his character suggest him to be such a man. Even when I attacked him, he had only stopped me and shoved me to my backside. His family was everything to him and I saw the pain cross his face when their abuse was brought up. An abuse he hadn't been able to stop. A mother he loved that had suffered, and a wife that had used those wounds as a defense. Like the feral animal I was.

I bathed and shook my head of the concerns of the previous day. I was determined to go to Larkin again and start exporting our orchard saplings to the town by the end of the evening. I would not let my mixed feeling about Cassius cloud my mission.

"Devika," I called, staring into a drawer.

She had left me alone to dress. I didn't often wear clothing that required her assistance and she had stopped insisting on helping me. Though now as I stared into the drawer that normally held all the trousers I ordered, I found it to be empty. I pulled open another that held my plain cotton shirts and found that also had been cleared out. I stepped deeper into my wardrobe and found the four leather vests I had commissioned from the tailor had also been removed. The tips of my ears heated, and my hands clenched into fists at my side.

"Yes, my Queen," she answered from the doorway of the room that held the copious amounts of clothing and jewels.

"Where are my clothes?" I asked gesturing to the empty drawers.

Devika opened her mouth and then closed it. I raised an eyebrow at her and she took a deep breath. I knew it wasn't her doing but I also knew that she had known about it this morning and hadn't bothered informing me.

"They were cleared out," she said finally. "Can I help you into a stay and a dress or skirt?"

I glared at her and she took my wrath with grace.

"No," I said flatly.

There was a knock at the door. Devika left me to go answer it as I fumed in the closet. All my guilt over my words to Cassius vanished. He was not as guilty as I had thought of him, but I still hated him. It seemed we were each locked in this game of punishments. He had told me if I didn't stop visiting Larkin there would be consequences.

"It's Captain Brees," Devika called to me.

"I'm not training today," I yelled.

"The king has requested your presence," Brees said, and I could tell he was smiling. I sent him a glare that he would never see.

"Oh, has he?" Barely controlled rage accompanied the words.

"He's in a strategy meeting with his advisors, I'll escort you," he said, and I heard his footsteps retreat.

"Are you going to let me pick clothes for you?" Devika asked me from the doorway again.

I took a deep breath and shook my head. He wanted me to explode. He thrived off my outbursts. In the same way I looked for a reaction from him. I wouldn't give him the satisfaction of my anger. He hadn't talked to me for three weeks and then dared to call on me like a dog. Like a dog wearing high court clothing.

"Every action has consequences," I said to Devika instead and she frowned.

The only reason I was wearing undergarments is that Devika had begged me. I didn't want to humiliate her too extensively, so I wore a corset and bloomers. When I stomped out of the room, Brees' eyes had gone as wide as formal dinner plates. Though he only coughed to cover up a laugh and said nothing motioning down the hall. We passed a few people who did their best not to stare at my scantily clad form as my bare feet pounded against the tile. I was exposed to the entire castle, with my breasts barely contained and my hair wild and free.

When we reached the door of the room where I supposed the meeting was taking place, two guards stood outside and looked rather nervous as Brees and I stood before them. They all exchanged wordless conversations with Brees who nodded, and they stepped aside. I realized staring at the doors I was to enter, some of the nerve I had only moments ago was fading. My anger was red hot but often cooled quickly after I had already set to do something ridiculous. Though I realized there was no going back now so I mustered what rage was still left and threw both doors open at the same time.

Seven men were sitting at a table. Eight if you included my husband sitting at the head. My stomach dropped as he looked up. It wasn't my propriety. I hadn't the sense to care about modesty. It was his gaze that raked itself over my form slower than necessary as my skin prickled with a shiver. It was his white-hot anger that burned in his stare as his eyes met mine.

"Cassius," I said, dropping a perfect curtsey with invisible skirts. "You wished to see me?"

The room was silent. The other men sitting at the table averted their gazes from me. Though the only person I was looking at was Cassius and his eyes never left mine.

"Gentlemen, I need to speak to The Queen in private. Please excuse me for a moment," he said, voice-controlled and cold as the depths of the sea.

"Of course, King Dalion." Some of them answered as he got up from his chair and came around to me steady and threatening.

He reached out and grabbed me with no gentleness and picked me up, hoisting me over his shoulder. As he turned, I saluted the men left at the table and winked at Brees as we passed. His face was as stoic as a stone and he betrayed no humor. Cassius carried me through the palace with maids, servants, and guards looking on in shock. I waved at them all from my perch.

I was surprised at Cassius' strength. He was a head taller than me so it was nothing for him to pick me up, but he didn't grunt or show any signs of exertion. When we finally reached the doors of my room. He put me down and shoved me against them. There was nowhere for me to look, but up at his face.

He didn't say anything for a long time, only stared down at me his mouth pursed into a line. I looked back at him with an eyebrow raised waiting for the onslaught of angry words.

"You cannot parade around the castle in this. You're a queen. You're my queen. I know that means nothing to you, but you have to maintain the slightest bit of pride."

"You took my clothes," I retorted.

"I told you there would be consequences for defying my order," he growled, "And I left you plenty of clothes appropriate for your station."

"I never asked to be your queen. You saddled yourself with a pirate, don't be surprised when I act like one."

"You aren't acting like a pirate you are acting like a child." His head bent lower as he pressed closer to me so we were almost flush. "You are completely unruly and obstinate. I can get Camber to act more like a lady..."

He went on but his words blurred into more angry insults as I was focused on his mouth. It moved with words directed at me, but I only saw his scar that marred his otherwise perfect face. The cut that left it would have had to have been deep. I was so focused on it that I didn't register my hand that reached up under the cage of his arms. When it reached his face, I ran the pad of my thumb along the angry white line.

He abruptly stopped talking.

"How did you get this?" I asked him and the anger melted from his eyes replaced with bewilderment and something headier.

"My father," he answered uneasily. "A lesson in not questioning him."

"How old were you?" I asked as he breathed out against my fingers and my heart fluttered against my chest.

I felt another wash of guilt over my words the morning after I had been poisoned. His mother hadn't been the only one who suffered at his father's hand.

"Seven." His eyes were on mine and completely guarded as if he expected me to attack him with the information.

I winced at the words and looked away, unable to meet his eyes. I was imagining someone attacking a child and inflicting a cut deep enough to leave that kind of scar. With his midnight eyes on mine and his mouth so close that our breath mingled together, I felt the grief of it.

"I don't need your pity." He reached up to move my chin, so I was looking at him again.

"How about my anger?" I asked trying to ease the intimacy of the moment with a half-smile.

"I feel I've taken nothing but your anger for months." He smiled in a way I hadn't seen before, not fury or sarcasm or wicked temptation.

The air between us had shifted. The battle of wills subsided and took its anger and challenge with it. We were left standing there too closely, with his hand under my chin and my breath coming in short bursts of anticipation.

"How is it that you still smell of cinnamon and fresh ocean air though I have stolen you from your home?" he asked, leaning in and whispering the question against my ear like a secret.

I swallowed hard and closed my eyes. I was sure he would be able to feel the wild way my heartbeat answered him. With no clothing to contain the thud of it, I felt suddenly more exposed than before.

"Are you an ocean goddess after all? Have you saltwater flowing through your veins instead of blood like us mortals?" His mouth had brushed across my cheek and was now over mine, hesitating there, his words feeling like worship.

I was reminded of my promise to him. That I would rather die than offer him any romantic advancements. Him promising not to touch me unless I begged for it. If it were solely my heart and body in charge I would fall to my knees and beg. Though my mind was strong and willed me to stay on my feet.

"You'd have to cut me open to see," I whispered, opening my eyes and looking up into his.

"If you'd let me close enough Georgette, I might."

I shivered at my name on his lips. Unsure of what we were talking of anymore. Or rather, I was sure that we weren't at war at that moment, and I was in a state of disadvantage. My tongue was too eager to wield cutting words and my mouth unaccustomed to anything else. Though I knew I needn't speak, if I only set up on my toes and put my mouth on his.

Someone cleared their throat and Cassius stepped back from me, leaving a cold absence.

"My King, the advisors await your return," Brees said. I shot him a dark look and he grinned back wide.

"Your things will be returned to you," Cassius promised.

"Thank you."

He looked more affected by my thanks than our previous proximity. I opened the door to step inside my room, catching words between him and Brees.

"Right then seemed like the appropriate time to interrupt?" Cassius asked.

"I wasn't sure if you were about to bed each other or contemplating murder. I feared for your life!"

"I swear on Baya I am going to find another guard for myself. I have been itching for a public execution."

"Maybe I should have let you bed her; you might be less irritable. Since you haven't taken a lover since she arrived," Brees grumbled.

I went inside my room and closed the door leaning against it. I closed my eyes taking in the fact that I had almost just kissed Cassius Dalion. The most arrogant, pigheaded, entitled human I had ever encountered, had sent my heart tripping over itself. The thought of begging him for his lips to be on mine had seemed feasible. Not just his mouth either as my mind imagined a scene of him in my bed that sent new sensations of heat through me.

Damn the King of Southern Ralice.

Chapter Eighteen

Mercy

The ocean.

The ocean was a weighty thing. It lived and breathed just as any human had ever done. It called out to me and demanded my allegiance, and I was helpless to its lusty demands.

When my boots hit the deck of The Siren I almost began to weep. How a few boards of dark wood and clean sails could bring me to tears I didn't know, but I didn't feel silly. The wind whipped through the harbor at that moment. There was no light breeze or hair rustling whisper; it was violent. My auburn hair whipped in my face and Elias yelled, greeting Jones who walked over to us.

Harbor bells went off in the distance. Every ring was a call to sailors to stay inland, abandoning their ships for warm whiskey and bedmates. The crew of The Siren was still aboard their ship standing defiant in the face of the wind and the bells.

The ship itself was as immovable as a mountain with the sails snapping in anticipation.

"Mercy," Jones said, embracing me in a hug. "I am glad to see you well."

"It's nice to see you too," I said, embracing him back.

"Are we ready to sail?" Elias asked, the edge of excitement lined every word and I couldn't help but smile at him.

"Aye Captain. With the wind?" he asked.

"Yes." Elias did a sort of short four-step dance and twirled on the deck of his ship. "Let's take this old ship down the river boys!"

He shouted the words and the crew roared back with approval. He turned back to me, extended his arm out and I stepped forward to take his hand.

Once we had gotten on open water, the sails were taut with wind and the crew worked hard to get us out on the river. I watched them all more closely than I had before. Elias stood behind the wheel as I leaned against the half railing looking out at the organized chaos. It all moved how it was supposed to, like a dance that each man knew as well as he knew his own heartbeat. They sang a song together as the wind-tossed their words into the river below.

The Cras was a cruel mistress, and the troubled water threw waves against the ship's broadside. A light rain started coming down on us as the sailing started getting a little steadier. Jones was suddenly at my side with my hat that I had gotten back in Liven, and I secured it on my head pushing my hair back. He also brought me a green captain's coat I didn't recognize. It was a brocade floral with bronze buttons. I looked up with a question in my eyes.

"Captain Georgette's," he said.

I hesitated to put it on, turning to Elias who stared at the coat with unblinking eyes.

"I'm quite enjoying the rain, Jones, but thank you." I patted the top of the coat and Jones nodded stepping away.

"Jones," Elias called and Jones took his meaning, stepping behind the wheel with Jamie close behind him. The young surgeon hardly left the quartermaster's side and the man seemed to be treating him as a son.

Elias had taken the jacket and his fingers were wrapped around the fabric; his knuckles white. A silent battle waged within him, and his grey eyes looked less like beach water and more like storm clouds.

"Jones will man the wheel tonight, you must be tired," he said, his storm parting for a moment.

The darkness hinted at coming, as the sky turned purple. I took his hand and walked with him down the stairs. We stopped at Georgette's room first, and he opened the door to set her jacket back on her table. The room had not been touched and was in as disheveled a state as it seemed it always was. Elias lingered, looking over her dresser, unmade bed and all manner of baubles and bags scattered about.

"What is it?" I asked looking around for what seemed to be bothering him.

"Just a feeling." He still lingered, eyes roaming over everything before he shook his head. "Jones is back in his quarters where you slept before so I can have new sheets put on Georgette's bed or..."

"Or? You'll sling me in a hammock downstairs?" I laughed.

"You can sleep in my quarters," he edged out with uncertainty.

"Oh." I looked into his eyes.

"I wouldn't dream of asking anything from you. You've endured so much in the past couple of weeks. While I couldn't say my mind wouldn't wander with you in my bed all I'm suggesting is sleep, nothing more." His mouth quirked at my silence.

"No, I…" I didn't know what to say.

The cool temperature did nothing to help the warmth that radiated through me thinking of his arms around me while I slept. The comfort and content I might find there was a strong pull. Even if there was more than sleep, I couldn't deny that I wanted that, that I wanted that with him.

"But I can have Georgette's sheets changed and you are more than welcome to sleep here."

"I'll sleep with you," I decided, nodding, completely sure of my choice.

He looked pleased, which suited me just fine; we headed out of Georgette's quarters and walked across the deck to his room.

It was a tidy place, as orderly as Georgette's was disorder. His bed had been made and everything was in its place beside a stack of clothes that I recognized to be mine.

"You assumed I would say yes to sleeping in your quarters." I looked over at him.

"I assumed nothing of the sort," but he shot me a salty look.

"The audacity." I shook my head looking through the clothes to find a nightdress that Georgette had loaned me what seemed like a lifetime ago.

"Turn around then while I change, Captain, and show me you can be as gentlemanly as you pretended to be at court." I spun my finger in a circle, signaling him to turn around.

"There's a basin of fresh water over in the corner if you want to wash off." He pointed but did as I asked by spinning a chair to face the wall and sat down rather dramatically.

I stripped off my skirts and blouse and after checking at least a dozen times that his head was still turned I shed my undergarments. Half a day of riding horseback had left me feeling dusty and sweat clung to my skin. I dipped a thin cloth in the cool basin of water and began to wipe my skin off the best I could, re-dipping it as needed. There were two basins on the desk, I assumed one was for Elias. I was bent over wiping my feet when the sound of his voice startled me straight up.

"Georgette and I were looking for an uncharted island south of Southern Ralice. It is unmapped and in an area that isn't patrolled by the military."

"What?" I asked holding the cloth to my breasts realizing just how small it was.

"You asked why we made a deal with King Kosdel. We were hoping to use his peace treaty with Southern Ralice to make it to the island without being captured. Piracy is a punishable offense in Southern Ralice."

"Isn't it a punishable offense everywhere?" I asked, dipping the rag back into the water.

"Well yes, technically but only Southern Ralice and Coranthia take the laws on piracy very seriously. Even Adamas, with your hatred of us, your port masters are easily bribed to turn a blind eye to such misconduct."

"My brother would not like to have heard that." I made a few passes over my face and my hair.

"I suppose not."

I braided my hair back from my face without tying the ends and slipped the black nightdress over my head. One thing I remembered about Georgette is that she had exceptional taste, which had surprised me for a pirate. The satin of the nightgown was cool and soft like pulling on a cloud might feel.

"What's on this island?" I moved my clothes off his bed, placed them into a tidy pile on the floor, and slipped under the covers.

I was only half involved in the conversation as I was excessively aware that I was in his bed in a nightgown. Every move I made and every shift of his tone caused the middle of my palms to tingle. I pulled the covers up as I got the chills, but I did not think it was from the cold.

"Are you done?" he asked having heard me climb into the bed.

"Yes," I said too loudly and covered my mouth with my hand.

He chuckled and got up and began stripping off his clothes. He hadn't told me to look away and I found my eyes wandering to different points of the room only to come back to his now exposed chest. He was sun-kissed there like he was on his face and was strong from ship work. He wasn't brawny but I could see strength beneath his muscles as he pulled his shirt all the way off. He had a bouquet tattooed on one side of his ribs. Lavender blossoms, gladiolus, and foliage sprouted and bloomed across his side in a beautiful display of black ink.

"You do have a flower tattoo." I marveled thinking of how Absalom had teased him about it.

"Aye." His voice was deeper, I met his eyes, a heat flushing through me when I saw the obvious desire present there. "Perhaps you should turn around, I misjudged how affected I would be by you staring at me while I undressed."

"Is you being affected all that terrible?" I was feeling cheeky, the fluttering in my stomach giving me courage.

"It is if you want to sleep." He hadn't moved to remove any more clothing.

"What if I don't?" I swallowed hard. "Want to sleep?"

"Oceans deep." He breathed out turning around and bracing his hands on the desk.

I wasn't sure if he was upset, but a strange sense of insecurity fell over me. I had no experience in this sort of thing and I wondered if I was...propositioning him wrong? I felt exposed with my heart laid bare before him. I chewed at my bottom lip and stared down at the cover on the bed.

I heard him move toward me and he lifted my chin to meet his eyes. Though it wasn't one of his soulful looks, instead his mouth was swiftly on mine, capturing a surprised sigh in my throat. He kissed me well and thoroughly until the fluttering in my stomach turned into an ache.

"If that is what you want princess, I would gladly oblige you any time you like."

"I feel there is a condition coming," I said, gazing up at him as love drunk as I had ever been.

"You have just suffered several losses." Both his hands were on either side of my face. "When I love you that way, I want you to be comfortable and obscenely happy with nothing else between us."

I nodded and leaned into his hands closing my eyes. The reminder of everything he spoke of brought everything back up. I was overwhelmed with the emotion of loss and daunting tasks to come. I was to lead negotiations with King Dalion. I had never done anything so important, directing lives and convincing a monarch to support a woman-led country; In a country with monarchs known for pillaging what they want and leaving others to the wolves.

"Why don't you lie down my love," he said, pulling his hands from me and stepping to the basin, as he started washing his arms with water.

I laid down and casually glanced at him as he stripped his trousers off and looked away shyly as he stripped off his undergarments replacing them with new ones. After a time, he crawled over me, hovering over my frame for a moment and placing a kiss on my forehead. He lay next to me and pulled me to him tucking my body against his, his arm curling around my middle.

"Georgette and I paid for some information about a lost treasure on the island we sought... or seek, we will resume our search as soon as we can." He didn't sound sure, but I wasn't going to bring that up now.

"Treasure?" I chuckled. "Why am I not surprised?"

"What else do you think pirates fill their days with if not treasure hunting, princess?"

"Philandering, taking things that aren't theirs, and all other manner of debauchery," I stated as he squeezed me closer, shaking with silent laughter.

"Indeed."

"What kind of treasure is it?" I asked trying to fight the drowsiness that was overtaking me.

"A treasure of an incredibly famous pirate that has been lost for nearly one hundred years. Could be a tale and nothing more."

"Why chase after it if it might turn out to be fictional?" I brushed my fingers over his wrist in a circular pattern.

"It isn't about the treasure, it's about the hunt."

We sat in silence for a long time after that. After I imagined sailing along with him on the hunt for hidden pirate treasure. The wind in my hair and the spray of the ocean on my face. Then I remembered the other question I had asked him weeks ago.

"What of your parents?" I asked quietly as not to disturb him if he had fallen asleep. "What happened to Hazel and Nathaniel Baine?"

He stiffened slightly but relaxed after a moment.

"A story for another night," he murmured.

I accepted that and pushed myself closer to him and reveled in the feeling of him breathing slowly as he drifted to sleep beside me. I wished I could have fallen asleep as easily, but my mind turned with everything that had been and was to be.

It felt surreal that the life I had been destined for half a year ago was no longer the course I was on. I wouldn't be married to a king. I wouldn't have to suffer the stuffiness of court. No more tight corsets and itchy skirts while people gazed on me with disapproval. I would be able to live mostly on the ocean under the stars. I could be in the arms of the man I loved.

Loved. Of course, I loved him. My only fault was not saying it back to him the moment he said it to me. Tomorrow after I presented my plan to him, I would tell him. It had to be after as I did not want to use it to sway his decision.

I was more than a little nervous to ask Elias about my plan to be the ambassador for my country. I realized the thought of him rejecting the idea wounded me, even though I hadn't asked. It wasn't the being on land part of it I worried about, but the fact that he would no longer be able to be labeled a pirate. He would be a Captain still, but we would no longer steal and build a fortune as he had before. How could I ask that of him?

Furthermore, what if I wasn't any good at representing Adamas as its ambassador. It was daunting to meet King Dalion to align our countries in a war. Holt had trusted him, and while it didn't count for a lot I would start with a hesitant trust as well. He had also married Georgette instead of killing her as he could have. Who knew the reasons for that, but he couldn't be all bad at least?

"Go to sleep, Mercy," Elias' sleep-laced voice said, startling me a bit. "Let tomorrow worry about itself."

I realized my body had gone tight with worry and thought, so I relaxed into him again taking a deep breath and let it out slowly. He lifted his head and kissed my cheek before nestling back into me.

Chapter Nineteen

Georgette

"Again!" Brees said, running at me once more. I stood my ground, rooting my feet, centering myself as he taught me.

I dodged his attack and as he passed, used my hands and shoved my open palms into his side causing him to lose his balance. He recovered rather quickly as he faced me again.

"Good." He nodded and I preened under the praise. "You're quicker than you were."

He attacked again using the broad side of his forearm and I grabbed it pulling him toward me. I knew I was supposed to pull him down and get out of the way, but I lost my footing and pulled him on top of me. He was not a small man, and the wind was knocked out of me as I made a groaning sound underneath him.

"Don't pull an attacker on top of you," he grumbled but he looked a bit concerned as he got up and gave me a once over.

"I'm fine," I groaned again as I got up. "You are not the first man that has been on top of me."

"Goddesses above, woman," he said, looking up at the sky shaking his head.

"Brees," I said, and my tone made him look at me more seriously.

"What is happening at the northern border?"

I wasn't sure he would answer me. I might still be the untrustworthy invader in the castle. Though I had grown tired of being kept out of things. With Cassius gone so often, I knew that something was happening, and the way he often looked exhausted I knew it was something big.

I hadn't cared before. I hadn't given a cockroach's piss what he was struggling with, and I certainly hadn't cared about his country or his politics. Though now I felt about as useless a queen as there ever was. I was planting an orchard, training to defend myself, and looking for ways to irritate Cassius. Not to say that irritating Cassius wasn't fun, but I felt as if I was becoming the kind of courtier I hated. A queen that sat by while her country had severe problems she ignored.

"There have been skirmishes where King Kosdel is sending men to attack villages on our side of the borderline. Several villages have been burned and several soldier camps have been attacked."

"Why?"

"King Kosdel had been inching his way into our land for over forty years. King Dalion Senior staved him off, but when Cassius took the throne, he came at the border harder than he ever had."

"Absalom," I said, "My friend in Kosdel's guard who died on the ship."

Brees nodded and winced a bit at the memory.

"He said Cassius was pushing into Northern Ralice territory. Said that Kings in Southern Ralice were greedy war seekers."

Brees barked out laughter that surprised me and I jolted a bit.

"No offense to your friend, George, I'm sure he was just as lied to as you were. We are not the ones that have a history of pushing borders. Cassius has no interest in starting a war. He would be stupid to go looking for one when he's barely begun to rule. No, King Kosdel had been attacking our border. He knows he couldn't beat us in a full-out war, our army is stronger than his, despite him having more territory."

"Will there be a war?"

He hesitated to take a long breath before responding. "You should ask Cassius."

"He won't tell me."

"Ask nicely."

I grumbled, going to shed the light armor I had been wearing for our training session. The air was more than crisp now as autumn had overtaken the summer. When I awoke in the morning the air was chilled and the maids almost always had a fire burning.

"Will you marry Devika?" I asked, partly to gauge his reaction as I did not think he would answer me.

"You have some nerve." He shook his head but at any mention of my principal lady's name his pale features flushed, and light danced in his eyes.

"Thank you."

"It wasn't a..." He stopped seeing the grin that pulled over my face. "Are we going to the Larkin orchard today?"

"Not until you answer me."

"How is this any of your business?" he asked, and I couldn't help but smile at the familiarity that had bloomed between us.

"It's not any of my business," I agreed. "Though I wondered if Cassius would be interested in knowing..."

"You wouldn't…" he stopped mid-sentence looking horrified as if he wasn't sure if I would or not.

That is exactly where I liked to keep people.

Brees reminded me a lot of Absalom; so black and white. His duty came before everything, and he was so private about anything that didn't involve his service. It had taken me five months to even learn that he had family that lived in the city. A younger brother who was a year away from joining the guard and a mom and dad who owned a thriving precious metal trade.

"Devika is royalty."

"She's chosen something different for herself," I reminded him.

"The reality still stands. She was born above me, and she is in line for the throne. Hestiege acknowledges female rulers, and she is not so far from it. Especially because her uncle seems unable to sire an heir."

"Who is to say one person is born above another person," I said, casting a look away feeling suddenly self-conscious in a way I had never before. "I was born to a prostitute on a poor island, adopted by pirates, and yet here I am, Queen of the snake kingdom."

"I take your point," he agreed.

"Unless there is no love between you, which I would not judge you or her for." But as I looked up it was clear in his eyes that that was not the case.

My sensible guard loved the goddess dressed in white.

"So let her choose," I said, facing him fully in unrepentant meddling. "One more question if I may."

"I am not quite sure I can handle any more questions," he said, leaning on the training stick he had been using to beat the tar out of me.

"What was Cassius' father like?"

His eyes slid to mine and narrowed a bit. I had a feeling the question was wading into sensitive territory. After Cassius' confession about his scar across his mouth and the truth of the stories about his mother's scored neck, questions had filled my days.

"Also, another question I feel you need to ask Cassius."

He had gone from open to fully guarded. Even when I had asked about Devika his posture had been more open than it was now. Now it was protective. He and Cassius had been friends since childhood as the tale went. He was one of the few people that referred to Cassius by his first name and I recognized a sibling bond that had formed between them. I knew better than anyone the lengths one would go to protect their brother.

"He hurt them, more than physically." It wasn't a question. "His presence lingers in the hallways of this place; I feel him."

"King Aamon was..." he struggled for the words.

"Brees," I pleaded, and I wasn't sure if it was the begging in my tone, or the exasperation lingering in my eyes, but he softened a bit.

Something had shifted and I wanted to understand. To better know Amara and Camber and even Cassius.

"He was evil and his death didn't come soon enough," he exhaled. "Cassius lives in the shadow of a man who raised him to be just as wicked as he was. Every decision he makes he compares to the way his father ran his kingdom, with snakelike conniving and a blood-drenched sword."

"Why strive for something like that?"

"We all often struggle to break free of who we were raised to be. To become something that is our own is to escape from a certain prison. His prison is that his heart is not rotted as his father's was and to him, that feels like failing."

The answer touched too close to insecurities I held within myself. Of captaining a pirate ship at the training of my parents, while dreaming of a different life. Each of my daydreams felt like I was failing their vision for my destiny. Every fantasy spoke of my ingratitude for their tutelage. While my parents never abused me or shaped me to be a darkened ruler, I understood the pull to live up to the expectations that were set for you.

"Let's go, Brees," I said with none of my former humor or wit dancing on my tongue.

I paced in my room that evening. My nerves were flayed, open, and tender. I had sent Devika off for the night and I stalked in front of the fireplace with no peace. The sheer layers of the gauzy green nightgown breezed across my ankles.

I had gone to stare at the portrait that had been painted of Aamon Dalion that hung in the castle gallery. He looked a lot like Cassius, with harsh briery features, and eyes as depthless as the ocean. Though Cassius had gotten his mother's freckles which softened his sharp edges a bit. The man in the painting was cold and distant, even for a painting. His eyes stared back into mine daring me to make a mistake in his presence, much like I imagined he had looked at the artist of this portrait. He was handsome and the painting had been done when he was Cassius' age. I turned to find Cassius' portrayal, and while the two men looked similar, there was humanity behind the eyes of the depiction of my husband. A hesitancy as well, like he was unsure about something important. Hesitant humanity was better than assured malice.

I was irritated and that irritation bloomed into anger, as my irritation often did. So, I was pacing my room, restless, in my satin nightgown. My locks of hair were still damp from my bath as it swished against my shoulders. Anger mounting, I grabbed my jeweled dagger off a table in my room and went to the door at my wall.

It could have very well been locked. Cassius could have not been on the other side. Perhaps he was so disgusted with me that he opted to sleep somewhere else. He hadn't seemed disgusted when we had almost kissed, however. Perhaps his feelings for me were as jumbled as my own.

When I turned the knob of the door and pushed it in, the hinges gave way silently. My husband was in fact in the room, sitting on the bed. He seemed to have been in the middle of rubbing his hands over his face.

His shirt was untucked and loose exposing his throat and the head of his snake tattoo I had seen most of. His head shot up and his eyes met mine at first with panic but once he saw me, he let out a breath and just leveled me with an unimpressed stare. I wasn't sure what my plan was. I was standing in the doorway with my dagger out, plain as day, in a nightgown with my husband staring at me like he didn't have the time nor the energy to deal with me.

"The door was not locked," I accused as his eyes shifted to the door between our rooms.

"The maids must have forgotten to lock it," he said, voice tight.

"Hm." I moved toward him, and his eyes followed me as I approached, keeping a wary eye on my dagger.

Once I approached the bed, he leaned back and looked concerned as I pressed forward climbing on top of him straddling him with my legs on either side of him. I forced him to lay all the way down as I pressed the knife to his throat. I searched his eyes, but they held no fear, only curiosity and something darker and more suggestive that sent a spike of heat through the core of me.

Perhaps this was your plan all along. Part of my mind prompted as I shook the thought aside.

"Have you come to kill me?" he questioned as a signature grin slipped over his face.

"Perhaps I have."

"Very well, do your worst my queen." He completely surrendered to me, using the same words he had spoken to me on our wedding day.

"I'm sorry for what I said about your mother." I broke the silence that followed with my careless apology.

"You brought a dagger to issue an apology? Is this a pirate custom?"

In case I felt the urge to kiss you again. My brain supplied but I kept that to myself.

"Well, you are forgiven and you may now remove your blade from my throat. Unless..." he said as his hands found their way to my thighs and he worked them up to my hips. "The apology isn't the only reason you've come."

The movement threw off my balance and I felt myself pitching forward which caused me to panic. I pulled the blade away and sat up straighter, but his hands didn't move, only gripped me tighter. My heartbeat quickened as I tried to keep my breathing even. This is exactly why I had brought a dagger. My body betrayed me.

"Aren't you tired of pretending you don't want me?" he asked, sliding his hands down and then back up feeling the curve of my waist. "Six months of abstinence for a pirate of the world seems like it might darken your disposition."

"I hate you," I swore but it was too high and too quiet like I was telling myself and not him.

"So, hate me." His hands slid up to my ribs, as he tugged me forward to lean over him again.

My hands lowered to be braced on either side of his head with one still clutching the blade that was faced away from him now, sinking into the covers of his bed. Heat pooled in my abdomen as one of his hands abandoned my side to brush a piece of hair behind my ear. His thumb came back to graze the line of my jaw.

"Hate me, while I lie you back in my bed. I'll show you all the ways I've dreamt about making your pulse quicken and your eyes flutter closed, with my name on your tongue." His thumb was on my mouth, my lips parting slightly for him.

I was aware I wasn't breathing. I was aware of the way my insides reveled in his words. Every nerve I had begged me to lean into his hand and let him show me if he could do what he promised. His hand worked its way to the back of my neck and his fingers wove themselves into my hair as he gently ran them through my wavy tresses.

I fell forward on my forearms with my face over his, our noses almost touching and our breath mingling together. Both of us were breathing quickly and I took small comfort in knowing he was as affected as I. His one hand kept working through my hair while the other brushed casually up and down my side.

"Cassius?" I whispered looking down into his dark eyes.

"Hm?" His tone was casual, but his eyes were dark and sharp on mine.

"Why didn't you tell me that you were helping find Mercy for her brother and that the man that killed Absalom worked for him? Why not tell me that you made an agreement with King Landlight to kill me and Elias, but married me instead and accepted my word that Elias was dead? Though I suspect you knew it was a lie."

He had frozen and had pulled his hand out of my hair and away from my side leaving me a little too cold.

"I think you should go." His eyes had gone from heady and wicked to cold and distant. He retreated into himself as I had seen him do before. I had gotten too close to something he guarded.

I tilted my head a bit to study him, and he frowned under my scrutiny.

"Eager to bed me, but only if I hate you? Or at least don't seek to understand what secrets you keep?" I asked sitting up, but I was still atop him. While I had no doubt, he could remove me if he wished, he just stared up at me.

"A familiar narrative to you?" he implicated, throwing up a defense with the words.

He was right. It was just sex if you didn't like or didn't know the person you were pleasuring. So, while you got whatever physical release you were looking for, you didn't have to be vulnerable. So yes, I knew it well.

"What are we doomed to then, husband?" I asked, head still tilted to one side and my hair had fallen in my face.

He took a few shaky breaths and reached up to tuck my hair back behind my ear.

"Goodnight, Georgette," he said, letting his hand fall, there was a finality to the gesture.

I climbed down off him with the heat receding from me and the blush seeping off my skin. The regret set in as Cassius did not move from where he was lying.

I had used the word *we* in relation to us. It was the first time I had ever thought of him and me as *us,* and not separate hurricanes battling on the same beach. The word itself proposed more questions that I was not ready to answer. After asking Brees about the war to the north, it had started gnawing at me that I was starting to picture myself as a permanent facet of this castle. I had slowly slipped from thinking of this as an unfortunate temporary problem and... *and what?* I didn't know.

I also thought of Absalom as I moved toward the door. His kind eyes and his hand in mine. Our matching scars and the love between us that had been doomed to fail. I hadn't felt the least bit of guilt or hint of betrayal when I had been on top of another man, a breath away from letting him make good on lascivious promises. Now I wondered if I should have. Though Absalom was gone, did it speak to darkness in my character that my heart seemed to have softened slightly to my husband? I didn't know.

What do you know?

I locked the door on Cassius' side and shut it without saying another word.

Chapter Twenty

Mercy

It was six days of sailing during the day and sleeping in Elias' arms at night. During the days I learned more and more about sailing. I read in the ship's small library, and we took every meal with the crew, as they all told us what they had done the sixth months that the ship had been ported in Hestiege. Each day I woke up earlier, excited to be a part of the ship's morning routine. Everyone welcomed me and were all patient as they taught me how to do chores and routine maintenance.

Every night Elias' and my kisses became fevered as our clothes became much too tight, feeling like a thick barrier between us. Then Elias would slow down and tell me we should rest. I was becoming frustrated with him the last night we sailed, and he just smiled as I huffed my frustration. He enveloped me in warmth and comfort.

"Elias," I demanded as his breathing slowed.

"Yes?"

"Why don't you want to be with me?" I asked turning over in his arms meeting his open eyes with my searching ones.

"All my life being with women hasn't meant anything," he said honestly. "To be a pirate means to never stay in one place for too long, and so it never made sense to pursue anything but enjoyable casual relationships."

"Oh," I said, feeling my face had colored with a blush and I was glad it was dark.

"You are not casual, and I am unused to worshipping a woman who also holds my heart. It's a new sensation for me. I would beg you to be patient with me as I try my best to honor you as you should be honored."

Whatever I had expected him to say it was not that.

"I thought it was me."

"You should know by the reaction of my body against yours that it has nothing to do with you at all. Just my own mind that is causing me to hesitate."

"Well done princess," he said brightly as we pulled into the harbor and he gave the order for the anchors to be lowered.

"Keep the ship docked here. I don't anticipate it being more than a month until our return but if it is longer, I shall send word," Elias said and Jones nodded.

"You keep him in line boy." Elias winked at Jamie, and Jamie grinned back as Jones shook his head goodhumoredly.

I misjudged what a full day of horseback riding would look like. I was sore from the tips of my toes to the back of my shoulder blades, as we took our first roads through Southern Ralice Territory. They were rough and unforgiving. We passed through several towns and ended up staying at a tavern in a town about an hour outside of Hallow for the night. I was too exhausted to even clean up and fell asleep on top of the bed in my clothes.

Chapter Twenty-One

Georgette

"What's this?" I asked coming out of my bathroom, as Devika zipped around the room cleaning up what I had dropped on the floor.

This was not her job; she just couldn't stand my untidiness.

"The women from Larkin made it for you," Devika said, stopping next to me for a moment, as I admired the overdress that was laid out on my bed.

It was rust-colored and tiny trees had been embroidered all over it with golden thread. The smallest sparkling crystals were woven in as the leaves. I couldn't imagine the work it had taken to make.

"You needn't wear it if you don't want," Devika said. "I can get you your trousers and coat."

"Wouldn't that be rude?" I quirked an eyebrow at her.

"You're the queen, you may do as you please."

"I'll wear it," I decided. "And something whimsical in my hair."

Devika took whimsical to mean a ruby and gold leaf circlet. She plaited my hair and secured the delicate crown on me as she stained my cheeks and lips. Over my undergarments, I wore a stay and cream-colored dress that fell off my shoulders. The overdress tied on either of my shoulders and laced in the back. I slipped on boots under the dress and Devika looked too pleased with my appearance.

"Will you join us?" I asked as we walked to my door where I knew Brees would be waiting.

"I think I will if you'll have me."

"I think Camber and Amara would love that."

Today was the day that we celebrated the planting of the final sapling in Larkin. Just under four hundred saplings had been transplanted into the ten acres that used to be home to the most prosperous trees in one hundred miles. The high priest had been out in the dead of night to bless the fields. That is what I had been told at least, because in Southern Ralice, no one was supposed to look upon the abhorrent man.

Kian had also told me that the burned earth would nourish the future trees quite well. It had been my pleasure to watch the last weeks as the town of Larkin had gotten some of its colors back. All the people had come out to plant the saplings, and they banded together like a family. Even Dola seemed less spiteful than she had been a few weeks ago, like she could finally see the horizon of a very dark day. I had gotten to know all her children quite well and felt a responsibility for the town that had endured more than its share of bad luck.

Lady Amara and Camber would join us, and I couldn't help the jittery nerves I got when I thought about her reuniting with Kian for the first time. While I was no grand romantic like my brother, I couldn't help but feel like it may be a fresh start for the woman I had come to admire.

I had also invited Cassius but he had just stared daggers at me across the dinner table. He hadn't made any more attempts to punish me for my disobedience. The last weeks hadn't been so hostile between the two of us. There was a slight tension about unspoken things, and I had so many questions I wanted to ask, but his demeanor always dissuaded me from the quest for truth. I found myself concerned with his approval and countenance. This irked me more than I cared to admit.

"You look lovely," Brees said, nodding his approval as I opened the door.

"Because I look like a proper lady?"

"I don't know that I would say proper," he teased, and I shot him a look as he chuckled in good humor. "Lady Amara and Lady Camber await you in a carriage at the front entrance." He doubled over in a half bow, which was also a mocking gesture.

I shook my head at him but got a glimmer of satisfaction from Devika scowling at him for his behavior, yet again. We made our way through the halls, and I caught myself looking for Cassius around every corner. Though I knew more than likely he would be off attending to something much more important than the planting of some trees.

Chapter Twenty-Two

Mercy

The next morning Elias was patient with me as I was slow to get up and moving. We ate a quick breakfast which I scarfed down like it was the first meal I had eaten in weeks. When we finally got back to the horses we had bought in Zanfil, I groaned as I climbed aboard my mare whose coat was the deepest black I had ever seen. Elias chuckled at me but said no more as we continued the last bit of our journey.

We came upon Hallow and I stared in amazement as the city rose to meet us. I had thought Molina was an opulent city. The pink stone wall surrounding this place was topped with pure bronze spires, which promised an exceptionally beautiful end to whoever tried to climb them.

Once inside the city, I marveled at the architecture of the buildings and the beauty of the perfectly placed stones underneath. The tales went that when the first king of Southern

Ralice built his home, he built it to be the envy of every other kingdom. I would say at least part of the tales were true. We reached the market on horseback and wound our way through people selling silks and crystals and all manner of food.

"Isn't it incredible?" Elias called back to me, and I remembered that he had been here to see Georgette before he came to Adamas.

"It is indeed," I marveled at the bounty of wares and open shop doors before me.

We made our way up one hill to the main gate of the city that wound up a hillside. The castle itself was protected by a wall as well, and even far away I could see how well guarded it was. I wondered if King Dalion was always expecting an attack.

There must have been three dozen guards at the front gate when we rose and stopped in front of the gate which was barred to keep everyone out.

"What business have you at Hallow Manor?" a guard asked, his voice husky and mildly threatening.

"I am Lord Tristen Kaloqey and this is Princess Mercy Landlight of Adamas. We are here as Ambassadors of Adamas, and King Dalion is expecting us," Elias said, his words weighted.

The man who spoke straightened up and bowed to us both as if suddenly embarrassed that he had questioned us at all. The guard started to move aside, and the gate opened as we were allowed access.

"Princess, forgive my rude questioning. The king and queen are expecting you."

"Thank you, sir." I nodded as I passed, and another man met us on the inside of the gate who was also on horseback.

He motioned that he would lead us, and Elias nodded as we followed. I was too busy taking in the new area, and what a great sight it was. Hallow Manor was indeed a splendid thing, with spires and windows glittering the sun's pure light. Ponds, hedges, gardens, and aged trees rose above us as if to speak of the owner's wealth. I caught Elias looking into a few gardens himself, though I knew he had been there before as well.

We stopped in front of the castle with its grand stone staircase leading up to a massive, rounded door, gilded in the same copper of the spires atop the wall. Large sections of plush grass sat either side of the stairs, and an explosion of ground ivy covered every other area with deep blue blooms that reminded me of the Southern Ralician flag.

"The King has prepared rooms for each of you, and he and the queen shall return to welcome you shortly." He dismounted and we followed suit. He paused for us at the base of the stairs as we all went up together.

Ten guards milled around the front entrance of the palace and opened the door so we could enter. Another guard was waiting for us at attention in the entryway. I ignored him for a moment forgetting my manners, to walk into the impressive entryway beyond. A fountain bubbled and was surrounded by a domed ceiling covered in busy paintings.

"It makes sense that you are still alive. She barks like a city dog, but knowing her now, I didn't think she would have had it in her to kill her own brother," the guard spoke.

My attention snapped to him, and Elias turned to face him as well. He was broad-shouldered and handsome. With long dark hair that was pulled away from his face. Elias looked defensive, but it made sense that he was recognized, as there was no doubt a warrant out for his arrest in Southern Ralice.

"I'm sorry?" Elias spoke.

"You needn't." The man waved him off casually. "I'm Queen Georgette's guard, my name is Brees. Without your beard, you might as well be female and male copies of each other."

"I pity any man tasked with guarding my sister." Elias smiled and I was surprised by his sudden ease.

"As you should, she's given me more than my share of trouble."

"You don't sound as if you loathe her for it, though." Elias was curious and Brees looked between each of us.

"I think that's a gift of hers, is it not?"

"Indeed." Elias smirked and stepped forward to extend his hand to the man. "Elias Baine."

"Brees Fogg," Brees said, shaking his hand before pulling back and dropping a low bow to me. "Princess Mercy, it is a pleasure to host you at Hallow Manor."

"The pleasure is mine, Brees," I said, dropping a curtsey.

"King and Queen Dalion are in the town outside the city right now, overseeing a political matter, but they will be back before the end of the day and have requested that you join them for their evening meal. I shall escort you to the rooms that have been prepared for you if you like, so you can rest and refresh. I can also give you a tour after as well."

We started following him up one of the black marble staircases, all the while taking in the manor around us. There was no denying the fact that it was lovely, but I felt suffocated by it, just like I did at home. It was grand and expensive, but I felt out of place amongst the ornate details. When we reached a set of doors Brees motioned for me to enter.

"These are your rooms and Captain Elias yours are just there." He pointed to a set of doors on another side of the hallway.

"When dinner is ready, I shall come to escort you to the dining room. Until then, warm baths will be brought for each of you. Your horses will be housed in our stables and shall receive the best of care."

"Thank you, Brees," Elias said, and Brees nodded and with an unreadable smile on his face, he turned and left us alone.

"Can I see your room?" Elias asked as I opened my door to peek inside.

"Why?"

"In case I like it better than mine, I'll make you switch with me."

"Such chivalry."

"I'm a pirate, not a prince," he reminded me as I opened the door wide enough for him to step inside.

"You have more chivalry than most princes, Elias." He winked at me as he clasped his hands behind his back taking in the bedroom beyond.

I told myself it was time to ask. I couldn't put it off anymore.

"Elias?"

"Hm?" he questioned, walking to the bathroom and looking inside.

"I..." I stumbled, which caused him to look back at me curiously, but he waited for me to begin. "I talked with Temperance and Prudence the evening before we left."

"Okay." He took a seat in a pink velvet chair.

"I named Temperance as steward over Adamas instead of myself." My gaze flickered to his face, and he looked surprised for a moment before nodding. "I..." I made an irritated noise in the back of my throat as I tried to articulate my thoughts properly.

"Come here," he said, motioning for me to come closer.

I walked over to him, feeling stupid but as I ended up in front of him, he pulled me down so I was sitting in his lap and he brushed a soft kiss against my lips.

"What is it?" he asked, twining the fingers of his hand into mine.

"I want to marry you," I announced and then covered my mouth with my free hand. "I meant to say that at the end."

The smile that filled his face caused warmth to bloom in my chest making me feel light and glowy. He pulled my head down to kiss me. His mouth worked over mine slow as his smile kept returning between soft kisses.

"You have to stop before I forget what I'm trying to say," I said, though my eyes were closed, and I found my hands on his shirt holding him to me.

He pulled back, but only slightly.

"I told my sisters I would take the mantle of Adamasian ambassador. Which consists of traveling to other kingdoms and negotiating trade deals, peace treaties, and things like that."

"Okay," he said, and his face seemed a little hesitant which doused my glowing joy.

"That is to say, you are under no obligation to agree, but I'd hoped..." I struggled again and he squeezed my hand encouragingly. "You might agree to be the captain of the crew I sailed with during my travels, and Georgette too, of course."

"I see."

"If you need time to think it over, I understand and of course you'll have to discuss it with the other captain of your ship."

"Mercy?" he asked, interrupting my thought as my eyes met his.

"Yes?"

"Do you love me?" he asked, and I couldn't have broken our eye contact if I'd wished to.

"Yes," I whispered, letting the answer out for the first time.

"I'll talk to Georgette," he said, reaching up to pull my face to his again. "But I would follow you around Marecult for the rest of my life, princess. You needn't be nervous to ask if I'll sail with you, there would be nothing I would rather do."

"I don't want you to lose something you hold dear. It would be different than pirating," I admitted, not denying the fact I was nervous.

"Love is sometimes synonymous with loss. Though what you gain is almost always better than what you sacrifice."

"I love you, Elias Baine," I said at normal volume, letting the weight of my declaration sit between us.

"And I've been waiting for you, Mercy, ever since my father told me about a love that could slay dragons."

I leaned forward and rested my forehead against his wondering if I had ever imagined that I could be as happy as I was at that moment.

Chapter Twenty-Three

Georgette

The rumble of hoofbeats came up to us as I surveyed the beauty of the infant orchard that would grow into a mighty thing. I turned with my warm mug of cider and nearly spit it out because of who I saw approaching us. The horse stopped and I looked up into the eyes of my husband. More surprising than that, was that instead of his traditional mostly black ensemble, he wore a vest that was embroidered the same as my own. A white shirt underneath and a bit of his throat exposed. I watched as he dismounted, drinking leisurely all the while, not ashamed for anyone to see that I was watching him. He made his way to me, his eyes never left mine, until he came to stand next to me, and then his eyes shifted to look out over the orchard and to the side where the celebration was taking place.

"Do you know what these people are calling you?" he asked after a silence so unbearable I almost broke it. I answered with a slight shake of my head and a loud slurp of my cider. "Queen Georgette, Fil's chosen."

"The peace goddess?" I screwed my face up at the implication and a laugh escaped Cassius' lips. It was such an infrequent sound I looked over to him in surprise.

"My sentiments exactly," he said after his laughter gave out. "Though it seems, they are loyal to you as I hear it. This town has had no loyalty to the crown for nearly twenty-five years."

"Perhaps if they had been shown a sliver of kindness in those years it could have been different," I accused. "Why are you telling me this?"

"Because I wonder if you are intentionally trying to turn my subjects into queenship loyalists, or if it's merely a side effect of your wanting to spite me."

"I don't know that I could separate motives at this point." I grinned up at him.

"I don't know if I find that frustrating, or charming."

"Let me know when you decide."

"There's a picture of my father in the hall of portraits, where he has his hunting dog next to him," he started, and I was unsure of the reason for the change in direction, but it was one of the first civil conversations we had had that hadn't turned into threats or sexual promises. So, I went along with it.

"I've seen it," I said, looking back out over the field. "The dog has a bloody bird in its mouth. You look a lot like him. Your father, not the dead bird."

"Yes, thank you for the distinction." He smiled again, and I wondered then what could have possibly put him in such a good mood. "He used to make me look at that picture frequently and say 'Cassius you will either be the dog or the bird in life. You can shed blood to keep the peace, or someone will have you in their mouth before long'."

"If you were to be the dog, who was the hunter?" I asked.

"I suppose he was."

"Well, your father sounds like one of the most abhorrent men I've heard of." I slipped my hand into his but didn't meet his eyes as he looked down to our entwined fingers, but he didn't separate them. "Also, he's dead. So, you needn't be his hunting dog anymore, and you needn't be the kind of king he raised you to be either."

"And what kind of king would you have me be, my Queen?"

"The good kind?" I shrugged a shoulder because even to my ears it sounded too simple a solution, but he didn't mock me for it.

"My King," Kian's voice came to us, and I went rigid pulling my hand away from his and tucking it behind my back. He smirked at the reflex and turned to face the man who had fallen in love with his mother all those years ago.

"Sir Nikkita," he said as proper and haughty as ever, and I wanted to elbow him in the gut.

Kian bowed low to Cassius before meeting his gaze unashamed. "We are truly blessed by the goddesses that you have come to our small celebration."

"You've suffered much," Cassius acknowledged. "I hope this brings a bit of prosperity to your town."

"Thank you, my King. We shall not forget your kindness."

"The kindness was my wife's, if it is praise you wish to spread, spread it on her behalf. I'm learning not to stand in her way when she's set on something."

"You've found an excellent queen to rule at your side," Kian said, bowing again to me and I rolled my eyes.

"I think so too," Cassius agreed, and I looked over at him incredulously as Kian left.

"Do you want some cider?" I asked struggling with the words in my throat.

"Perhaps one cup, but I've really come to fetch you."

"Why didn't you send Brees?"

"I had to leave someone behind to receive our guests."

"I didn't know we were expecting company." I didn't know much of anything.

"Yes, I only got their letter of intent to visit a few days ago. I do believe you know them both."

"I know them both?" I turned to face him fully hearing the play of dark humor in his voice.

"Yes, Lord Tristan and Princess Mercy. The man you gave a title to, and the princess you kidnapped." He searched my eyes for the truth, waiting for me to share some honest bit of myself.

He had ambushed me with this on purpose because he knew I could not control my initial reaction and had hoped to glean something from my face. Though he wanted me to offer him a bit of truth. How could I offer him the truth when he had been deceptive and kept this from me? How could I be honest with him if he refused to extend the same courtesy? He pulled away any time I tried to pry open the lid off his truth.

"Let us forego the cider and head back then," I said, my heart hammering in anticipation of seeing my brother.

He nodded as if he had anticipated this, and I scowled at him. I made a point of saying goodbye to Amara and Camber who assured me they would be fine with the Castle guards.

Camber was running through the trees, with streamers made of paper ribbons and squealing as Dola's children chased her around. Amara was speaking with Kian on the edge of a table laden with sweets and cider. Their conversation was hesitant, but it made me smile all the same. We accepted thanks from many townspeople, even though Cassius looked as uncomfortable as I had ever seen him.

I glared at the single horse that Cassius mounted and held his hand out to me to help get onto.

"Did you not think to bring me my own horse?" I complained, situating myself behind him, trying my best not to touch him more than necessary.

"I think you are under the impression that thoughts of you, and your welfare, run unbridled through my mind all day Georgette, and I can assure you they do not."

I smiled, throwing my previous caution away. I leaned into him and wrapped my arms around him, too low for anyone's comfort. He turned his head as much as he could to give me a displeased look and I smiled up into his dark eyes.

"Is that the truth, Cassius the liar?"

"Baya, consume me," he breathed out before spurring the horse into an uncomfortable run and the wind stole my laughter from me.

I barely waited for the horse to come to a full stop before I dismounted as unladylike as possible falling to the ground in the process. I didn't care or even look back to see Cassius' reaction, as I grabbed my skirts and bolted up the main marble stairs and through the front doors where I collided with Brees.

"My Queen," he shouted, holding my shoulders to steady himself.

"Where are they?" I asked, out of breath as he let me go, a smile crept over his face.

"Your brother and Mercy are touring the throne room," he said, and I took half a second to narrow my eyes at him but didn't have the time to care.

I flew down the halls of what had been my home for the last half a year, panting as I came to the tall throne room doors. I straightened up and smoothed my skirts out. I was sure my gold and ruby circlet had been displaced and so I didn't even attempt to fix it. I opened the door and walked through, my heart in my throat and tears on the edge of my eyes.

I had meant to walk calmly toward them, I truly had, but when my brother turned as the door shut, he smiled at me. I broke out into a run again. His smile never faltered as he caught me in a tight hug.

"Queen Dalion," he said through laughter.

I pulled back and punched him hard in the shoulder before turning to Mercy. She smiled at me and curtseyed in such an awkward display of greeting. I shook my head at her as I embraced her into a hug and she let out a surprised sound. She stood stiff for a moment before relaxing into it and wrapping her arms around me.

"It's nice to see you alive and thriving." She pulled away from me giving me a shy smile.

"It's nice to see you too, Mercy." I slung my arm over my brother's shoulder. "Did our dear Lord Tristan find his way to you without any trouble?"

"Indeed," the princess answered.

The door opened and my arm slipped from my brother's shoulder as Cassius walked down the middle of the marble aisle toward us. Elias had gone rigid and stiff as all the relaxed happiness seeped from him. Mercy also seemed to stand straighter, and I caught the hint of fear in her eyes as Cassius approached us as silent as ever. While his nails were painted black and his hair was pulled back, the rust-colored vest did something I thought to soften his threatening presence. It was his face that was the real trouble, his lips always rested into a frown, and his dark eyes, if not smiling seemed wicked.

Mercy bowed to him as he stopped before us but Elias did not. They both addressed him by his full title, but Cassius wasn't looking at them. His eyes held mine; letting me know it was my move in our game of strategy. I looked over my shoulder at my brother, then at Mercy, and back to Cassius.

Chances were that he already knew who Elias was and was now waiting for me to lie to him again. I had half a mind to, after he had tried to stir up a response from me at Larkin by surprising their arrival on me. Though if each of us was always looking for a way to outdo one another in spite, there would never be any trust between us. It was then I realized the deep aching want I had for him to trust me.

Despite the darkness in him, and regardless of the hatred that I had harbored for him for so many months, I found that it had melted away. It hadn't been all at once but slowly, over time, the ice of my will had melted one drip at a time. So now I stared at him challenging me to lie to him, and I wanted him to know the truth.

"Elias," I said, using his real name, and my brother was at my side before his name had left my lips. "This is my husband Cassius. Cassius, this is my brother Captain Elias Baine of The Siren."

Elias's eyes slid to mine, and I gave him a small nod which he reciprocated and stepped forward extending a hand for

Cassius to shake. Cassius looked shocked as his brow furrowed and he blinked a few times too many. He had not expected me to tell the truth. He turned finally and put his hand into my brother's.

"Captain Baine." He nodded. "It's a pleasure to meet you."

"I think that's the first time a king has said that to me." Elias grinned openly. "I am torn now though, between thanking you for taking care of George, and slitting your throat for kidnapping her."

"Infuriating, isn't it?" I commiserated.

"Quite," Elias said. He was still looking at Cassius and the two seemed to be caught in their own wordless conversation. I didn't want anything to do with it.

"And you as well, Princess Mercy." Cassius bowed to her and she nodded. "Hallow Manor welcomes you with anything you need."

"It's rather impressive," she said, gesturing vaguely at the walls that surrounded us.

"Yes well, when people have something to prove they often overcompensate." He looked around the room as if he hadn't seen it before. "What do we owe the pleasure of your company?"

"I've come to negotiate the terms of war with you King Dalion, on behalf of my country."

"I'm surprised your brother sent you, after your kidnapping, I thought he would keep you under lock and key until you died," Cassius questioned.

"My brother was murdered," Mercy said distantly and I turned to look at her shocked.

"What?" Cassius asked, tone matching my feelings. "Murdered? Holt?"

"Yes," Mercy said, her words brave and resolute. "Our Archbishop was in league with King Kosdel or his Archbishop. He murdered all my brothers save the youngest, Herold."

"Spineless maggot," Cassius cursed out, and if not for the tone of the conversation I would have smiled at the raw honesty of the reaction. "I am sorry for your loss, Princess."

"Thank you, I wish to discuss this further with you, is there somewhere we might do that?"

"Yes, let us discuss over dinner, it seems much has changed but the support that I promised your brother has not." He nodded to her, and her shoulders fell like it was confirmation of something she had been worried about.

"Unfortunately, I've eaten through all the goods you brought for me," I said, throwing a smirk at Elias who winked in my direction. "So thankfully, our meal will be enjoyable. I'll show you both to the gardens, they are beautiful and I know you'll enjoy them."

I happened to catch Cassius' gaze as I spoke and stared at him quizzically as I couldn't read his expression. The look he was giving me was unfamiliar; something akin to happiness.

"I'll see you at dinner then," he said to what seemed like everyone, but his tone was soft and he looked only at me.

A flutter started in my stomach and a feeling of shyness like I had never experienced overcame me, followed by irritation that I was feeling that way. I nodded at him as he turned away.

"You're very flushed," Elias said eventually, and I stuck my tongue out at him as Mercy's laughter bubbled out of her and spilled into the empty throne room.

Chapter Twenty-Four

Mercy

We all sat at the dinner table eating and drinking. Cassius and I stayed silent as Elias and Georgette shared information back and forth about what insignificant things had filled their months apart. The conversation was mostly the endless laughter that they shared, except when they discussed what they had each done to honor the memory of Absalom. There was a lull in conversation after that, where the only thing you could hear was the sound of everyone eating.

I took a deep breath and started the conversation I wanted to have, without waiting for Cassius to bring it up.

"I would like to discuss concerns about the treaty you had with my brother, before his unforeseen death." Cassius' eyes met mine across the table where he sat next to Georgette who was looking at Elias. They were now having one of their silent conversations.

"Of course, Princess," Cassius said, sitting back in his chair with a small glass of green cordial.

I sat back as well, reaching for the matching glass which had been filled with the same liquid. I sipped it to find a piney sugared liquor that was thick and syrupy on my tongue. I let the flavor permeate my mouth, having not tasted anything like it before.

"As you know, all my brothers were murdered by our Archbishop, who I believe to be working with King Kosdel. His intention was to have all our three kingdoms united under one religion."

"Northern Ralice's religion, no doubt." Cassius nodded but let me go on without anything else.

"My youngest brother was spared but he will not be of age to take the throne for many years," I said, waiting for Cassius to say something demeaning but he waited silently for me to go on. "My sister Temperance shall sit on the throne as a steward until Herold comes of age. She is younger than me, but her temperament is better suited for a ruling. She is only seventeen but well beyond her years."

"I understand," Cassius said, and I thought him such a funny contrast to the many-worded woman sitting next to him. "What would be the concerns you have?"

"I..." I faltered for the words suddenly acutely aware of my lack of experience talking about war. I had thought he would object immediately to Temperance, or any woman being on the throne until my brother was old enough.

"If you thought I would object to a female ruler in the place of your brother you were mistaken." He said it kindly, not to correct but only to assure. "I am harboring a woman in line for the throne of Hestiege. Her father and I have an agreement that whenever the current king of Hestiege meets his end the woman in my protection will take the throne."

The way he worded it made it seem like the king of Hestiege would meet his untimely end very soon, and I balked at his candor. Georgette's head slowly turned so that she was looking at him with eyes as wide as dinner plates.

"She doesn't know that," Georgette said, horrified.

"No, it would make her complicit in conspiracy and murder. I meant only to protect her reputation by keeping her out of it," Cassius said easy as a breeze, despite him having all but admitting that he and another man had a plan to murder a king. "King Ning is a cruel man who neglects the needs of his people. He asked me to strip his niece of her title so she would not be a threat to his throne, but a new age of rulers is coming, younger and less attached to tradition than the age before. She will be a much better ruler for Hestiege than her uncle is."

"Why would you tell us this?" Elias asked and I turned to him as his shoulders were up with tension and his eyebrow was raised. "We could go to King Ning with this information that you've worked so hard to keep private. Why tell us now?"

"I don't believe you have loyalty to any crown, Captain, if I've learned anything from your sister. I am telling Princess Mercy to gain her trust by sacrificing a bit of truth to her." After answering Elias with a bit more superiority than Elias seemed to find necessary, he turned his attention back to me. "If you don't mind me asking Princess, what is your role to be in all of this?"

"I've taken on the role of Ambassador of Adamas. I will also speak on behalf of our kingdom on diplomacy and negotiations for war."

"Very well." He nodded and I saw no hesitation on his part in the face of my sex. "Your brother had requested soldiers, weapons, and other resources to win his war against Northern Ralice. I was somewhat hesitant at first to agree because I am new to my throne. Though recently, King Kosdel has been pressing heavily into my borders along the Lapulous lakes, and I feel I have no choice but to push back."

"In your opinion, do we have a good chance of victory?" I hoped I didn't sound too naive.

"My army is the largest in Marecult, we are fortified and well developed. Adamasian forces are nothing to balk at either. If my sources in Northern Ralice are to be trusted, King Kosdel was heavily relying on the hope that your brother would be swayed by an offer of an alliance against me. It may be a bloody war, but victory leans heavily in our favor. Your brother and I had agreed that neither of us had the reach to take over the entire kingdom of Northern Ralice, so their price for the loss will be money and resources, as well as the loss of some land along our border."

"We intend to honor the terms set with our brother," I said confidently.

"Well, it seems for now we have little to discuss then. When we overtake King Kosdel I am leaning toward killing him, but I could be persuaded to spare his life."

"No." My voice rang out across the dining room, and I was surprised to hear that Georgette's voice joined mine in chorus.

Cassius began to laugh as if it were some great joke, eliciting an irritated gaze from Georgette.

"Well, then I shall send him an invitation for a banquet and ball. Merely a formality, he has made it clear that his intention is war, and no peace treaty shall be struck, but some traditions are worth keeping," he said after his laughter subsided.

"I'm sorry to interrupt my King, but there are courtiers from Coranthia who have come unannounced," Brees said from the door with more than a little hesitation in his voice.

I watched Cassius turn with an eyebrow raised to his Captain of the Guard, and the man shook his head and lifted his shoulders.

"What do they want?" Cassius asked making no move to stand up.

"They came alone and unarmed," Brees stated, "Just them on horses, said they know the queen."

"What?" Georgette said, breaking the formality of the conversation. "I can count the number of courtiers I'm acquainted with on one hand, and two of them are sitting in this room."

"I have them in the throne room with a guard, I told them to await word from you."

Cassius' brow furrowed as Elias looked at Georgette, who looked like she was trying to figure out who would be calling and using her as a point of contact. Cassius was now looking at her with waiting for her response.

"Lord and Lady Prestige," Brees started, and my heart jumped at the sound of chairs scraping across the floor.

Georgette and Elias were on their feet having pushed their chairs away from the table. Cassius and I looked on in question as the twins stared at each other.

"Why are they here?" Georgette asked Elias, her eyes narrowing.

"I told Jones to inform them of the situation if I didn't return to the ship after a set amount of time," he defended, and my brow furrowed in confusion.

"Elias!" Georgette smacked her palm into her forehead.

"Don't act as if they wouldn't have heard anyway. The entirety of Marecult knows of Georgette the Pirate Queen, you think they wouldn't have come eventually?"

There was a silence between them as Cassius and I looked on completely lost.

"Race you there," Georgette finally said.

"Georgette I think we are beyond such childish things..." Elias began, but partway through his sentence he left my side and bolted for the door. He was almost all the way out before Georgette let out an indignant cry and raced after him.

"Filthy cheat," she yelled as she cleared the door and Brees who had moved out of the way of the racing pair.

I sat back in my chair and grabbed the crystal goblet of spiced wine that had been placed in front of me. Part of me was glad that there was a distraction from more serious topics, but I wouldn't race after the two pirate twins. Their antics were too sporadic for my blood. I stared across the table as Cassius sat back down and took a small sip of some wintergreen-colored cordial from a small glass. He set it down and folded his hands under his chin resting his elbows on the table.

"I have no idea as to what just happened," he admitted.

"I think we will both find that happens to us a lot as long as we keep their company." I took another drink of wine.

"That is disconcerting." He sat back, and we enjoyed comfortable silence for a few minutes.

"Shall we go see what all the commotion is about?" I asked after a bit, standing up slowly and smoothing out my clothing.

"I suppose we should," he agreed, standing. "I cannot tell you how much trouble Georgette has caused during her time here, the thought of her and a twin running unsupervised in Hallow Manor is very unsettling."

"I would say there is warrant for that concern," I chuckled. A small and what I supposed to be a rare smile, crossed over Cassius' face.

Chapter Twenty-Five

Georgette

I didn't catch him. I had never been faster than him and as he was in a full run, I knew there was no way I would beat him there with his head start. My heart was pounding from more than the exertion, and as I saw Elias slip into the throne room door ahead of me, I felt a wave of emotion crash over me. I stepped in front of the door to gather myself and catch my breath.

I felt overwhelming anxiety to face the people behind the door. My insecurities all rose to the surface at the same time. There were few people in the world I cared what opinion they had of me, but the weight of their approval settled over me like a storm cloud on a sunny day.

I opened the door slowly and slipped into the room that was only lit by a few lanterns that cast eerie shadows on the marble floor. I walked slowly toward the small group amassed at the end of the room by the thrones; a happy reunion taking place. Then a figure lifted their head to meet my eyes.

The kind smile of my father greeted me, and I ran the rest of the way to them as he held his arms out for me.

"There's my girl." His weathered gravel voice felt like a blanket, and I began to sob into his chest as he pulled me tighter.

I tried not to slip into resenting my parents for raising us to be pirate captains at the soft age of fifteen. It had been their plan all along to raise a captain to take their stead. They had never lied about their intentions, and so when they passed the wheel to Elias and me four and a half years ago there had been no room to be upset. They were asking it of us at so young an age, but it had always been expected. They had groomed us for it with no deception. I knew they loved us deeply, but they had left us to captain the ship all the same. I couldn't bring myself to hate them for it, though some might see it as cruel.

We didn't speak of our parents to many people. Rumors circulated of course, most assumed they had died. Neither Elias, nor I contradicted those rumors. It protected them.

"Let me see her," a voice like honey in tea said, and my father let me go and I turned to receive a critical once over by my mother.

Hazel and Nathaniel Baine, or Hazel and Nathaniel Prestige if they were parading as courtiers. Both were dressed properly and would both manage fine in the high court. They had trained us after all in how to survive in any situation.

"You look like a queen," my mother said to me, and it did not sound like a compliment. She extended her arms to me, and I fell into them squeezing her tight.

There was a bit of time where we all just stared at each other as we hadn't seen our parents in about three years. Not since the last time we risked visiting them in Coranthia, where they were retired and living in a large home in an ocean town. My father looked older somehow, with greys in his hair which he had once worn in long braids but now kept short. My mother looked the same if somewhat softer, with her figure a little less toned than it had been before, which was to be expected.

"So, what exactly happened?" our father asked, and my eyes slid to Elias who was already looking at me to get our story synced before we began to talk.

"Don't look at each other like that, we want the truth," my mother demanded.

"Well," Elias began, and I kept silent to let him talk. He had always had a way of making regular words sound silver. He especially had a way with our mother, to soothe her irritation. "What happened is we were following a lead to Valloe's treasure, and in order to follow the lead we had to make a few deals with some less than scrupulous characters."

"I would like to inform you before you continue, Elias William Baine, that Jones has already told me his version of the story," my dad said, with an eyebrow raised at us but he didn't look irritated, he looked entertained.

"Ah." Elias rubbed the back of his neck.

"We really should have thought more carefully about keeping dad's best friend on as our quartermaster," I grumbled, and my father began to laugh as the doors to the throne room opened again: Brees, Mercy and Cassius walked in.

I went rigid as all my feelings about my parents and my king husband, collided. There was no way that either of them would approve of...*approve of what?* My mind asked and I silenced it and looked to Elias who looked slightly less nervous than I felt. He nodded to me as we turned to greet Cassius and Mercy. Brees stayed by the door.

My heart sped up again as I met Cassius' gaze and he looked behind me to my parents. We were, yet again, at a moment where I could choose to be honest with him. Only this time I wasn't exposing my brother who I knew trusted my judgment, but my parents. What if I told the truth, only to put them in danger?

"Do you trust him?" Elias whispered, and I turned to meet his eyes. Again, I met no judgment, there was only genuine curiosity.

I turned back to look at Cassius who stood in front of us with a wary expression. There would be no doubt who Elias' question was about. Though he had whispered it, everyone had heard and now I was either going to admit to its truth or deny it.

I reached out for Cassius' hand with anxiety butterflying in my stomach. His eyes flashed surprise for a second and I smiled happily to have caught him off guard. His face went back to its stoic resting, but he stepped forward and accepted my hand and it gave me a bit of courage to turn and face my parents.

"Cassius, these are my parents, Hazel and Nathaniel Baine. The original Captains of The Siren. Mother, Father this is Cassius Dalion King of Southern Ralice, he also happens to be my husband."

My mother's eyes went wide but my father was too busy sizing up Cassius, who was not retreating from his stare. Cassius faced him confidently, just as he had done with Elias.

"While we are making daring proclamations," Elias said, pulling Mercy to his side who had a scarlet blush over her face. "This is Princess Mercy Landlight of Adamas and I am irrevocably in love with her."

Laughter burst from me as a surprising sound came from my mother who looked now both horrified and dumbfounded. Cassius squeezed my hand twice and I looked up into his eyes and he winked at me, looking as close to happy as I had ever seen him.

"It seems," my father said, wrapping his arm around my mom's shoulders. "Our children have strayed from the narrative we set for them, but then again I might be disappointed if they hadn't."

"There is a room waiting for you in the west part of Hallow manor. You are both welcome to stay here as long as you wish," Cassius said, bowing slightly to them which was humorous, as he was a king, and they were old pirates.

"Perhaps we shall retire then, for the night," Father said, "Seeing as how our children are healthy and alive and seem to be in good spirits."

The last half was for my mother whose brows had knit together in disapproval.

"We can tell you the full story over breakfast," Elias supplied, and he took a couple of steps forward to kiss mom on her cheek.

"I'll show you to the room that has been prepared," Cassius said, and his hand pulled away from mine which I felt myself hating. When I looked at him, he was staring down at my empty hand, he stopped and put his hand back into mine pulling me along with him.

I retired to my room after walking Elias and Mercy to their rooms. I almost laughed out loud as they lingered in the hall. Mercy was unwilling to say out loud that she was planning on sleeping in Elias' room with him, and Elias was unwilling to cause her any emotional distress. I would have made fun of them but felt like everyone had enough emotional trauma for the night and walked alone back to my chambers.

I passed Cassius' door and his guard wasn't present which meant he wasn't inside. I wondered where he had gone after showing my parents to their room but didn't ask the guard stationed at my door. I slipped inside my room and found Devika reading by candlelight in a chair in the greeting room.

"Devika," I nearly shouted, and she looked startled even though she would have heard me come in. "I'm so sorry you haven't retired to your room yet."

"Nonsense, it was a big day for you," she said, closing the book with a snap and smiling up at me kindly. "Your brother and your parents in one night, after all."

"News travels fast."

"Gossip travels fast, actual news travels as slowly as molasses pours from a jar." She stood. "I've just had a bath warmed for you, and set an itinerary for the next few days, and things you must attend."

"An itinerary?" I asked tilting my head. "I've never had an itinerary before."

"I thought with how well you handled the situation in Larkin, you would like to do similar things around the kingdom. So, I have produced several proposals for you to look over."

I could not tell her now of course, but I thought Devika would make a fabulous Queen.

"Proposals?" I asked. "Devika I... I don't think I will be here long enough to start anything of that magnitude and see it through."

She stared at me in the dimly lit room, and I wished to shrink away from her knowing gaze and disappointed posture. She let out a long sigh and I drew away as if struck. I hadn't discussed my plans with anyone, but after the conversation with Elias, Mercy, and Cassius earlier, I would only be in Hallow until King Kosdel was dealt with, and that end seemed to be approaching rather soon. Then I would leave with my brother and return to life on the ocean and my ship. As I thought it, my heart began to tear itself apart at the thought of me leaving Hallow. The thought of leaving Cassius caused emotions to surface I wasn't sure I could untangle.

"Georgette, one is born into this world for a purpose. Sometimes we are so blinded to that purpose that we fight against it with everything we have, swimming against the current of the role we were created to fulfill."

"I don't believe in your religious convictions," I said like an insult, but she had the composure to not respond in anger.

"I'm not talking about religion, my Queen, I'm talking about seizing the thing your soul was created for. You were created for Hallow and Southern Ralice. I know you can feel it, as much as I've seen it change you every day since you arrived. If you wish to leave, I won't bother you about it again, and I'll let you go back to your life of piracy. But you could do something here, for these people, for yourself, and our king. Don't squander that."

She didn't give me a chance to respond, not that I would have anyway, but she walked out of my room without another word, leaving me angry and hollow. I stomped into my room and removed my clothes viciously. I petulantly threw them on the ground and sank into the warm water, laced with sweet almond oil as I rolled my anger around in my head.

I had no right to be angry with Devika because I had always encouraged her to be honest with me. I was mostly angry with myself because so much of what she said struck true within me. Perhaps I hadn't contemplated my leaving Hollow since my brother's letter because I hadn't wanted to. I slipped beneath the water so it could wash my angry tears away. I sat under the surface until I thought my lungs would explode. I came up and reached for the bar of cinnamon soap that Devika had found for me. She knew I found the smell of cinnamon comforting and so it had been a special gift. I scrubbed my skin with it, hoping to erase some of my confusion. I washed my hair and rinsed off, stepping out of the tub. I dried off with my sheet and put it back where it went as I picked my clothing up and set them in a neat pile on the table in my room. I put on a midnight blue nightdress and silk dressing robe that Devika had laid out for me.

I intended to go sit on my balcony beneath the stars that had never failed to answer me when I was distressed. I walked to the set of doors and pulled them open as the chill of the air bit against my exposed skin. I turned and realized the other set of doors to what would be Cassius' balcony, were wide open. I furrowed my brow as I heard the sound of destruction coming out of them. The distinct sound of glass shattering came to me as I rushed back into my room and to the door that led into the hallway. I could have tried the door in my room that led to his, but my fragile ego would be wounded if I found it to be locked.

I nodded at my guard who looked nervously sideways and as I came out of the room and headed toward Cassius' set of double doors, I was surprised to find Brees standing outside of them. He looked angry and his gaze only softened when I stood in front of him with a questioning gaze.

"What is happening?" I asked after he didn't speak.

"We received some very distressing news from one of our large border camps on the edge of the Lapulous lakes."

"Will you tell me what the news was?" I asked quietly to show I wasn't in the mood to berate anyone.

"Our soldiers have a tradition if they are stationed at a camp for the sixth month running, their wives visit for one night every two months. They get the day and the night off to spend together."

"Okay?" I questioned not understanding his point.

"This camp was inhabited by men from the town of Gorsh to the north. A strong group, like brothers, and last night was the traditional night for them to spend with their wives. But in the middle of the night, the camp was overrun by North Ralician soldiers. They imposed on them with sheer numbers waiting until the camp was asleep to kill all inhabitants."

"The wives?" I asked despondently because the cruelty of war knew no bounds.

"And some children, babies who were too young to be left at home." His tone was as black as night as I watched the boiling anger surface once more. I winced away tears pricking at the corners of my eyes.

To surprise sleeping soldiers was one evil, to kill their wives that lay next to them was another, and the cold blood-covered sword that would kill a defenseless baby was another evil entirely. I shivered as a chill ran up my spine.

"I didn't know King Cyril was declaring outright war as of yet," I said, still quiet.

"This is a new low, even for that cowardly murderer."

I reached around him to open the door to Cassius' room, and Brees put his hand on my shoulder.

"George, he can't..." he breathed out slow and I saw the pain behind his eyes. "He can't take any more tonight."

"I'll be gentle," I said, but he still looked hesitant, unable to take my word. "I promise you Brees, on my honor, I will walk softly."

His hand fell from my shoulder as he allowed me to enter the room. The receiving room was trashed as tables had been overturned and furniture was in disarray. Anything that had been glass was shattered to pieces on the floor. I shut the door behind me and took care of my bare feet to not step on any shards of glass. I walked down a short hallway to Cassius' room, my heart fell as I saw him sitting on his floor leaning back against his bed with his head resting on his knees.

"Cassius?" I called to him, moving closer as if he were a wounded animal.

"Has my wife come to revel in the chaos?" he asked, though the question was muffled as he didn't lift his head.

"Not tonight." I sat down across from him.

He raised his head to look at me then, and I stayed silent in front of him while he stared. For the first time, he looked like a boy. The boy that had been left a crown and lived in the shadow of a cruel man. Normally he wore it well enough to where I doubted anyone could see it, but I saw it tonight.

I moved slowly as his eyes followed my every shift. I slid one of my knees in between his and rested forward so I could look at him with our knees interlocked. He ran a hand through his hair, drawing my attention to how disheveled he looked, broken and disarrayed.

"I won't keep you here," he said finally after the silence started to eat away at me. "If you wish to leave, I will let you, and I will not come after you. As long as you are in waters under my rule you will be protected. I would never, could never, keep you here against your will."

"Thank you."

"I'm sorry, for..." he stopped, setting his head back down. "Well, I'm sorry for a lot. For taking you from your home and forcing you into this marriage." He sounded so distraught and not all like his general condescending self.

"I accept your apology." I started drawing nonsensical lines on the side of his trouser-clad calf.

"How will I tell them..." he asked, and his mood shifted as he retreated into himself again. "Tell the town, tell the children that their parents have died because their fathers served in my army?"

He can't take anymore.

Brees's warning came to me as I sat in silence, not at all conventional for me.

"Perhaps," I started, suddenly self-conscious about sounding like an idiot. "You don't have to pretend the lives that were lost meant nothing to you." He raised his head a little to look at me with an eyebrow raised.

"I only mean that it might help if you show that you are distressed as well, it may serve you better than cold indifference," I said quietly, and his eyes never left mine and I was drawn in by the intensity of his stare.

I reached out without meaning to, running my hands through his hair, tucking some of it behind his ear. He closed his eyes and leaned into my touch as I brushed my thumb along his cheekbone. My breath caught in my chest as I realized how badly I wished for Cassius to succeed as a king. I wanted him to be a good ruler and I wanted him to feel like someone saw through the darkness he thought he had to project.

"I'll come with you," I surprised myself by saying.

He pulled his head all the way up as a boyish hope filled his eyes. My hand started to fall from his face, and he reached out and grabbed it, pressing my open palm to his face again. I raised my other hand and placed it on the other side of his face.

"I wouldn't ask you to," he insisted, but there was no way I could go back on what was said now. Not with the way his eyes grazed over my features like I was some sort of wonder.

"You don't have to ask."

"Will you sleep with me?" he asked and as soon as the words left his mouth, the most ridiculous blush crept over his pale cheeks. For a married man, he seemed over-affected by the question. "I mean, just to sleep. I'm afraid this is a dream."

"I could do something inappropriate to convince you otherwise," I smirked.

"Tomorrow." He smiled back. "Tomorrow, continue your crusade of being the most unconventional queen Southern Ralice has seen. But tonight, would you stay with me?"

I nodded, too unsure of myself to say anything else.

Chapter Twenty-Six

Mercy

Once Georgette had gone, I slipped into my room to grab a nightgown that had been supplied by the lady who was assigned to me. I hesitated to call her by any title because I knew in different countries women who served as court ladies were called different things. In Southern Ralice it was a position of high esteem, and the women were compensated just as well as any man at court.

I brushed my hair out, braided it back in a single rope and splashed some water on my face. I was determined and running off the emotional high of meeting Elias' parents and his gregarious proclamation of love.

I opened my door and looked down either side of the hall making sure no one was there as I dashed across the hallway into Elias' room beyond. I didn't knock or announce myself, opening the door and slipping inside, finding my pirate captain splayed out on the bed. His feet were on the ground, but he was laying on his back with his arms over his head.

He lifted it when he heard the door and his mouth quirked up into a smile.

I felt brazen coming into a man's room late at night dressed in nothing but a nightgown, but I couldn't find it in me to be ashamed or even hesitant. Not tonight, and not with Elias.

"Hello, my love," he said as easily as if he had been saying it his whole life.

"Hello," I said smiling, walking up to the bed.

"Are you enjoying the finery of Hallow Manor?" He propped himself up on his forearms as I stepped in front of him.

"I'd rather be on the ship," I said honestly, as I felt the call of the ocean already.

My admission pleased him, and I saw it all over his face as he stared at me in wonder. It gave me the push of courage I needed to make my way up on the bed. With each of my knees on either side of him, he lowered himself back down now with his arms behind his head, a surprised grin on his face.

"Hello," he said again, looking into my eyes with his storm grey ones.

"You've already said that."

"Am I not allowed a hello more than once?"

"You mean to distract me from what I came for."

"What is it you've come for?" One of his eyebrows quirked up, and I could tell he was enjoying the banter. Something that came so naturally to him but had never been easy for me. That was until I had fallen in love with him and now, I could flirt with him.

I leaned down and felt his hand come up my back as he pulled out the leather cord I had just put in my hair. He gently worked his fingers through the braid until my hair hung like a veil blocking the world out. I placed a kiss on his mouth and his hand that had been working through my hair, pressed at the base of my neck to keep me to him.

"I've come for you," I said, pulling back slightly. "If you'll have me."

"If I'll have you?" He did not smile, only grazed his knuckles over my cheek. "It is you who will have to agree to have me, Your Highness. For the night may love the day, but how could he hope to woo her?"

"I've been successfully wooed, Elias. Show me what else dawn and dusk have to offer." I shifted my weight, working my nightgown over my head, and tossed it aside but his eyes never left mine, never strayed to my figure. I took one of his hands and placed it on my waist. Only then did his eyes wander fervently over my frame.

"Very well, my love. I will weave you a tale of passion under a blanket of stars on a bed much too comfortable for a pirate."

"And by what means shall you weave your elaborate story," I asked, trying not to sigh as his thumb brushed the bare skin under my breast.

"Oh, by whatever means necessary."

I leaned in again, capturing his mouth with my own, and fell along with him as our hearts wove the tale of intimate adoration.

Breakfast the next morning started quiet, and it seemed like Elias' mother was as irritated that morning as she had been the night before. We all had gotten word that Georgette and

Cassius had to attend some sort of business, so it was just the four of us at the opulent dining table as servers brought out a decedent breakfast for us to eat. I was cutting into a crepe filled with thickened cream and fresh berries when Nathaniel spoke to me.

"So, Mercy, what is a princess of a country doing galivanting with my son?" He didn't seem to mean any harm in the question, but Elias still shot him a look and shook his head sharply.

"She's..." Elias began but I raised my fork at him to interrupt.

"I can answer for myself," I said as kindly as I could manage, but Elias didn't look offended, only pleased that I had spoken. His mother, Hazel, offered me a smile as well.

"I have taken up the mantel of Ambassador to my country and so I came to discuss the terms of the war that is upon us with King Dalion, who will be our ally."

"The kings of Southern Ralice don't often stir their fingers in other people's wars," Hazel said, but it wasn't directed at me but Elias.

"I think you might find that Cassius seems to be a bit different than the kings of this land before," he responded carefully as his mother scoffed at him.

A rage boiled in me that I did not know frequently, but it seemed, in the face of someone discounting what Elias had to say, my temper flared.

"Lady Hazel, I know how you don't understand fully of my history with your children and what we have been through together, but one thing I have come to admire from them is how they don't judge people by their title alone. Something I thought certainly they had learned from you, and something every soul in Marecult could use more of."

Hazel looked taken aback at the rebuke and Elias was looking over at me with wide eyes and an unreadable expression. Nathaniel coughed into his napkin to cover up a laugh and his wife shot him a glare that would wither a fresh spring flower.

"And tell me, Princess Mercy, how did you come to admire my children's better qualities?"

So, I began my version of our mighty adventure, and I thought I was getting rather good at it.

Chapter Twenty-Seven

Georgette

I had ignored the pointed looks and raised eyebrows Devika had given me all morning as we prepared to leave for Gorsh. I hadn't been in my room when she had come to get me ready. I had been in Cassius' room. In his bed. Fully clothed having only slept, but that didn't matter to my principal lady.

If Devika had one flaw, it was that when she thought she had been right about something she gave off an air of it that could shake a mountain.

I had awoken next to Cassius, his hand wrapped around my middle, with me tucked against him like I had been made to fit there. I thought perhaps once he woke, he would revert to the cold ruler I had seen so frequently since arriving, but as I listened to his long breaths become shorter and his fingers and limbs had stretched the sleep away, he did not retreat from me.

"How did you sleep?" he had asked.

I had to swallow hard several times before the answer *I slept fine,* came to me, my emotions as sticky as molasses pudding.

Brees greeted me at my door and walked me from my room to escort me to the carriage outside.

"What will the banquet be like?" I asked him. "Receiving another king you plan to go to war with seems so...strange to me."

"It's mostly a show of power. The way something appears is often as powerful as what something actually is." He said it so pointedly with a thin veil of resentment directed at me that I frowned over at him.

"What is it Brees, are we not beyond your disappointed words directed at me with no clear meaning?"

"There are rumors of things King Kosdel has been spreading to the other rulers of Marecult," he huffed out, upset that I chastised him.

"What sort of rumors?" I asked stopping to look at him.

"If I am being completely honest with you, my Queen, he is circulating doubt to Cassius' ability to rule, and how he is easily manipulated."

"What foundation does he have for such claims?" I asked, finding myself more defensive of Cassius than I would have ever been before.

"You," Brees said flatly.

"Me!?" I all but shouted in laughter. "What do I have to do with Cassius' ability to rule?"

"While Cassius meant to use your...wildness, as a display of the mad crown of our country, King Kosdel has begun to twist it into something else. That Cassius is incapable of controlling his wife, and a man who is unable to control his wife is easily overtaken. They've heard that you refuse to bow to him and that you don't address him as king. That you wear men's clothing and act like a wayward pirate who occupies a queen's seat."

"What an idiotic sentiment," I swore as I continued to walk. "Why hasn't Cassius said something to me about it."

"I've urged him to, and he's refused." Brees' exasperation was apparent. "I thought you may listen to reason."

"It is not reasonable for a man to judge another for the actions of his wife," I muttered. "Also, I do not know what you wish me to do with this information, for I cannot change what men think based on one king's slander."

"I'm not sure if there is anything to be done now, I just wished to make you aware."

"Why?" I asked as we reached the large front doors of the manor.

"Because I know you care about him." Brees swept past me without leaving me room for a rebuttal. I was left with my mouth open as I stepped through the door and saw Cassius coming up the stairs smiling up at me with a happiness that softened every defense I had against him.

The carriage ride was quiet all the way there, with Cassius looking as sober as ever. We had to skip breakfast with my parents, and I sent a note to them that I would come to find them when I returned. I was dressed in trousers of iridescent purple with a matching vest with silver buttons. I was playing with the sleeve of my linen shirt with belled sleeves trying to think of something useful to say, but Cassius seemed content to sit in silence. A silver crown with clear crystals sat on my head with enough pins to secure it, that I was sure I could fistfight someone without it coming off.

When the carriage came to a stop, Cassius took a deep breath and let it out slowly; I felt as if I were seeing a completely different person than I had been presented with the last six months. The man before me was burdened and grieving, not something he would have let me see even weeks before.

He exited the enclosed carriage and reached back to help me out. I took his hand and stepped out, almost slipping at the sight before me. The entire town had gathered in front of the carriage and there was not a friendly face amongst them. There didn't even seem to be a respectful face; they all looked angry. I understood why, but while Cassius may have been expecting it, I surely hadn't. I scanned the face of every man, woman, and child. The men left were well into their twilight years, or too young to have been soldiers. The women had red-rimmed eyes and my heart ached for their loss, as children hung from their arms, a lot of them now without parents.

"Good people of Gorsh," Cassius said, facing them. "I come to you today to express my deepest condolences for the severe loss you've suffered."

The crowd didn't so much as shudder, and their faces of stone did not change at his words. Cassius' guard stood behind him, shifting uncomfortably, and I stood at his side staring openly into the people's eyes, daring them to contradict him.

"The loss of your families' lives was an act of violence that was unexpected and cowardly on Northern Ralice's part, but regardless of fault I cannot imagine your suffering."

As Cassius opened his mouth to speak again something flew out of the crowd and hit him square in the chest. I stared at the item on the ground which was a now destroyed tomato. I stared at Cassius' chest where it had landed, while he stared at the wet stain on his clothing. I looked back up to see a young boy of about twelve who had stepped forward and was breathing ragged, as tears streamed down his face. The guards moved to step forward and I almost yelled for them to stand back when Cassius held his hand up and they stopped.

"We don't care about your worthless apology!" the boy yelled at Cassius.

"Boy." A woman from the crowd chastised him and reached out to grab his arm. "Do not speak to the King that way."

"Let him speak," Cassius said as the crowd went more ghostly than it had been before.

"You've taken everything from me!" the boy went on as tears started forming in my eyes. "My father and my mother were in that camp as well as my little sister that was born not three weeks ago!"

Pure rage, white-hot and unrelenting lay in his eyes. He hated Cassius for what he thought Cassius took from him.

"I am sorry," Cassius started.

"You aren't sorry! My dad was a good soldier. He served your father before you and was treated horribly under your father's rule and you are no different than he was, sending men to camps to be slaughtered at the border."

"What is your house name son?" Cassius asked and the boy had the good sense to look a little taken aback.

"Mistlork," he replied curtly.

I winced at his words and Cassius did a little too. I opened my mouth to defend him but as I formulated the words Cassius fell and knelt on one knee before the boy who had walked forward and spoke.

A king kneeling to a boy in the dirt. My king kneeling in the dirt to a commoner.

"I cannot offer anything more to you than the promise that justice will be served to the king and his kingdom that took your family from you. This will not bring them back, but it is all I have to give you. I promise you as a man promises another man, Master Mistlork your family will be avenged."

The guard behind me knelt behind Cassius following suit so that the twenty guards we had brought with us were all kneeled in front of this boy, whose tears had started once more. I took a knee beside my husband and bowed my head to the boy as well. A murmur swept through the crowd.

"Your promises mean nothing to me," the child said with a shaky breath.

I stood then, stepping forward and leaned in, not unkindly, as the boy stared up with eyes full of terror.

"Your King does not break promises," I said harshly. "Your loss is great and life is brutal. This will not be the last tragedy you suffer, and you would do well to mind your tongue in front of those who hold the ability to take your life from you."

"Yes, my Queen." He bowed his head, but I put my fingers under his chin and lifted his eyes back to mine.

"Your father and mother would have been proud of you. You're brave, but do not let your bravery turn to stupidity. Your King is known as Cassius Dalion Oathgaurd, you would do well to take his promise to you as truth." I mustered every bit of high court in me to sound as queenly as I could.

"Yes, my Queen."

"When you come of age, you ask for an audience with me, and we will see what is to be made of you."

"Thank you." He nodded as all the anger seeped from him and a brokenhearted boy stood before me. He receded into the throng of people who looked at me and Cassius now with something less than hatred, but also less than trust; that would have to be earned.

I took the crown off my head which Devika had pinned on so well that I ended up ripping a few strands of my hair out with it as I set it on the seat next to me. I smoothed my hair and scowled, rubbing my scalp where the crown had pulled too hard. I looked up and Cassius was staring at me with a ghost of a smile on his face. He looked as handsome as he ever had in his twisted crown of metal, dark clothing, nails black, and tattoos.

"What?" I asked, shifting uncomfortably under the scrutiny. "These things are heavy; I have no idea how you people wear them for so long."

"Cassius Dalion Oathgaurd?" he questioned, his mouth lifting into a full smile.

"You should be called something other than *the mad king*," I shrugged.

"The mad king is a title that has been made up over centuries of the ruling, Oathgaurd has never been uttered by anyone besides you."

"It will be now," I assured him, crossing my arms. "I think it had a nice ring to it."

"We've come a long way from Cassius the Liar."

"Yes, that was intentional." I looked out the window, suddenly very ashamed I had ever said such a thing in seriousness.

"I doubt it will catch on, as noble as it was."

"Pirates are well versed in the art of the tall tale Cassius, if I say you are Cassius Dalion Oathgaurd, then that is who you shall be. I will see to it single-handedly."

"I fear then that everything I've heard of pirates is untrue."

"That's the wonder of it, you can never be sure."

After a long silence, I looked from the window to him and colored at the fact that he was still staring at me openly.

"Oh, for goodness' sake, stop looking at me like that Cassius." I furrowed my brows.

"I'm in love with you." He sighed as if it were the worst fate in all the world.

I couldn't stop the smile that spread over my face while cursing myself, for I had the terrible misfortune of smiling when I was taken off-guard. My heart dipped into my stomach as I stared at him wide-eyed and smiling, like a fool.

"I'm not saying that to get you to stay, though I know I could never hope to make you do something you didn't wish to. I just, I've been in love with you and I thought, for the sake of being honest, that I should tell you."

"And at what point, Cassius, did you fancy yourself in love with a pirate?" I sat back in my seat across from him and crossed my arms.

"Perhaps from the moment you blew me a kiss as I stood on the pier," he said, and I reveled in the hesitancy of his voice. It wasn't commanding or even sure. He was nervous and I heard it in the breathy delivery of his words. "Though perhaps that was simply rapture. So, maybe it was when you threatened to slit my throat if I entered your bedroom on our wedding night. Though perhaps that was just a twisted lust imagining if you would have made good on your threat."

"I would have." I met his eyes sparkling with humor.

"But then again, it has been every memory of you cursing my name and the way it sounded so sweet on your lips, even while you hated me."

"What a strange man you are, to fall in love with a wild creature who hated you so." I leaned in then and he followed suit so that our faces were only inches apart.

"I've been called many things worse than strange."

"I know," I said, reaching out to cup his cheek in my hand. "Some of those things have come from my mouth."

As the words left me, his eyes lingered on the curve of my lips as my face started to warm and my breath became less available. I was nervous in a way I hadn't been in a long time about a man's proximity. Cassius seemed to have that effect, making me feel like I was doing all this teasing and flirting for the first time.

"Perhaps you can use your lips for something other than disparaging my good name."

"Firstly, I feel like the good name is a bit of a stretch, and secondly, do you have any suggestions of what to preoccupy my mouth with?"

Darkness flashed in his eyes and unfettered desire was displayed on his face. He leaned forward slightly, and I retreated to my seat nearly giggling as his mouth opened slightly in protest.

"Retreating from fear, George?" he asked using my nickname for the first time, causing a spike of heat to snake through my stomach.

"Not at all, but while all the maids you've wooed before surely handed themselves to you on a silver platter, you'll have to come to get me if you want me, my King."

He sat back; his eyes ravenous as he surveyed me. The first time I had ever addressed him as *my King* and the admission of it, along with everything else sat between us. It took everything in me not to climb on top of him in that carriage and give him everything we both wanted, but I was enjoying the game too much to give in now.

"Let's make a wager," he said wickedly, still staring like he was undressing me.

"What will the stakes be?"

"No stakes but victory alone, a winner and a loser."

"Ah, the privilege of bragging." I grinned back. "Alright Cassius, what is the wager?"

"The rules are simple, the first to beg for a kiss, loses."

"Agreed," I said, reaching out my hand and we shook on it. Each of us with the thrill of a challenge in our eyes.

Devika met me at the entrance of the palace as Cassius and I climbed the steps.

"What have I done now?" I asked as Cassius stood behind me.

"You have an appointment for the tailor, to choose your attire for the ball to receive King Kosdel and his company," Devika said, bowing to me and Cassius before slipping inside and leaving us alone once more.

"What fun." I rolled my eyes, though I was honestly thrilled to visit the tailor.

"Georgette," Cassius called and I turned back with an eyebrow raised. "Might you do me a favor?"

The walls of defense I kept around my heart rose immediately as I began to panic. Of course, I knew this would come. Him asking me to change. The conversation with Brees earlier came back to me and I opened my mouth to defy him.

To defy any change that he intended to make to me, to fit the mold of his queen.

"King Kosdel will no doubt try to use any means to cut you when you see him at the banquet," he went on, and I closed my mouth that was about to spew vicious rejection. "He will use the tip of his words to dig into your deepest wounds to get a reaction. I fear he will bring up your friend Absalom as some sort of flippant attempt to cause you to react. He will not stop there; I would beg you not to allow him the satisfaction."

"Oh," I said, releasing the rigid posture that I had taken.

"Your reactions of love and anger are too precious to be wasted on such a man," he said, passing me and leaving me with everything under the stars to ponder.

I was headed to my room with words and feelings swirling inside of me, my head cast down on the tile, deep in thought. When I reached my hallway, I looked up and was startled to see my mother leaning against my door.

"Mother, I was going to call after you and father as soon as I got done with my appointment with the tailor," I said, trying to shake my conversation with Cassius off.

"I wanted to speak with you without your father present," she said, and my heart dropped into my stomach. This was rarely a good thing.

"We can speak in my room." I nodded toward my door which she opened, and we both stepped inside.

"I believe I was too harsh with you at our reunion last night." She sighed and a bit of my hesitation lifted. "I did not mean to sound so disappointed in you."

"I understand your disappointment." I nodded to her. "You escaped the high-born life so that you might be free. You fought to be respected and accepted for what you could do rather than a name or sex you were born to."

"I know this was not your choice," she went on. "Though even if it is your choice, I did not fight for freedom my whole life so that you might not be offered the same."

"You handed the ship down to us. Our life..." I stopped my voice tight, and my eyes full of tears.

"No, I wanted only to hand you a life of choice. I am sorry for my reaction yesterday; it was rooted in fear of my past."

As I opened my mouth to speak, I noticed the painting of Baya that decorated one of the walls of my receiving room. I stared at her golden halo and the blush gown that she wore, it trailed into the part of the mural that was to be the ocean.

"I've missed that look." My mother matched my mischievous grin.

"What look?" I asked, stepping over to her quickly as I embraced her in a hug which she returned with tight arms around me.

"The look of my fierce daughter coming up with a plan to take the world by storm."

Chapter Twenty-Eight

Mercy

I was walking through the gardens that evening by myself, having spent most of the day with Elias and his parents. They spent the afternoon swapping stories and laughing as only a family could. Hazel's mood seemed to lighten little by little as Elias told her stories of how Georgette had been doing the past couple of months.

Hazel and Nathaniel were a proud sort of couple, which I found to be quite odd. For while Hazel was high born, I learned that Nathaniel was an orphan in Northern Ralice when he had gotten his start. They reminded me of Elias and his sister which I supposed was only natural, but I marveled at how the twins had learned their behaviors from a generation before them.

Nathaniel never spoke down to Hazel or belittled her in any way. They were equals in conversation and rank it seemed. And the love that Elias had once told me I would see burning in their eyes, was as pure as he had described it. I had also learned that they retired and now lived in Coranthia in a house at the base of the Shipidor mountains, and when the Corinthian winters hit, they moved into a home they had in a village nearby.

Everyone dispersed when Georgette and Cassius returned. I took the time to have a bit of quiet, away from any questions or expectations. Elias seemed to understand and allowed me to wander off. I was thinking of my siblings, and how I should retire to my room to write a letter to Temperance about how the negotiations had gone. I wondered how they were fairing and if the country had fallen into mourning about my brothers.

Doubt started creeping into my mind about the choice I had made to name Temperance as the Steward of Adamas. The voice of my mother and father harped with ghostlike reminders in the back of my head. Self-doubt settled around me as I sat on a stone bench and pressed the heels of my palms into my eyes until I saw stars. Could I even be an ambassador? Wouldn't someone be better suited than I? Certainly, Temperance was better suited for the throne, but would I be able to carry the mantel of the Adamasian Ambassador. Or had I merely been born to follow orders? To be a good and quiet wife?

"Oh, be quiet," I said out loud.

For the first time, I felt like my life was headed in a direction where I had steered it; surrounded by people I wanted to be around. I had made choices to set myself on this journey and I was strong enough to do what I had set out to. I was neither Georgette, with her loud and certain air about her, nor was I Temperance, with her steady and rigid countenance. I was Mercy, firstborn Princess of Adamas, and the first female

Ambassador my country had seen, with a love of the sea, and eyes only for a pirate captain.

"Are you alright?" Georgette's voice came to me, and I looked up startled, pulling my hands away from my face.

She was standing before me in a purple set of trousers and vest with pearl bangles and tinted cheeks. It should have looked ridiculous, but I only found her lovely and uniquely herself. She was holding her tricorn hat, which I knew Elias had brought here for her. It was about the only thing on her that looked out of place.

"Yes, sorry, lost in thought." I fixed my posture as she came to sit next to me and began turning the hat in her hands.

"Yes, I often yell at myself in the garden," She smiled a little. "Very good for releasing frustration."

"No one had been meant to hear that," I admitted, smiling over at her, seeing the lines of worry on her face.

"I shan't repeat it." She hesitated and then began again. "I am off to see my tailor and was wondering if you might accompany me. You will of course need a dress to receive Cyril and I thought we might...go together?"

"Certainly," I said, standing up, but she did not.

"Also..."

I was unused to seeing her so hesitant, so I sat back down with my brows raised and a question on my face.

"Well, I fear there is no uncomplicated way for me to phrase this and you are the first person I've told."

"Alright," I almost whispered, as to not interrupt her thought.

"It's just that, I haven't talked to Elias, but I assume you plan on sailing with The Siren."

"Yes," I said, realizing Elias would not have had a chance to tell Georgette about my proposition. I wouldn't wait for him to explain it while she was here with me now.

"I've taken on the title of Ambassador for Adamas and I had approached Elias about you and him heading up my crew while we sail all over Marecult. Of course, he didn't agree to anything, and I told him if he had any qualms I completely understood. It will be a much different lifestyle than the one you are both used to."

"I see," she said, but didn't look too shocked or worried about the information. "Well, I think that will be a conversation for you and Elias to have."

"I would never usurp the relationship between you two, it's your vessel and I know what the trust you have means. I would never overstep in such a way, George."

"No, Mercy." She rubbed her free hand over her face. "I mean that I won't be getting on The Siren when it departs this time."

When I looked up at her in panic, tears were starting to drop from her eyes to trickle down her cheeks. I understood then. The looks between her and Cassius. The way she seemed to effervesce in this setting. Elias' looks into her room on the ship.

"Have you told Elias?" I asked, voice still small.

"No, not yet." Misery seeped from her.

"I think he knows. I don't know how, perhaps it's a twin intuition, but he suspects."

"Yes, he's always possessed that talent." She reached over and set the tricorn hat in my lap and tears started to form in the corners of my own eyes.

"I can't..."

"You can," she said, steadier than her voice had been a minute ago. "Your life has been full of *I can't* Mercy. It's time for you to know you can. The Siren needs two captains. That's the way it has always been. The ocean calls to you the way it calls Elias, the way it has never called to me. I love it to be sure, but it does not possess me; doesn't drive me. I don't..." She swallowed. "I don't miss it anymore. I did at first, but now..."

She started to cry again, and it was such a sight to behold. For Georgette was a steel blade of determination, quick in its path and sure of its target, but I supposed even blades had their limitations.

"That isn't shameful," I assured. "Your love of court is no more shameful than my love of the ocean."

"Yet," she exhaled as she stood wiping tears off her face violently as if that would erase them. "It feels like a betrayal all the same."

I didn't know the words to assure her that it wasn't, because I didn't have the words to assure myself. I could only nod and stand next to her. Hoping the message that I understood what she was feeling was felt.

After Georgette and I drank spiced wine and laughed our way through the tailor appointment, I was in much better spirits as I slipped into my room to prepare for the evening meal. Elias was there waiting for me, having already bathed and changed. His hair was curling around his temples and still a bit damp.

I smiled at him, and he started to smile back, but his eyes snagged on what was in my hand and I was filled with a certain kind of embarrassment. I held Georgette's tricorn hat and Elias stared at it with such intensity I thought it might explode. I fought the urge to throw it down and instead waited for his response. He stood slowly and made his way over to me, eyes never leaving the hat. When he was in front of me, he tugged it from my hand and I let him take it, watching his eyes for any shift.

He ran his hand along the inside and nodded solemnly before setting it on my head and tipping it slightly.

"Are you alright?" I reached up and touched his face, running the back of my hand along his cheek. My heart ached at the tears I saw building in his eyes.

"I will be, my love." He pulled me in for an embrace and I squeezed him tight against me, wishing I could steal the pain he wore and carry it for him.

Chapter Twenty-Nine

Mercy

Weeks later, I came into the ballroom and was bombarded with just how lavish Hallow Manor was once again. The floor shone a polished marble, and the room's size was immense. It seemed in Southern Ralice, a banquet was a feast and dancing all at once. So, at one end of the large room was a long table with food enough for an army that looked almost too perfect to eat. While on the other side was a band of players that continually poured music into the room. While there must have been four hundred people in attendance, the room didn't look full in the slightest. From the large double doors of the entryway, you could see straight to where Cassius stood with King Kosdel who had arrived earlier that day.

I was thankful that I hadn't run into him around the castle, though I thought that was by design. He had a man standing next to him and a woman looking uncomfortable standing behind them. I could tell that Cassius said little in the conversation, and King Kosdel was doing most of it.

I turned about the room to admire the large murals that were set into walls, decorated with glittering gold paint. The detail of each one could keep someone entertained for hours and their equal I hadn't seen. Some of them were quite depictive of sexual acts and drunken revels and I laughed whenever my eyes grazed any particularly comical scene.

"Shall I paint you a mural?" Elias' voice came from behind me, and I jumped a little but fell back into his frame.

"I didn't know you painted, only whittled bits of wood," I teased.

"Well, you never know, perhaps if I tried it, I might be quite good."

"Who is that man with King Kosdel and Cassius?" I asked him. "Do you know?"

Elias tensed immediately and his arms went stiff around my middle.

"That's Absalom's father." His voice was controlled but angry. "Master Gerald Church."

"You're angry with him?" I asked, feeling stupid for having to ask.

"He would have known he was putting Absalom in danger by sending him with us, and would have known that ultimately the king's plan to have you killed would mean he would die too. He sacrificed his own son for his loyalty to the crown and for that, I will always hate him."

"Will you introduce me?"

"Are you mad? I don't want to get near him for fear I may gouge his eyes out here and now."

I turned in his arms and looked up into his eyes which were fraught with questions and terrible rage.

"This is how the game of war is played, I must go see them as the Ambassador of my country but if you don't wish to look at him, I understand. I should want his eyeballs gouged out as well. After all, he is the man that I was to be married to, and he tried to kill me before I could so much as arrange tea with his other wives." I hoped the ill-timed joke would lighten his mood.

"I'll go with you," he sighed eventually. "Just in case he says something stupid, and I have an actual reason to inflict justice upon him, and the vile king he serves as a dog."

We made our way over to them and Cassius looked a little relieved that we had come. He turned to us and bowed as I curtseyed in the simple grey satin gown that I had ordered from the palace tailor. The back was low but other than that and the sleeves that belled out, it was marvelously unfrilly.

"King Kosdel, Princess Mercy Landlight of Adamas and Ambassador of her Country and Captain Elias Baine of The Siren, my wife's brother." Cassius introduced us though we had already met, and I bowed to him noting that Elias didn't move from his rigid standing position.

"So nice to see you again Princess, your loveliness has come to me in dreams many a night."

"I am sorry to say, I forgot you almost as soon as I left your presence the first time," I responded demurely.

"This is Gerald Church, master of Kosdel's armies," Cassius interrupted, not giving King Kosdel a chance to respond to my insult. "And Norrisa his new bride."

"You wed your dead son's betrothed?" Elias asked behind me, and my eyes went wide as I looked past Gerald to the woman behind him who turned a deep shade of red.

"Her father agreed that I was a suitable replacement as she had already been promised to Absalom before his tragic passing."

The way he said it caused me to clench my fists and I could feel the anger radiating from Elias without having to turn around. I took a long breath in and let it out.

"I don't mean to keep you from the party gentlemen, enjoy your evening." I turned and looked to Elias who was staring directly at Gerald, a pure hatred in his eyes I had never seen displayed before.

"I believe I saw some punch," I said, and Elias' eyes slid to mine as he nodded holding his arm out to me.

"King Dalion, do you know when my sister is to make her appearance?" Elias asked and Cassius gave him a small smile.

"I do not, but I have no doubt the room itself will shift and murmur so that you will know when she does."

We left him with the vipers, though he seemed able to handle his own, and made our way to a table of food.

"I'm sorry, it may take me a bit to acclimate to being better with politics, where I don't say things to embarrass you." Elias sipped out of a crystal punch cup I had handed him.

"Nonsense, you didn't embarrass me in the slightest. Also, I feel much braver with you at my side, always." I slipped my hand into his.

"Will you sleep with me tonight?" he asked in my ear. "I fear I may never again sleep well, without you by my side."

"Well for the sake of your rest, it would be rude of me to decline."

"I couldn't agree more, though I was speaking more of not sleeping."

"Elias Baine!" I gave him a disapproving look which he returned with a wicked grin.

"Yes, Captain?"

The thrill of being called a captain shot through me. The conversation I had with Georgette a fortnight ago, seemed much more like a dream and less like reality. She still hadn't spoken to Elias about it, but he had told me he thought she was worried he might be disappointed. So, he waited patiently for her to bring it up in her own time. It was something I admired about him. His ability to sit on something and let the other person divulge what they were thinking in their own time.

He was patient but sure, like the ocean. He had been so sure of his affection for me so early, unquestioning in his devotion. Yet, I hesitated to return his love even while he declared it. My hesitation never caused him to be less sure.

I reached out and pulled his face to mine, placed a kiss on his lips and one on his cheek for good measure.

"What was that for?" he asked, winding his fingers into mine and squeezing once affectionately.

"For letting me find my way instead of telling me which path to take."

"I'm a little concerned that me offering you a simple right of living gets me a kiss, not that I'm complaining, but you are worth much more than that."

I leaned in and kissed him again slowly as his hand unlaced from my fingers and found its way to my cheeks. He tasted of punch as he deepened the kiss and I sighed against his open mouth.

"We will draw a crowd if we keep this up," he murmured.

"Let them look." I looked up into his eyes.

"Pirate," he accused, and I laughed a burst of sparkling happy laughter that I felt to the tips of my toes.

Chapter Thirty

Georgette

I walked to the doors where I would be announced and took in a long breath with Devika at my side.

"I'm proud of you," she said, dressed in the finest crimson velvet gown I had ever seen. For the maidens of Baya wore red, so for this, Devika had conceded and not worn white.

"I have not done much here for you to be proud of," I admitted. "But I hope to learn."

"And that, friend, is what makes you a good queen." She touched my arm and stepped in front of me to set the stage for me to enter.

My gown was all shimmer and champagne gauze. A corseted top and billowy sleeves that tied at my wrists. Gold and silver stars of metal thread were stitched on every part of it, so it shone like a blush-colored sky. High points of my skin had been painted with gold paint so that I too shimmered in the light. Deep berry-red tinted my lips, and my head was not adorned with a crown, but with a headpiece that resembled the halo that Baya was often depicted wearing. I wore my hoops in my ears and nose and the tentacled siren necklace my husband had given me on our wedding day. It was the first time I had worn it since.

I stepped through the door, thoroughly feeling as if I were about to retch. I searched the room as the herald announced me, and the world turned to watch my entrance. I paid no mind to the chatter that filled the hall, or the way I felt exposed with the open neckline of my gown. I just looked for him. If I could just catch his depthless eyes, I would be able to walk through the crowd of people.

And then there he was, dressed in all black but for a gold crown sitting atop his head that I had never seen before. He was in a conversation with King Kosdel but when our eyes met, he turned away from him and met me with an open expression of astonishment. I smiled and as I passed, people dancing and talking gave me a wide berth for me to reach him.

"King Kosdel," I said curtly to the King who had tricked my brother and me.

I looked at Master Gerald Church who stood at the ready at his side. I stared at him for a long time, sure that anyone with a set of eyes could see the hatred radiating off me. He had the good sense to look a little uncomfortable shifting from foot to foot and avoiding my eyes. A woman was standing to the back of him, much younger than he with chestnut-colored hair and pretty brown eyes. She stared right at me with a curious expression as if I were a traveling show.

King Cyril Kosdel grinned as if I were playing into his hand exactly, but as he opened his mouth to say something I turned to Cassius. In a dramatic swirl of skirts and stars, I kneeled before him. I was well aware that the room had gone silent. I looked up at him like a beggar asking for water and put my hands out to receive his. I had to bite my tongue to keep from laughing because he looked both pleased and horrified. He managed to hold his hand out to me as I placed a kiss atop it.

"My King, it is a pleasure to attend at your side."

"Hm?" he responded, looking now like he was going to laugh.

There would be no mistaking the picture. The goddess Baya snubbed Northern Ralice but bowed to the King of Southern Ralice. Even if I was only a pirate dressed as the goddess herself. King Kosdel may have woven tales of what kind of king Cassius was, but tonight his pirate goddess wife bowed to him alone.

Cassius helped me back up and spun me around, so my back was against him and snaked his arm around my middle, making me feel more secure.

"The tailor would not tell me what you were to wear but she did tell me to accent in gold to match you," he whispered, and I looked down, noticing his normally black painted nails were shimmering gold in the chandelier light.

"I must admit you have changed," King Kosdel said, breaking the intimate moment and I stared over at him.

"That's the nature of life," I said simply, trying my damndest to put on a face of indifference. Though rage boiled my blood so terribly I wanted to charge him and strangle the man with my bare hands.

"I've had some of your things brought," Gerald said. "Things you had kept at Absalom's, have been delivered to your chambers."

My muscles tensed and my jaw clenched at the bastard's use of his son's name to get a rise out of me.

"How kind Master Church," I managed through clenched teeth.

"This is my wife; we were recently wed. Norissa, this is Georgette Dalion..." He pulled the woman in front of him like some sort of shield. *Coward.*

"Queen Georgette Baine-Dalion," Cassius growled from behind me.

"It's alright, my King, this is the woman that my friend Absalom was to marry before he was murdered." I tried my best to make my voice as devoid of emotion as I could. "It seems after sacrificing his son to country, Master Church took his betrothed as well."

The girl looked like I slapped her, which was not my intention, but she had been in my line of fire. Gerald glared at me, showing a bit of anger I had heard about from Absalom but had never seen in the man myself. Gone were his soft glances my way and cooing over my wellbeing.

"Absalom hardly spoke of anything, other than you and Elias the couple times I met him," the woman said in a quiet voice and my eyes met hers begrudgingly.

She was pretty in an everyday sort of way, she would neither stand out in room nor offend anyone's eye. She was small and delicate, and my mind supplied me with an image of her hands holding Absalom's face that caused a soft smile to surface on my face. I smoothed my features, taking a deep breath. It was unlikely this woman had a choice in her fate and likely that after Absalom had died, Gerald finagled a bargain where he secured a wife thirty years his junior.

"Yes, well he had some decency of character, it's a pity you came to be married to the lesser of the Church men," I answered, and she didn't look as if she disagreed.

"What a whip of a tongue your bride has on her Cassius. Might I have your hand for a dance then Queen Dalion?" King Kosdel stepped forward, extending his hand out and I debated my response.

"You know well enough that the first dance of the evening belongs to my King," I said curtly.

"And if you think you are going to touch, let alone dance with my wife, Cyril you're mistaken. If you so much as look at her with anything other than a passing glance, you'll leave my kingdom in a grave-cart, cold and stiff," Cassius said as his arm tightened around me. I smiled up to the King of Northern Ralice who looked briefly confused before stepping back and looking at Cassius with disgust.

"Cassius, I thought you too sensible to fall in love with the first woman you married. Your father would be disappointed in your lack of will. I also assumed you would be smarter than to threaten to kill me," King Kosdel spat, which just made my smile grow wider.

"My father is dead, and I will not be the one to kill you Kosdel. Georgette is more than capable of handling you herself. She has sharp teeth under those beautiful lips of hers. Now if you two gentlemen will excuse me, I am going to dance with my wife."

I waved to Gerald and the King as Cassius pulled me away to the dance floor. The band stopped in the middle of the song they were playing to begin a new one for us alone. A traditional slower-paced tune began as Cassius pulled me into perfect form.

"You were magnificent," he praised.

"Aren't you afraid to dance with a sharp toothed pirate woman? What if I bite?"

"I'm hoping you do." He winked at me, causing warmth to spread over my face.

"I want to kill them," I said after a while of us dancing in silence. "I cannot believe Gerald brought Absalom's betrothed here and has married her."

"You haven't told me anything of Absalom." His voice was quiet, like a secret. His words pulled the strings of grief in my chest.

"I loved him," I said, swallowing hard.

"You were lovers?" he asked as if he had already assumed.

"No," I sighed. "Never lovers, just friends, perhaps in another life something more but not in this one."

"I see, what did you love about him?"

"I..." I started, as it became increasingly hard to talk. "He was a good friend, loyal to my brother and me despite our differences. He felt things deeply and he followed every rule to the last letter."

"A good man then," Cassius was drawing small circles on my shoulder with his thumb.

I couldn't answer him as the tears that I was holding back could not handle another word about it. I felt a burden lift that I hadn't known I had been carrying. Some part of me wondered if I would have to keep silent about Absalom at Cassius' side to not wound his ego, but he didn't seem bothered by my admission in the slightest.

"You didn't need to..." Cassius started looking for the right word as he looked at my dress. "You didn't need to do this for me, it doesn't matter to me what Cyril, or anyone that aligns themselves with him thinks."

"The only person who is allowed to speak poorly about you is me," I said. "Also, the game of kings is as frivolous and ridiculous as any I've seen, but it seems the game must be played regardless. Still, you haven't told me how lovely I look."

"I needn't tell you," he said, as a smile played at the corners of his mouth. "Every man in this room, save your father and your brother, are looking at you with enough desire for the compliment to be moot."

"But I didn't don this ridiculous dress and halo for them, Cassius." I reached my hand up to run my fingers through the hair at the nape of his neck.

"Then, my Queen, I have to inform you I have no words to explain how lovely you are tonight. Though I prefer you in trousers, they give me a better visual of some of your assets that I admire."

"You should be ashamed of yourself," I said, but true laughter burst out of me, as he brought me closer to sway in the music.

"Might I steal my sister for a dance Cassius?" a voice came to the left of us, and I smiled at my brother who had a face full of trouble.

"You certainly may, but only if you return her, it seems I can't bear to be parted from her for long." I felt color stain my cheeks, but I refused to look away from them and instead shook my head.

"I shall indeed then." Elias stepped in as Cassius winked at me, before turning in a whirl of black into the crowd.

"I would like to remind you of what a fuss you made when I fell in love with a princess, and in your hypocrisy, you have fallen in love with a king. A notoriously wicked king at that." Elias started leading me before I was ready and pulled me along with a scoff on my lips.

"Don't try and deny it. Your face is radiating happiness and you two are dripped in unfulfilled desire, it's a little sickening." He spun me too forcefully trying to knock me off balance and I kicked his shin.

"I wasn't going to deny it, you crusty barnacle. I simply think you remember me making a fuss when in actuality, you were the one that made a fuss."

"Perhaps so." He smiled at me as I rolled my eyes at him.

"I'm glad you're here," I said seriously. "I am not accustomed to being separated for so long."

"Nor I, us being raised to depend on the other, I missed you fiercely." Emotion pricked at his eyes. "Though, I think, if my inclinations are correct, and they usually are, that we will have to become accustomed to that feeling. Shall we not sister of mine?"

I faltered again; my feet unable to make sense of what my brain was telling them to do. Elias kept in step though, with a sad sort of look on his face all the while.

"Mercy told you?"

"No, George, I'm just not blind. You're in love with the King and you shall not be returning to The Siren...will you?"

"I..." My breathing became labored as a heaviness settled itself in my chest.

"It's alright," he assured, but his face spoke of the same pain I felt. "After all, if I'm going straight, and I fear my beloved will not have it any other way, ambassadors visit the capitals at least once a year if not more, so it isn't so dismal."

Tears slid down my face. Too much, too warm, my chest too tight.

"You belong here," he went on. "Look at you, I've never seen a queen as perfect as you." I kicked his shin again. "Ouch, I was being sincere."

"Stop it," I begged as I stopped dancing to wipe my tears from my face and he pulled me into his side to embrace me tightly.

"You are dearest to me in the world, George."

"Aye," I said, wrapping my arm around him, squeezing back.

Chapter Thirty-One

Mercy

The night wore on and Cassius had been right about Georgette's entrance. Everyone watched her make her way into the ballroom and our eyes trailed after her star sewn gown and gold-painted skin. She looked as goddess-like as I had ever seen anyone look. My conversation with Absalom returned to me when he compared her to Baya and now, I could see what he saw in her, a fierce defender.

I danced with Elias most of the night, save when he danced with his sister and his mother. I danced once with Cassius who was hardly ever away from Georgette, his eyes trailing after her always. I danced twice with Nathaniel, which was the most lively I had ever danced, and he brought laughter bubbling out of me.

"Tell me," Nathaniel asked, after one dance where he led me off the dance floor. "Your story is so similar to my wife's I have to know, what made you want to live a life on the ocean?"

"I'm not sure if I could rightfully explain," I said to him. "The ocean itself calls to me, the desire to do something for myself without anyone directing my fate, Elias, and perhaps the stars too if I am being poetic."

"You seem a bit pragmatic for poetry," he confided.

"I suppose that is mostly true."

"Good, a storyteller needs a solid pillar to bring him back to the ship deck every once in a while," he said, smiling at his wife who furrowed her brows at his mischievous grin.

Though soon she was swaying with him on the dancefloor, a smile gracing her face as bright as I had seen.

"I'm going to ask Norissa to dance," Elias said as I stood at his side. "The poor creature looks miserable."

"That is probably a kindness she would appreciate."

So, I watched him from where I stood in the background, content to take the party in silence, observing couples, music, and gossip. I let the melody spill over me and smiled as Elias danced with his sister once again and they laughed together when the song was done. Each of them spoke to each other with wide hand movements and knowing looks. They sat against the wall opposite me, and I watched them happily laugh for what seemed like an hour. Each of them was equally animated.

"I'd always wondered how the Pirates Baine were so young yet maintained such a robust reputation." I was startled as Cassius' voice came to me.

"What conclusions have you drawn?" I asked, now leaning back against the wall as he did the same, looking in the direction of the Captains who were none the wiser of their audience.

"Seeing them together, I understand."

I smiled and Elias caught my eye from across the ballroom, he said something to Georgette and she too looked over at us. She made a joke which had Elias laughing so loud I could hear him from where I stood. No doubt the joke was at our expense, but I couldn't bring myself to feel anything but joy.

"Tell me, how do you think we will fare being in love with pirates, Cassius?"

"Seeing as how I have lost myself completely to the admiration and wildness of my wife, I cannot say. I hope you do not suffer from such affection as I do," he admitted, and I found myself looking over at him to find he was being serious with no hint of mocking in his face.

"Elias would say there is no other way to be in love."

"Well, at least I know I am doing it fully." He offered me his hand.

"Would you suffer me one more dance, Princess?"

Chapter Thirty-Two

Georgette

Cassius hardly left my side the whole banquet. If I wasn't dancing with Elias, Brees, or my father, I was dancing with him. His watchful eyes were on King Kosdel the whole time. Then when I felt myself waning, he told Devika, who danced most of the night with Brees, that he would escort me to my room.

So, we walked through the darkened corridors together in silence, him seeming right at home in the void of noise, and me itching to break it. The silence accepted him, the dark shadows claiming him as one of their own, while casting me out. I was too loud, too careless against his silent thoughtfulness.

"So, you'll leave with your brother and Mercy?" he asked, and the ache in my chest from talking to my brother throbbed again. "It won't be long, surely, if Mercy is to be the Ambassador for Adamas she'll be busy trading and striking deals with Hestiege and Coranthia."

"Will you miss me?" I tried to play off my heartache with cheap humor.

"Heavens no." He smiled back easily, not looking disappointed in my reaction, only accepting. "You are the thorn in my side I should have been rid of months ago."

We had reached my door, and I turned to look up at him.

"Why didn't you," I asked hesitantly, feeling needy. "Get rid of me?"

"You know why."

"But you'll let me leave now?"

"I've kept you too long for selfish reasons." He reached, cupping my cheek with such gentleness, that it didn't feel real. "First, you were the jester in my show, the jewel in my mad crown, and I used you for my own ends. Then, as I began to realize that hating you wouldn't be an option, I kept you here because I was worried I would never find anyone quite like you again."

"And now?" I leaned into his touch.

"Now I realize if I force you to stay because I love you, keep you in captivity, it would be torture far worse than losing you."

I cannot become your jailor, George.

His sentiments were too familiar, too similar to a conversation I once had not so long ago. Only this time when I asked myself if this life would feel like a prison I was met with a different answer in my heart.

I was a little ashamed having wrestled with the guilt of loving Absalom and then seemingly falling in love with another. Was it a betrayal? Elias had spoken some words to me which softened the pain.

Absalom wasn't yours and you were not his.

"Are you mine then?" I asked without thinking, and then became a little embarrassed by how childish it sounded.

"I've never belonged to another person as I belong to you Captain Georgette Baine of The Siren. As much as one can belong to another, I belong to you. When you leave, I shall only beg you to visit me every so often so I might tell myself I will see you again."

I'm yours too. The words wouldn't leave my mouth. So funny how everything else fell quickly from my lips but the declaration of love was lodged in my throat, refusing to come out. I only nodded quickly, stepping away and feeling a coward as I opened my door.

"Goodnight, my King." I shut the door on his knowing face filled with understanding.

I stood inside my receiving room door with my back against it for a long time crying. The tears slipped from me; from a wound I was sure had partially closed. The thing I found about grief was that its trauma could be ripped open and bleed anew with any sort of prompting, large or small. My heart ached for all the right reasons. For love, and for loss and the choices I had already made, to start a new life.

As I stood and walked to my room, I realized as I dried my eyes with my fingers, surely leaving gold shimmering paint in their wake, that I would not be able to get out of my dress on my own. The corset on the dress had taken Devika on her own to strap me into and there was no way I could unfasten it without help. My eyes worked over to the door. It was either ask him for help or sleep in the dress that did not allow me to breathe properly. I took the halo out of my hair and set it next to me.

I sat on my bed for several minutes and let my breathing become regular before getting up and stepping to the door.

It was open, and I let out a sigh of relief as I pushed it in. Cassius was in his room, standing at a fireplace with a small cordial glass in his hand. He had taken off his coat, vest, and boots and had untucked his white linen shirt. His neck and part of his chest were exposed, and the firelight flickered against the undone version of him.

He looked up at me as I stepped forward slightly, and then leaned back against the doorway. He didn't say anything, only stared at me in that way he had, which sent a riot of fluttering through my stomach. My face grew warm with just the way he surveyed my figure, lingering on the dip of my hips and the swell of my breasts. I had never been shy, but I felt hesitant under his scrutiny in a way I hadn't before. I didn't give bedfellows much time to examine me before, or hadn't noticed if they liked what they saw. I hadn't cared.

"Have you ingested more poison?" he asked as he raised an eyebrow. "Perhaps a delicious pastry was left by your bedside?"

"Do I look as if I have been poisoned?" I certainly felt as if I had been. My heart raced and I was lightheaded.

He didn't answer, only stared.

"Cassius," I said too loudly and too quickly. "Come here."

He hesitated only a moment before he obeyed the command, strolling over to stand in front of me, an arm's length away. I made a displeased sound which sounded almost like a growl in my throat as I reached forward and slipped my fingers into the waistband of his pants pulling him to me.

"This is what I meant," I said, looking up at him as he gave me a half-grin.

"You should have been more specific." He reached up to push a lock of my hair behind my ear and his fingers slid along my jawline.

"Cassius," I whispered now, but I hadn't needed to, as his eyes had never left mine.

"Yes?" he asked as his thumb brushed over the bow of my lips.

"I'm not leaving."

He stilled. Everything about him stopped it seemed, even his breathing.

"Mercy is going to take my place on the ship and I'm going to stay here with you, in Southern Ralice. Unless you irritate me too terribly, in which case I might return to a life of piracy." I smiled, but he was not smiling. He was still as a stone carving in his gardens. "Also, I love you, if that wasn't apparent to you already."

He moved then, lifting me against him while I yelped as turned us toward his bed. He set me down and used a hand on my chest to push me back so I was laying down.

"Say it again," he demanded, voice rough and breathless, warming my limbs.

"If you irritate me, I'll leave you?" I grinned up at him as he climbed on top of me, caging me in with his arms. He frowned as I laughed, and he lowered his head and put his hand under my chin forcing my head sideways so his lips grazed my ear.

"Say it again." The command was heavy, and heat started to build in my center.

"I love you." He moved my chin back so I was looking at him, his eyes darker than I had ever seen them, with a glint to them that was somewhat predatory.

He traced my features with his fingers, ran his hand through my loose strands of hair and then went lower to my collar bone, brushing his fingers gently against my skin.

"I need your help to get out of this dress," I said, trying to cool the riot of emotion in my stomach. Trying to remain in control of myself despite the losing battle.

"Very well." He sat upon the edge of the bed, and I took a moment to school my expression before I got up and stood with my back to him.

If I had thought Cassius hadn't been with many women before me, that would have been the moment that delusion would have burst. He removed the top tulle layer of the dress with its sleeves and let it fall in a pile next to him. Then he began unlacing the back of the corset with a deftness that even Devika might have found impressive. When it was loose enough for him to pull over my head, I let out a great breath.

"You needn't wear such a thing ever again," he assured me, pulling down the other two layers of skirts, though I could have done that myself.

"I shall not," I assured him. "Though I did love the way your eyes were on me the whole evening."

"My eyes are always on you George, from the moment we were married, you've just never noticed."

I stood with my back to him in a slip that was a champagne color that matched the dress. With nothing else between us, I whirled on him and stepped closer. He reached for me as if he expected it and ran a thumb along my cheek and pulled it back, revealing a slight golden shimmer. When I said nothing, he reached out again and traced my features lightly, going over my shoulders and then letting his hands feel the curves of my hips.

"Are you going to kiss me sometime or shall I leave?" I asked sharply, after minutes of him touching me delicately had wound my nerves so tight, that I thought I may snap.

"Is a kiss all you came for?"

"No," I ground out, my body aching at the thought of stopping at a kiss.

"Then why are you rushing me?"

"Cassius," I warned, as his fingers traveled lower leaving fire wherever he touched.

His stood and dipped his head low to mine as my breath caught. He smiled, self-satisfied and my eyes narrowed. His mouth was hovering just above my own, and my eyes were fluttering open and shut as our breath mingled together. I pulled his shirt up and over his head to do some exploring and touching of my own until he seemed as well worked over as I.

He pushed forward and I pulled back pushing him away ever so slightly, with my hand flat against his chest.

"Beg me for it, Cassius."

His eyes were open and looking into mine, the ache in his gaze growing at my words.

"Is that how it is to be?" he whispered, but it almost sounded like praise.

I said nothing, only smiled as my hand made torturous circles on his abdomen before slipping my fingers into the waistband of his trousers once more. So, this is what it was to be, a constant battle of dominance. I waited to see if he would bend for me.

"Queen Georgette Baine-Dalion, Captain of the sea," he started, as his mouth found itself at the base of my neck, his tongue flicking over my pulse.

"Hm?" I answered him as I tried to control my breathing.

He picked me up again and sat me on the edge of the bed.

"Would you." He dropped to his knees before me, his hands sliding down my legs tortuously slow. "Allow me a kiss?" He placed a kiss to the inside of one of my knees.

"Please?" I chided him, though it was now physically painful to resist.

"Please," he ground out as a sharpness came into his voice.

"I suppose…" I didn't finish and I didn't remember what I was going to say because he moved too quickly and pushed me down once again on the bed using his arms to trap me. All that came out of me was an embarrassing noise that was between a sigh and a moan. His head lowered so his mouth was below my ear.

"I will not be made the only one to beg for something tonight, darling, I promise you that."

I had no time for a salty rebuttal. No time to challenge him with a stare because the next second his mouth was on mine.

It was soft at first, making me wonder where the hard edge of him was, as his mouth was so thoughtful and lovely as he worked my lips over before pressing his tongue to the seam of them. I opened for him, as my body reacted on its own using my fingers to pull him closer, his chest on mine not seeming enough.

"You feel divine," he said, having broken away from me even though I let out a sound of protest.

"True." I pulled my hand up to trace his scar again as he kissed the pad of my thumb.

"My arrogant pirate wife." It was reverence in his tone that I soaked up like dry soil during the first rain.

"I believe you threatened to make me beg for something." I snaked my fingers into the waistband of his trousers again, brushing against ridged muscles as his eyes closed and he inhaled with a shaky breath. "Kiss me and don't stop this time, or I shall become very vexed."

"Yes, my Queen." He dipped his head once more to kiss me, but I turned aside and reached up to bring his ear to my lips.

"That's Captain, to you."

"I'll kiss you silent, you sinful creature."

And he made good on all his threats.

Chapter Thirty-Three

Mercy

A rattling woke me as I sat up in the dark and heard the distinct sound of a door closing. It came to me from outside the entryway of the room Elias and I were occupying. I sat up quickly and shoved Elias. He sat up as quickly.

"What is it?" he whispered.

I slowly reached down, hearing the steps get closer, I grabbed my twin swords at the side of my bed. They clattered together and the steps quickened. Elias was up standing on the bed in the dark. I stood as well and slipped the pommel of one handle into his hand. Three figures appeared in the doorway, one of them holding a lantern casting light into the room. They were wearing Northern Ralician military red and all three had weapons drawn.

"Politics." Elias sighed as he hopped off the bed and rushed the three men at the door with what I swore was a smile on his face.

The men hadn't seemed ready for us to attack them. Elias was in a thin pair of undergarments, and I was wearing a floor-length nightgown but that didn't stop us from attacking them with everything thing we had. They were trained well but not as well as us. The three of them fell easily and quickly. Moments flew by as our steel met theirs. I didn't have time to realize I had killed two men in a matter of minutes, but Elias seemed unfazed as he wiped my sword on his undergarments looking around the room.

"Put on something quickly, if you wish, and we must go to Georgette and Cassius." I nodded, taking the dressing robe off the armoire and slipping it on, tying it in front of me as Elias tugged some trousers on, and threw the linen shirt he had worn to the ball over the top of himself. He started to wipe his bloodied hands down it but looked up as the sounds of more footsteps approached, and we raised our weapons at the ready.

"Oh, thank the goddesses," Nathaniel exhaled, as he rounded the corner.

Elias' dad sagged in relief seeing us alive.

"Where is mom?" Elias asked, concern lacing every word.

"She went to Georgette," he said, turning to leave as soon as he had come. "They took the guard by surprise; they've tried to take the castle but weren't prepared for the military presence that King Dalion keeps here. They have all been thwarted, but they sent men to each of our private rooms to execute us in our sleep. Seems that while King Dalion may not be as slippery as most kings, King Kosdel had every intention of taking his kingdom from him in the dead of night by killing the unarmed and sleeping."

"Imagine his shock when he encountered pirates, and an armed princess," I said.

"The way I hear it Mercy, you're more pirate than a princess," Nathaniel responded with something like admiration in his voice.

Chapter Thirty-Four

Georgette

I woke to blissful comfort as Cassius had fallen asleep against me after we enjoyed each other's company for a fair amount of time. I ran my fingers through his loose black hair, and he nuzzled against me like a cat looking for affection. I moved away from him as his arm snaked out and pulled me back.

"Where are you going?"

I chuckled removing his arm from me.

"This is the time Devika has my bath drawn for me and we have a full day of things to plan and a war to start."

"You are leaving me to go bathe before first light? Have I that little influence on you?"

"It's a very big tub."

His head lifted as I slipped out of his bed and put on the thin chemise that had been under my dress.

"Is that an invitation?"

"If you are unable to discern that, Cassius, I fear I cannot help you."

"Such harsh words after my name sounded so sweet repeated on your lips last night." He sat up and looked around for what I supposed were his trousers.

I blushed but turned away so he couldn't see.

I slipped into my room, closing the door between us quietly. Devika was not in the room, but my bath had been drawn as I could see the lanterns had been lit. I went to my closet to grab some clean clothes to wear, already daydreaming about slipping into a bath with Cassius across from me. I shook the silly vision away and went to step out of the room when I heard a commotion coming from my receiving room. The door opened and I stepped out thinking Devika had come, only realizing too late that it was too many sets of footsteps to be Devika, and they were much too sturdy.

Two men rounded the corner with their swords drawn on me.

"Hello," I said, surveying my surroundings.

The men were Northern Ralice military and it was apparent they hadn't come to take tea with me. They said nothing as they advanced, and I ran to the table next to my bed to pick up the dagger that Cassius had given me. Though a dagger in a sword fight served no real purpose, at least I was armed.

"Perhaps we could discuss this, gentlemen, over some breakfast," I tossed the sheath of my weapon on the ground and brandished the perfect thin blade in front of me.

I realized as they rushed me, and I backed against the wall that I was going to die. I had not expected to live forever and when I was a pirate, I had even realized there was a very real possibility that I might die young. I suspected I was going to die when I was taken by Cassius a lifetime ago. Now with two men rushing at me, swords drawn and my back against a tapestry, I realized I was much less invincible than I felt most times.

As one of them knocked my dagger from my hand with their sword cutting my fingers in the process. I dropped it and swallowed hard as a flash of movement caught my eye beyond them. A man placed his blade against my throat and leaned in with a vicious smile of missing teeth and breath bad enough to kill on its own.

"Any last words pirate filth?" he asked as the other stood back with his sword extended.

"You're very ugly and your breath smells horrendous." I decided on as he growled and pressed his blade into my throat as I closed my eyes.

"Unhand my daughter!" A yell came from across my room and before the man had time to react, I reached up and pushed his blade away with my bare hands as it sliced through my skin, I slipped to my knees as my mother came up behind the men who had barely any time to catch her blade as she attacked them. I scrambled for my dagger on the floor and sprang up, stabbing one man in the shoulder with it. He yelled dropping his sword and tried to reach back to remove it while my mother ran her sword through him. The other man, with terrible breath, caught my mother on her arm with his weapon as she pulled her blade free to attack him. I ripped my dagger from the man's body and my mother and I advanced until he was against the wall.

"Not too bad for pirate filth." My mother winked at me, and I smiled as she held her sword against the man's throat. "Why have you come to kill Queen Dalion?" she demanded.

"An order, from my King," the coward sang like a crow. "We were to kill Princess Mercy, Queen Georgette, and the pirate boy."

"Why?" My mother shouted at him a fierceness in her eyes. I wondered if one could only experience such a thing when defending their child.

"King Kosdel means to take the Southern Ralice throne by force."

"How will he do that without..." I asked eyes wide. "Cassius,"

"Go," my mother said, "Take a sword, George, and save him."

I didn't respond, just took the sword that the dead man had dropped on the floor in one hand and my dagger in the other. The handles burned the lacerations on my hands, but it was as if the pain was distant and unimportant. I ran to the door that joined Cassius' and my room and threw it open.

Inside Cassius was sitting in a high back chair, and standing in front of him was King Kosdel with his sword drawn on Cassius. My heart dropped in my stomach as I saw a bleeding wound in Cassius' chest. Could I make it across the room before the blade went into him again? Cyril turned to see me in the doorway not looking worried that I stood there with two weapons.

"Ah, Captain Georgette." He smiled. "Just in time to watch your love die. Perhaps I'll keep you as a court harlot when I restore Ralice to its former glory under one king and one religion."

I watched Cassius grit his teeth at the threat, but King Kosdel's blade pushed into his throat. Cyril turned back to Cassius, and I watched as the blade drew blood. I had no time to decide if what I was doing was smart, or practical, or would even work. I felt the weight of the dagger in my hand and flipped it so I was holding it like a throwing knife. The weight was different than the practice knives, so as I wound back and threw it through the air, I put a little more force behind it. I hadn't meant to close my eyes, but it seemed I had. I heard a cry I prayed wasn't Cassius'.

I opened my eyes and saw that King Cyril had dropped to his knees and my dagger stuck out of his upper back. He seemed to be struggling to remove it but it was very well stuck in place. I looked to Cassius who was staring at the man with wonder and relief.

"You could have hit me," Cassius said as his chest rose and fell with labored breathing.

"But I didn't."

"I've seen you train with a throwing knife; you aren't proficient."

"You are sounding terribly ungrateful." I walked over to Cyril whose eyes were wide with pain from where he had fallen to his knees. I stepped in front of him and placed the stolen sword at his throat.

"Would you beg for your life, coward?" I asked him, as he looked up at me with fear in his eyes.

"No," he managed, though I could tell his body was failing him.

"Good, for Absalom alone, you don't deserve the opportunity." I slid the blade through his throat and used my barefoot to kick him over. Leaving the sword lodged in him.

I turned to Cassius who was attempting to stand despite the wound on his chest.

"No," I said, pushing him down and smearing my blood all over his shoulders from the open wounds on my hands.

"Georgette!" I heard a shout from my bedroom and turned to see my brother rush through the door like a sea storm. Mercy came behind him, and then my parents. All with weapons drawn looking ready to take on an army. Judging by some, would seem they already had.

"Cassius," another voice called from Cassius' reception room as a set of heavy boots came down the hall. Brees appeared with a nasty-looking cut on his cheek but other than that, appeared fine.

"I'm perfectly fine Brees," Cassius assured him.

"No, he isn't, he needs attention," I said to Brees who nodded at me.

"King Kosdel's remaining men who surrendered, including his son who seemed to know nothing of this cowardly grab for power, have been rounded up and are being held in the war room."

"Well, it seems we have avoided a war," Cassius said casually. "For now, at least. Mercy might you sit in on negotiations. Your country was betrayed as much as mine, and Northern Ralice's new ruler shall have a hefty price to pay for his father's inadequacies."

"Of course, King Dalion."

"But perhaps we should all bathe first and be bandaged. No need to bleed all over the war room table," Cassius suggested.

There were a few chuckles as Brees went to fetch a healer. Elias came to inspect my wounds and when he was sure that I wouldn't die from them in the next hour, shuffled off with his arm around Mercy. My father embraced me, and my mother did as well.

"You look like a queen," she said to me for the second time, only now she sounded proud instead of disappointed, bringing tears to the corners of my eyes.

When they left, I turned to Cassius who was slumped into the chair looking more irritated than anything. His wound was not bleeding much, and I suspected it hurt worse than it was.

"Would you like me to move you to the bed?" I asked him as his eyes met mine.

"I think this would be an inappropriate time for us to pleasure each other."

"That isn't..." I trailed off as a glint of humor shone in his eyes. "I hate you."

"Oh, good. After you just saved my life," he said, grimacing as he stood up on his own. "I thought that you had developed feelings for me."

"Oh, heavens no, I just didn't want my opportunity to rule a country to be squandered."

He pulled me into an embrace, which must have been a sight, as we were both covered in blood and half-dressed; then he kissed me soundly. "Thank the goddesses, what a relief."

Chapter Thirty-Five

Mercy

Standing next to the throne of Southern Ralice, I realized why Cassius had gotten his reputation of being cruel, or at least kept it after his father died.

Dressed in all black, including his dark twisted crown, and black ink on his knuckles looking out over the successor of Northern Ralice who knelt before him, he was an intimidating presence. His pirate wife also sat next to him dressed in black brocade trousers and vest with her crown perched on her head looking equally as formidable. I would not have wanted to be King Kosdel's son, Hannan, for all the spice in Hestiege.

"While I do not take you at your word that you had no knowledge of your father's plans to take my kingdom from me while I slept, the kingdom of Adamas and the Kingdom of Southern Ralice have chosen to offer you clemency and allow you to keep your throne. However, each of us has stipulations for the ten-year peace treaty that you will have to sign, and I will let Mercy speak for her country. For Southern Ralice the only terms I have set is a fifty-mile border push and a solid agreement that the Lapulous lakes belong to our country. Our border will extend thirty miles into Northern Ralice, you have three months to relocate any of your settlements and citizens."

He went silent as I stepped forward and Hannan looked up at me.

The rounding up of Northern Ralice's military had been swift and happened while none of us had been present. Captain Brees had expertly taken his company and thwarted their attempts of the overthrow, with extraordinarily little effort. The Priest that resided here in the castle had confessed to having drugged the guard at each of our doors so they would be easily incapacitated while we were unaware. It seems King Kosdel had been planning this for many years and used palace priests and Archbishops to execute his vision for Marecult under one rule.

If only he had accounted for a princess turned pirate and a pirate turned queen.

"Yes, outlined is monetary and resource compensation for the damage you have inflicted upon our country. These reparations will last the full ten-year term of the peace treaty." I spoke with as much authority as I could muster.

"If you breach this treaty on the Adamasian side, you will suffer the full force of our army as well as theirs," Cassius gifted.

"Likewise, if you refuse any of the terms set by King and Queen Dalion we will stand with them and take your crown from you," I said sternly, and the man before me looked overwhelmed.

He had not been prepared to be the ruler of his country today. Had not been prepared that we would offer mercy either.

We did not speak the fact that neither Cassius nor Adamas could suffer a war of this size right now that would end up with us having to split the land and resettle citizens. We didn't have the stability nor the resources but let the new king think we did.

"One other stipulation my wife has insisted upon, is that Gerald Church is kept here and serve his sentence for treason in Hallow the remainder of his days. His wife will be given an annulment by your priests and shall also remain here in Hallow."

"What will their fates be?" Hannan Kosdel asked, turning to his side where Master Gerald Church stood with his eyes forward and his jaw set.

"That is no concern of yours." Georgette's voice came as commanding as her husband's and the man closed his mouth and simply nodded.

We had discussed our plans together before we called this meeting with Hannan. Gerald's wife would be offered a choice of life aboard The Siren as a crew member of the ambassador of Adamas, or she would be trained under Devika as a Principal lady to replace her when Devika was offered the throne of Hestiege. Whatever wages she made would be her own and would not be sent to her father. These had been Georgette's only demands as she seemed mostly satisfied by the revenge she had taken on Absalom's life. Now she seemed determined to make right what she could, by providing for the woman he had been betrothed to.

The reparations offered to my country would make us stronger while Temperance gained her confidence on the throne. I had written her that morning to inform her of the events of the past two days and told her I would be returning home shortly to help her with anything she might need. Elias and I decided the best course of action was to spend the next six months in Adamas, to support my sister before setting sail under the new flag of The Siren. The flag of broken anchor and stars would be traded out for an Adamasian flag flown beside the flag of Marecult.

A letter had been sent to King Jacob Vaxa of Coranthia and King Gedeon Ning of Hestiege of our victory over Northern Ralice as well as the promise of a future visit of the new ambassadors of Adamas. There was also a section of the letters that informed them that Adamas, Northern, and Southern Ralice had pardoned The Siren and its crew of any crimes of piracy.

As Hannan Kosdel stood up and stepped forward to sign his name in his blood, Cassius stood, and I stepped forward on behalf of Adamas.

"To the start of a new generation," Cassius said when it was all over. Hannan shook his hand and bowed to Georgette and me before he turned, and all his remaining company was ushered out of Hallow Manor; save Gerald Church who would suffer Georgette's hatred locked in a cell for the rest of his miserable life.

"Why don't you get married before you leave?" Georgette asked from her chair in the dining room.

Her legs were crossed up on the table and she was drinking wine, each sip she took was punctuated with a subtle slurping sound.

"Mercy may wish for her family to be present," Elias chastised her. "Also, I have not asked her about marriage yet, and you are sticking your queenly nose where it doesn't belong."

Cassius was sitting back with a half-grin on his face as his eyes followed the conversation.

"Pirates needn't get married anyway," Hazel added. "Nathaniel and I have never married in the formal sense of the word. We refer to each other as husband and wife but there has never been any paperwork between us."

"Yes, but if they don't get married here then I shall not get to throw a party for them," Georgette said, as if that were the most important bit of this decision and I began to laugh.

I looked over to Elias who was sitting next to me, staring daggers at his sister who was still slurping away on her goblet of wine. He ended up looking at me with what I assumed was an apology for his family, and rolled his eyes looking back to his plate which contained only his peas which he pushed around.

"If I were a pirate, perhaps a wedding would be unnecessary," I said, casually looking over to Georgette and winking. She immediately put her feet down in anticipation of what I was going to say. "But since I will be the ambassador of Adamas perhaps it would be prudent."

"You would agree to marry me for the proprietary implications?" Elias asked, eyes shifting to me and a chuckle in his voice. "I would be more concerned with what people will say about you being married to a pirate."

"A mid-day wedding in the fall gardens would be lovely," Georgette added.

"Would you be quiet?" Elias said, pointing a fork he had in his hand at her.

"Children," Nathaniel warned as if they were ten years old.

Amara chuckled from her chair where she sat with Camber at her side. The child beaming at the people gathered around the table.

"I think I'd like to get married in the garden if it's alright by Cassius to use his home." I looked at Cassius who still wore the same entertained expression, only now he was staring at his wife.

"I know better than to stand in Georgette's way." He smiled looking at me. "Of course, you are welcome to."

"Elias? Of course, we can wait, there is no rush." I slid my hand to his knee as the table went dead silent waiting for his answer.

"I would marry you in the deck of our ship on a raging river, Mercy." He squeezed my fingers. "If you wish to be married in the garden here at Hallow, I would be deliriously happy to be standing beside you."

Georgette gave out a holler that rang out across the dining room like fire from a cannon.

Weeks later, I sat in a chair with my knees tucked up under me reading my letter from Temperance and Prudence. There had been a mourning festival in the capital city for my brothers. Prudence swore that the stars shined brighter than they ever had before. Temperance's information was as factual and structured as one might imagine with facts and events listed off like a list of food items. They each ended their letters with a salutation of being glad to see me when I arrived.

"Have the words changed since you read them earlier today, Captain Baine?" Elias came out of the bathroom shaking his wet hair like a dog to dry it, as I gazed at his undressed form, admiring the man who had become my husband earlier that afternoon.

"No, Captain Baine, the words have not changed." I tossed the letters on a small table in the room we had claimed together the last three weeks at Hallow Manor.

Tomorrow morning, we would leave before the sun rose. Set a course for Adamas, and then after we ported there for our set time, we would be off sailing around all Marecult. I would better my country with my travels and speak on behalf of our government on political alliances. I planned to see everything, visit all kingdoms and ports, and educate myself on lifestyles and cultures I had been ignorant to before, with my husband at my side.

Elias came up behind me, wrapping a bath sheet around his waist and I frowned in disapproval which elicited a smirk and a shake of his head.

"Will you be sad to leave?" I asked, voicing a question I had been hesitant to ask.

He was silent for a while as he came to sit beside me in a matching chair. He rolled his head back and his foot began to sway back and forth which was a sure sign of a restless mind.

"I will be glad to be back on the ship, on the ocean."

"Both true, but not what I asked." I smiled. "You and your sister have a way of trying to use the truth to tell a lie."

"I've never set off on a journey intentionally without her, with no intention of returning to get her." He swallowed hard, as emotion filled his voice.

I got up and sat on the ground next to his chair, letting my head rest against his legs, and he started running his hands through my hair. Nathaniel and Hazel had left earlier that day to return home, after our wedding ceremony had taken place. There were so many goodbyes being said in such a short time.

"We needn't leave so quickly, Elias, if you want to stay longer..."

"No," he decided. "She is safe and happy, and we will eventually have to learn to be apart."

It was a painful sort of confession that started an ache in me.

"Enough of this melancholy mood. It is our wedding night after all my radiant bride," he said, and I tipped my head to look into his eyes.

"So it is, did you know I was once engaged to a king?" I smiled as he descended upon me to press a kiss on my forehead.

"Is that so?" he asked, kissing my nose. "What became of him?"

"I believe he was killed by a pirate."

"Probably served him right." Elias slipped on the floor next to me taking my face in his hands and leaned his forehead against mine.

Chapter Thirty-Six

Georgette

I had never experienced heartbreak so fully in my life.

Watching my ship pull away from the pier had my heart twisting in my chest, in such pain I could barely breathe. It wasn't the dark polished wood or even the tentacled siren carved into the front. It was the people aboard. The crew I wouldn't see every day. It was the future that I was so sure would be mine.

It was my brother. It was taking my brother away. I would see him again, but our path's which once had been wound so tightly together, were now split and he was sailing away on our ship, leaving me to a life I chose.

I wouldn't change my mind. Even then as my chest ached, I knew I belonged in Southern Ralice. I belonged with Cassius. I was as sure of that as I had ever been of anything, but it didn't stop my tears.

Didn't stop the wave of nausea as my brother came into view on the back of the ship. The knowledge that I was standing next to the one my soul loved, did not stop the sobs that racked my body as my brother called to me across the distance.

"Morning Captain!"

"Morning Captain!" I shouted immediately, though my voice broke partway through.

He waved as Mercy stepped up beside him and they both stood on the back of the ship until they were no more than pinpricks on the horizon. I sat down on the dock with my legs dangling off the edge as Cassius came to sit next to me.

"I'm sorry, we can go soon," I assured him as he slipped his hand into mine.

"We shall stay as long as you like. In fact, if you wish to live here on the dock, I will simply move the castle to this shoreline."

"Hallow Manor by the ocean." I closed my eyes and leaned against him as my tears dried but my heart continued to ache. "Sounds quite lovely."

"You'll have to live there by yourself of course, as I have no taste for the ocean."

"Perhaps I shall meet a handsome sailor."

"I wouldn't wish you on the worst of sailors, let alone a handsome one," he mused. "But then perhaps I'll see if Jessamine Vaxa would consider returning to Hallow."

I gave him an incredulous look as he chuckled, pulling me closer.

After a long time and after all my tears had dried, I stood up and held my hand out to him. "Let's go home, Cassius."

"Yes, my Queen."

Chapter Thirty-Seven

Elias

I made my way up to the back of the ship as The Siren pulled away from the dock. Taking a deep breath, I stepped up to the railing to look out over the back. Steeling my emotions and holding my courage, I clenched my teeth together.

Mercy stood at the wheel of the ship. Our ship. She nodded to me, acknowledging my heartache with a soft smile.

Looking up at me was Georgette. I tried to ignore the reaction her tears pulled from me, as saltwater pricked my own eyes. I reminded myself, while it felt like I was leaving a piece of me behind, she looked like she belonged where I was leaving her. That thought brought me to look at the man who stood beside her, steady and as resolute as a mountain. He nodded to me as our gazes met and I nodded back. A promise between him and I, to take care of the one whom my soul had been tied to since birth. The sun peaked over the horizon, and I waved to my sister.

"Morning Captain!" I called as the distance between us continued to grow.

"Morning Captain!" she returned the greeting.

Mercy came up beside me and slipped her hand into mine. She stood with me until the dock was out of sight. I used my free hand to wipe a traitorous tear off my cheek. I stayed silent unsure of what to say or how to go on without Georgette. Certainly, I knew practically what to do, but it seemed a little like I was lost. Mercy's hand squeezed mine and I pulled her into me, closing my eyes and taking a deep breath of ocean air.

Epilogue:
18 Months Later
Cassius

"This is ridiculous," I complained, wiping sweat from my brow. "We should give up this fruitless search, we've been on this damned island for four days."

"My pampered king," Georgette patronized me, and her brother laughed with her...or at me, I wasn't sure. Mercy nodded at me in apology.

"I know you tire of hearing me say this, but if there was a treasure to find in Southern Ralice's waters, my father would have found it. He loved little above his wealth and if he had the chance to increase it, then he would have."

I walked through a spider's web at that exact moment and did my best to hide my disgust as I wiped it off my face. We were currently exploring a series of rock caverns on the island that Georgette and Elias had led us to. With The Siren anchored offshore, as well as an Adamasian exploration ship, and a small warship from my fleet, I had given the deadline of five days for this ridiculous exploration before I would demand we return home. While my mother would no doubt make a fine steward of Southern Ralice I was eager to sleep in a bed, and not on the sandy beaches of a distant island, eaten alive by bugs.

"You didn't have to come," my brother-in-law reminded me.

"I wasn't going to send my wife, the Queen of Southern Ralice, to an uncharted island with pirates, while I sat on my throne at home." I narrowed my eyes at Elias.

"I was a pirate before I was a queen, Cass," Georgette said, lifting up on her toes to press a kiss to my cheek leaving me a little less irritated.

"You don't have to remind me."

We happened upon an underground spring of water that I was sure we had seen before and wondered, not for the first time, if we had been going in circles.

"Have we been here before?" Mercy voiced the question that I was thinking.

"I think so..." Elias said, looking around the cavern and the small pool of water that was emptying through several waterfalls all around us. The water poured loudly over rocks across the naturally made room.

Georgette made her way toward the large waterfall and climbed rocks to be right up next to it. She sat down on a flat rock, situating herself as she reached out to cup some of the rushing water in her hands. She was wearing pirate clothes, relaxed trousers, a crude vest, and a linen shirt. Though, a woven circlet of rubies sat atop her head in complete contrast to the rest of her attire. In a year and a half, I had not grown accustomed to how much I wanted her. Every moment, and every word from her, made me value her more than the day before. She drove me absolutely mad at times, but she always had honey on her tongue to soothe any anger she had intentionally stirred at night when we lay together. She was as wild as the day I stole her away from her ship.

The people loved her. Queen Georgette Kingslayer they called her, and her unique approach of visiting towns and cities within Southern Ralice had resulted in support for the crown I wasn't sure had ever been in Southern Ralice's history.

The Siren had also gone through the conversion from a pirate ship to an ambassador's vessel for Adamas. Though there were rumors of it detouring to do some less than legal ambassador business. Such as this demented mission we were on now, looking for lost pirate treasure. I looked to Mercy who was leaning against Elias, who had his arm wrapped around her. His eyes scanned the cavern ceiling. I looked up where his eyes were gazing to see if I could see what he was looking for.

The only reason I had agreed to a split of the imaginary treasure, was because I knew it didn't exist. Southern Ralice and Adamas would split fifty percent of the treasure evenly and the other fifty percent was to be given to Elias and Georgette to split amongst themselves and the crew of The Siren.

I looked back to Georgette and was startled when I didn't see her on the rock where she had last been. I scanned the cavern and did not see any sign of her, but had not heard her climb down from her perch either.

"George," I called out but got no response.

"Where is she?" Mercy asked now, pulling away from Elias who was looking around as I was.

That is when the soaking wet face of my wife emerged from behind the waterfall as she did her best to push her hair away from her face. A splitting grin graced her features, the likes of which were rare and not always welcomed. Before I could move, Elias was up the rocks she had climbed. She reached out a hand and pointed to something I couldn't see. Elias looked where she had motioned and let out an excited yell before disappearing behind the wall of rushing water.

I started the climb up the rocks followed by Mercy as I reached out to help her up on the rock platform Georgette had been sitting on. I looked where she had pointed, and deep in the rock had been carved a broken anchor and three stars. The pirate flag of Marecult.

"If this treasure turns out to be real, she will be insufferable for years to come," I grumbled, motioning for Mercy to step into the waterfall before me. She was now grinning, and a flush of excitement was present on her pale features as she all but jumped through the water.

The waterfall had soaked me all the way through and as I wiped the water from my eyes, I focused on a small room beyond, barely tall enough for me to stand in as my head almost grazed the ceiling. Beyond where we were standing, was a small untouched area with about two dozen sealed barrels in a room the height of my wife, who wasted no time jumping down from the small stone platform, over to one of the barrels. She removed a dagger from her belt and began to pry the lid of the barrel off. Elias had to bend his head a little as he made his way to help her. Mercy and I seemed to hold our breath as we peered over the edge to see what was inside as they lifted the lid.

The twins began to laugh and Georgette spun around in what was a jig of some sort as gold coins and a few precious gems of green and sapphire winked back at us.

"Oceans deep!" I exhaled, having picked up that particular pirate slang from my wife.

Elias dove his hand into the gold and scooped up a handful of the riches, letting them slowly drop back into the barrel.

The treasure had been loaded onto the ships and brought back to the mainland. We all sat at a table in a tavern in Brits. The last night we would spend together before journeying back to our homes with our portion of Valloe's treasure in tow. The bittersweet air of a successful expedition and subsequent departure hung around all of us. Two of us headed back to rule a country, and two back to sail the seas for the sake of peace.

"I would like to propose a toast, to the twin Captain's Baine," Mercy lifted her glass. "May history not forget you."

"To pirates who hoarded their treasure!" Elias said, raising a glass.

"To my disbelieving husband and the extra forty silvers I've won simply by being right!" Georgette said across from me as she shot me a wicked grin. She raised her glass, showing off the tattoos on her fingers that matched my own. Only now we all had four circles instead of three.

"To our fortunes and fates." I raised my glass. "Might there never be a cold bed among us, or a moment dully wasted."

The

End

Author Note

There is something surreal about finishing this story. Since it started rattling around in my brain, I have been chasing Elias, and Georgette across the Seas of Marecult. I have been rooting for Mercy to find her place in the world, and wanted Cassius to find true love. These characters taught me many things, though I did not set out to learn anything from them

This story will always be dear to my heart as it was born of a grief from losing my brother, whom I loved dearly. Some terrible things can give way to beautiful joys.

Oh reader! You have no idea what you reading my story means to me. You have given a dreamer more happiness than she can say. This part-time writer, full-time wife/mom will never be able to express the joy of my soul that you picked my book up and followed my words to their end.

May your next escapade be marvelous.

Acknowledgments

As always, I have so many people to thank, because there is no way this would have made it out into the world if I was the only one in charge.

The Lord carries me through every keystroke.

Thank you to my husband and biggest supporter. I love you, Barrett, 'till the end of the line. My two little munchkins, you guys are such a blessing. Willis, my favorite sister, thank you for reading everything I push at you and for talking through my plot holes. Brits, to whom this book is dedicated, love you babe.

My Alpha reader Celeste (your encouragements make this possible), my critique partner Persephone, my cover artist Primmepgx, my editor Natalie with Shrimp Books, my beta readers, my ARC readers, (Ali, Emma, and Reanna you guys are heart of my heart).

To my supporters and readers who waited for this second installment.

To anyone who ever encouraged me. You made a difference.

CPSIA information can be obtained
at www.ICGtesting.com
Printed in the USA
BVHW030641090422
633873BV00004B/86